*This volume of YIVO's Yiddish Voices Series was prepared for publication with generous support from the family of Harriet R. Yassky*

YIVO Institute for Jewish Research

# THE MOTHER OF YIDDISH THEATRE

**Published Titles**

*Three Yiddish Plays by Women: Female Jewish Perspectives, 1880-1920,*
ed. Alyssa Quint
*The Mother of Yiddish Theatre: Memoirs of Ester-Rokhl Kaminska,*
ed. and trans. Mikhl Yashinsky
*The Destruction of Dubova: Chronicle of a Dead City,*
Rokhl Faygnberg, ed. Elissa Bemporad

**Upcoming Titles**

*Mississippi (1935) By Leyb Malakh: A Yiddish Play about the
Scottsboro Boys,* ed. Alyssa Quint

# THE MOTHER OF YIDDISH THEATRE

Memoirs of Ester-Rokhl Kaminska

## Edited and Translated by Mikhl Yashinsky

BLOOMSBURY ACADEMIC
LONDON · NEW YORK · OXFORD · NEW DELHI · SYDNEY

BLOOMSBURY ACADEMIC
Bloomsbury Publishing Plc, 50 Bedford Square, London, WC1B 3DP, UK
Bloomsbury Publishing Inc, 1359 Broadway, New York, NY 10018, USA
Bloomsbury Publishing Ireland, 29 Earlsfort Terrace, Dublin 2, D02 AY28, Ireland

BLOOMSBURY, BLOOMSBURY ACADEMIC and the Diana logo are trademarks
of Bloomsbury Publishing Plc

First published in Great Britain 2025



Cover image: Membership application form, Yidisher Artistn Fareyn, circa 1922, Esther-Rachel
Kaminska Theater Museum Collection © From the Archives of the YIVO Institute for Jewish
Research, New York. Piece of white paper tear © Piman Khrutmuang /Adobe Stock

Headshot and other details from Kaminska's membership form submitted to Poland's Yiddish
Actors Union, in which she provides: her signature; her indication that she has no pseudonym;
her address in Warsaw (11 Oboźna Street, apartment 24); the date of her first appearance on
the Yiddish stage ("30 years ago"); and, as an answer to where she has performed: "in various
theatres and countries." YIVO, RG 8: Esther-Rachel Kaminska Theater Museum Collection, Box 60,
Folder 462, https://digipres.cjh.org:443/delivery/DeliveryManagerServlet?dps_pid=IE11103681.

Memoir originally published in Yiddish, after the author's death, as *Derner un blumen: der veg fun
mayn lebn—memuarn* (Thorns and Flowers: The Path of My Life—Memoirs), in thirty-two weekly
installments in the Warsaw daily *Der moment*, from June 11, 1926 to January 21, 1927.



Bloomsbury Publishing Plc does not have any control over, or responsibility for, any third-party
websites referred to or in this book. All internet addresses given in this book were correct at the
time of going to press. The author and publisher regret any inconvenience caused if addresses
have changed or sites have ceased to exist, but can accept no responsibility for any such changes.

A catalogue record for this book is available from the British Library.

A catalog record for this book is available from the Library of Congress.

ISBN: HB: 978-1-3503-2106-9
PB: 978-1-3503-2107-6
ePDF: 978-1-3503-2108-3
eBook: 978-1-3503-2109-0

Series: Yiddish Voices

Typeset by Deanta Global Publishing Services, Chennai, India
Printed and bound in Great Britain

For product safety related questions contact productsafety@bloomsbury.com.

To find out more about our authors and books visit www.bloomsbury.com
and sign up for our newsletters.

For my own mama, Debra Weiss Yashinsky, a teacher.
And for her mama, Elizabeth Elkin Weiss, a Jewish actress,
who came into this world three months before Kaminska left it.

—MY

**FIGURES 1 AND 2** Photographs of Kaminska as a young woman, during the period depicted in her memoir. The stamp indicates that this particular copy of the book containing these images was held by the Vilna Jewish Teachers' Seminary. Ester-Rokhl Kaminska, *Briv fun ester-rokhl kaminski* (Letters of Ester-Rokhl Kaminska), ed. Mark Turkow (Vilna: B. Kletskin, 1927), 64, 96.

# CONTENTS

# FIGURES

# PREFACE

## *TOVAH FELDSHUH*

What do I, Tovah Feldshuh, an actor of the American stage and screen, have in common with Ester-Rokhl Kaminska, legend of the Yiddish theatre, active a full century earlier, from approximately 1892 to 1925? From reading her memoirs, originally titled *Thorns and Flowers*, which began to be published in 1926, a year after her death, alongside my memoirs, *Lilyville*, published in 2021, one might surmise: everything, and nothing, all at once.

I'll start with "nothing." Compared to Kaminska, I was to the manor born, raised in the affluent suburb of Scarsdale, New York, under the watchful eye of two nurturing parents: my war-hero father, Sidney, a pillar of unconditional love, and my extraordinary mother—doting and scrutinizing in equal measure—Lillian Kaplan Feldshuh. Hence the title of my memoir, *Lilyville*. Kaminska was born to a poor family in a rural town that is now part of Belarus, but was at the time in the region of the Russian Empire labeled the Pale of Settlement. Whereas my childhood was characterized by matching outfits, fancy schools, and piano lessons, Kaminska's upbringing was one of chores that involved manual labor, cooking, and cleaning, with only some respite for study and even less for play. She did not learn to sing by pursuing a degree in a conservatory, she writes, but rather by listening to peasants as they walked to and from their work in the fields, and to the chanting of yeshiva boys. When she arrived in Warsaw to join her sisters, she led the precarious life of the working class, doing factory work and helping her sisters care for their children in exchange for a roof over her head.

But there are common experiences that bond actor to actor, no matter the time and space that define our individual worlds. Kaminska and I share a passion for the stage, a passion that we both felt before it could promise us even a hint of celebrity or a lifestyle promising any security or predictability. Obviously, Kaminska's commitment to her passion played out differently than did mine. Never did I have to sing with an orchestra pit consisting of only a woman who played the French horn as she breastfed her baby (kudos to both women in that unlikely scenario!). Nor did I ever have to wheel out manure from a stable before I invited audiences into it so that it could serve as a performance venue. I give Kaminska credit for doing so and I give her even more credit for her willingness to share such details with her readers. Chapeau!

But I can certainly relate to the dream of becoming an actor while coming from a family that wanted something else for me. I love when Ester-Rokhl describes how she came to wed Avrom-Yitskhok Kaminski because her sisters refused to allow her to join a traveling troupe of Yiddish players unless she was married, fearing scandal. "But here's the real scandal," she writes. "If some mystery man had appeared before me then, God knows who, I would have gladly married him, as long as it meant I would be allowed to go off and play upon the stage." A woman with priorities, I thought to myself, as I read her words in our fellow actor Mikhl Yashinsky's robust and lively translation.

Moreover, I could certainly relate to the camaraderie she shares with her actors on the road. She writes touchingly about her journey to Płońsk, for instance:

And as the sand got deeper, the men simply climbed out to lighten the wagon's burden and accompanied it on foot. As they walked and we rode, we rehearsed songs from the operetta that we were to play in Płońsk, to the rhythm of our feet and rolling wheels. It was such a balm to our hearts that we felt we were the richest people in all the world. As the dusk began deepening, we finally sighted the shtetl.

These spontaneous moments of fellowship offstage or behind the camera are the magical moments that sustain us as performers. This memoir reminds me of how timeless they are.

Perhaps the most obvious parallel between us, however, lies in the way we are perceived and shaped by our Jewish audiences, as both of us became embodiments of *di yidishe mame*, the quintessential Jewish mother. I found some of my richest dramatic material in the Jewish mother roles I have been honored to play, from Judy, the mother of the title character in the cult-classic film *Kissing Jessica Stein*, to the matriarch-politician Golda Meir in the Broadway show *Golda's Balcony* by William Gibson. I am only just completing my run as *Funny Girl*'s Rosie Brice, mother of Fanny Brice, as I write these words. Likewise, Kaminska discovered the reaches of her talent through the vehicle of such Jewish mothers as Jacob Gordin's mighty heroine Mirele Efros and the deeply feeling mama at the center of the silent film *The Vow*, a performance so beautifully analyzed by Yashinsky in this volume's introduction. We both intuitively understood, so I surmise, that Jewish mothers are enduringly complex: they nurture and through that nurturing set standards, teach, and lead. They wring their hands when life challenges their young. They also force themselves to let go when they must. The complexity and the tensions in these Jewish mother characters allow for endless theatrical possibilities.

When I was invited to read her memoirs, I wondered to myself: what if not these pages will finally make legible the invisible threads that bind my acting career to a legacy of Yiddishkeit, of Jewishness? When I think about it, more than many of my Jewish acting peers, I opted for this Jewish legacy as early as when I changed my stage name from my given name Terri Sue to my formerly little-used Hebrew name Tovah. True, the name Tovah earned the first stamp of approval by an early non-Jewish boyfriend of mine. (To earn my mother's approval of the name took several decades!) But when I think about it, "Tovah" changed the landscape of my career; it isn't crazy to think that behind my name change was not only the wish to have a name that was more grown-up and sensual, but also a subconscious desire to connect to my Jewish past through my craft. Perhaps this is why I am deeply touched by another one of Kaminska's experiences in a shtetl to which she journeyed with her troupe. She writes:

> All day Friday we sold tickets, and Saturday evening we headed off to the theatre. We made ourselves up, got into costume, and sat down to wait for our audience. But the clock struck ten, and there was not a living soul in sight. We had to wait for the Jews to finish the evening prayers and the havdalah service marking the end of Shabbos.

In her memoirs, the shtetl residents are starved for Yiddish performance, but they give their Jewish observance top billing. Likewise, she describes the generosity of one landlord who insists on housing and feeding the troupe for no charge other than the simple pleasure that the Yiddish performances bring him. Little from Kaminska's gritty depiction of her life as a woman and an actor made me envy the particulars of her life experience, no matter the storied place in history that it earned her. Hers was a life of accomplishment but equally one of many difficulties and even tragedies, including the cancer that took her from this world too soon. But there are moments, such as that post-Sabbath performance in the shtetl, when she portrays a Jewish culture of such wholeness and cohesion that she pierces my heart. Yes, I think to myself, I would have loved to know firsthand the texture of that experience—these memoirs help me touch it. And yes, something from that night, Kaminska and her troupe putting on a play under the stars for their fellow Jews as they stream in following havdalah, I carry in me to this day.

# INTRODUCTION

# THE THORNS THAT GREW THE FLOWER[1]

*MIKHL YASHINSKY*

## Kaminska's Meticulous and Monumental Art— and Its Humble Origins

Mother bids a final farewell to her son before he leaves for the war. It is a scene easily imagined, one treated with reverence and dollops of dripping sentiment in a great many photographs and paintings. The sweetheart in John Everett Millais's canvas *The Black Brunswicker* (1860) comes to mind, her regimental lover going off to fight Napoleon as she slyly pushes the door closed behind her, blocking his departure. In the form and face of Yiddish actress Ester-Rokhl Kaminska (March 16, 1870[2]–December 27, 1925), however, performing in the silent film *Tkies-kaf* (The Vow),[3] this scenic genre becomes a masterclass in precision. She demonstrates how a whole story of the heart can be told in a seamless sequence of expression and honest gesture. Her acting is neither schmaltzy nor exaggerated, as one might expect of movies of the era, neither glamorized nor fake, but rather simple, spare, surprising, and real.

The grande dame of the Yiddish theatre, its most famous star in her era, Kaminska is captured here in her final screen performance before she would succumb to cancer at the age of fifty-six. She was already ill when the film was shot. Despite this, here, as Mrs. Kronberg, she is at the height of her magisterial powers. She looms large in the frame, with broad shoulders and an imposing stature, as photographs of her give testament to, but reveals a deeply vulnerable heart. Her lips are painted darkly—high-contrast features being necessary in a story told in black and white, wordlessly, where the body and face are all—and she wears a checkered dress with a striped apron. Soldier boy is at her side. Her movements are so specific, especially those of the hands, and shift so fluidly from one to the next, like the disappearing and reappearing act of a stage magician, that it is worthwhile to delineate them in full, to give the reader a sense of her evanescent art, most of it lost to the ages. And so let us grasp here the rich narrative web Madame Kaminska so deftly weaves in a shot lasting just half a minute:

1.  With her son distracted as he hoists his baby sister into his arms, Kaminska as Mrs. Kronberg takes the opportunity to wipe away her tears. This she does not with a gentle dabbing, but with both hands gripping the handkerchief, covering her entire face with it. So that none can glimpse her streaming eyes? Because she cannot bear to look? Because the outpour is so profuse that she needs the whole of the cloth to catch it? It is an unexpected choice, and a textured one—it may be any and all of these.

2.  The hands grasping the kerchief enfold it, as Kaminska moves them to a clasped position at her chin, eyes upturned, lips moving slightly, as if in silent entreaty to God—a prayer for salvation.

3.  The son hands his baby sister over to his father and turns to face his mother. It is as if she were not expecting his full gaze—or indeed has been expecting it all her life. Her face, after passing evenly through gradients of intermediate emotion, turns resplendent with joy. With her eyes, she drinks in the beauty of his face, the face she created. Her hands spread apart to behold him, and he seizes them. She nods as if to say: Yes. Now is the moment. Hold me.

4.  The embrace. Here, again, a surprise. One might guess that the actress would fling both arms around him. Not Kaminska. Too simple a choice for the actress who had seen and experienced so much. Though the right hand moves to clutch the son's back as he presses her close, the left does not follow. Instead, it returns to her

face, handkerchief still in hand, covering it again therewith. She cannot give in fully to the ecstasy of holding him, knowing it will melt anon. Her grief remains, but Heaven forbid she reveal it to him. And so, the concealing kerchief, and one hand held back from the embrace.

5. Then that hand to his face, feeling his cheek, glorying in it. The other hand now sprawled wide over his shoulder, needing every digit to feel the firm presence of him. The face turns away. She cannot let him be unnerved by the sensation of a falling tear.

6. Her body shakes with her sobs.

7. She showers him with kisses.

8. She clutches his face, whispering unheard words. They are for him alone.

9. The hand holding his face drops to her breast, vainly trying to still the mad beating of her heart.

10. He descends upon the hand; now it is his turn to cover her with kisses, his face pressed against the hand held at her bosom. With her other hand at his neck, she presses him down—may he hear the throb of the maternal heart once more.

11. Their affection, their urgent need of each other, conquers. She surrenders her valiant defenses; she will let him touch her face, with its rivulets of tears. She presses it to his, unmitigated by the handkerchief now. She closes her eyes and lets the camera capture her visage fully as she goes cheek-to-cheek with her son. They are as if fused together, their hearts beating with the same wounded and boundless love (Figure 3).

12. But they cannot remain so. She vibrates with sobs, inadvertently pushing him backward with the force of her agony. He takes the opportunity to leave. Kaminska clutches desperately at his arm, trying in vain to prevent his going, like the determined inamorata of *The Black Brunswicker*.

13. But unlike Millais's supplicant, whose face remains serene, pure anguish has taken hold of Kaminska's. She is more like Cassandra now, ancient auguress of doom—a scene later, Mrs. Kronberg's son will die a hero's death on the battlefield, in service of the tsar. It is as if she knows it. As he exits the room, Kaminska collapses

into a chair. Her hands now lie resigned in her aproned lap, her face exposed in a mask of tragedy incarnate. The actress's striking features are lined with loss and with years of hard living on the road. It is not a face of easy charm, but it is fascinating, sharply hewn, and practical for her purpose—the tool of a master craftswoman, and she uses it to full effect. Her body is ample and robust. She is capacious enough to feel worlds of pain, as we see her doing here, abandoning her physical strength and melting into sorrow. But by the same release, she gives worlds of comfort to her audience, through the recognition of a shared plight. In her broad palms, she cradles the hearts of a people. Such was Kaminska's art.

The performance amounts to an extraordinary series of dramatic beats, a rush of intermingling pain and pleasure. By the end of the filmed sequence, Kaminska has given her audience a new gesture, posture, or glance about once every two seconds. And yet her work is not frenzied. The attitudes drip into each other like molten lead, smooth and sparkling, pouring through the tunnels of a linotype machine, and emitting, as linotypes do,

FIGURE 3 Ester-Rokhl Kaminska, in the role of the fiercely devoted mother Mrs. Kronberg in *Tkies-kaf* (The Vow) (1924), holding her son before he leaves for war.

the text of a story. And there, fully formed on the screen, we witness what the woman so desperately wished to become in those salad days covered by these memoirs: an *artistke*. By it, she means an actress on the Yiddish stage. But she had become more than that. As the prima donna Tosca says of her lover, the painter Mario Caravadossi, in Puccini's opera named for her, "Ecco un'artista!" Behold, a true artist.

The command of her craft showcased in the film was not the product of a few moments of shooting. It was built up in the early years that are the scope of these memoirs, which describe approximately the first half of the author's life, from 1870 to 1900. The early years of her career were marked by wars with her family, resistance against tsarist suppression of Yiddish theatre, struggle to stake out a career as a professional woman in a misogynistic society, and tragedies experienced as a mother. During those years, on the road with her troupe and in intimate communion with the humblest of small-town audiences, she laid the foundation for the actress and cultural leader she would become, and simultaneously, for generations of Yiddish theatremakers.

Though her memoir does not actually cover the period of her greatest fame, as Kaminska passed away before she finished writing, it is significant as an origin story. In its pages, she recalls days of joy and days of woe that she would eventually channel into her emotionally authentic performances, expanding the professional and artistic breadth of the Yiddish stage. She learns from and lives among shtetl types—rabbi and rebbetzin, merchant and mendicant—whose personalities and behaviors would inform the creation of her own characters. She undergoes the transition from a religious and cloistered shtetl girl to a cosmopolitan urban woman, a process of becoming modern that is at the heart of Yiddish plays and the history of the genre's evolution. And she builds crucial audiences among the masses during the precarious early days of Yiddish theatre. This was a fragile period when a theatre for the Eastern European Jews in their own idiom was first coming into its own, buffeted by forces of religious convention and governmental suppression, its success and endurance by no means preordained. By picking up on these varied threads of Kaminska's material, the reader is allowed to behold a marvelous tapestry, one that displays the very genesis of an artist and her art form.

As an institution in Europe, the incipient Yiddish theatre was in its most fragile state during the years covered by Kaminska's memoirs. Yiddish actors who had accrued the most stage experience in significant urban venues left the Russian Empire after a wave of anti-Jewish suppression led to a governmental ban on theatre in the language in 1883.[4]

The ban uprooted Yiddish theatre troupes entirely from Odessa, where it was strictly enforced, and forced them out of long and lucrative relationships they had with theatres in other cities. Kaminska, in her memoirs, remembers crossing the path of Avrom Goldfaden, the preeminent steward of the Yiddish theatre, who granted her one of her first auditions. Not long after that meeting, in 1888, he would throw up his hands at the government's restrictions and leave for New York, where he largely failed in his pursuit of New York audiences.[5] His absence on the continent of his birth left a void filled, in makeshift fashion, by a small number of European Yiddish actors, many of them eminently inexperienced, who formed motley troupes. One of these was Kaminska's. It was hers that would emerge to have the most lasting significance, with its actors remembered as pioneers.

But this took time and effort. For years, in order to successfully produce Yiddish theatre, she and her troupe had to rely upon their raw talent, devotion to the art, entrepreneurial instincts, shared know-how of shtetl life and imperial bureaucracy, and willingness to work and endure physical trials. With these qualities, Kaminska and her colleagues successfully bridged the years of the ban until 1905, when its enforcement slackened and, through the exertions of Kaminska and her colleagues, the art form was able to claim venues and audiences of prestige and greater commercial viability. With actors she had trained and a chance to reach her audience without overdue governmental interference, Yiddish theatre blossomed anew. In part, it did this by looking toward America—especially the work of high-minded New York playwright Jacob Gordin—where Yiddish theatre was allowed to grow without hindrance. Meanwhile, the theatremakers began innovating artistically back at home in Warsaw, as an avant-garde repertoire and approach to stagecraft began to take hold in a newly independent Poland in the years following the First World War. Much credit for the significance, artistry, and popularity of the scene there is due Kaminska: her dogged pursuit of Yiddish performance in the towns and villages (even unto the end of her career), her loving cultivation of actors, and her instinct for good theatre and good roles (Jewish and not Jewish—she would even come to play Strindberg translated into Yiddish, some of the most forward-looking repertoire available to her), notwithstanding her lack of formal training. She would only see a few years of Yiddish theatre's most established and artistically refined period, but it was Kaminska, more than any other figure, who had set the stage.

# The Artist as Matriarch

By the end of the shot in *The Vow*, as Kaminska cowers in her chair, the body of this artist convulses with the force of parental grief. She embodies the personage she so often played in her various starring vehicles, the role for which she gained greatest renown—that of the universal *yidishe mame*, the Jewish mother, made manifest in the body, the eyes, and the hands of this one courageous woman born into poverty in the shtetl of Porozove, in what is now Belarus. There in that chair, her hands in her lap, wailing, she grieves along with all the mothers of her tribe. As a critic for the Russian-language newspaper *Odesskie Novosti* (Odessa News) wrote of her in the role with which she was most closely identified, Mirele Efros, the determined businesswoman and beleaguered matriarch (an apt combination for Kaminska!) in Jacob Gordin's eponymous drama from 1898 (Figure 4):

> Two feelings wrestle with each other in Madame Kaminska: the feeling for veracity that compels her to present the role in such colors as will draw us near to reality, as well as a higher and more complex feeling, a feeling that tears through the conventional exterior wrappings of the stage image and endows her with dashes of the universal, of that which belongs to all mankind.[6]

This critic captures the dual attainments of Kaminska's art: on the one hand, it bore emotional truth on an intimate and personal level, informed by the turmoil of her own life. At the same time, by the forcefulness of her acting, with her voice echoing the wail of a tortured people, comprehensible to all of anguished humankind, she built a theatre of compassion that could resound globally.

Kaminska was not just one unto herself, nor just the mother of an accomplished brood of actors (both her actual children and the performers she mentored in her theatrical troupe), but rather one unto all the world, representing Yiddish theatre to audiences all over as its most important female interpreter in her day. She was extolled as a mother of her people and widely recognized as the mother of her art form, being known by the honorific *di mame fun yidishn teater*, the mother of Yiddish theatre. The acting was no mere act—or perhaps it was so persuasive that it lifted her beyond the realms of art and into the family of her audiences.

FIGURE 4 Production photograph of Kaminska as Gordin's heroine Mirele Efros, known to generations of Yiddish theatregoers as "the Jewish Queen Lear," as, like Shakesepeare's tragic hero, Efros finds her empire in the sights of her covetous children. Kaminska appears here with her own daughter Ida (1899–1980) playing Mirele's grandson Shloymele. Ida, who would herself become a leading Yiddish actress of her day, begins her own memoirs with an account of her mother. She remembers Ester-Rokhl, by then an accomplished businesswoman like Mirele herself, telling Ida that as she had reached four years of life, it was high time that the girl join her onstage by playing her grandson. The play then was Dovid Pinski's *Di muter* (The Mother). Ida quotes Kaminska: "Reginele [Kaminska's elder daughter, Regina] is already too big for the role. Siomkye is the same age as you are, between four and five." Ida would go on playing such roles at her mother's side for years, for as long as she remained "a drobne" (a tiny slip of a thing), as her mother used to call her.[7] By the time Ida had graduated to playing Mirele, it had become a tradition—her own little daughter Ruth then took up the challenge of playing the grandson, just as Ida had done alongside her mother. Sandrow, *Vagabond Stars*, 155.

# A Name That Would Be Remembered

Even the names given to the girl at birth may have struck her public as tokens of the status she would attain. "Ester" recalls the Jewish queen-consort of Persia who saved her people from destruction. Kaminska affirms in her memoir that she was named after her and felt a certain affinity with the ancient heroine, taking great delight in playing her onstage. And the little Ester-Rokhl was born on the Fast of Esther, immediately before Purim, the holiday marking the salvation of the Jewish people by her queenly namesake. Before the advent of the *haskole*, or Jewish Enlightenment, in the nineteenth century, Purim-tide had been the only period during which traditional Ashkenazic communities permitted theatrical performances. Fitting, perhaps, that in the late winter of 1870, in the Hebrew month of Adar II, while the town's merrymakers would have been going doorstep to doorstep, entertaining Porozove's householders with *purim-shpiln* (song-filled spectacles based on stories of the Bible, often that of Esther), a child was being born a few houses over who would one day bring such theatre out of the confines of private homes and the religious calendar, and into the year-round public square, according it the refinement of carefully cultivated art.

Her second name, meanwhile, which she was called by those close to her, sometimes in the sweetly intoned diminutive "Rokhele," is that of the biblical matriarch Rachel. Rachel was the most beloved wife of Jacob and has been known to Yiddish speakers through the ages as *"di mame rokhl,"* Mother Rachel, who is said to weep for her people and provide them comfort from on high.

Thus, on some spiritual level, the great woman's title was presaged from her birth, and so was she remembered at her death. At Warsaw's chief Jewish cemetery, established in 1806 and still one of the largest Jewish burial grounds in the world, her gravestone stands tall amid its surrounding monuments, outsized only by the ornate mausoleum dedicated to three writers considered leading pioneers of modern Yiddish literature: Y. L. Peretz, Sh. An-ski, and Yankev Dinezon. Kaminska's stone bears an elaborate bas relief in marble by noted Jewish sculptor Fishl "Felix" Rubinlikht,[8] carved with emblematic creatures of the Bible, tribal tradition, and folklore that identify her as an artistic scion of the Jewish nation (Figure 5). There is an eagle with wings outstretched, snakes, a lion's head[9] supported by a bear and a deer, and a peacock. A golden peacock, in Yiddish lore, is said to fly the world over as a symbol of the resilient, itinerant, and artistic Jewish

FIGURE 5 Kaminska's gravestone at the Jewish cemetery on Okopowa Street, in Warsaw. In the Yiddish script, she is identified as *"MAME / ESTER ROKHL / KAMINSKA."* Photograph by Jolanta Dyr.

spirit. Here it has seven plumes, like the branches of the ancient menorah. And below this menagerie, etched in solemn Hebrew letters: מאמע—*Mame.* Not the more formal choice of *Muter*, but rather the intimate one—a woman beloved of her children.

So she would remain even to the succeeding generations. Poet Kadia Molodowsky, a leading light of her own day, though in the field of letters rather than theatrics, was, like Kaminska, born in a small shtetl in the Grodno governorate of the Russian Empire, though a generation after. Using the pen name of Rifke Zilberg (the protagonist of one of her own novels), Molodowsky memorialized the actress in a series of biographical portraits of iconic women, among them such giants as George Eliot, Golde Meyerson (aka Golda Meir), and Greta Garbo ("di legendare geshtalt fun di muvis").[10] The essay on Kaminska comes directly after the one on Queen Esther in the sheaf found among the author's archival typescripts. There, she writes of Kaminska,

She did not borrow any tricks from anyone. She was real and honest on the stage—and thus did she become Ester-Rokhl Kaminska—the mother of Yiddish theatre. . . . She was an actress who descended from a poor people, and she crowned this people's poverty. . . . In the last months of her life, in the year 1925, while suffering from illness, she traveled to perform in a shtetl, in order to help, with her arrival, a group of actors who were poor and hungry. . . . The Jewish assimilationists in Poland, who considered themselves "Poles of Mosaic confession," were none too curious about Jewish happenings, but they were in the habit of going to see Ester-Rokhl in the Jewish theatre. She truly belonged to the whole of the people, even to those who felt themselves estranged therefrom. That was her power.[11]

Such was her purpose and so was she remembered: "the mama Ester-Rokhl." This was also, tellingly, the title of a 1953 biography of Kaminska, *Di mame ester-rokhl*, by Yitskhok Turkow-Grudberg, the brother of Zygmunt Turkow, who had married Kaminska's daughter Ida. Ida remembers in her own memoir that even Ida's father never addressed Ester-Rokhl by name, but rather only as "Mama"—though she was, in fact, his wife.[12] In keeping with the eternal image of a Jewish mother—she who would run for her child "in vaser un fayer," through water and fire, as the classic song titled after the *yidishe mame* has it—such tributes as Ida's, Molodowsky's and Turkow-Grudberg's recall her as unpretentious (Molodowsky describes her as "on fliterlekh," without sequins)[13] and emotional; loving and selfless; inevitable and magnetic. Try as children might to escape their home and hearth, and chart out a new destiny for themselves (as Kaminska herself did), they are pulled inexorably back to the matriarch. As a child cannot forget her mother, so even the assimilationists, moving away from a purely Jewish culture, were drawn to Ester-Rokhl, who, after all, embodied a synthesis of the traditional (playing out Jewish themes in the language of her people) and the modern (charting out an unprecedented career, and advancing her art to meet the tastes of a new century).

## The "Mame" as a Daughter

But in these memoirs, which she labored over throughout the final year of her life and left unfinished before she died, the revered matriarch is no mother at all, at least not until the closing chapters. She is a daughter—a curious, precocious, rebellious girl, fixed firmly to the earth from which she sprouted, but dreaming of higher, untested branches. When she receives a raise of two rubles a month at the shoe factory in which she had found menial employment in Warsaw, she puts the extra cash into buying clothes, letting people see her the way she saw herself: "Just imagine my joy! With the money I earned, I managed to dress myself quite finely, so that everyone on Pawia Street came to know me as the *aktorke*, the little actress. And I would think to myself, 'Dear God, when will it actually come true?'"

Here was a shtetl girl who would become a star of international stature—"the Jewish Duse," another of her honorifics.[14] In her diary-like chapters, she allows us a glimpse of this girl, the personal experiences and struggles that lay behind the silent mask of her acting in the soundless film. We get to hear her voice. Meanwhile, we come to understand not only the genesis of a Jewish artist but also the person herself: a striking, complicated, extraordinary character containing volumes, but in her origins, a perfectly commonplace figure of her place and time—a girl of a poor shtetl family with few prospects, drawn to the city and the bubbling atmosphere of opportunity it offered. Not commonplace, however, in the specific case of the modernizing Yiddish artist, was how Kaminska would never actually abandon the world of the shtetl, as other writers and performers did, but rather returned to it again and again as she built up her career and her art.

She was born Ester-Rokhl Halperin[15] in Porozove, then part of the Pale of Settlement, the stretches of the Russian Empire that Jews were legally permitted to inhabit. The seventh and last offspring born to the family, she was a child of her father and mother's relatively old age. In his earlier years, her father Khaim had been employed as a cantor and ritual slaughterer, but by the time she came into the world, her aging parents and those children who remained at home were chiefly living on the community's charity. Kaminska remembers Khaim in a short autobiographical sketch as having been, during her lifetime, a luftmensch without a stable profession.[16] Still, being the daughter of a man who had been a cantor—and the sister of two brothers who served as cantors, one in Germany and another in Poland— was an early auspicious sign. So many of the great stars of the Yiddish stage and screen were the children of cantors,[17] raised with a consciousness of how an individual may hold sway over a gathering of people with his own artistry, voice, and spirit.

But as Sholem Aleichem cautions in his story of another preternaturally talented child of a shtetl cantor who dreams of a life of fame, *Yosele solovey* (Yosele the Nightingale) (1889), "A beys-hamedresh iz nisht glaykh tsu a teater"—a house of prayer is not the same as a theatre, and a cantor interceding for his congregation before God, unlike a player treading the boards, must be "a mentsh fun gute mides, a laytisher yid, nit keyn hefker-yung" (a person of good virtue, a respectable Jew, not some lawless youth).[18] An actor is not subject to the same religious demands. Such worries would plague Kaminska's pious parents and sisters as she began to express her aspirations toward the stage. When a recently ailing Porozove inhabitant returns to the shtetl after having visited Warsaw to see doctors, she informs Ester-Rokhl's parents of the teenager's dangerous dreams. They subsequently fulminate to their Warsaw daughters who have charge of Ester-Rokhl, in a furiously long missive decrying the glaring contrast between the solemn piety in which the girl had been raised and the morally dubious world she was entering: "Surely you are not, for God's sake, tolerating such savagery! And yet it seems you are? That a child of ours should work as a two-bit magician! A comedienne?!" The letter ends with the dark warning that if the girl did not want to end her parents' lives before their time, she should quickly end her new career.

Such opposition was in vain. As Kaminska makes clear from the start of her memoirs, she was too resolutely invested with her own sense of who she was and what she wanted. When, as a teenager, she sees her first performance in a theatre, Gounod's opera *Faust* being performed at the Summer Theatre in Warsaw's Saxon Garden, she watches the performers rapt, unmoving, convinced they are something like divine beings, not believing they are real until she is taken to the stage door to see them up close, and in so doing, becoming convinced that their trade is one she, too, might someday ply.

Even in the memoir's early scenes, we see this is a person with an innate sense of the theatrical. When one midsummer night, the household hears strange voices coming from the shtetl synagogue, she narrates the scene with all the suspense and humor of a sensational melodrama. She is a sharp-eyed student of her environment, telling the reader that she did not learn to sing by pursuing a degree in a conservatory, but rather by listening to vigorous young Gentile rustics as they walked home from the harvest harmonizing, scythes and sickles slung over their shoulders, and to the chants emanating from the throats of the yeshiva pupils, poring over their volumes of the Talmud. She is also an enterprising young doer, so confident in her own skill and intelligence that her narration sometimes verges on the comically boastful. She recalls that while she easily made friends with the boys of her shtetl, she looked down on the girls for not being as clever as she, who could polish her family's candlesticks infinitely more brightly than they did theirs, and whose family samovar shone with such splendor after she was done with it that it was "impossible to tell whether it were just brass, or actually pure gold." Still, the writing is not vainglorious: Kaminska has pride in herself, but also, always, a simple joy in doing good work, and an appreciation for the sincere love of others.

When Passover approaches, and it comes time for the girls of Porozove to circulate around the homes of the shtetl assisting in the production of matzo for the holiday, this talented girl is in high demand. She writes that "it was well-known in Porozove that Rokhl, Khaim-Yoykhenen's daughter, could roll out matzo dough better than any of the other girls," and that "the rabbi himself used to say that my work was the most kosher, as well as the most beautiful." This radiant self-confidence—a staunch belief in her own talent despite the difficulty of her circumstances—characterizes much of the writing in her memoir, giving it a certain humor and a glitter. Such is the voice of one born to be an actress, and not merely an actress, but rather a prima donna, a leading lady, a diva.

At the same time, she was known to her friends and to all the theatre world as a kind, generous, selfless, and plainspoken person. As the theatre historian Zalmen Zylbercweig writes in his biography of her that began as an unusually long entry in his multivolume *Leksikon fun yidishn teater* (Biographical Dictionary of Yiddish Theatre) and ended up being published as its own monograph, she was awarded her exalted status in the pantheon of Yiddish actors for her

> great humanity, which she gifted to every role, the friendship and love with which she acted toward her colleagues and toward the Yiddish theatre in general, her respect for the playwright whose work she was performing and to every writer with whom she came into contact.[19]

And underneath that "great humanity" and all-embracing magnanimity, there is that assured sense of self throughout the memoir, that "eygnartiker ikh" (unique "I," as Zylbercweig describes her personality),[20] which lends Kaminska another dimension. In her narration, in which she is nearly always the best at this and at that (and perhaps she was!), Kaminska gives us an account of the supreme faith in one's own qualities and capabilities, fearlessly demonstrated, that is a key element in the birth of a star. In fulfillment of the teenage girl's dream, hers was a star that would join the celestial ranks of those near-divine beings she saw that one summer's evening in the Saxon Garden, when the "Jewel Song" of Gounod's heroine Marguerite left her dazzled.

# Shtetl and City—
# Between Two Worlds

In the course of the memoir, with womanhood approaching, Ester-Rokhl persuades her orthodox parents to allow her to join her older sisters who had settled in Warsaw, which she does in 1885 at the age of fifteen. It was a journey undertaken by many others like her in the same period, making the testimony an important historical document of this move toward cities and all they offered, both bad and good, for Jews from the provinces. In the 1880s, Warsaw's population swelled enormously with newcomers, especially, like Ester-Rokhl, Jewish in-migrants from other towns and cities in tsarist Russian-controlled Congress Poland.[21] But the move, like the girl's daring decision to pursue acting, was also a choice considered to be fraught with danger. As Warsaw was flooded around the turn of the century with townspeople from around Poland, the city gained a reputation in the Yiddish press as a threatening, immoral environment in which its naive new Jewish residents, especially women, struggled desperately to make a living and were frequent victims of both petty and violent crime.[22] The memoirs provide us with a captivating first-person account of just such a working-class woman from the provinces who has come to the big city at a time of massive inflorescence and flux. The work is all the more precious because it was written by a woman of humble background, rather than a highly lettered man more well situated to contribute an account of the time that gets passed down and read. It is revealing that despite Kaminska's lasting fame and the popularity of the memoir genre in Yiddish literature, Kaminska's memoirs were never granted the honor of publication as a book in their original language, only having appeared in serialized form in a daily newspaper, and largely forgotten since that point, owing to the ephemerality of the medium.

Kaminska at first struggles along with the women of the city, gaining employment at a series of factories. One job has her wrapping labels around cigars; at another, stamping shoes with the name of the manufacturer, and serving as charwoman; at yet another, sewing on umbrella canvases. But eventually, the fluidity of identity and pell-mell of diverse experiences that the city offers—hallmarks of the new-fashioned Warsaw—prove to be the key to her self-discovery. The teenage girl defies her family by auditioning for Avrom Goldfaden. This was the playwright, composer, and impresario known for professionalizing the Yiddish stage, with productions that date back to 1876 Romania—the man remembered as the "father of Yiddish theatre," just as Kaminska would come to be known as its "mother." She ends up pursuing ingénue parts in the city.

Soon her mother and father express their stern objection to such a course on the grounds that its attendant immodesty and frivolity amount to a *khilel-hashem*, a desecration of God's name. Though she does not name it, the popular perception that blurred the lines between sex work and the work of an actress, as well as the explosion in the trafficking of Jewish women in Warsaw in the period,[23] likely compounded the parents' fear. Ester-Rokhl dutifully returns to them and the shtetl life. But upon their deaths, she returns to Warsaw and her dream. There she takes a role in an operetta: Mirele, the ill-treated good girl of Goldfaden's *Di kishef-makherin* (The Sorceress).[24] Not long after, she sets out with a wandering troupe of vagabond Yiddish players, who entertain one shtetl after another with their rollicking, if somewhat ragtag, renditions of operettas, historical romances, and parodistic send-ups of conventional Jewish society written by Goldfaden and other populist playwrights.

Goldfaden had at that point given up on presenting Yiddish theatre in the Russian Empire, having formerly produced in the great metropolises of Odessa and St. Petersburg until the establishment of the ban.[25] Self-identifying as an "aristocratic" gentleman and being attracted to the affluent Jewish middle classes, he had focused on the cities instead of the provinces during his career as an impresario in the empire. He typically spurned the chance to present his work in the shtetlach, with their lack of infrastructure for the performance of theatre and scarcity of true aficionados. He would eventually tire of working around the tsarist ban on Yiddish theatre entirely, formerly having sought to circumnavigate it by repackaging his work as German-language theatre, as Kaminska's troupes would do. Indeed, the name she and her husband give to the troupe they establish, in which Kaminska appears for the bulk of the performing narrative, is the Daytsh-Yidish-Teater—German-Jewish Theatre.[26]

Kaminska and her fellow artists never abandoned the repertoire, though, nor their *landslayt*, their Eastern European compatriots. They worked in the shadows of the ban by presenting their shows in the western reaches of the empire and throwing themselves into the presentation of their work in the shtetlach, recognizing a craving for it in those places. The memoirs cover these crucial years of growth and dissemination of the genre, when Yiddish theatre gained its true foothold among the Jewish masses, a period following Goldfaden's greatest success. It was these rough-and-tumble tours that forged within Kaminska her own unique artistic soul, a talent true, without pretension, and at one with the folk, a people that she nourished with her art. Her art was, in turn, fed by these everyday women and men, shaped by their own distinct character and strivings.

# An Interpreter of Stories, Now Telling Her Own

The recursive style of Kaminska's storytelling that emerges distinctly as her destined career gets underway is, like her resolute sense of her own worth and talent, another distinctive attribute of her voice. Just as she does not hesitate to heap praise upon her own personal qualities, neither is she afraid of repeating an idea—for instance, her ambition to become an *artistke* upon the Yiddish stage—or a scene structure. The tours, madcap and highly pressurized and full of amusing misadventures as they are, eventually start to resemble each other. The players pack their few properties, stray beards, well-worn costumes, and themselves into a rickety wagon (those who don't fit walk beside it); make off to the next shtetl; set about finding a firehouse or barn or stable that could house their performance (professional year-round theatre being new to the Jewish masses, and playhouses being few and far between); nail some boards to some discarded, overturned sleighs for a stage, maybe cut down some trees in a nearby forest for scenery, and clap together seats for the audience by laying some planks across a bunch of barrels and setting up the "orchestra"—one single fiddler—atop an oven and his score upon a mound of barley (these particular measures they took when they played Goldfaden's biblical pastiche *Shulamis* in the malt-drying room of a brewery's basement); seek the official permission for the performance from the local officials; post the bills to advertise the show (on which, hopefully, the official would have placed his authorizing signature); sell the tickets; and finally, play for the gathered crowds, who are almost uniformly enchanted. Distinctly unenchanted would be the tsarist censor or gendarme who would sometimes turn up in the back of the hall, checking to ensure that the performers were not playing in Yiddish. When these officials did appear, and the artists had happened to ease into their mother tongue, they would haphazardly switch back to an insecure and half-garbled Teutonic Yiddish, some having a greater command of German than others (and Kaminska is always keen to point out which ones have got it and which ones don't). Then load out of the makeshift playhouse, pack into another wagon, and shove off to the next shtetl down a tortuous country road.

This repeated structure, in various permutations, makes up the bulk of the theatrical portion of the narrative, with Kaminska's anthropologically rich account of her shtetl childhood and emotional memories of her early period in Warsaw taking up its first half. But what a fine close look the repetition provides us at the life of a road company, while throughout, the structure is leavened by intermittent episodes swinging between comedy and tragedy. Such episodes include the much sought-after girl's entangled series of swains and fiancés;[27] the deaths and disappointments of cherished family members; abbreviated and rather practical romance with director, playwright, and fellow actor Avrom-Yitskhok Kaminski (1867–1918), with whom she began acting in a traveling troupe as a young woman; births and two child deaths—a daughter, Leye-Shifre, and a son, Yoysef-Hirsh; the troubled raising of children, Kaminska regretfully leaving them to be taken care of by her sisters as she continued on the road; and the perils of dangerous border crossings and dangerously leering men, both of these being topics of intense discourse in today's world, adding shades of surprisingly contemporary relevance to Kaminska's century-old memoir. That many of these episodes are punctuated by earthy dialogue, animated by bustling movement, and anchored by the construction of tangible scenes and the establishment of place, is testament to Kaminska's strength as a theatremaker. She transfers her skills from the stage to the page and presents to her audience the drama of life.

But even when her story cuts along set pattern lines—another shtetl, another show—just as her unabashed boasts give us insight into her star material, so, too, the repetitions of the memoir have their hidden function. Throughout, even whole sentences read remarkably like ones before. But in this very sameness is a mirror of the life of the actor itself. In the theatre, every day can feel much the same as any other. The play, no matter which paupers or dignitaries are in the audience, no matter how sick or anguished or joyful the actors feel, ends how it is scripted to end. The star-crossed lovers always take their own lives in the crypt at the close of Shakespeare's treasured teen tragedy. Or, to take an example from one of Kaminska's vehicles, *The Sorceress*: the witch is always burned at the end in the fire she set herself, Mirele and her straitlaced paramour Markus are blissfully reunited, and the merry family gathers to crow in grateful chorus, "Der vos grobt a grub far yenem / Falt aleyn arayn!" (He who digs a grave for another / Falls in it himself!). So it is in the theatre! Night after night, things are very much the same. And so it is in Ester-Rokhl's memoir. There is a comfort to that, and an emotional truth. No life is full of infinite variety, not even a bohemian actor's—perhaps *especially* not an actor's, at least not one committed to a set repertory of pieces like Kaminska and her fellow players are. "Oylem goylem," as the Yiddish aphorism goes—the audience is a fool, and must have its laughs, its tears, its neat moral at the resolution, and the same again the night after . . . and after . . .

But here, in the resolution, Kaminska's memoir differs from her theatrical art. We do not get a moral at the end. In fact, we do not even get an end.

The author was gravely ill throughout her last year when, on her sickbed, she endeavored to finish committing her memories to paper. At first, she dictated them to Turkow-Grudberg, the kinsman by marriage and devoted protégé-admirer whom she had, to his delight, appointed as her private secretary. But in time, she decided to first write them out herself by hand and only then leave the editing to him, telling him that, "Reflecting comes easier when one is quite alone—then I'll let you figure out my chicken scratch."[28] She would not finish this "khezbn-hanefesh"—accounting of her soul—as Turkow-Grudberg calls it, perhaps quoting Kaminska,[29] before she died in 1925, leaving the incomplete work to be organized for publication by him and his brother Jonas Turkow.[30] Jonas had acted with the Kaminski Troupe, run by Ester-Rokhl and her husband, from 1917 to 1920, and served as tour manager when the players traveled through war-torn Eastern Europe.[31] The memoirs would be published posthumously in one of Warsaw's two Yiddish-language dailies, *Der moment*, in thirty-two weekly installments from June 11, 1926, to January 21, 1927.

In the final entry, the narrative finds her in the important industrial center of Łódź, having had a series of affirming successes, now, at last, beginning to play regularly in larger cities and prestigious theatres purpose-built for Yiddish theatre. She even writes, acknowledging that she is getting ahead of herself, of winning critical admiration in St. Petersburg ("But we will leave that for now and carry on recounting in the proper order," she redirects, heartbreakingly—as that would be the penultimate sentence she managed to set down). Gone were the days when she and her troupemates were forced to dodge horse manure when entering for their introductory arias in stables-turned-playhouses. At the close of the memoir, she has earned the friendship and approbation of a famed Hebrew and Yiddish modernist poet, Dovid Frishman (1859–1922). That relationship is also a milestone, with Frishman, in his capacity as a leading cultural critic, being a significant early champion of her talent at a time when other critics were more hesitant. The last chapter of the memoirs is named for him.

The most well-known period of her career, which saw her giving the highly regarded performances that guaranteed her lasting fame and cemented her status as the "mother of Yiddish theatre," was still to take place after the chronicled events.[32] In this regard, Kaminska's memoirs do not shower her readers with what some may have sought from the promise of her memoirs' original title, *Derner un blumen* (Thorns and Flowers)—the endless bouquets of accolades to follow the many thorns she so carefully documents. Those performances as a true celebrity took place after she settled down in Warsaw in 1905 and began playing in loftier dramas of the "literary" style, feeling freed by the contemporaneous softening of the

Russian imperial government's restrictions on Yiddish theatre. In 1907, together with her husband, she would found the first permanent Yiddish ensemble committed to such repertoire, the Literarishe Trupe, heralding in a credible and psychologically rich style of acting, and beginning to play her series of mother roles for which she would become most famous.

The content of her memoirs would have turned out entirely differently had Kaminska heeded the advice of one famed expert. After inquiring into the possibility of publishing the work in the "World's Largest Jewish Daily," as the official stationery of New York's socialist newspaper *Forverts* proclaimed, with an illustration of the grandiose *Forverts* building on East Broadway looming in the corner, a response was sent back to her by the secretary of the paper's imposing writer-editor Abraham Cahan:

> He will be very pleased to print your memoirs. However, he proposes that you begin, from the very start, with your dramatic career, and delay for the moment [the description of] your personal life until later. You will obviously understand that the public is highly interested in theatre—and so if you start with that, it will be "oll rayt."[33]

Kaminska was excited by the tastemaker's interest in her work. After Cahan sent a subsequent missive asking for more entries,[34] she wrote to her own personal editor and transcriber, Jonas Turkow, "I have this very minute received a very good letter from the *Forverts*," noting, however, that Cahan would not publish the couple of entries she sent without her sending in advance at least ten more.[35] But it was not to be. She notes in the same letter to Turkow that she planned to show Cahan's letter to Tsvi Pryłucki, the editor of Warsaw's *Moment*, who would eventually publish the memoirs. It seems that Kaminska could not be persuaded to write her memoirs backward, even knowing, amid her battle with cancer, that she might not get to the end if she carried on chronologically (it is likely that the illness is largely why Cahan asked her not to do so, fearful of never receiving the stories he was most eager for). Kaminska knew that her origins, and the origins of her art, were just as worthy of attention as the juicy backstage material from her marquee years that Cahan assumed would most fascinate his audience. And as one of her greatest advocates, the venerated author Peretz wrote in his play *Nokh kvure* (After the Burial): "A mame veyst shtendik, vos tsu ton"—a mother always knows what to do.[36]

The period covered in Kaminska's memoir was so crucial to her, perhaps, as it constituted both her youth and that of the Yiddish theatre itself. Goldfaden gave his first performances in Iaşi, Romania that would mark the start of the professional modern Yiddish stage in 1876, just a few years before Kaminska hit the road with a group of performers playing his wonderfully colorful and tuneful pieces. As a young person discovers the world, so were her theatrically untutored audiences discovering the world of drama right along with her, as she laughed and trilled and capered for their delight. During her career, her audiences grew from just having their eyes opened to the form to being insatiable, relentless fans thereof, like a teenager discovering a rock star who meets her exact needs, whose poster on her wall becomes the icon of all her anxieties and latent desires. In a 1914 fan letter from an admirer in Odessa, an abundant spray of violets printed on the card curls around passionate remarks sounding like the ravings of a besotted youth, addressed, "Der harts-bahersherin fun yidishn publikum"—To her who rules the hearts of the Jewish public.[37] A card of devotion bestowed by a group of youngsters, signed simply "Dvinsker yugnt" (The youth of Dvinsk, the Latvian town known today as Daugavpils), hails her using the Yiddish informal register, which is how children would address their mother ("Ere dir, muter fun yidishn teater!"—Honor to you, mother of Yiddish theatre!).[38]

And as Kaminska came into adulthood, so did the Yiddish theatre and its increasingly discerning audiences, taking on a more mature character. In both phases, she was a pioneer, first in the widespread dissemination of the art form itself throughout Eastern Europe, then in its reconceptualization, its attainment of a level of artistry that would give it a place on the world stage. Kaminska would seem to insist, with the attention and detail she devotes to recalling her early years, on their importance to both her trajectory as an artist and to the art form itself. The program for her anniversary gala performance in Warsaw, marking thirty years on the stage, underlines the significance of her very first parts. On that night, she would pay equal tribute to both phases of her career, the sensational and the psychological, by playing *both* of her two great Mireles: she would direct herself as the stony matriarch of Gordin's *Mirele Efros,* with which she had solidified her reputation as an accomplished thespian in Warsaw; and she would play it right alongside the sweetly singing sixteen-year-old Mirele of Goldfaden's *Sorceress,* her first-ever principal role on the stage, now reprising it at age fifty-two.[39] On that night, organized by a committee featuring such luminaries of Yiddish Warsaw as the writer-photographer Alter Kacyzne, and introduced by the journeyman writer Mendl Elkin, the aging actress would remind her public of the glories of the soprano role that first brought her before the eyes of the wider world, precisely as she does with her colorful reminiscences of the early Goldfaden crowd-pleasers throughout the memoirs.

What followed those early roles—the entire second half of her blazing trajectory—Kaminska did not ultimately have the life within her to describe. And so, at the close of the memoirs, she and her band of peripatetic play-actors pack up their carts, leave Łódź, where they had been playing in the splendid new Groyser Teater (Great Theatre), and set off for yet another community to which they could spread their merry gospel of Jewish art. It is almost telling that she does not inform us exactly whither they wandered. Their destination is wherever we might dream, perhaps. There is no moral, no final triumphant chorus of lessons learned and sacred purposes fulfilled, no aria of cathartic, saga-ending woe. The wagons go on wheeling. The reading audience wonders. And curtain.

And yet, what rich value there is in all that Kaminska was able to give her readers. How genuinely funny sometimes they are! How delicious it was to find, in translating this author's testament, that there are still so many instances of blithe, effortless humor in her narration that cause me to laugh aloud, even while taxing my eyes over the close examination of tiny newsprint from a century ago (as but one trivial example—when Kaminska casually quotes her disapproving sister issuing a tirade against Ester-Rokhl's activities, name-dropping the Warsaw Yiddish theatre "Eldorado," but in her ignorance, or in a poorly conceived attempt at mockery, calling it the "Tulderada"). It was a quality that she appreciated. Ida remembers her mother being so good-hearted, so quick to admire a person, that when defending someone she was fond of whom everyone else disparaged, she would sometimes say, "But he can tell a good joke."[40] She goes on to praise her mother's ability to toss off witticisms even in the direst of situations. When acknowledging that no great biography has been written of her mother (and to this day, no full-length one has yet been published in English), she goes on to state her belief "that her personality could best be depicted by a collection of her *bon mots*, puns, and jokes."[41]

It is a pity that we still have not been graced with such an Ester-Rokhl Kaminska jokebook! In the meantime, this translated memoir may serve as such an artifact of her personality, and a capsule of her narrative style and thoughts. Her writing vibrates with the emotion of a life fully lived, and the thrill of remembering it. Therein lie all the rich texture, comic incident, danger, nerves and excitement, failures and ovations—indeed all the dirty details—of a nineteenth-century actor's life on the road.

# The Artist's Bumpy Byway

Kaminska emerged as an actor in an era preceding the establishment of Yiddish theatrical unions that followed the First World War. She first performed when Yiddish theatre was ad hoc and officially illegal. Being a woman under such circumstances did not make things easier. Kaminska was continually surrounded by unscrupulous admirers and hotheaded, ambitious artists as she charted a course that was unfamiliar and disdained for one of her sex, especially one with such a rigorously traditional upbringing. As a mere child, we witness her fierce self-advocating in order to attain some formal education, so that she might learn to read and write as well as a boy. Later, she paints an understatedly disturbing scene at a private dinner in the hotel suite of her troupe director, to which he has invited the local government censor along with other small-time Russian officers. The officers become drunk and flirt with the young Kaminska, with whom they are able to get on more easily because she speaks a more articulate German than the rest of the troupe. When one invites her on a private sleigh ride, and her director encourages her to accept it (wanting to win over the authorities so that the censor might relax his overview of their performances and they might be permitted to play in Yiddish), the stakes are clear—especially in the eventual repercussions for the troupe that result from her and her fellow actresses not giving these men what they seek (for the bizarre denouement of this particular drama, see Chapter XXVIII—"An Official Sparks Scandal in Tomaszów").

That she sets this scene directly after an account of her playing Mirele, the damsel in distress of *The Sorceress*, is perhaps no coincidence, though she does not draw attention to the parallels. Mirele is sold by that piece's titular witch into something resembling sexual slavery in Turkey, where she is forced to perform in scanty apparel for café customers to the accompaniment of a malicious organ-grinder. The drama onstage mirrors the reality: both Ester-Rokhl at the dinner and Mirele in the Istanbul café are forced, under the threat of severe punishment, to sing to the tune of a tyrannical man.

Throughout the memoirs, there are rhyming situations like these, and hidden depths below the surface of Kaminska's writing—fascinating juxtapositions, and significant things left just barely unsaid. Underlying the episodic play-by-play is an actress's great sensitivity and vision, and an understanding of her life as a drama with strong narrative threads running through it, with a struggling but strong heroine driving it all forward.

After marrying Kaminski and conceiving, she is made to wear a corset—a "neshome-kvetsher" (soul-squeezer), she calls it—to tamp down her pregnant belly when onstage, as the dresses she owns would not fit over it without her body being painfully constricted. Soon after, she is met with the fearsome difficulties of having to give birth and rear babies on the road, cope with the tragedy of infant death, and make the quite modern decision to commit herself to her career and share out some of the burden of childcare to others. Here is a woman beset with stumbling blocks, from both inside and outside of her close artistic community, a woman who would have to look out for her own interests and sense of self in a world that often sought to undermine and exploit them.

Her memoir, distinguished by all of this toil, this anxiety, the twinned pain and passion of the business of show, is grimy and unglamorous but consistently glorious from installment to installment, priceless as an account of this time and place, this theatrical scene, the very birth pangs of an art form. The author has a near photographic memory of her past, filling in the register of her activities and interactions with skillfully chosen details and idiomatically rich dialogue, though never quite painting each scene with all the sights, smells, sounds, and psychological soul-searching that a contemporary memoirist might. There is a sense of movement, of one thing and then the next, of the show that must, under any circumstances, go on.

One quirk appears as a perennial leitmotif. Ester-Rokhl continually seems to be made nervous and overawed, to the point of nearly fainting, by new and imposing sights: the towering edifices of Warsaw; the vastness of the crowd in a train station or a theatre audience; miraculous opera singers and the grand figure of Goldfaden; a makeup artist named Antoni (this sequence being one of the great set pieces of the memoir, in which she expresses horror at having to go onstage in a pair of trousers and her face being daubed with pork schmaltz). But then—always—the girl plucks up her innate chutzpah. She takes a deep breath. And she performs.

As she tells herself while sitting and watching a performance of Goldfaden's national-historical opera *Bar Kokhba*—a characteristically plainspoken expression of her immense stores of self-confidence—"Well, once I've learned the music, I'll be able to carry it off just as beautifully. After all, there can't be some great trick to it, if you already speak Yiddish" (Figure 6).

FIGURE 6 In a production photograph (*c.* 1892), Kaminska appears as the Jerusalemite maiden Dine, enamored of the rebel leader who is the title character of *Bar kokhba, der zun fun di shtern: oder, di letste teg fun yerusholayim* (Bar Kokhba, the Son of the Stars: or, The Last Days of Jerusalem). At her side is Leyb Shtrasfogl playing her father, the pacifist sage Reb Elieyzer. Dine is one of the roles she plays in the course of her memoirs, and she writes of her early dreams pertaining to the role in one poignant passage: "Ever since I had returned from Porozove, some *takhles*, some suitable, practical aim in life had been sought for me. My sisters had thought that aim could be to become a milliner or seamstress, while I thought it could only lie in becoming Dine, the heroine of Goldfaden's opera *Bar Kokhba*."). Zalmen Zylbercweig, ed., *Albom fun yidishn teater* (Album of the Yiddish Theatre) (New York: Elisheve, 1937), 31.

# As the Possibilities for Yiddish Theatre Expand, Kaminska's Star Ascends

Here was a sense of assurance that would serve her throughout her career, especially as bold new horizons opened for her chosen field. Toward the end of the memoirs' chronological scope, Kaminska's traveling operetta troupe, once confined to the shtetlach, now plays in such burgeoning cities as Łódź, still, however, having to avoid speaking Yiddish onstage lest their performances be instantly boarded up by the government censors. But one monumental shift would follow another for the Kaminski players—first into the cities, then out of the shadow of the ban on their art.

Kaminska's long years of service to her art and her audiences in the shtetlach, honing her craft and her understanding of what her public desired, prepared her to seize her moment in this approaching dawn and guide the form to meet its expanded potential. In 1905, coterminous with the first Russian revolution, the tsarist ban on Yiddish theatre—and restrictions on Jewish culture generally—slackened.[42] The legalization of Jewish daily newspapers would also make consistent coverage of theatrical happenings possible, a step indispensable to the promotion of the art. In the same year, Kaminska and her husband settled down in Warsaw to found their own Yiddish theatre, the Bagatela, in Mokotów, then a suburb of the city and now a neighborhood therein. It opened with a performance of the Yiddish actor-writer Zigmund Faynman's *Khanele di neytorin* (Khanele the Seamstress).[43] The Jews of Warsaw would come out in droves, even battling freezing temperatures in the dead of winter, to enjoy the company's new artistic repertoire. It included dramas by the historically minded playwright Dovid Pinski and the theatrical reformer Jacob Gordin,[44] in whose artistically ambitious pieces Kaminska would excel, and with whose female roles—among them the title characters of *Khasye di yesoyme* (Khasye the Orphan Girl) and *Mirele Efros*—she would come to be associated. In time, the troupe would turn even to her husband's Yiddish translations of the most highly regarded European plays, both classic and au courant, including Molière's *L'Avare* (The Miser, or in Yiddish, *Der karger*) and Gorky's *Na dne* (The Lower Depths, or *In opgrunt*).

Their much-lauded successes at a series of theatres in Warsaw would attract the notice of the entire region, and in 1908 Kaminska performed the unimaginable by playing six weeks in St. Petersburg, the crown jewel of the empire, where most Jews were still not permitted to reside. There, she became the darling of the Jewish intelligentsia and even the Gentile, Russian-language press, being invited to the grand homes of the upper classes and lavished with banquets in her honor, as she in turn brought them into an intimate acquaintance with her beloved Yiddish theatre.[45] In 1909, and again in 1911–12, she would set foot in America, touring there and being greeted as a celebrity.[46] In 1912, following Kaminska's performance in Gordin's *Khasye* at the fashionable Belasco Theatre in the nation's capital, and previewing her imminent return performance there in Z. Libin's 1905 drama *Di vilde* (The Wild Girl),[47] a theatre reporter for Washington D.C.'s *Sunday Star* recorded that the renowned actress had a success "so pronounced that another presentation for tonight was arranged for." Underlining her and her fellow players' crossover appeal, the reporter added, "The histrionic work of these Yiddish players is attracting the attention of English-speaking playgoers and dramatic critics of the daily press. So realistic is said to be their art that one can follow pretty clearly the story of the play without a knowledge of the Yiddish tongue."[48]

Earlier on that tour, which she undertook with the troupe of Kenny Lipzin, a diva in her own right and a sort of American-based counterpart to Kaminska, she performed *Mirele Efros*. Though the role, on American soil, had been owned since the play's 1898 première by Lipzin, that actress, recognizing her rival's prowess, gave her "special permission" to play it with her own eponymous company.[49] The matchup, and the drama of Kaminska's potential success or failure on American soil, proved irresistible for the country's Yiddish theatregoers and literati. The comic newspaper *Der groyser kundes* (The Big Stick) from one of the weeks she played in New York, headlining the Lipzin Theatre at 235–237 Bowery, depicts an anxious Kaminska remembering the passionate admiration she had won on her first American tour, now disappointed that the New York public is not showing her as much favor on her second. Amid her reverie, she plucks the petals of a flower and tosses them to the ground, each reading either "Libt mikh yo" (Loves me) or "Libt mikh nit" (Loves me not) (Figure 7).[50]

Even Cahan, the revered editor of the *Forverts*, after "finally" getting the opportunity to see Kaminska in the part, weighed in with an article bluntly titled "Ver iz a besere 'mirele efros', madam liptsin oder madam kaminska?"[51] (Who Is a Better "Mirele Efros," Madame Lipzin or Madame Kaminska?). Cahan acclaims Kaminska for her "modern," "realistic," "natural" acting, declaring that her performance achieves true authenticity: "Zi redt vi a idene un zi geyt vi a idene" (She talks like a Jewish woman and walks like a Jewish woman). Still, he feels Lipzin (the hometown heroine, after all), with her style belonging to the "classic" school and delivering a

אסתר רחל קאמינסקי : ערשט פאר־א־יאָהרען אז מיין געליעבטער (טהעא־
טער־געהער) איז געוווען שטערבליך פערליעבט אין מיר... און היינט? לאָמיר
אקאָרשט זעהן : ער ליעבט מיך יא; ער ליעבט מיך ניט; ער ליעבט מיך יא; ער
ליעבט מיך — אָוי, א בראָך איז מיר! ער ליעבט דאָך מיך טאַקע ניט!

FIGURE 7 Kaminska caricatured in the New York humor magazine *Der groyser kundes*.

Mirele that "smacks not of Lithuania, but rather Shakespeare," makes the greater impression in the role.

Indeed, despite Kaminska's intermittently brilliant success in the New World, it seems that owing to the subtlety and fine strokes of her acting (as in her precise choices made in the silent film, described at the beginning of this introduction), she was too ahead of her time for some New York audiences still accustomed to the histrionics of melodrama and the cheap laughs afforded by vaudeville. As Ida quotes a New York writer paying Kaminska tribute after her death in 1925, "Ester-Rokhl came much too soon to us in America. Only now, after the Yiddish Art Theatre has already been performing for several years, are they acting in the style that Ester-Rokhl utilized years ago."[52]

Demonstrating her readiness for the challenges set by modern, sophisticated work, in time Kaminska's repertoire expanded, with the tormented heroines of Dumas's *La Dame aux Camélias* (The Lady of the Camellias, or *Kamelyen-dame*) and Ibsen's *Et dukkehjem* (A Doll's House, or as it was more simply known in Yiddish, after the name of the protagonist: *Nora*), as well as the work of such avant-garde Yiddish playwrights as Perets Hirshbeyn, namely his eerie folk drama *Di puste kretshme* (The Empty Inn).[53] In selecting the latter play, she exhibited the selflessness for which she had become renowned. When she suggested it, amid her feverish quest for new dramatic voices, Kaminska was questioned as to whether it had a role that suited her talents (the central female role is a much younger person, an anguished, sexually daring girl named Meyte). She responded tersely and piquantly, "Ikh vil mir zoln shpiln di pyese, nisht mayn rol" (I want us to perform the play, not [simply] my role).[54]

After Kaminska returned to Warsaw following one of her tours, Kaminski, leveraging the profits from his wife's work, undertook in 1909 the remodeling of the Golgotha, a giant round circus arena seating 1,500, into a new Yiddish theatre known as Kaminski's Theatre.[55] Building it up at No. 1 Oboźna Street in an area of town where more upscale, assimilated Jews lived, far from the traditional center of the Jewish community, Kaminski intended that folks rich and poor should honor his and his wife's art by making a special pilgrimage.[56] Yiddish theatre would be performed there until 1917, though with mixed results—the venue was, after all, a trek for most of the city's Jews, and rather too enormous to fill, especially with the hard sell of the more serious-minded repertoire that had become the stock-in-trade of the Kaminskis' forward-thinking troupe.[57]

Ida remembers her father's hubris upon deciding to establish his theatre on Oboźna Street, quoting him as saying, "I don't want a ghetto," insisting that even Jews in kapotes (long coats worn by religious men) and *peyes* (curly sidelocks worn by the same) "should come to a fine, large theatre in the center of town."[58] It was a callous attitude that seems to have distinguished him from his open-hearted and sympathetic wife. Ida mentions in her memoirs his handsomeness, height, and large gray eyes—as well as his ease in attracting women, particularly once he had become manager of a theatrical troupe. Soon after in her text, she recalls that when he, who could not bear to lie, "mercilessly betrayed my mother, he also mercilessly reported this to her."[59]

The woman's suffering and sorrows, her *yisurim* and her *tsores*, feature often in the chronicles of her life.[60] No doubt some of these accounts obliquely allude to Kaminski's infidelity along with the struggles they state more plainly: her own bouts with illness, the difficult life on the road, the ups and downs of the business itself and its hold on audiences, having to leave her children with her sisters who largely raised them so that she could pursue that career,[61] and the deaths of younger children precisely because of the dangers of strenuous travel. One arresting scene in the memoir has her playing Queen Esther on the very day of the burial of her son. The boy had been shockingly suffocated to death on a wintry-cold wagon ride from one theatrical destination to another, his wet nurse unwittingly smothering the baby while protecting him from the freezing temperatures. Of her performance shortly after, Kaminska remembers, "It was no coincidence that the next day, people all over town were raving about how the queen had performed as though she were actually undergoing some excruciating ordeal," just like the biblical heroine. The spreading fissures of Kaminska's heartbreak extended to her playing and gave it the wrenching quality of life, the same quality we see in the face of the prematurely grieving mother as she bids her son farewell in *The Vow*.

Though she had won international fame by the time she set down her memoirs, she was insistent on recalling these least glamorous, most painful parts of her life in her handwritten pages. The thorns stab, but they are there on the flower-stem of her career. They, more than a relation of endless glories would, tell a tale of who the woman was, and how she was formed, on her journey to becoming an actress-*impresaria* of renown. As is true of the best blues singers, her art was said to be deeply informed by the pain and struggle that were her daily bread. Nokhem Lipovski, the theatrical producer, placing her in "the center of the Yiddish theatre's martyrology," remembered her thusly, writing that "For no other Yiddish actor was life as rich with dramatic collisions between ideal art and the harsh realities of existence, and so full of personal torments and hardship, as it was for the late 'Mother of Yiddish Theatre.'"[62]

The children that this mother lost in the course of her memoir would not be the only ones she buried before her own untimely death. Her daughter

Regina, born in 1894, whom Ida remembers being acclaimed the "beautiful" one and she herself the "clever" one, would die of liver disease in 1913, leaving the family in a state of both misery and destitution, the girl's need for good doctors having used up much of their resources.[63] Owing to the economic situation, *di mame* Ester-Rokhl had to do what she always did: wiping her tears, which carried on flowing for months, the woman packed up and left for a theatrical tour, this time to Paris, London, and Baku, so as to earn all that was needed to keep her remaining children clothed, housed, and well educated.[64] The show went on for her, in spite of everything, and Kaminska did what she felt she must to satisfy both her own artistic hunger and the needs of her family (Figure 8).

The image of Kaminska as ur-mother is complicated by her not having been a physically present mother to her own children throughout long stretches of performing, but that discrepancy also revealingly illustrates the tensions of a career woman's life in the period, the distinction between public myth and private reality, and the braided strands of artifice and truth in the construction of a stage image. Still, even from afar, it is clear that

FIGURE 8 Ester-Rokhl Kaminska with her family in Warsaw, 1903. From left: daughter Ida Kaminska; Ester-Rokhl; daughter Regina Kaminska, who died in late adolescence in the year 1913; husband Avrom-Yitskhok Kaminski; son Yoysef Kaminski. Photograph (YIVO, RG 119, Folder "Kaminska, Esther Rachel," Item 2).

Ester-Rokhl was taking care to manage the upbringing of her children. Her frequent and lengthy letters home are filled with solicitations as to their welfare and directives on matters as prosaic as buying an overcoat for her son Yoysef (whom she refers to tenderly as Yoysefke or Yosinke), or getting their photograph taken so that it might be sent to her.[65]

In one letter to Yoysefke,[66] written in the throes of her illness the year that she died, she pleads that he make sure to eat enough (and at the proper times!) in Berlin, where he was at the time studying music. She expresses regret that she does not have a home in Berlin so that she might feed him herself, or alternatively, that his music professors are not in Warsaw. The letter culminates in typical fashion, with a number of almost-endings, each time returning to lavish her "zunele" (little son) with further expressions of affection: "And so, my Yoysefke, I don't have anything more to write you," though she then writes with more news for a paragraph more; then an entreaty, "My child! Your Aunt Rivka [who took part in raising Ester-Rokhl's children] has become somewhat agitated by your not writing her separately with your greetings"; then after asking about his finances and residence, "Ikh gris un kush dir toyznt mol, dayn traye mame" (I send my love and kiss you a thousand times, your devoted mother), and her signature—but it's not over yet! After the signature, she adds "Write often, Yoysefke," following it with the communication of greetings from the others at home in Warsaw, and further news of her own doings, reflecting her own constant push to advance her art and secure an existence for her family free from the penury in which she herself was raised.

When world war had erupted, and the tsarist government returned to limiting the production of Yiddish-language theatre, Kaminska again figured out a way forward—and language-hopped once more. She toured for five months in the Kherson governorate, which included cities like Odessa and Nikolaev, with such Gordin chestnuts as *Mirele Efros*, *Khasye the Orphan Girl*, and the Faustian morality play *Got, mentsh un tayvl* (God, Man, and Devil)—only now all in Russian. Returning to Warsaw a few days before the Germans occupied the city on August 4, 1915, Kaminska took over the direction of Kaminski's Theatre until 1918, when her husband died in Łomża, Poland, following an acute asthma attack, at the age of fifty-one.[67] The tireless artist would then set off again for tours of Ukraine and Lithuania in a rapidly shifting Eastern Europe. She played under one government then another, performing eventually in Communist state theatres under the authority of the Soviets in Moscow and Kyiv, though, due to her celebrity, commanding a higher salary than her fellow actors in the workers' ensembles.[68] She gave a mixed report to the Warsaw press following her return from this two-year Soviet tour. Describing the pressures of playing in a region devastated by post-First World War pogroms, she claimed, however, that theatre artists were regarded as "privileged proletarians" among the Bolsheviks and, with a few notable exceptions, treated with "consideration" (as the American press transmitted the content of her remarks) by marauding pogromists "amidst general Jewish slaughter."[69] Still, she acknowledged the banning of the works of her beloved Gordin among the Soviets, all of his plays except for *Mirele Efros* and *God, Man, and Devil* being prohibited, and his widely admired *On a heym* (Without a Home) being dismissed as "trash."[70]

A Russian ban on the art she held dear—the new development would not have seemed new to her at all, but rather an ugly reminder of the desperate conditions she had worked in during the early part of her career, under tsarist rule. And yet she does seem to have expressed some degree of appreciation in her remarks. Here is the carefully measured speech of one who had, in her years of experience, grown not only to be a mistress of her art, but the business thereof, too. From the shtetl years documented in the memoir, she had learned that Yiddish theatre is akin to a saber dance. She is well acquainted with the necessarily subtle steps sideways and the clever feints, the lunges forward and the concealments, to allow one to carry on practicing one's art, in the face of a regime far less than friendly.

In 1920, she left to tour the provinces again, such theatrical nomadism as is covered in the memoir having remained a fundamental, though taxing, part of her career. The programs of the period attest to her importance in her company and in the theatre world writ large. She received top billing in these latter tours, her name appearing above the title on playbills, an honor accorded only to the biggest stars. In a performance at Vilna's Shtot-Zal (City Auditorium), the bill announces a tour of "der velt-barimter kinstlerin" (the world-famous artist) Kaminska—her troupe going without mention. Her name appears double the size of her fellow players' names in the cast listing for the evening's entertainment, a translation of Russian realist Alexander Ostrovsky's *Bez viny vinovatye* (Guilty Without Guilt, or in the Yiddish version, *Umshuldik shuldik*).[71] After touring, she settled down to perform at Warsaw's Teater Tsentral, which, under the direction of her son-in-law Zygmunt Turkow, came to be known as the Varshever Yidisher Kunst-Teater (VYKT, or Warsaw Yiddish Art Theatre).[72] In it, she was well and truly enthroned as the queen mother of a group of experimental young Yiddish actors who had grown up with her as their great model and who covered her with reverence and adoration until her final year when, as cancer took hold of her body, she mostly stopped performing (Figure 9).[73]

FIGURE 9 *Di mame* Ester-Rokhl and her theatrical brood, Vilna 1923. Kaminska sits in the center, surrounded by the young artists of the Warsaw Yiddish Art Theatre, in which she acted and served as sagely mentor to the coming generation of artists. Looking off into the distance, in a lighter-colored dress, is Ida Kaminska, with Ida's husband and the director of the troupe Zygmunt Turkow seated in front of Ida, one arm folded over the back of his chair. Photograph (YIVO, RG 119, Folder "Kaminska, Esther Rachel," Item 5).

# The Curtain Falls

After Kaminska received her cancer diagnosis in Warsaw, she underwent an operation in Vienna.[74] When she returned, weakened though she was, Kaminska was eager to ascend the stage again, which she did as Mirele Efros in Vilna. She had been invited there along with her son-in-law Zygmunt and daughter Ida. Though Ester-Rokhl was still doyenne, Ida now shone as a leading lady in the company, with a starlight all her own. She no longer played her mother's toddling grandson, but instead her chief foil in the play, the conniving daughter-in-law Sheyndele. When she first appeared onstage, Ester-Rokhl was greeted with an ovation that lasted a number of minutes. "I stood backstage," recalled Ida, "dressed in my wedding gown for the role of Sheyndele, my heart beating like a hammer and tears streaming from my eyes. My mother's performance was magnificent, and it was hard to believe that she was struggling with an awful illness." What follows in Ida's account is so devastating, so true to who Ester-Rokhl was—exhibiting the same poignant marriage of onstage drama with off that continually presents itself in her own memoirs—that it bears reproducing in full:

> During the second act I had to say to Mirele (that is, to my mother), "Do you think a person can live forever?" but I could not utter the final part of the question. I got as far as "Do you think . . ." but the rest of the line remained stuck in my throat. Seeing this, my mother did not let me finish and replied, "I know what you mean. Don't worry. I know that a person cannot live forever." At the end of the act my mother embraced me. "My poor sweetheart, you couldn't say those words. But don't worry. Everything is all right, and I feel well."[75]

Not long after, Ester-Rokhl Kaminska passed away. A tragedienne to the end, her final words were reported by relatives to be "*Di forshtelung vert geendikt*" (The performance is over).[76] Ida and her brother Yoysef, now twenty-six and twenty-two, respectively, were left without a mother and father. But according to the grieving Jewish masses, it was not just those two who were orphaned. *Literarishe bleter* (Literary Pages), Jewish Warsaw's leading periodical documenting arts and culture, described her passing in characteristically apt turns of phrase, in a black-bordered box on its cover a few days after her passing:

> Mir fareynikn zikh tsum algemeynem troyer (We join ourselves to the general sorrow)
>
> tsulibn toyt fun (caused by the death of)
>
> ESTER-ROKHL KAMINSKA
>
> di mame un dos kind (the mother and the child)
>
> fun nayem yidishn teater (of the new Yiddish theatre)
>
> un drikn oys undzer tifn mitgefil der familye fun der farshtorbener un di faryosemte yidishe artistn (and express our deep sympathy to the family of the deceased and the orphaned Jewish actors).[77]

Along with Kaminska's son and daughter, all of the artists then treading in the trail she had furrowed with her unceasing wagon wheels were now left without a mother. And Kaminska herself, the journalists noted, had been not just a mother of her art form, but a child, too—one who had grown up right alongside the Yiddish theatre, which had now reached its adulthood.

The grandeur of her funeral, as portrayed in contemporary news reports, reflected a collective grief felt by an entire culture: from the early morning of December 29, Oboźna Street, where she had lived and died and maintained her theatre, was filled with mourners of every stripe, carrying funeral wreaths from their various organizations and bearing testament to how well beloved the actress was "among all classes of Jewish Warsaw."[78] Kaminska's younger protégés, along with dozens of theatres and literary societies (including delegations from America), followed in the massive procession behind those elder artists who had first played alongside her, including such showmen as Berman, Rotshayn, Shvartsbard, and Faynshteyn, as well as her first director, Yulius Oskar—all of them names that turn up frequently in her memoirs. By the time it reached the Jewish quarter, the number of mourners in the cortège apparently stretched to 80,000. Before her open grave, one of the most legendary cantors of Europe, Gershon Sirota, sang elegies with his choir, and an address was delivered by the esteemed Yiddish writer Hersh Dovid Nomberg, whose own mentor, Kaminska's artistic collaborator Y. L. Peretz, lay hard by under his own tombstone.[79]

# Seedlings Blossom in Her Wake

The great lady was gone, but she left a significant legacy. A theatrical museum posthumously founded in her name initially took up residence in her own apartment. Today, its vast collections, now housed at the YIVO Institute in New York, represent one of the world's largest extant archives of prewar Yiddish theatre materials, crucial to the study of the art form.

Her children, themselves artistic luminaries and leading exponents of their crafts, formed her legacy in flesh and blood. Ida, as an older woman, was nominated for an Academy Award for her performance as a Jewish shopkeeper during the Nazi occupation of Czechoslovakia in the 1965 Czech film *Obchod na korze* (The Shop on Main Street), a remarkable achievement for an actor who worked primarily in Yiddish. She was the first and only actor to ever turn in an Academy-recognized performance in a film produced on the other side of the Iron Curtain. Kaminska's son Yoysef, the composer and violinist, was concertmaster of the Israeli Philharmonic until he retired at the age of sixty-nine.[80]

Meanwhile, the still-active State Yiddish Theatre of Poland, today known as the Teatr Żydowski im. Estery Rachel i Idy Kamińskich, was established in 1949, and in 1955, at a ceremony marking the thirty-year anniversary of Kaminska's death, dedicated in her own name (later, her daughter Ida's was added).[81]

The very art form she pioneered remains vibrant into the twenty-first century. This is the art form of which Kaminska's acolyte Turkow-Grudberg wrote consolingly in her wake, "Ober dos folk blaybt lebn, un dos teater iz a lebediker eyver fun folk" ("But the People remains living, and the theatre is a living limb of that People").[82]

And as her final act, Kaminska bequeathed a legacy in pen and ink: memoirs she drafted with the last of her strength, only ever published in Yiddish in serialized form in the newspaper, now appearing as a book that will hopefully be worthy of her, and for the first time in English (Figure 10).

The scene of my work, as I bent low over the scans of *Der moment* and construed each word of Kaminska's, was typically in my dressing room backstage—while performing in Yiddish theatre. Often, it was while appearing in *The Sorceress*, the operetta that gave Kaminska her first professional acting engagement—as it did for me. While she played the tormented girl Mirele, I played that girl's tormentress, the scheming and

FIGURE 10 Kaminska in Vienna, recovering from an operation to save her life, 1922. The photograph, taken at a desk and showing the actress with a reflective gaze, grasping what appears to be a pen, was perhaps taken to commemorate her writing her memoirs, a project she undertook during this period. Zylbercweig, *Di velt fun ester-rokhl kaminska*, 269.

dubiously magical Bobe Yakhne, traditionally played by a man en travesti. Once, upon returning from playing the scene wherein the witch traps the girl in the marketplace of Botoșani, I sat down in my braided wig, corset, and bodysuit, and, with my ludicrously long plastic nails, tapped out her harrowing account of the same scene (in which Ester-Rokhl catches a cold midway through, performing barefoot on a frosted-over stage in the dead of winter).

She was with me as I trod those boards, as she is with us all who labor in her chosen discipline, whether we realize it or not. Yiddish actors today do not typically have to clear the hay and filth out of a barn in order to procure a playing space (though just as Kaminska's troupe put on *Shulamis* in the brewhouse cellar, a young and scrappy collective of ours recently had to clear beer bottles out of one member's Brooklyn basement for the purpose of putting on a Yiddish cabaret there; and, when rehearsing a new Yiddish play that I wrote, my fellow actors and I had to push aside mannequins and bits of bangles and brocade, as our rehearsal space was an embroidery workshop in the heart of Manhattan's garment district). Neither do we, thankfully, have to dodge the strictures of an antisemitic regime by fitfully flitting between languages (at least not yet). But still, despite occasional explosions of success, our precious and unique theatre maintains a place between the mainstream and the fully underground, a delicate position in and out of the shadows that allows us to experiment and play and progress, as did Kaminska and her various troupes.

How wondrous it has been, in simultaneously translating her words and plying her trade, to feel that we are not alone in this history, that we are players in an ongoing drama going back centuries—that we all of us have a mother.

# A NOTE ON THE TRANSLATION

As I have labored these past seven years to set Ester-Rokhl Kaminska's dramatic narrative on the stage of this volume, many others have whispered invaluable advice from the prompter's box or heroically assisted from the wings to help her story be heard. Among these partners in our joined endeavor, to whom I toss the bouquets of my sincere gratitude, are the scholars who are editing this series, Alyssa Quint—who avidly and amiably stewarded this translation project from the very beginning—and Elissa Bemporad; dear Amanda (Miryem-Khaye) Seigel, among those who first brought Kaminska's memoirs to my attention; Barbara Henry, with her keen and insightful editorial suggestions; the family of Harriet R. Yassky, who have made the work possible; the living descendants of Ester-Rokhl Kaminska's family, who honor the memory of their venerable ancestress; Rhodri Mogford, Gabriella Cox, Amy Brownbridge, Mohammed Raffi, and all others from Bloomsbury Publishing and its production management team, each of them so patient and supportive throughout the preparation of the book; YIVO photography archivist Vital Zajka for sending on scans of the precious images that appear here, as well as the other dedicated archivists who assisted me as I spent long hours in the YIVO reading room; Mirosława M. Bułat, Polish translator of Kaminska's memoirs, with whom I enjoyed a friendly and fruitful correspondence as we worked on our individual projects; and my erudite Yiddishist comrades Philip Schwartz and Sandra Chiritescu, respectively in Vienna and Zürich, who never tired of my daily *frishtikn* (breakfasts), as we came to call them—requests for input on this or that fine point of Kaminska's language, which, during the period of my proofreading late into the night in New York City, greeted them most mornings when they awoke.

Following are a few notes on the orthographic conventions observed in this translation and the style for which I have aimed:

In other volumes, Kaminska's name is sometimes given in its anglicized spelling, Esther Rachel Kaminska, but here, the spelling adheres to the Yiddish transliteration standard established by the YIVO Institute for Jewish Research. In still other works, Kaminska's last name may be rendered as Kaminski (the neutral version of the surname, unlike the specifically female version that is used for Madame Kaminska in Polish and very often in Yiddish) or indeed in its accepted Polish orthography, Kamińska. For other names in the volume, anglicized spellings are sometimes used if the person is a well-known figure—Sholem Aleichem, for instance—or if the individual's name is rendered in an anglicized form in the *YIVO Encyclopedia of Jews in Eastern Europe*.

Yiddish words throughout the translation are transliterated according to the accepted YIVO standard and are italicized, unless the word happens to be in common use in the English language, in which case a spelling appearing in the *Merriam-Webster Dictionary* is used and left in roman (if, however, Webster's spelling diverges too dramatically from the standard Yiddish pronunciation of the word, then it is sometimes given in the YIVO spelling in italics).

Place names are typically rendered in the spelling used in the country in which the place is situated today, if it is more or less a phonic match to the name by which Kaminska knew it. If there is a common English name for the locality (as in "Warsaw"), then that is preferred. If the place's contemporary name diverges dramatically from the Yiddish name used by Kaminska, and there is no well-known English alternative, then Kaminska's rendering of the name is sometimes given. Though these tsarist-era names may be uncomfortable for some readers, they reflect the period during which Kaminska found herself in these places. In many cases where this divergence presents itself, endnotes provide the locales' present-day names to help readers situate them. Outside of the body of the memoir, names reflecting contemporary usage are often preferred—thus Kiev to match Kaminska's language when she mentions the city, but Kyiv when it is referenced in the introduction and notes.

When figures in the memoir use such languages as Russian and Polish, I have sometimes preserved their speeches in those languages or, occasionally in the case of German speakers, found a style that preserves the Central European flavor while relaying their words chiefly in English. Sometimes I have even retained Kaminska's original Yiddish when the original phrasing seems particularly piquant or important. In all these cases, I have made sure to also provide a translation or otherwise make the meaning of Kaminska's original lines clear.

A translator is like an actor, it has been said, endeavoring to capture, in every gesture and utterance, the unique personality of the character speaking the given lines. May the wandering spirit of the wandering actress Kaminska smile on my efforts. Throughout, I have made efforts to deliver her reminiscences with the greatest fidelity and to transmit the antique charm of her style, the author's prose now being a hundred years old. But I have also found room for play, considering it important to evoke the freshness, vivacity, and poetry with which Kaminska writes about her salad days, endowing them with the excitement and uncertainty of youth while at the same time looking back with the twinkling eye and ironical wisdom that are the gifts of age.

As each new leg of her theatrical tours commences, we are riding alongside the young, untested actress and her older narratorial self, half-dreading and half-dreaming about what will be in the next city or town. I hope the reader's journey beside us all (the elder Kaminska, the younger, and myself) will be a pleasant one and that you appreciate every detail Kaminska points out to you from atop the juddering boards of her overladen wagon.

# I HOME

I was born in the year 1870 in the shtetl Porozove, in the Volkovysk district,[1] which was within the Grodno guberniya of the Russian Empire.[2] A tiny little shtetl, containing just a few streets: Mill Street, Kropivnits Street, Novidvor Street, *Shul-gas*, where the synagogue was, and *Tsigayner-gesl*—Gypsy Lane. Mill Street bore that name because it was adjacent to the water mill. But it had another name: *Mizrekh-gas*, East Street, for the Jews faced it, as they faced Jerusalem when they prayed. And yet another name, Church Street, because at one end of it, before you reached the water mill, stood the Polish Catholic church.

Gypsy Lane was also called Cemetery Lane, because it terminated at the Jewish cemetery. And it was called Gypsy Lane because, because for as long as I can remember, a Gypsy family resided on the street. The man dealt in horses, and his wife dealt cards to divine her clients' fortunes.[3]

You can imagine from the number of streets what a very small shtetl this was. It seems to me it was the smallest shtetl in all of the Grodno governorate. Still today, no train reaches it. Two times a week, the mail is brought in on a wagon from the town of Volkovysk. I can still picture clearly how we used to all run up to our little town office, where they would hand out the mail every Shabbos and Wednesday.

But it was a shtetl with glorious air. A narrow river meandered through its middle, and a little wooden bridge stretched across the river. It originated somewhere in the mountains and ran through various fields until it reached us. We called it the Porozovse. It must have been after the river that the town got its name. Very often at Passover, when it thawed, this narrow little river would grow wider and higher, and the little bridge would float away with it, along with the little blacksmith's forge that stood right beside the riverbank. A couple of cottages would get dragged along, too, a few little barns—anything that stood on the banks of this "River Jordan." It was terrible luck for the Jews who lived on the other side of it. For a number of days, they found themselves unable to get to the shul to pray.

We were the lucky ones—we lived right on the *shulhoyf*. This, the synagogue courtyard, consisted of a circular plot of land, not gated or fenced in like typical courtyards, but rather abutted by a little hillock, overgrown with grass, with an old study house atop that. It had been standing there since before I was born. And behind that was our own little house with its thatched roof and two low windows that nearly touched the ground, which looked onto the windows of the study house.

The shul, a tall stone building with a shingled roof, was built when I was a very young girl, but I can still remember its construction. Some time later, a little wooden building was erected on the same courtyard. This building served as the *hegdesh*, the poorhouse.[4] Wagons full of poor folks, wandering from city to city, would turn up there, and these people would spend the night. And when a dead body was brought up from a nearby village, it would be brought there to be washed. It was given the honor that it was due and then conducted away to its eternal home.

All of this was just opposite our little house, where I grew up in utter terror. Terror, yes—because I had heard tell that in a shul, after midnight, corpses come to chant the evening prayers.

Once, in the dog days of summer, we had gone to sleep outside in our yard, for our little plot was enclosed with a fence, unlike the shul courtyard. In the middle of the night, I heard it myself—the corpses wailing in the shul. I woke my brothers and mother, and they heard it, too. We all ran into the house, our souls just about scared right out of our bodies. This was Friday night. When Shabbos morning came, Father explained to us that there was a nest of doves in the shul, and that doves wail, just like people.

Still, it all made a fearful impression on me. Oh, that stone shul, that poorhouse . . . Whenever I had to walk home a bit later at night than usual, I don't know how I kept my soul from flying right out, that's how terrified I was. Anywhere else in the shtetl, I could walk freely, without fear, but when I approached the shul courtyard, which I had to do when coming from Gypsy Lane, and my glance fell upon the poorhouse, I would jump out of my skin and bolt, and the faster I would run, the higher my terror would rise within me, until I had to start screaming: "Mama! Mama!"

And always, Mama would be waiting to run out and welcome me with a holler of her own: "*Sha, sha,* be quiet! I'm here, I'm here!" And I would fall into her arms, nearly fainting.

Still, to this day, I do not know why they chose to build the poorhouse right on that courtyard. A nice ornament it made to the shul! Probably they did it just to add to my terror.

The community eventually installed a family to take up residence there, headed by a fellow alternately called Motl the Chimney Sweep, Motl the Water Carrier, and Motl the Whitewasher, the latter because every Passover, he would perform the service of whitewashing the Jews' houses. In time, he took on another name: Motl the Poorhouse Man.

I suffered on his account, too. He would walk around covered with whitewash from head to toe, such that only his eyes could be made out, which would frighten me. Or he would be covered in ash and soot from sweeping chimneys, and that would frighten me half to death. Or he would come by during the month before the High Holidays to knock on the door, calling the men in the house to come to shul for *slikhes*. Those three knocks, and that terrible cry, "Shteyt oyf tsu slikhes!"— Get up for the penitential prayers! I still shudder to think of it.

But when the poorhouse was full of the wandering poor, it was much better. The paupers would tell all kinds of stories, and a cartload of boys would come racing over to listen, me right alongside them. I used to like bringing the poor folks bread and potatoes from our house. And they used to like to scare me, teasing me that when it was time for them to go, they'd snatch me up into their wagon and take me along with them.

The rabbi's residence, built as part of the study house, was also on the shul courtyard. Now that study house, that was something else! A truly holy place. Our house still stands across from it today. The windows still look out onto each other. In summertime, they would all be open to the fresh air. I can still hear the intoxicating melodies chanted by the yeshiva bochurim, the young scholars, as they pored over the Talmud the whole night long. Such divine music it was! It seems to me I'll never be able to forget the ecstasy I felt upon listening to those splendid tones of the boys' studying.

When I wanted to have a look at the yeshiva bochurim, I would stride into the study house on the pretext of asking what time it was. I was no stranger to them, as I sometimes accompanied my father to pray on Friday evenings, and when I would, I'd be the first of the young children that Avreml the sexton would hand the goblet of wine to after the cantor finished blessing it. All the youngsters envied me for it. But I was useful to this Avreml. He used to have me help him light all the candles in the chandeliers before services on Friday evening, and whenever it was a holiday, or the anniversary of Moses' death,[5] there were a great many additional candles to be lit surrounding the bimah. And it would be my honored duty to light them all with a candle that was attached to the end of a long stick.

I had few other pastimes as a girl. My entire childhood was spent in a thick layer of dust and dirt brought in by the sheep that used to trot in from the surrounding fields. And how I used to love to trot in, through that cloud of dirt, right alongside them.

What do you make of my simple pleasures?

# ▌▌ MY CHILDHOOD

On the path of my childhood, I found stones and sand, along with thorns and pinecones that would stab at my bare feet as I gathered mushrooms and wild berries in the forest.

As I was his last child, I have no memories of my father as a young or vigorous man. He was already old when I was born, white-haired and weak-limbed, unable to do very much at all. He was a luftmensch, anyhow, with his head in the clouds, living off little more than the fresh air of the shtetl. We never rose above poverty. But he was an honest, respectable man. Even before I came along, he was already quite deaf but was given a post as overseer of the newly built shul, with its congregation of the restless dead. The great keys to its doors were kept at our house.

But my father was not charged with doing very much. His chief task was to rise at dawn and recite psalms for the community. Even in my deep sleep, the tones of his chanting would come buzzing into my ears. Having finished the prescribed psalms, he would walk over to the study house and daven the morning service there. Then he would come home, slurp up some barley soup for breakfast, and go back out again.

Our neighbors called us the "*kle-koydeshnikes*"—the shul mice—or the "congregation kishkes," the community's guts—in which the community's money was freely digested. Our family consisted of my parents and their seven children: four sisters and three brothers. The older ones had set off to make their way in the world by the time I was born. I remember, many years later, when my eldest brother returned to Porozove to visit my parents. He was by then employed as a shochet[1] and chazan[2] in Germany. My feet, which were black from running around outside, were given a good scrubbing for the occasion. It was then that I received my first pair of shoes, which my brother bought especially for me at the store of Beyle Hertskes. Our neighbors even sent a bottle of wine along for Shabbos, in honor of our guest, and welcomed him with a special Friday evening service. He was dressed in a modern clerical cap and robe he had brought along with him, and he sang the prayers in an operatic fashion, as his pulpit was in a grand, modern synagogue with a choir. Meanwhile, our neighbors muttered to each other, "Who even knows if he's still a Jew? He looks more like a priest to me."

It was this brother who chiefly supported my parents once they had reached their old age. My father received no salary from his daily duties at the shul, though he would receive a sexton's fee if he had to help arrange a wedding or a circumcision, twenty or twenty-five kopecks per. But when Chanukah or Purim would come along, why, then we'd turn into real tycoons! For on those holidays, the congregation's more well-off families would send a nice bit of gelt our way.

When it was Purim, I'd sit by my father at the table, on which there stood a white wooden salt cellar covered with a slotted lid. And I'd get to drop the coins in that the congregants had sent their children to deliver to us in little paper packages. I would tear them open and call out to the children, just as I'd heard Mama do, "Thank your papa for us!" Sometimes a rather grown young man would come with a parcel, and as soon as I blurted out, "Thank your papa for us!", a fierce tug on my sleeve from my own papa would make me realize that the young man, for quite a while at that point, had no papa.

In these parcels, you would find coins of all sorts. Each contained around three big copper ten-pieces, five copper six-groschen coins, and about ten three-kopeck coins. Those ones had been polished to a perfect smoothness from so much handling over time. And the richer congregants would typically send along a big silver piece, or a forty-groschen coin. Altogether it would amount to a princely sum, up to three rubles, and sometimes even more. After Purim, I would be given a kopeck a day as pocket money. With that, I'd go to the market and buy a hot bagel, then gobble it up on the way home. And as I'd walk, I'd have this terrible urge for everyone to look at me. I didn't understand that it would have been better for me to just walk along inconspicuously with my bagel, even though in my quarrels with the neighborhood children, I was routinely teased for being the "congregation kishke"—a freeloader.

Later, I would come to understand why it was that when my mother, say, wanted to buy some plums to cook up for compote, or a few raisins for a cake she was baking, she would have to wait for all the other matrons to leave the shop. Otherwise, they'd look askance at us, as we were living off the donations of the congregation, and here we were indulging in dainties. But in actual fact, it wasn't the congregation's money that sustained us. My eldest brother and my sisters, all of whom had left home young, would send my parents all they could, and it was really from their donations that we got by. For example, my eldest brother, on the first night of Passover, would always send us a sum of twenty-five rubles, which at that time was a serious bundle! He'd write that it was for Passover expenses and for "building up our garden."

See, behind our little house, we had rather a sizeable fenced-in yard. But as the house and yard were situated on the shul courtyard, every Purim the rowdy merrymakers would tear off half the fence so they could use the posts to make a racket and stamp out the wicked name of Haman when it was chanted in shul. That's why my brother would write at Passover of the need to "build up our garden," by which he meant mending the fence,[3] and also planting what we needed.

That began soon after Passover. There was a great deal of work for me to do then. A great deal of fun to be had, too. First came the plowing, which meant getting to watch a Gentile man who came over to cut furrows in the yard with a pair of oxen, with me following close at hand carrying an apronful of cut-up potatoes. Step by careful step, I'd march behind the oxen and toss the potatoes, which I had halved earlier with mother, into the deep rows lining the ground. What a scream it was to hear Ryhorka the plowman ordering the beasts around, as I walked right behind him, always with Mama at my side.

And after that came the work of harrowing the field, that is, stirring up the clods of soil, once the potatoes had begun to sprout. We'd hitch up a horse with a harrow, then attach a large stone to its wooden frame, and the horse would trudge over the field with it, grinding up the dirt and smoothing out the surface. I myself would hold the reins and drive the horse, and when I'd grow tired, I would hand them over to Ryhorka and climb up onto the harrow. It would really do a number on my insides, shaking my kishkes up and down, but what a thrill it was! And after that, the work of making sure all the potatoes were well placed and covered up, and then planting all sorts of other vegetables, including carrots, beets and beans, turnips and swedes, radishes, and so forth.

What a sublime joy it was to observe how God helped as everything grew and grew, showing due appreciation for all of our efforts. As my dear mama used to say, "Look, daughter, our toil has been worthwhile, thank God. Everything, *on eyn-hore*, may the Evil Eye keep away, is coming right up, good as gold. It's a sign we'll have a bountiful harvest." The only difficulty came when we'd get no rain and would have to shlep up water from the well outside the shul and cover the whole of the yard with it. That job was no laughing matter, but I did it with pleasure if it meant being a help to my sweet mother.

And so we spent our time, year in, year out, planting the garden in the spring, and in the fall digging up the potatoes and pulling up the rest of the vegetables, then storing the potatoes in our cellar and the rest in the attic. I know how small I must have been then—for when we were drying the carrots in the oven to prepare for winter, I used to crawl in there myself once the job was done, to pick out the desiccated carrots from the back corners. And that's how we had carrots to cook up all winter for our tzimmes.[4]

Often I'd wake up early in the morning and order Mama: "Dress me!" And Mama would ask me back in her long-suffering tone, "What should I dress you in today?" And I'd simply say, "Why, just tie me up with this bit of rope, good and tight!" Because in those days I used to walk around dressed only in a peasant's shirt of rough homemade linen, gathered at the throat with a red porcelain button. And since the shirt was too long, it had to be fastened with a rope. And that was the whole of my summer wardrobe.

When winter approached, they would make a wadding-stuffed skirt for me, along with a little red jacket, quilted like a blanket, together with a pair of horse-leather shoes, fitted with iron-reinforced soles. It was in just such a rustic pair of shoes that I first came to Warsaw, as you will see later.

*   *   *

When I grew a bit older, I noticed how the children of rich families would go off to study under Ester the Rebbetzin.[5] So I started begging to go, too, to be sent to the cheder, the classroom in the rebbetzin's home, where I could learn the Hebrew alphabet. I even taught myself at home to prepare, and it worked—I was signed up for a summer semester in the classroom of Ester the Rebbetzin, or Ester the *Zogerin*, the prayer leader, as she was called, for it was she who read out the prayers for the other women to repeat in the women's section of the shul. She was truly formidable in her command of Hebrew and led a class of up to twenty girls from the better families. Her classes cost three rubles a semester.

The studies began with Hebrew reading, prayers, reciting psalms, and translating from the Hebrew Bible into Yiddish. I learned all of it easily in the first term, and by the end of it, I knew Hebrew quite well. What came less easily was scrapping together the three rubles to pay for another term. My passion was there, to go further in my studies with a teacher of Torah and the rest of the Bible, but the money was not. Such teachers commanded high fees, and anyway, I had a brother who was three years older than I. It was considered absolutely necessary that he study, but not so with me. "A girl doesn't need to know much more than how to pray." And as they told me it must be, so it was.

Right around that time, a teacher from some other town showed up in our shtetl. They called him Hershl the Writer. And when I saw girls walking with sheaves of paper under their arms, carrying pens and ink in their hands, right up to the house of Hershl the Writer, my heart beat wildly with the yearning to learn. But what could I do?

When I grew a little older, I was set to other tasks, including picking berries. Before summer even started, the gathering would begin. The reading of *Parshe shmini*[6] from the Torah at shul meant the return of the stork. With *Parshe koyrekh*[7] came the little blue bilberries. We used to wake at four in the morning, rustle up a whole gang of women and girls, and sometimes a few layabouts, young men who had nothing better to do, along with black bread and cucumbers and great big pails or pitchers for collecting the berries, and stay out gathering till nightfall. Oftentimes I wouldn't get back until after maariv[8] was completed. But as soon as I did, Mama would come running out to help me lug back the big pitcher, now heavy with berries. Mine were always the prettiest: clean and smooth little specimens, free of any leaves. We could get a couple of meals out of the haul, boiling them down with sugar syrup and spreading that on bread. We'd have that for dinner two times a week during picking season.

*　*　*

Thus did I spend my childhood years.[9] Even summer was all work and no play: the garden, the field beyond, grazing the goat, and so forth. We always had our own goats. I remember that once I forgot to lead the goat into her stall, and so she spent the whole night just outside our window, lying on the bench of sod that flanked our house. In the middle of the night, we heard a scream coming from this beautiful snow-white creature. When we woke in the morning, she was nowhere to be found. I called for her, I hollered for her. But she would not come.

So we set out onto the open fields, and there she was—ripped apart by a wolf.

You can understand how much the population of Porozove suffered when wolves would come to prowl freely around our shtetl. We were even more susceptible—our house on the shul courtyard was just on the outskirts of town, touching the fields beyond.

Winters were terrible. Often, when there was a snowstorm and the snow would pile up, when we'd wake in the morning, we couldn't even open the front door due to the mountain of snow that had accumulated just outside it, reaching all the way up to the roof. I'd have a nice bit of work to do then. Once we'd manage to get the door open, we'd have to go out with shovels and clear paths to the well outside the shul so that we could go to retrieve water. The toil warmed us up considerably, though, and got some color into our cheeks—precisely as if we'd just enjoyed the finest meal.

And after such hard work, we'd get it, sitting ourselves down for the heaping bowl of barley soup with potatoes that was waiting for us on the table. It contained no meat, of course. Meat was a rare thing for us in Porozove. We wouldn't have it during the week, but for Shabbos, they'd slaughter a calf or a barren cow. First, it would have to be slaughtered according to our law and properly koshered, and even then, the rich folks would get the first pick of the meat. It would often happen, however, that the slaughtering was in some way mismanaged, and the meat ruled *treyf*,[10] then no one in the shtetl would get any meat at all for Shabbos.

I, at least, wasn't much bothered by it. For me, a bowl of barley soup with milk poured in was more than enough, together with a bit of rye bread. I'd stuff it in with such gusto that I'd get quite stuffed myself. When I'd finally lift my head up from the bowl, my head was in a daze, and my cheeks and eyes were red, as if they'd been well roasted over the fire.

For my father, we'd often buy a bit of lung in a pot of broth for three kopecks. Now that was considered a dinner worth admiring. My father hated dairy meals, and my brother would always say, whenever he'd come home and see a dairy dinner laid on the table:

"Fine, let me have my drink of dinner now!"

Then he'd seize the milk-doused noodles and the farfel, and, straight from the bowl, no spoon, slurp it up until his belly grew quite full. Oh how I'd laugh when he used to say, "Lemme have my drink of dinner!"

# ||| BOYFRIENDS AND GIRLFRIENDS, SHIKSES AND SHKOTZIM[1]

That brother, the one who used to "drink up his dinner," was three years older than I. He would often say to me, "Let's get out of this place. What could possibly become of us as long as we stick around here?" But I couldn't leave my mother. I loved her so, more than I did my father.

This brother had friends who used to come visiting. When winter fell, we would all go skating, traverse the snow in cavalcades of little sleds, and build snowmen. I would invariably join in on the fun. I always preferred boys as friends over girls. The girls of Porozove seemed too foolish for me. Everything I did, I did better than they ever could. Whenever we would gather at the river to polish candlesticks, my four candlesticks always shone far more beautifully than theirs. When I would polish our samovar, it would be impossible to tell whether it was just brass or actually pure gold.

When Passover came around, and we needed matzo, we did not go about it the way they do in the big cities, where people would simply buy matzo or bring their flour to someone who would bake matzo for them. No, for us it was quite different. Before Passover, all the matrons, even the richest ones, would go out themselves or send off their daughters to "earn helpers." That is, every married lady or young woman would have to go to ten or twelve homes to help roll out matzos, and then those ladies whom they had helped would go to help the others. For example, I had to help roll out matzos for ten or twelve matrons, after which they, or their daughters, would be expected to come to our home to help with ours.

For me, this business of "earning helpers" was easier work than for anyone else. It was well-known in Porozove that Rokhl, Khaim-Yoykhenen's daughter, could roll out matzo dough better than any of the other girls, and so all the mistresses would come calling for me. I even found the work pleasant. I would have to get up at dawn (for the rich families used to bake their matzos early, in the oven's first load of the morning) and remain on my feet rolling out dough for three hours or so, sometimes twice a day. Later, when it was our turn to bake matzo, all I had to do was run about and call up our own helpers and tell them it was time to come to us.

Once we had finished it all, with God's help, I had one additional task: rolling out our rabbi's special *shmure* matzo,[2] for only young girls, like me, could be employed for that duty. It was my special duty every year to round up the other young girls and roll out the rabbi's matzos with them. It fell to me to gather the troops because his family and mine were neighbors, both of us living on the shul courtyard.

It was always very cozy at the rabbi's when we would go to help with his matzo. His sons would always be there—all very fine young men—and the rabbi himself served as mashgiach, watching over the process to guarantee that everything was done by the book. He made sure that no dough was left over on the cutting boards or the rolling pins.[3] In this detail, too, I was exceptional. The rabbi himself used to say that my work was the most kosher, as well as the most beautiful.

I was like one of the family in that home. I used to help the rebbetzin prepare for Shabbos and other holidays, and therefore was present for all manner of interesting occurrences. What didn't I see at the rabbi's home! A gett, even! Yes, I witnessed the official arguments in a ritual divorce unfolding in that house. For weeks, all day and all night, people were debating what the wife's name was. The husband called her "Tsirl," but everyone else in the shtetl called her "Tshirl."[4] Whether "Tsirl" or "Tshirl," people went on being churls over it for a good number of weeks, until finally the couple made up and returned home together in peace.

I even saw a *khalitse* at the rabbi's house, the procedure that exempts a man from his religious obligation to marry his brother's wife upon the death of said brother. It was rather a terrifying thing. I could not stand too near, for I was told that behind the table on which the corpse had been ritually cleaned before being buried, which was set up in the room as a partition, was the dead man himself, standing guard—the late husband of the woman who was bringing the *khalitse* suit. I stood there quaking. But I remained— out of curiosity, though keeping my distance—until the whole business was concluded.

I am sure that in the big cities, even if a person lives to a hundred years, they could not see and experience all the things I did just in my childhood years in that tiny shtetl of Porozove.

How much sweetness surrounded me on a typical evening in summertime, when all the other children and I would sit in a great big circle in the courtyard, with little clay bowls in our laps and wooden spoons in our hands, waiting for one of our mothers to bring out a massive bowl filled with sweet milky noodles. When she appeared, all the children would dart to her side with their utensils and remain there until she filled their bowls to the brim. Then they would slowly, carefully bring them back to their spot in the circle, and, hunched over the bowls, eat up the noodles while listening to the sweet song of the Gentile boys and girls who were returning from the harvest with their scythes and sickles slung over their shoulders. The shikses were all in vigorous good health, wearing lightweight dresses of pink, white, and blue, with kerchiefs tied around their heads, each in the arm of a shegetz,[5] joining their song with the young men's in delicious harmony.

I wonder now: how did these peasants come to sing so beautifully, and in multiple vocal lines, with nary a single sour note among them! Now I know that songs are classified as duets, or trios, or quartets, but I knew nothing of such nomenclature then. I only knew that the songs were lovely. And so was eating the noodles and milk. The singing would continue late into the night, and the echoes from the fields would resound through the entire shtetl.

In the evenings, the singing of the peasants in the fields; in the mornings, the singing of the yeshiva bochurim in the study house. My soul was always saturated with song.

When I would march out into the woods with a company of friends to forage for berries or mushrooms or hazelnuts, I would make a point of bringing along only those friends who had strong voices, with whom I could practice beautiful music. Naturally, it was all synagogue music— that was what was most familiar and dear to me. When we would go out foraging thus, stooped over from dawn until midday, we would discern from the position of the sun itself when it had turned twelve o'clock and was time for lunch. At that point, we called together the whole company and would engage in my system of getting the kinks out of our backs, sore after so much bending. We would all lie down with our bellies to the ground. Then everyone would take turns climbing onto the person next to them, stretching out their shoulders for them. After that, we would all eat the hunks of rye bread we had brought along, together with a cucumber, a bit of cheese, or indeed the berries we'd foraged. After that splendid lunch, I would give the cue to start up a song, which sounded no less lovely than those of the shikses and shkotzim.

Once, I remember, during one of these rousing sing-alongs, the heat was so intense that even in that impressive forest with its towering pines, we could not hide from the stabbing sun. I issued a command to the company for us to head home earlier than we had planned. As soon as the words emerged from my mouth, thick quilts of cloud emerged to cover the blue sky, which we could barely see through the dense canopy of trees. It grew darker and darker in the forest, so that it became difficult to find the paths that would lead us back to the shtetl. But we all came together as one and strode ahead. We did lose our way for a while in that overgrown and wild forest, but we eventually hit upon a path—an altogether different one, terminating at a village called Brustove.

As we neared the fields outside the village, a nasty bit of thunder and lightning began to make its presence known in the wood. The lightning lit the paths we could take, but meanwhile, we began hearing the crash of falling trees. Every thunderclap nearly turned me deaf. When we finally emerged onto the open field, everyone was seized anew with fear. We saw no living soul. Even the birds had hidden somewhere to escape the veritable hurricane! We all stood there despairing, until one girl in the company persuaded the rest of us to make our way forward and enter the village Brustove. Thus, all of us clutching close to each other and I, naturally, standing beside the girl who led the way, pressed onward through the rain and hail, the crashes of thunder and flashes of lightning.

We walked in this way until we noticed a peasant upon a wagon piled high with hay.[6] I ran toward this Gentile and found some sense of protection at his side. I had heard it said that when the nations of the world mingle freely with each other, thunder itself cannot exert its dominance over them. So had my mother taught me. We were all now reassured that we would not die because there was a Gentile among us, and he had a horse, and, moreover, the great mound of hay atop his wagon offered defense against the hail.

The peasant drove us to the little village of Brustove. At every thunderclap, the peasant crossed himself, and I whispered, almost soundlessly, the blessing, "Shekoykhoy ugvurosoy moley oylom"[7] and from time to time a "Shma yisroel,"[8] until we arrived in the village, and a scene I shall never forget:

Wherever we looked, little cottages with thatched roofs were ablaze, having been set aflame by the lightning. A little farther on, a cow was lying on the ground, and beside it, almost in a seated position, was a Gentile woman. She leaned on her milk pail, which still brimmed with the milk she had drawn from the cow. Both of them had been struck by lightning and were dead.

*   *   *

When we finally returned to our shtetl, we could hear heartrending cries emanating from a multitude of voices. It was clear something had also happened in our town. Leaving my company behind, I took off for home, my long, slender feet carrying me as fast as they could. At the shtetl's edge, I met my mother and sister, who were also running. Their eyes were red and swollen from crying, both believing that I had been killed in the storm.

On our way home, they said nothing to me. I entered our house feeling barely alive, still holding my pitcher half-filled with berries. Throughout our whole travail, I had not cast it aside. As I sat down to eat something, I glanced around the room and noticed a large bowl of water sitting on the hearth. I remembered my mother having taught me that during a terrible thunderstorm, water should be set out near the windows. Once I had finished eating, I asked, confused:

"Mama, why were people crying so at the cemetery?"

But this only made my mother break out into fresh tears, and she told me that Mikhle, Nakhmen's daughter, had been killed in the storm. I wonder now how the news did not instantly drive me out of my wits.

Mikhle, Nakhmen's daughter, as she was always called, was one of my dear girlfriends, though she was richer and a little older than I. I would often spend time with her and sit with her on the porch of her beautiful house that stood on Novidvor Street. My heart clenched with pain when I ran toward it and did not see Mikhle. Behind the house, in the family's spacious yard, almost the whole population of the shtetl stood in a big cluster. And there in the center of the yard, buried up to her neck, was the beautiful Mikhle. All waited, hoping that the earth might somehow absorb the lightning from her thunderstruck body and restore her to life.

I began to inquire into how the disaster had occurred, and her sister told me how Mikhle had been sitting on the porch, and after a while, had entered the house. Calling her sister's children into the house, too, Mikhle proceeded to shut all the windows but forgot to shut the door. She then went to the salt cask to get a bit of salt, and as soon as she leaned over the cask, a lightning bolt as long as a Lithuanian rolling pin stole in through the doorway and then out through the chimney. On its mad dash through the home, it had singed the long, red braids of the beautiful, fair-skinned Mikhle as it dragged her young, innocent soul along with it to heaven, leaving her robust figure still leaning over the cask of salt.

One could never imagine such a sight until one has witnessed it oneself. A big, hearty girl with a strong body, made to stand erect like a living person, only her long, coppery hair in disarray. Just standing there, having been placed in a pit in the ground.

The shtetl had no doctor. There was no one even who could formally establish and certify the death, just some quack who had made his way over to the dead body and was now dragging the fleshy hands up out of the ground. He struck a vein, but no blood flowed from it. Then they rubbed her hands with rough brushes, and the white skin did not redden. Then somebody remembered that one customarily sticks a feather under the nose. When the feather did not rustle, it was finally affirmed that she was dead. They pulled her body up out of its temporary grave and brought it to the proper burial place.

*   *   *

The tragic scene of the thunder and lightning and Mikhle, Nakhmen's daughter, made a frightful impression on me. I began to think that there really was no point in remaining in Porozove. It seemed I would eventually have to tear away from my poor, goodly parents, and make my own way in the world. But how? By what miracles? After all, even for the shortest journey, one had to have a bit of money.

When my father used to come home from prayers, he would drink a glassful of coffee and eat a bit of challah. We always made sure to leave enough challah uneaten on Shabbos for Papa to be able to enjoy it all week long. The rest of us would subsist on black bread. Once he had finished eating and saying the blessing over the meal, then would quit the house once again to go and carry out some transactions at the store of Beyle Hertskes, I would always bid him farewell with this wish:

"Tatele, gefin epes a koshere metsie!"—Dear Papa, may you find a nice kosher bargain!

On one of these occasions, the following happened:

In Porozove, agricultural fairs were a regular occurrence. Peasant men and women would travel to our shtetl from the surrounding villages and estates, and when they would come, there would be such a crowd in the streets that a body couldn't walk without being jostled on every side. It was like that, too, in all the inns and taverns—each of them crammed with peasants.

At one such fair in autumn, my father went as usual to the store in the marketplace. It was bad weather out, so he stopped over after in the home of the proprietress, Beyle Hertskes. "Fat Beyle," she was also called, for she was a very stout woman. She was always pleased to host my father and welcomed him with a glass of hot tea, fresh from the samovar. There he sat in her house, which also served as a tavern, while it filled up with tobacco smoke—and with peasants. A wet and spreading layer of mud coated the floor. Before long, my father was desperate to leave, but then he noticed a little piece of paper stuck there in the mud. He bent down and grabbed it—it was a hundred-ruble bill!

He took it, placed it in his sleeve, and made a round of the room, keeping his ears perked to see if anyone was searching for the money. He knew he could not go home now, though it was already evening. Suddenly, he heard some ruckus in the tavern, but he couldn't make it out well, for he was rather deaf.

It turned out that the estate owner, Khaiml, a very wealthy Jew, was the man who had lost the hundred. He was running in and out of the tavern, poking his head into all the nearby wagons, looking everywhere, wringing his hands as if he had lost his entire fortune. My old father went up to him and asked, "Khaiml, what are you looking for? Perhaps I know?"

But the man shoved him off, screaming, "Get out and leave me be, you old imbecile!" But my honest father would not leave his side, insisting, "Just tell me what it is you're looking for." When the fellow finally answered, in a fit of anger, "A hundred rubles! Did you already know?", my father removed the bill from his sleeve and showed him. "Could it be this?" my father asked, handing over the muddied bit of paper.

The rich, corpulent man grabbed him and kissed him. "Come have a drink, on me!" But my father turned and went home, not even answering him.

When he returned and sat down to his spot of barley soup with "nothing" (the poor man's version, lacking meat or milk), he told us the whole story.

Soon it was the talk of the entire shtetl. "A hundred rubles! To find such a treasure, then give it away? It would've been enough for Rokhl's whole dowry!" our neighbors insisted, trying to contain their convulsions of laughter. But my father would answer, "My Ester-Rokhl is priceless. And God will take care of her, too!"

And so I remained at home, no opportunities of leaving for someplace else yet revealing themselves.

Thus the years ran on. I grew up tall. By my ninth or tenth birthday, I had already reached a grown-up's height. My mother found this something to lament over. "Such a big girl as you," she would say, "and I let you go barefoot?" They had to make me a new pair of shoes. They could ill afford it. But still, the pair was made for me, hewn from horse leather and fitted with iron horseshoes, with six holes apiece for the red laces to go through. These were the last shoes I had in Porozove, the same in which I would later be brought to Warsaw, where they made their unexpected début on old Walowa Street,[9] as you will see later on.

# IV  TO WARSAW!

My three sisters had left home when I was still a child, the eldest even before I was born. Each one brought the next sister to Warsaw after her, until all three had become Warsovian ladies, with Warsovian husbands.

In the 1880s, when the pogrom took place in Warsaw,[1] my sisters' shop on Pawia Street[2] was looted. For a long while after, they were terribly afraid that eventually all the Jews of the city would be slaughtered, and so my two sisters who lived in the city decided to seek refuge back in Porozove. One came with her six-month-old.

Their husbands remained in Warsaw for a short while, but soon they came to Porozove, too. Both of these men were natives of Warsaw, so one need hardly describe what an impression my shtetl made. Everything seemed absolutely wild to them—and they seemed wild to me, and to the rest of Porozove, too. Their dialect, their singsong intonation as they spoke! Whenever one of them chanced to say the words *yakh* or *yo*, *ets* or *enk*,[3] everyone exploded with laughter at these sillies. "Well," I thought to myself, "I suppose I'd be laughing, too, if they weren't *my* sillies."

My older brother-in-law was a tinsmith and a real artist at what he did. He remained in the shtetl for several years and made a good living off the patronage of the local landowners. The other had been a teacher back in Warsaw. Once in Porozove, Hershl the Writer became his competition. My brother-in-law established a secular secondary school, renting out a long, low house for the purpose. He set up two wooden easels inside it, placed a chalkboard on each one—and voilà, he had an academy.

All the rich girls of the shtetl made a beeline to learn from this new Warsovian teacher, who was indeed a very good instructor of Russian, German, and Yiddish. But I had no such luck. My sister had a small and sickly child, and so it was more convenient for the family to make me into a nanny rather than a scholar.

That's how things were for a short time, until my brother-in-law realized he did not like teaching the young ladies of Porozove, and he returned to Warsaw, his home. At first, he lived alone there until he could find some new position. Once he had it, he sent for his wife and child, and also, as it happens, me.

I did have some concept of what Warsaw was like. I had picked up the dialect from listening to my sisters talking to each other, and could really speak it, before I had ever set foot in the city. Whenever they prattled on about Warsaw, my sisters compared every little thing to Porozove. For example: "The courtyard of the Mławer Shul is as big as the entirety of Porozove." Or they'd say: "In Warsaw, on Tłomackie Street, there's a shul we call the Daytshe Shul[4]—why, it's as big as the entirety of Porozove." Or: "On the theatre square, there's a theatre. It's as big as the entirety of Porozove." So I asked them once, "*Reboyne-shel-oylem*, Master of the Universe! How big is the entirety of Warsaw, then?" But they would just laugh at me. So I didn't ask them anything else about the city, and decided in my heart, "If it is my destiny, I'll just have to see it all for myself."

*   *   *

But first, I would have to make the journey.[5] My brother had received a position not in Warsaw, but nearby it, in the town of Skierniewice.[6] He sent us money from there, and a new dress was made for me with it, and a headscarf purchased. Shoes I already had. All in all, I was ready to travel. Mostly. First, we had to arrange for the documents I'd need. I didn't even have a birth certificate! So, what did we do? My father brought me to the *izborshchik*, the official who used to evaluate Jewish boys for service in the Russian army, so he could now evaluate me.

In those days, boys in our community who had reached the age of military service would be brought in to be "evaluated," and this is how that went: when the young man was "evaluated" to be twenty-one years old, he was conscripted, and when he was "evaluated" to be twenty-four years old, he was released. That was how so few Jews in our town ended up serving in the military—they didn't shave their beards, so they all appeared much older than they were.

One of my brothers was blond and looked very young. Still, by the time he turned twenty-one, he already had a wife and, I think, two children. When he had to face the draft, our father brought him to Volkovysk.[7] There they visited a barber, who darkened his blond beard with black pomade, so that he would look older.

My mother and I also helped. When Papa went off to Volkovysk with my brother, we went off to Porozove's cemetery, to weep. For two whole days, we lay prostrate on the graves of grandfathers, great-grandfathers, good friends, and righteous people, pleading that they intercede for us in Heaven. And from the cemetery, we went to the Holy Ark in the shul, and from there back to the cemetery. At night, when we returned home for just a few hours, I fell asleep quite quickly, having spent the whole day lamenting and praying. But my mother did not sleep. She sat up till dawn reciting psalms.

In the morning, our neighbor Blume, the dressmaker, came charging toward our house, banging on the windows, and screaming with a note of utter rapture in her voice: "Leye-Shifre, your son Yekl is free!"

My mother asked her how she knew. And our neighbor explained that my mother's brother Yoysef, who had been dead already for perhaps forty years, came to her in a dream and told her that my brother had been evaluated to be twenty-four years old and was let go. And that is exactly what happened to him.

Now I was to be evaluated by the official in the same manner. I was no older than eleven, but a tall girl, and so the man evaluated me to be thirteen. I think he did so because issuing passports to those who were under thirteen wasn't allowed. And so I was judged by my height and given a passport good for a month. Now we could begin our preparations for the trip in earnest.

But my mother's constant sobbing absolutely lashed at my heart. Poor soul, she cried out the same plea over and over again: "Dear little daughter, perhaps you ought not to go? Our own barley soup, our own rye bread—why shouldn't you go on eating it alongside us?" But I was able to gather myself together sufficiently to ask her to allow me to go, promising I would never forget about her, and that I would come visiting often. Anyway, I would not be traveling with strangers, but rather with my own family. And in the end, I had to seek out some purpose in life.

And so a covered wagon was hired. It was in the middle of winter, with bitterly low temperatures. My mother stuffed the carriage with bedclothes and a great lot of hay so that we wouldn't get cold. And now there began a series of farewells to beat the band.

First, with the whole shtetl, all of my boyfriends and girlfriends. The most interesting farewell was at the rabbi's house, with the yeshiva bochurim. Some of the young scholars even extended their hands to me, but only, of course, when no one was looking, as any physical contact between boys and girls was strictly forbidden. They wished me happiness and promised to think of me while they studied so that their learning would be counted as a merit in my favor and assure my well-being. The farewell of the young man from Yurberik,[8] who ate lunch in our home every Sunday, was especially heartfelt. He expressed deep regret that I would be leaving because it was always I who made sure he had enough good and filling things to eat when he came over.

Once I had bidden farewell to the rebbetzin and her sons, I went into—that is, the rebbetzin led me into—the rabbi's own office, and she said to him, "Avrom-Dovid, listen. Rokhele is leaving us, going all the way to Warsaw!" (And she pronounced *Varshe* as *Varse*, because her *sh* always came out as *s*.)[9] Our wonderful rabbi approached me, kissed my head, and murmured something I couldn't make out. Then he expressed his wish that I always be healthy and happy wherever my feet should lead me, and that I become an estimable personage, and well-known, and that he should only hear good news about me. After that, he took me by the shoulders, led me off to one side, and said to me, in tones of profound gravity:

"Know this, Rokhele: Warsaw is a big city, and a sinful city. You must be careful of yourself, and always remember that you are a virtuous Jewish daughter, and that you are leaving behind virtuous and elderly parents. You must, God forbid, never bring shame to them at their age."

Our saintly rabbi's words made my hair stand on end, and I broke out in sobs. I vowed to him that I would forever heed his holy words, that I would protect myself, and not traverse a wicked path. And I promised him, in a trembling voice, that I would bring honor to my parents, and to him, too. My eyes fit to overflow with tears, I bade him farewell. He then gave me one more kiss on the head, while I gave him one on his coat sleeve, and then, still weeping, trudged slowly away from his home, as I heard the rebbetzin calling after me, "Go in good health and return in good health!"

I returned to my own house, where I packed up my wardrobe, which included just one more shirt beyond the one I was wearing at the time. There, I said goodbye to my mother and father, and the assembled members of our extended family. My sister and her child, meanwhile, seated themselves in the covered wagon, and the driver set off.

The whole family and I, with an added company of neighbors and strangers, accompanied the wagon until it reached the Kropivnits Mountain. There the leave-taking and the kissing and the weeping began all over again, after which I was finally able to make my way into the wagon to join my sister. I took her child in my arms and covered myself with the featherbed.

The coachman urged on his horse, and the wagon juddered as it made its way up the mountain. I could still hear my mother's voice crying out, "Hashem yatsliekh darkekho"—May God grant you a successful journey! Over and over I heard her repeating the same bit of Hebrew, until the carriage began its rapid descent down the other side of the mountain. Then I could hear the echoes of my mother's dear voice no longer, nor the voices of my friends, with whom I'd grown up in such close companionship.

Suddenly, I rose and handed over the child to my sister so that I could steal one more look back from the wagon. But Porozove was already too far. Only the brass cross that rose from the steeple of the church, which stood in the middle of the marketplace, higher than all the thatched and shingled roofs of the town, could still be seen, glittering in the distance. I remained in that position, looking back, until even that, the very top of the spire, disappeared from view, as we continued our descent down the mountain.

I dried my eyes, sat back down, took the child from my sister, twirled the feather bed around me again, and recommenced my sniveling, only now more quietly. But my sister quickly silenced even that when she began telling me about all that I'd soon be seeing in Warsaw, and all that I could become there: a dressmaker, a hatmaker; in a word, anything. Anything I could ever wish to be.

She had managed to calm me. Now, sitting there in the carriage, I began to think, "Oy, if God will only help me, I'll be able to start earning money, and I'll send it back to my mother and father, and they'll have enough to live on!" With such thoughts occupying my mind, my heart filled with confidence and joy, and I fell asleep.

# V  EN ROUTE

When I awoke, and the coachman said we'd soon be arriving in Svislach,[1] I was very happy.[2] First of all, I'd get to rest a bit after all the jostling of the carriage, and second, I'd get to experience, for the first time in my life, a big and impressive town. I had always heard that Svislach, compared to Porozove, was as good as Kraków.

When night fell, we arrived and stopped over at the home of some acquaintances of ours. We spent the night there, bade them farewell in the morning, and continued on our way. We had already traveled 5 miles and had 9 left to go. That day, we traveled 4 more, until we reached an inn. There we stopped, had a meal, and stretched our legs a bit.

As we sat there, I heard a group of coachmen talking about the Białowieża Forest, how it was the largest forest in all of Russia, and that the tsar himself did his hunting there, where there were a great many wild beasts to be found. It was the same forest that we'd have to cross on our way to Białystok. And so I asked our own driver, in my earthy Russian, "What is it they're going on about?"

"Ah, they're not talking," he answered. "They're blabbering, never mind them!"

This reassured us. It was not his first time driving through the forest, he said, and nothing had ever happened to him there. Still, it was better to traverse it in the daytime, so we decided to stay the night at the inn.

In the morning, we made a good start on our journey, passed safely through the Białowieża Forest, and arrived in Białystok that same day, a Thursday. It was fine and sunny out, with a dry frost coating the ground. As soon as our little covered wagon turned onto one of the lanes leading into the city, I stuck my head out and saw before me great brick buildings with shining tin roofs. I could barely believe my eyes. When the coach turned onto an even lovelier street, with even taller buildings, I craned my neck to get a glimpse of the very top stories, and asked my sister, "Tell me, dear one, are there such houses in Warsaw, too? And do people really live up there at the top?"

She smiled and answered me with a cool air, "You'll see soon enough." As we were talking, I saw beside the buildings a troop of little children sliding about on the clean, smoothly swept pavement. When they caught sight of our coach, they began to shout in unison, "Gypsies! Gypsies!" This they did with such a shocking clamor that I felt I would faint. I stood straight up, and in so doing, managed to rip apart the very covering of the covered wagon. In mere moments, I had torn off nearly the whole of the canvas. The coachman shouted at me as his vehicle rolled along, saying I was tearing the cloth. Meanwhile, the three wagon bows across which the canvas had been stretched stood naked, and I, myself exposed as I stood among them, was now in full view of the little rascals on the street.

When they saw me there, with my dark features and red headkerchief, they began to chase the carriage with its bare frame, calling out in Russian with renewed vigor in their voices, "*Vot tsiganka*, look at this Gypsy girl! A little Gypsy girl!"

At this point, my sister and I were laughing so uproariously that the coachman thought we'd gone out of our minds—and he started to cross himself.

We turned onto a wide street that was called Piaskes.[3] We had a distant relative there, a woman who owned her own house, and in it, a tavern, and besides all that, a little textile factory, too. This woman, a dark-haired and dark-eyed Jewess, admitted us into the house. I didn't know her, nor she me, but she recognized my sister, and asked her, "Who's the girl?" As soon as she heard I was the sister, she welcomed us both very warmly. Having brought in our things from the now *un*covered wagon, she led us into a little nook of her establishment and furnished us with tea and rye bread.

We ate our fill, treated our coachman to his own portion of bread and a glass of sweet tea, and paid him his fee. We also gave him back the blankets that our mother had given us to wrap ourselves in on our journey, and a letter, all of which he was to deliver home for us. I bade farewell to this Gentile and asked him to pass on the same fond greeting to our family, and to tell them that all was well with me and that I was very happy.

The Białystok relative, Henye, wanted terribly for me to stay with her. She wouldn't treat me as a servant, no, no—she would treat me as her own child. And I could hang around in her tavern, and when a respectable young man would turn up someday, she'd marry me off to him, and would see to it that all would go just right for me. But as for myself, I couldn't wait for Sunday to come, the day of our departure for Warsaw.

And God be thanked, Sunday came on quickly. We had all our things packed and had gone shopping for things to eat on the road: a few precious, fresh bagel sprinkled with poppy seeds, and rye bread sprinkled with caraway, and rolls that in Białystok are called *hulnik*,[4] which are great big flat rounds of bread, for just three kopecks apiece.

It all gave off an aroma of perfect freshness—Białystok had always been famous for its baked goods. And though we'd already filled a sack with them, our relatives still gave us a few more for the road, and we departed with fond farewells. I told them that if things went sour for me in Warsaw, I would surely return to them. Then my sister and I set off for the train, in a droshky fitted with springs.

What a sensation! I could barely comprehend what I was experiencing and started to laugh loudly. Here I was, sitting on a soft seat in a carriage, like an aristocrat, while the *drontske* (as it was called in Białystok) bounced me this way and that as it went rolling along on its springs. And I could feel my insides bouncing right along with it. Still, I wasn't afraid for myself. I had no fear of falling out—more than once, in Porozove, I'd been in carts that had flipped over. But I was afraid for my sister and her child. At every bend in the cobblestone road, I yelped, "Oy! Oy!" and held tightly onto the child. At last, God intervened, and we arrived at the station. Still today, Białystok's streets are paved pretty frightfully.

My sister told me we had made it. I hauled down our luggage from the *drontske*, and we all went inside. Stretching out on a bench, I took the child in my arms and and sat there quite sure that I was already on the train. But then my sister told me we would soon have to climb aboard. I still didn't know what it all meant, and so decided I'd better just keep silent and await my destiny.

My sister told me to wait where I was as she walked away to buy our tickets, then got instantly swallowed up in the vast hora of men and women swirling around the station. I tried to look for her from where I was sitting, but I couldn't see her, couldn't pick her out from among the crowd. The tumult in the station was rendering me nearly deaf. Finally, she returned and handed me two green slips of paper, telling me these were the tickets, and that each cost two rubles and thirty-five kopecks, and for the two of them together, four rubles and seventy kopecks. My hands flew to my head! "Oh well," I thought to myself. "That's just what these things cost, I suppose."

So there we sat at the station, the *vokzal*, as I learned then such places were called. Every minute some kind of pipe blew a shrill note, and I asked my sister, "What's all the whistling about?"

"That's the whistling of the train," she answered. "The very one we'll soon be riding."

*   *   *

At last, the time came.[5] We grabbed our luggage and the child, and made our way onto the platform outside along with a great many others, all of whom pushed and shoved me as we proceeded. I held fast onto my sister's sleeve so that I wouldn't lose her because, strange as it was, whenever she left me for even a couple of minutes, I could never find her again in the swarm of people. She always had to call my name so that I could figure out where she was.

"Could it really be that all of these people are also going to Warsaw?" I asked her as we forced our way onto the train and into the little compartment with the bench seats, just like the ones I had sat on in our shul in Porozove. But this was no synagogue—it was our train, finally.

We placed our luggage on the appointed shelves and made ourselves comfortable in our seats, just as if we were at home. I heard a ringing and was dying to ask what it was, but was too embarrassed—I had already resolved not to ask any more questions. And besides, we were surrounded on all sides by strangers. By no means was I going to speak in front of them. But my sister understood and said without my having to inquire, "That'll be the first *zvonok* ringing. In a little while, there'll be another, and then with the third, we'll be on our way!"

Just opposite me, next to the window, sat a Warsovian man, around thirty years of age. He started off our time together by poking fun at the dialect of us Litvaks[6]—for instance, how he had overheard my sister using the word *zvonok* to mean "bell."[7] He asked her, "Are you all traveling to Warsaw for the first time?" "No," said she. "I'm already a Warsovian by now, but it's the first time for the little one, my sister."

That opened up a world of jokes and wisecracks for the man, one after another. He began gibing at me, "You know what's coming, Miss? It's our custom in the city that when you get off the train in Warsaw, you have to give someone three kisses." I could tell this jester wouldn't let me off so easily, so I snapped back at him, "If one is expected to give kisses, then I suppose I will . . . to myself." That shut him up good.

Soon I was saved by the bell, too, as it rang three times, a whistle accompanying it, and the whole compartment with its bench seats began to move. I looked out and saw the station disappear behind us as we journeyed forth from the city, crossing into the fields beyond. I simply had to get up and peer through the window, then couldn't tear myself away. The fields were spinning, the trees galloping past, and the little houses vanishing in mere moments—all as I stood in place, my face pressed to the glass. I became lightheaded and was barely conscious of the fact that I could sit down if I so chose. But the fields and forests wouldn't stop whirling across my vision.

Eventually, I pulled myself together and started in on our sackful of goodies. I took out a couple of bagel and some cheese and began to eat, also handing some to my sister. As I sat there and nibbled, I thought to myself, "How great are God's wonders! Here I am sitting in this funny little room, and at the same time, I'm traveling miles and miles, and they even tell me I'll soon be in Warsaw!"

Night fell and it grew very dark. We must have been sitting close to the locomotive because when I turned to look out the window again, I saw long, snaking sparks flashing past us. It gave me such a shock. I could no longer keep as calm and quiet as I had been, and asked my sister in an undertone, "Dear one, look at those sparks—is it not dangerous?"

But though I made a point of asking quietly, the clown sitting across from us still overheard and began afresh with his harassment of me. I talked back to him, giving him a good telling-off in my saltiest shtetl language, until I got him to keep quiet for good.

Eventually, the four and a half hours had flown by, and the train arrived in the big city.

# VI  IN WARSAW!

I became altogether disoriented when I saw the crowd descending from the train. It was more people than I had ever seen in one place in my life. But soon, we had to start making our exit, too. Our talkative neighbor helped us with our luggage and helped my sister and her child climb down the steps from the train. He helped me down after them, taking me by the arm. How strange it felt, to be held like that by a man who was a complete stranger . . .

People stood on either side of us, outlandishly dressed, with brass buttons and these funny little hats. And they wouldn't stop shouting. "The Hotel Saski!" cried one of them. "The Hotel Angielski!" piped up another. Others grabbed at people's sleeves. One of them seized my bundle and shouted, "Cab!" I snatched it back from him and called out to my sister, "Gevalt, Keyle, what do they want from us!" And again he tore my bundle away. My sister, who was always very jovial, laughed at me now with such enthusiasm that she almost let go of her child. Still cackling, she tried to put me at ease, saying, "Don't be afraid, Rokhele, they're not gonna do anything to you, they only want to take us where we're headed."

Pushing our way through, we finally made it out of the station, and the very cabman who had grabbed my bundle got what he wanted. There we sat now, in his cab fitted with glass windowpanes. Our luggage was thrown on, and we told him to take us to 48 Pawia Street.

After we'd been driving for a little while, I asked, "Are we in Warsaw yet?" "No," my sister answered. "This is still Praga, a suburb of Warsaw." A bit later, she said, "We'll soon come to the Praga Bridge," which we crossed shortly after.

"Now whaddya say to that?" she commented. "A touch bigger than our bridge back in Porozove, eh?" But I was simply struck dumb with amazement and couldn't get a word out in response.

As I gazed silently, we passed over the bridge with its hundreds of streetlamps. And then, all those beautiful, wide avenues. Every minute our cab went past some tall pole which held at its pinnacle a splendid lantern with shining glass and such a strange, luminous fire, casting such a very far-reaching light.

I had no need of asking anything, really, because my sister pointed it all out to me: "That's the palace, and this is the famous street known as the 'Krákow Suburb,'[1] and here's Senatorska Street, and there's the theatre square," and so forth, until we reached Pawia Street. Here it was much darker, and a deep layer of mud coated the ground.

It was so dark out that the cabdriver had terrible trouble finding the address number 48 (which now, as I write, has become number 84). He decided to stop his vehicle and barked back to us in his thick Warsaw dialect, "Nu, you can get out now! You've dragged me along on a real wild goose chase, right into this nasty bit of mud. It's time to get out!"

When we began to do so, with the small child in tow, our older sister immediately recognized us, emerging from the shop she owned in the front of the courtyard where we'd stopped. After hugging and kissing us, she quickly led us into her home, served us tea and fed us, then conducted me to my room on the third floor.

As I walked up, I felt hollow wooden stairs under my feet, just like the ones we had in the shul in Porozove, leading up to the women's balcony. But that staircase at shul only had about ten or twelve steps, whereas here I just kept climbing and climbing. I thought they would go on forever!

# VII SIREN SONG

My first stroll through Warsaw's famous Saxon Garden[1] made a wonderful impression on me, because of this: when I went there with some girls whose acquaintance I had recently made, strolling down one of the pretty tree-lined paths, we heard singing coming from somewhere. It turned out an opera was being given in the Summer Theatre in the park—the Winter Theatre had burned down. As soon as I heard the music, it was as if I had been welded to the fence that encircled the playhouse. Many others were standing there, too, and so I wasn't ashamed of staying fixed to the spot until the singing stopped.

"What is this?" I asked my companions.

"An opera," they said. "Being played in the big theatre."

I asked them how much a ticket cost, and they told me that you could get one for thirty kopecks if you didn't mind sitting way up high. I walked back with a heavy heart that day, wondering when the day would come when I could enter such a theatre. So I made a firm resolution, deciding the thing as I walked: that when I began to earn money, I would eat one roll fewer each day, and that way I would be able to save up slowly, one kopeck after another, and I'd eventually have enough to go, at least once, to the theatre.

But things turned out quite differently. A couple of young men started to visit us at home. They had been raised in our shtetl Porozove but for a good while had been living in Warsaw, where they were making a good living. One of them, a certain Moyshe Kohn, was an avid theatregoer, and said to me once, "You know, Rokhl, *Faust* is on at the Opera tonight.[2] Come with me."

I nearly collapsed from excitement. I could hardly believe my own ears. But I gathered myself together sufficiently to ask my sister for permission, and threw on my things. Barely a minute passed before I was fully dressed for the theatre, in an adorable dress and dainty slippers. Oh, I was quite the little mademoiselle!

# VIII GOLDFADEN

We arrived successfully to the Saxon Garden, and this time not just outside the fence of the theatre, but within it, and not just within the fence—but within the theatre itself, in the first row of the balcony.[1] As I remember it, we were the first ones there, but soon people began pouring in. I looked down from my seat and instantly felt vertigo. The tops of such a multitude of heads! It was getting full above us, just as it had filled up below. My gallant escort said to me, "Down there, the ground floor, that's called the 'parterre,' and those boxes are called 'loges,' and above us is the 'gallery.'" But now I couldn't stop looking at the massive chandelier with its myriad little flames.

A bell sounded, and the orchestra began to play. My heart nearly jumped out of my body from sheer excitement, and I continued looking all around me, rapt.

"Look down there, see the curtain?" said my young man. "Soon it will rise, and you'll see the singers playing there on the stage." He continued: "The one who's playing the Devil is named Seideman, and that one is . . ." Eventually he started running through all the details of the plot, but who could listen to him?

All I could do was sit there, stock-still, never moving until the curtain finally fell. I was as if in a drunken haze. I felt embarrassed to say it, but it came out of me anyway: "These cannot be ordinary people." The last act, with the heavens opening up, and the angels, discomposed me entirely. When it was all over, I finally woke up from my beautiful dream.

"What's got you so out of sorts?" my young fellow asked me. "Yes, they're ordinary people, just like you and me!"

"Well then I'd like to see these supposed 'people' up close," I answered.

"Come," he said, "I'll introduce you."

Leaving the theatre, he led me to the stage door, where we waited until all of the singers had come out. I stood as if I had been soldered to the spot.

But when my young fellow called all these performers by their names, I did finally believe they were actual people.

When I arrived home, my sister asked me, "Nu, how did you like it?"

I couldn't say anything. I was simply stupefied. When I went to bed, everything I had seen on the stage played over again in my head. And when I woke up, I found that I had already memorized much of the score: the "bang-bang!" heard during the duel scene, the marches . . . I couldn't stop singing it. My home audience was bemused to find what a little "musician" I'd become, and several times I heard one or another family member saying, "If we let her study the stuff, who knows what she could become." But that kind of talk never rose above just that, mere talk.

Still, they did send me to study—with a seamstress. I did not stay with her long but picked up her craft quite easily. I didn't like it, though, and fled from her with the excuse that I could no longer sit at the sewing machine because it made my head hurt. My sisters loved me, so they believed anything I told them, and I returned to my life of chores around the house.

*   *   *

One fine, sunny day, my brother came round and said to me, "You know, I recently met some Yiddish actors from Goldfaden's troupe.[2] There's a fellow called Goldshmidt,[3] he lives on Nowolipie Street,[4] and he told me that Goldfaden is producing a show at the Theatre Bouffe (later the Eldorado, today known as Bogusławski's Theatre) and is looking for a girl to play kid roles."

So I started begging him, "Yosele, won't you bring me there?" He promised he would, and it wasn't long before we both snuck out of the house and ran off to see Goldshmidt. Even his apartment made a powerful impression on me: a tiny little place, in the basement of a small wooden house, and very poor. My brother was already quite at home there, though, and he introduced us. Goldshmidt gave me a good once-over and proclaimed me too tall for juvenile roles. My brother replied that I was still quite young. And Goldshmidt said, "Yes, I can see that, but still . . . she's grown quite big."

I thought to myself, "There it is, my mother's lament all over again: 'Such a big girl mustn't walk around barefoot!'"

Nevertheless, he asked if I'd like to learn how to read music from him, and if I had any desire to become a Yiddish actress.

"I would like to very much," I said, of course, my cheeks turning quite red. "But I don't know if I can."

"Sing something," he said to me. I didn't have much time to think. My brother gave me a pitch, and we sang a little piece for two voices. Then I sang something by myself. I apparently pleased the maestro, as he then said to me, "I shall introduce you to Goldfaden."

I am quite unable to express the fullness of what my heart underwent at that moment. Suffice it to say that I said goodbye to him and ran home beside myself with joy. My sister told me she would permit me to leave the house to study for an hour each day. And so I began going to Herr Goldshmidt, and he began teaching me how to read music. Before a week had passed, I could already sight-read the first chorus from *Shulamis*: "Ongelodn mit al dos guts."[5] But I wasn't singing the lyrics yet, rather just the solfège syllables:

> Fa la do do re
> Re do fa sol la
> La si sol fa.

Every day, I walked along Pawia Street with a book of music under my arm. Whose happiness could have equaled mine! Then one day, Goldshmidt said to me, "We're going to visit Herr Direktor Goldfaden."

I put on the best clothes I had, and we crossed Krasiński Square, passed underneath the massive pillars of the grand Baroque Krasiński palace, and entered the first floor, which then served as a hotel where many Yiddish actors lodged. I was led into a room where there sat a handsome, well-fed man. I heard Goldshmidt telling him, "This is the girl I was telling you about."

Goldshmidt then turned and said to me, "This is Herr Direktor Goldfaden."

I was so terrified, I felt the floor begin to tremble under my feet. Goldfaden noticed, and said to me, "Don't be afraid, dear girl. Sit a while and rest, then you'll sing something for me."

I collected myself, took courage, and told him that I wasn't at all tired.

So Goldfaden sat himself down at the piano and struck a couple chords. "Sing something that you know," he instructed.

Goldshmidt piped up, "Sing the first chorus from *Shulamis*."

Little by little, I settled down, being very much warmed by Goldfaden's affable nature. And so I stood up and sang through the whole of "Ongelodn," accompanied by Direktor Goldfaden at the piano.

It was a hit.

"Very good," he said. "You may come to observe our rehearsals at the theatre."

As we walked from there down Smocza Street[6] to Long Street,[7] where the Theatre Bouffe was, Goldshmidt kept pressing upon me one demand: that I mustn't be so bold as to get too friendly with the actor known as Tantsman[8] and the other stars. I must do my best to only engage with them from afar. He repeated it over and over, enough times to strike fear in me.

But Goldfaden had told him to bring me to rehearsals at the theatre, after all! I couldn't stay afraid too long. I said goodbye to him and flew home as though a gust of wind were carrying me.

"Nu," my sister said when I arrived. "We'll have to wait and see what comes of all this."

Soon the day came when Goldshmidt, my teacher, brought me along to rehearsal. In front of the building was a gate, and above it, inscribed in great big letters, "THEATRE BOUFFE." Passing through it, we walked into a courtyard with a garden. Once we entered the theatre, Goldshmidt instructed me to sit down on one of the bench seats in the house, while he ascended to the stage. They were rehearsing *Bar Kokhba*.

It was Tisha b'Av[9] and I was fasting. But being filled with the pleasure of observing the rehearsal, I soon forgot the emptiness of my belly, forgot about my fast entirely. I felt something quite different now to the emotions I had experienced in the goyish theatre where I had seen *Faust*. Here, they were speaking the same language that I did.

Once they opened *Bar Kokhba*, I went to see a performance with my brother. I was stunned by how beautifully they carried it off. But I also thought, "Well, once I've learned the music, I'll be able to carry it off just as beautifully. After all, there can't be some great trick to it, if you already speak Yiddish."

By the next morning, we were already imitating one number after another from the operetta, singing them with the right words and everything. I did the prima donna Madame Tantsman's[10] parts, and my brother took Spivakovski's.[11]

I carried on in this way for a while, continuing to take music lessons from Goldshmidt twice a week. But it was not in the cards for me to remain that happy for much longer.

# IX MOTHER AND FATHER TAKE FRIGHT

Right around this time, a woman from my shtetl, Sore, Isaac's daughter, took ill, and as there was no doctor in Porozove, she traveled to Warsaw, where she headed straight to the house I shared with my sisters.[1] Just my luck. I was charged with bringing her to the doctor and all around the pharmacies. She stayed for a couple of weeks with us and spent the whole time interrogating me, "Tell me, Rokhele, where is it you go every day?" Singing lessons, I told her. Little did I know that in telling her this, I was digging my own grave.

Eventually, she recovered from her malady and returned home to Porozove, where she passed on to my mother and father the warmest greetings from their children, sons-in-law, and grandchildren in Warsaw. But at my parents' last question, "And how is our Ester-Rokhele doing?", the woman grew silent. My dear mother and father were much frightened, but she quickly tried to calm them down by providing this answer:

"She is well, but goes out every day with a book under her arm, then she's out for an hour or so, and when she returns, she shuts herself into her room and tra-la-la-las the whole day away. She's learning how to sing, you see. She wants to go work in some 'treeter,' I think it's called, and become an actress."

Once my very pious parents heard this, not two weeks passed before my sisters received a missive. It must have been ten pages if it was a page—and all about me: "Surely you are not, for God's sake, tolerating such savagery! And yet it seems you are? That a child of ours should work as a two-bit magician! A comedienne?!" And so on and so on with the same kinds of fulminations, ending with the statement that if I did not want to end my parents' lives, I should quickly end this career of mine.

So what happened? My foot no longer darkened Herr Goldshmidt's doorstep, nor did I attend any more rehearsals. I did once walk to Long Street and stood outside the Theatre Bouffe hoping to catch him, so that I could return his scores. It was going to be so hard for me to part from my music. But then I saw our physician, a certain Dokter Shantser, who liked me very much.

"What are you standing here for, dear girl?" he asked me.

I told him the whole story, complaining about my fanatical parents.

The doctor, after taking it all in, took hold of me and started making monstrous noises (he always spoke in his own patent version of German, so as to sound refined):

"Vat do you vant to become?" he shouted. "A jüdische ectress? Return to your haus, schnell, or I vill vallop you mit mein cane! I vill tell dein bruder-in-law, and Gott knows vat he'll do mit you! Jawohl, you must go home at vahnce!"

And so I ran home with my scores and returned to my old, gray, workaday existence: cooking breakfast each morning, feeding the children, sending them off to school, then toiling away as I cleaned every room both upstairs and downstairs.

All of it had become so dreadfully boring, and I missed my mother. I asked if I could be sent home to the shtetl for a short time. My sisters agreed. They fitted me out with some new clothes and sent me home. I had indeed been seriously longing for Porozove, but truth be told, my greater longing was to show up there with a couple of nice new dresses, a hat, and a pair of ankle boots without iron soles, and a parasol, too. "Well isn't that something?" I wanted everyone to say. "A true-blue Warsaw mademoiselle!"

When I did return, there was no end to the glee of my sweet elderly parents. I felt rather gleeful, too. Even the snottiest, richest girls came to gape at my "modish" Warsaw dresses and fancy blouses. There were three very pretty frocks: one blue, one gold, and one made of black velvet, with dainty pink flowers (it was bought for me off the rack for three rubles). In the eyes of Porozove, I looked like the Countess Potocka![2] The sons of the rich families all came swarming around me like flies on honey, but they were not to my taste.

As the lady who visited us in Warsaw had spread the news far and wide of my having become a *shpilerke* and *zingerke*, a genuine actress and singer, ladies started inviting me over to come demonstrate my skill. It did not take much begging for my entire repertoire to begin pouring out of me. It consisted of Elyokem Tsunzer's[3] ten new songs, and bits of *Bar Kokhba* and *Shulamis*. The shouts of "Bravo!" reached to the very heavens. Gentiles lined up on Novidvor Street, outside the windows of the houses where I sang, and applauded right along with the crowds inside. Twice a week I gave such recitals.

And so I achieved a certain level of distinction in Porozove. It was entirely forgotten that I had once been taunted as the "congregation kishke," the daughter of a poor family that depended on the charity of the community. But I did not let my new status go to my head. I again became a constant presence in the rabbi's house, resumed my volunteer service helping the rebbetzin prepare the Shabbos meal, rolling out dough for noodles, and when our beloved Passover came around, rolling out the dough for the rabbi's *shmure* matzo.

Still, it didn't take long for it all to feel dull and commonplace again. Now I started to miss Warsaw. I wrote to my sisters, telling them I wanted to return, and my brother-in-law sent me five rubles for the journey back. I began to prepare: packed my few belongings, along with a pretty little pot of flowers I had planted myself, and said goodbye to all my near and dear ones in the shtetl, including, of course, the rabbi and the rebbetzin. Then I boarded a stagecoach for Białystok and from there, took the train to the big city. I had become quite a whole person: traveling on my own, just imagine it, and arriving on my own—and poof! There I was, back in Warsaw!

# X  AMONG THE YIDDISH ACTORS IN THE GRZYBÓW NEIGHBORHOOD[1]

In the summer of 1892, my young gentleman, the fellow considered to be my fiancé, came to visit and told me that a new Yiddish theatre was being established in Warsaw. And what's more, they were saying that it had already received a performing permit but was looking for actors. I asked him if it would be on the level of the theatre company that Goldfaden had operated with Shomer.[2] He said it would be. It was even to be in the same building Goldfaden and Shomer had produced out of, but now the theatre was called the Eldorado.

I looked at him hard and began to question him as to the source of his information. He told me that he had met a certain Shvartsbard (the Elder),[3] and that Shvartsbard had told him that his son-in-law, a certain Vaysfeld,[4] was getting together a troupe.

"And you know what, Ruzhele?" he said (for that's what my fiancé called me). "When you have a bit of time, I say we go and have a look at what they're up to."

So one Shabbos afternoon, my fiancé came over, and we walked together to Herr Vaysfeld, in the neighborhood of Grzybów. He was a teacher and maintained a school there, consisting of two large rooms. When we entered, it became clear that my fiancé had already told these people about me—I ascertained by how I was received by the crowd assembled there that I had been quite eagerly awaited. Why, it seemed I'd been talked up as the second coming of Adelina Patti,[5] or some other such celebrated songbird.

At Vaysfeld's, I found a band of young men joined by a great many girls and young women, all of them dressed in their Shabbos best, and some of them even in quite expensive and beautiful ensembles. The relations between them seemed very friendly, for they spoke loudly and joked with each other. It was apparent that it was not their first time meeting as a group, either, for they were speaking about what roles they would all be taking in the coming season.

But as soon as we entered, the mood changed entirely, as all started turning their attention toward me. My fiancé turned rather pale and grabbed me by the arm, as if he were struck with a sudden fear that someone would take me from him. Eventually, he regained his composure and began introducing me to the folks who were there.

I was presented to Herr Vaysfeld and Herr Shvartsbard, who was Vaysfeld's father-in-law (*Schwiegervater*, as my fiancé put it in German, trying to sound elegant); then to the three young Misses Shvartsbard: Sonye, Franye, and Ruzhe, as well as a son, Max Gustav Shvartsbard;[6] then to a small, chubby, but very piquant little lady named Triling;[7] and then another lady, formerly one of Goldfaden's chorines.

Countless pairs of hands were extended in greeting: rough hands, soft hands, quite delicate hands. By their various textures, it was easy to guess what kinds of people these youngsters were, and what various sorts of work they had been involved in. As we all introduced ourselves, I heard these names for the first time in my life: Herman and Adolf Berman (they were called "the big Berman" and "the small Berman," even though they were the same size),[8] Yankev Libert,[9] Herr Kaminski, Herr Abelman, Herr Polakevitsh, Herr Ronde, Herr Titelman, Herr Rotshayn, these introductions being followed by, "This is our director, Herr Yulius Oskar, and this is our chorus master Herr Lustig, and here is a German actor, Herr Berthold, the brother of the famous opera singer Rechtleben." But still there were more: "This is our heroic bass, Herr Gisyanski, and Herr Faynshteyn and Herr Rozenkvyat, also from Goldfaden's company. And this is Herr Gothard, our *souffleur*."

I had no idea that a *souffleur* was a prompter. I could have told you what an *artist* was. *Chorister*, too, because cantors in the synagogue also had choristers. But a *souffleur*? Not for the life of me!

After we'd all gotten acquainted, they peppered me with questions about what kind of work I was involved in, and how much I earned in my trade.[10] When I asked them why they wanted to know, the elder Herr Shvartsbard answered, "Because we are trying to figure out whether it will be worth it to you to throw aside your present occupation, and become a performer."

I did not know how to respond. What did he mean, "worth it"? Surely they would have to see first off if I had any potential. How could they possibly know that I even had it in me?

"Why shouldn't you?" the elder Shvartsbard went on. "Your fiancé told me that you are very musical and have a fine voice. And you've a fine figure, to boot, so why not?

"You see, Miss," he went on, "everyone here is a tradesperson, each a master of their trade. Nevertheless, they have all abandoned these trades in order to tread the boards. Here, for example, Miss Triling? Is a milliner. And Mr. Kaminski? A bootmaker.[11] Mr. Libert is a printer, Mr. Abelman a cork maker,[12] Mr. Rotshayn a ribbon maker.[13] But they have all cast their professions aside and taken up acting."

I sat there, quite still, listening with profound attention to his speech about how people manage to become theatre artists. The art they had all dedicated themselves to started to assume an altogether different sort of charm for me. I had thought actors were something like angels, like the bass Seideman and the tenor Myszuga, whom I had heard sing in the opera *Faust*. But in fact, they were just ordinary people like those before me now, these men and women at the dawn of their onstage careers. Was it not amazing?

I remained seated for a while, listening to each of them putting in their oar to contribute a little jest even sillier than the one before. Finally, the chorus master Lustig said to me, "Miss Halperin, sing something for us."

I did let the begging go on for a bit, but when they all came and stood before me, waiting, I relented. I blushed a little, but plucked up my courage and went to stand beside the piano. Lustig gave me the starting chord of Mendelssohn's "Autumn Song"[14] and I sang it with great feeling, according to all who were present.

The artists-to-be applauded me warmly and expressed their confidence that they had found in me the right prima donna for their newly assembled troupe. When I began to go, they surrounded me and pressed me with the persistent question, "When will you come to one of our rehearsals?" I looked at them in astonishment. What could they mean? Already?

"I shall of course have to ask my sisters first if they'll even permit me, and my brother-in-law, too," I said.

"One doesn't ask permission for this," they responded. "All celebrated actors and performers once had to leave their homes behind without asking, in their first step to becoming great artists."

But I said to them, "I will not run away from my home. One of you must come to my family and persuade them, and if they give their permission, then we'll talk."

# XI AT POLAKEVITSH'S FACTORY[1]

What did my home life look like? For a long time now, thank God, I had demonstrated myself to be a very industrious chore-doer for my sisters living upstairs and downstairs, so that no one could've ever said of me that I ate in their house for free. But such drudgery would not lead anywhere. I began asking if I might be allowed to gain some employment outside the home. The idea of being a hatmaker or a seamstress pleased me very much. But we would have had to pay for my taking an apprenticeship, and that was impossible for the family.

Across the street from us lived a man who was employed at Polakevitsh's factory. He advised that I could get work there pasting labels onto cigar packs, for which I could get a weekly salary of two rubles. But it would depend on how fast I worked. I grasped the opportunity with both hands.

So one sunny day, I went off with this neighbor to the factory on Bonifraten Street.[2] We entered a large courtyard. My word, but how many people were there! It seemed to me I had never seen so many people before in all my life. But I said nothing and just followed the man I had been brought to meet. Meyer the Cigar Maker, he was called.

He led me through an entrance on the left of the courtyard and up into the factory, then presented me to a round-bellied man who led me to a table where he showed me the work I was to do. It was not long before a great wave of people came rushing in. Every table was soon occupied by young men and women, who dove headlong into their labors. And with their labors began a song, in voices so resounding that you could go deaf from it. I sat down, and a basket full of packs of cigars was brought to me, along with an empty basket and a pack of long slips of paper—the labels.

I saw how others did their work and quickly caught on to the tricks of the trade. A board would be smeared with a starchy glaze and the labels laid onto it, after which the then-sticky labels could be wrapped around the packs of cigars. At the start, the work went slowly, but I grew quicker and quicker at it, and started tossing the finished packs into the empty basket with panache. Still, before my empty basket was even half full, the others had already started on new baskets. When the stout fellow approached me, he turned up his nose a bit at my progress, but when he lifted up a pair of my finished packs and regarded them closely, the finished product pleased him very much. The labels were pasted on nice and straight. He even called over others to show them how fine my handiwork was.

"Just do it a bit faster," he said to me, "and you'll be right as rain."

I worked at it until noon, at which point a large bell was rung, sounding just like the one that they used to ring in our shtetl when a fire had broken out. But when I saw everyone running off casually and noticed the time of day, I realized it was merely lunchtime, so I went out to take my lunch, too. All my fellow workers, one by one, were running down the steps and always getting stopped for a moment when they reached the exit, with its narrow doorway. I joined the line. Then I saw what they had been stopping for: when I got to the exit at the bottom of the stairs, a woman started tapping at my pockets, grabbing here and there. When I finally reached the courtyard, I thought to myself, "My God, what have I gotten myself into? Seems they think everyone here is a thief, that all of us should need to be frisked like that!" And yet I resolved that I would remain for the time being and see how things progressed.

I noticed everyone else scattered about very merrily, not looking at all bothered by having had to submit to such an inspection. Those who lived nearby ran home to eat their lunch, but I couldn't go all the way back to Pawia Street. Someone was kind enough to spot me a copper ten-kopeck coin, with which I entered a little shop on Bonifraten and bought bread for four kopecks, a bottle of oatmeal stout for four more, and herring for two. I gobbled it all up right there in the shop, just as I saw other factory girls doing. Then I rested for a short spell and returned to the illuminating work—ha!

Sitting there and pasting on labels, I got to thinking, "How could anyone be satisfied with such a stupid job, so satisfied as to sing while doing it!" But I did finish out my day there. When night came, people started to put on their things to go home. There were several ways out of the building, and, who knows how, but I found myself on one of the staircases which had a man inspecting the workers at the end of it, instead of a woman. There he was, ready to give me the old tapping treatment! Afraid and embarrassed,

I ran back up, then down again by another staircase, where I found yet another man! But seeing other women exiting by the same way, I did so, too, and once the search was over, hurtled myself through that door as though escaping an inferno.

Once I returned home, embittered and insulted, I asked one of my sisters, "What kind of work is this? And how can people allow themselves to be humiliated in that way? If their bosses suspect them of being thieves, they shouldn't deign to continue working there!" But my sister just laughed at me, so I went on, in my plainspoken way, "Fine, go ahead and laugh at me as much as you all like, but I certainly won't be going back to a job like that again."

No one said a word in response, and I went on living with them as before.

Not long after, I began asking again if some worthy employment could be found for me, and I was sent to work for a lady who made umbrellas. That pleased me much more. No salary was spoken of at the beginning—they said they would first have to see how I took to the work, which involved sewing the canopy onto the ribs of each umbrella. The method was demonstrated to me once and I caught on immediately. I would lay out the canopy, stretching out the material, then sew it to the ribs at the corners and in the middle, and then, turning the little umbrella around, drape the whole of the canopy over it, carrying it off with a good bit of skill. In a word, my work was *neat*.

After working manually in that way for a couple of days, they set me up at the sewing machine. There my progress was not quite as quick. I couldn't catch the pedal, and things did not go well. I broke several needles, and one of the women who was teaching me lost her patience. "Pea-brain!" she roared. I said nothing, just went right home and never returned. And so ended my promising career as a maker of parasols!

I returned to carrying out my chores dutifully at my sisters'. After a time, things started going better for my brother-in-law. He became the manager of the building we lived in, and we moved into a nicer apartment. And when he began to earn more, a pretty little dress and hat were made for me. I was developing quite nicely—people said I was turning out to be quite a pretty girl.

Around this time, one of my brothers arrived in Warsaw. He was three years older than I, and a rakish, clever fellow. He quickly secured a position in the well-known brewery of Herman Jung and began to earn wages that were nothing to be sniffed at. This was probably in the mid-1880s, when Goldfaden and Shomer's troupe was playing at the Eldorado. My brother would attend the theatre often, and upon returning home, would tell of all he had seen there, and sing every catchy tune he'd heard. My curiosity kept me on the very edge of my seat. But as for going myself, or asking if I could be brought along—it was more than I could even dream of then.

However, time would not stand still. Little by little, I was shaking off my old Porozove ways. Gone were the days when I'd have to spend long summer Shabbos afternoons, as was customary for us women, bent over the lessons in the Yiddish Bible I had brought along with me from home. Now I began taking the Shabbos day to do whatever I pleased. I was pretty, and as I dressed prettily, too, I became better friends with a couple of elegant young ladies who also lived on Pawia Street, both of them corsetières. Like me, they worked hard the whole week through, so we took advantage of Shabbos to enjoy ourselves together: going for walks, singing, and dancing the whole day through.

# XII AT THE SHOE FACTORY

Ever since I had returned from Porozove, some *takhles*, some suitable, practical aim in life had been sought for me.[1] My sisters had thought that aim could be to become a milliner or seamstress, while I thought it could only lie in becoming Dine, the heroine of Goldfaden's opera *Bar Kokhba*. At that time, my eldest sister was living at 78 Pawia Street, which was owned by a Gentile landlord. Every Shabbos, a large company would gather at her home, mostly young, musical people, many of them choristers at the synagogue, and they would perform bits of music popularized by the greatest chazanim, along with the loveliest ballads.

Often the landlord would stand under the window with other Gentiles and listen to the singing. Once he said to me after I had taken part in one of these sing-alongs, "Why don't you go sometime to the Towarzystwo Muzyczne, the Musical Society?"[2] I told him I didn't have the money to pay for lessons.

"I know a famous professor there," he responded, "who would teach you for free."

He even gave me a letter of recommendation to take along to the professor. It was like he'd spoon-fed me a big dose of instant happiness. Not long after, I set off, letter in hand, for the society. The professor listened to my introduction and said, "I will give an answer myself to Mr. Sopcinski (the landlord)."

After a couple of days, the landlord came to tell me that it would be a while before I could expect to earn anything from my talent. I would have to study long and hard, and then, if a spot eventually opened up, I could join the chorus of the Imperial Theatre. I did end up going back to the Musical Society a few times, obtaining free access to observe rehearsals as an auditor, and I was delighted by them. But what good was it when I still had to go and seek out employment someplace?

*　*　*

As I knew something of the shoemaking business, my sister having once worked in a shoe factory, she brought me to the same place where she had been employed, a wholesale factory, at 7 Nowolipki Street. It occupied the entirety of the ground floor and was made up of large rooms with long countertops, with great glass-fronted cases running along the walls. I was hired at a salary of eight rubles a month and would be working for a certain Aleksander Goldberg, a German-speaking Jew from the region of Courland, in Latvia.

Before a week was up, I was already a dab hand. It was my job to stamp the leather, turning the shoes on great iron lathes so that the name of the company could be proudly pressed onto the soles. It was not easy work, but I did it deftly. I would stamp out thousands of pairs, then pack them up in baskets. Great bunches of shoes are heavy, and I ended up having to lift whole poods[3] of them at a time. Indeed, what did I not do for my two rubles a week? I cleaned all the rooms of the factory myself, dusted all the massive cabinets, made the fires in the winter, and as if that were not enough, I would have to go wherever Mrs. Goldberg bade me, whether it was on an errand to the seamstresses, or the milliners, or what have you.

I suffered a great deal in that factory, but still ended up staying a whole two years. After a time, I was given a raise of two rubles a month. Just imagine my joy! With the money I earned, I managed to dress myself quite finely, so that everyone on Pawia Street came to know me as the *aktorke*, the little actress. And I would think to myself, "Dear God, when will it actually come true?"

But my dreams would not be fulfilled so soon. Meanwhile, the long, strenuous hours in the shoe factory continued. I remember one hot summer's day when, feeling very fatigued, I fell asleep, laying my head on a crate. The boss came in and when he saw me sleeping, he bellowed, "I pay you to work, not to doze!" But I endured it all quite quietly and patiently, consoled in the knowledge that I would not be staying in this profession forever. So I resigned myself to the work for a while and lived frugally.

From my ten rubles a month, I was able, on occasion, to send my parents a bit of sugar along with a few packages of chicory and coffee. I managed to do it by not taking the trams (still led by horses in those days in Warsaw), and instead, wheresoever I was sent, going on foot, thus saving twenty or thirty kopecks a week. I was given plenty of free shoes and slippers at work, but I used to give them away to poor women on Pawia Street, who would thank me to the high heavens for them.

Before I knew it, my childhood years had flown by. I had become a young woman, and soon the young men came courting. When I was fifteen years old, I became engaged to a carpenter. He was a good deal older than me, but one of my brothers-in-law, who worked with him, said that it was a good match. For his sake, I entertained the young man's advances. But once a week was up, and one of my girlfriends declared that she did not think the man particularly handsome, I broke off the engagement.

I made this man quite unhappy by leaving him! People informed me that his mother cursed me when she heard, damning me to remain a wanderer forever and never find my place in the world.

Some time later, I became reacquainted with a young man from our shtetl. One day I went strolling with him in the Saxon Garden and we ended up talking about someday getting married. Suddenly he asked me how much I would give him as a dowry. I said nothing in response, only told him I had to go meet a girlfriend. And left him sitting there on a park bench.

When I returned home, my sisters asked me where my young fellow was. I told them that he was sitting on a park bench—and that was the end of that.

Five times I became engaged, and all of my young men loved me to distraction, despite the fact that I had no dowry to speak of. Instead, they would fall in love with my lovely figure and my lovely voice. Such were the compliments they would pay me. They would all go absolutely mad for my singing. But in time, I grew to hate every one of them. I would inevitably find some fault, often a musical one—either this one had no ear to speak of, or that one had no voice.

Another engagement I broke off simply because my fiancé sat himself down in a droshky before I did. I let him sit there, but I left, and that was that.

My family would say to me, "Crazy girl! Your wildness will leave you a spinster till your braids go gray!" But I was not bothered in the least. I went on living life and following my daily routine: waking early at my sister's home, dressing the children, cooking breakfast, feeding the children, sending them off to school, then making myself smart and going off to the shoe factory, where I spent hour after hour working and singing to myself. I took to heart the lyric in Goldfaden's opera *Bar Kokhba*: "Flaysik tsu arbetn iz dokh a shpilekhl!"—Working with zeal is no big deal! And so this little workhorse spent her days.

# XIII THE DEATH OF MY MOTHER

One day, on the way to work in the shoe factory as usual, I ran into the postman beside the statue of the Virgin Mary on Pawia Street. He handed me a postcard and I read it. It was addressed to my brother Yoysef, telling him to begin saying Kaddish for our mother.[1]

With all breath gone from my body, I ran to my sister's house at 73 Pawia Street, where Yoysef also lived. I stormed in with the card in my hand, then immediately fainted. We had so loved our beautiful, intelligent mother. With her death, I was left without any zest for living. My rosy cheeks gradually turned white, and my sparkling eyes were constantly filled with tears.

I also lost any will to work. They grew unsatisfied with me at the shoe factory and gave me the sack. I went back to spending each day at home with my sisters. Soon I began experiencing persistent hallucinations that my mother was still living. I could see her before me, serving me food or lighting the Shabbos candles. Feeling a painfully intense need to return home and visit her grave, I campaigned to be sent back to our shtetl. My family understood my wish, and I prepared for my journey. But as I was terribly depressed, they would not let me travel alone, and my elder brother Yoysef was sent to accompany me.

By that point, the train went all the way to Volkovysk, the large town near our shtetl, and the journey was not cheap. The family gathered some funds for it, and my brother and I set off a few days before Passover.

When we met our aged father after our arrival in Porozove, his eyes were red from weeping. Upon seeing us, his laments tore from his throat anew. He was then living with an older married brother of mine, and other people now occupied our little house.

I wanted to run off to my mother's grave but was told that in the month of Nisan, one must not disturb the dead.[2] My brother and I stayed in our brother's house with our father. When it came time for the first seder, I witnessed my 84-year-old father sobbing like a child, and crying out, "My first seder without my sweetheart!" He barely spoke the whole night. He couldn't even utter the blessing over the wine. But we all steeled ourselves and carried out the seder till the very end.

Once Passover ended, I began to think about taking my father back with me to Warsaw, and within only a couple of days, we already had all our travel documents in order, including his.

# XIV A TREACHEROUS CROSSING

It was evening on Rosh Chodesh of Iyar.[1] My father came home from the evening prayer service and I served him dinner: milky noodles. He ate it all up and looked so well at the table that I said to my brother, "Look, Yoysef, how red Papa's lips are, may no evil come to him." I then tucked him into bed, and he recited the evening Shema[2] and fell asleep.

I lay awake in the same room, reading. Suddenly, my father awoke and said to me, "*Tokhterke*, dear daughter, you could ruin your eyes reading in this dim light, God forbid." I obeyed him and went to sleep, too.

The next morning, a Tuesday, I arose at about eight o'clock to meet the woman who came to us every day to buy our potato peelings to feed her cow. She remarked on my father's unusual position in bed, sitting up and leaning his head on his hand, and said to me and my brother, "Children, don't you see how sallow your father looks?" I went to him so I could drag out the featherbed from underneath him and cover him with it, but I couldn't move him. Then I tried waking him up so that I could at least move him into a lying position. Finally, I realized. He was dead.

I remained standing beside him as if frozen. I could not scream, nor even cry. All day I remained mute. I observed the people who came to perform the customary rites on him, for in our shtetl, the tradition was to purify the body in the home of the deceased. And I saw them carrying him out of the house. Still I could not speak.

I did not go to the funeral, following another custom of our shtetl: that the daughters do not go to a parent's funeral, only the sons. It was not until a few days later, while sitting shiva,[3] that I finally regained my faculty of speech. When the seven days were over, I sold my mother's brass candlesticks and a few other possessions, and returned to Warsaw an orphan.

I went back to my sister's home, but I could not bring my hands to do any kind of work there. I no longer felt like a child—it was as if when I lost my poor, dear parents, I had also lost my home and the name of "Child." Still, my family treated me very kindly, orphan that I was. They also began to think in earnest about marrying me off. But as there was no money for a dowry, they could not help me. It was decided that I should be sent to live with my eldest brother, the one who worked as a cantor and kosher slaughterer in the town of Thorn, which belonged at that time to Germany.[4] They said he was a rich man, and so it was decreed I would go to him for what in Polish was called *wspomaganie*, that is, financial support—in this case, for the purpose of getting married. My brother-in-law provided me with eight rubles for travel expenses. As I did not have a passport for going abroad, I was advised to smuggle myself across the border.

Lacking the money for a suitcase, I packed a pair of my dresses into a bundle and was accompanied to Warsaw's Vienna Station,[5] where a ticket for Aleksandrowo[6] was bought for me. My sisters wished me well, saying that I should travel and return in good health and bearing mountains of gold pieces from my brother. In the same breath, they warned me not to entrust anyone with the details of my destination or to breathe a word, God forbid, of my intentions to smuggle across the border. I could be betrayed to the authorities. They struck such fear into my heart that I wanted to turn right around, but it was no moment to be a fraidy-cat. And so I braced myself and set off on my covert journey, without a passport, from Warsaw to Germany.

*   *   *

When I arrived in Aleksandrowo, it was already dark, this being midwinter. I took my bundle under my arm and began asking around as to where I could find an inn. One owned by a certain Mrs. Z--- was pointed out to me. There I went, and entered a large, dark room. A gas lamp smoking on the wall illuminated the crowd of people that filled the space—men, women, and children, Jews and Gentiles. I asked which of them was Mrs. Z--- and was duly directed to a kind-faced Jewess.

As soon as I approached her, she burst out with "You need to get across the border, too?" I was struck with fear. My sisters had told me, after all, not to speak to a soul about my destination. But I told this woman anyway, revealing that I was headed to my brother in Thorn, Chazan Halperin. She told me that she knew him well and pointed out to me everyone else sitting there in the room—they, too, needed to get "over," or *darüben*, as she put it in German.

"But you, Fräulein, I'd advise to cross at the town of Nieszawa.[7] Visit the cantor of that town. He knows your brother and will be able to send you over with a safe escort."

A train was leaving soon for Nieszawa. I bought a ticket and before long was inside the Nieszawa cantor's home. After I introduced myself to him, he extended me a most cordial welcome. His wife then made up a bed for me and I spent the night there. In the morning, the cantor went to ask after a *moylekher*—what they called the smugglers who helped you steal across the border.[8] But he was not out long and came back with nothing. He explained that formerly, the border had been left open, for many people were only crossing over temporarily on their way to eventually settling in Brazil. But now that that the area had become overfilled, the security at the border had tightened severely. Just the night before, someone had tried to get across and was shot at, and their *moylekher* was actually hit, and killed.

Naturally, the news rather did me in. The cantor decided to send me back to Mrs. Z--- in Aleksandrowo. As my eight rubles were now considerably fewer, I wasted no time in asking the cantor if he would lend me a bit of money, assuring him that I would send back a reimbursement when I reached Thorn. But he could give me nothing—he, too, was very much a pauper.

Arriving back in Aleksandrowo, and Mrs. Z---'s inn, I found her front room crammed again with all the people from the day before. When I went over to take a seat at the bar beside the innkeeper, a tall dark-haired Jew, dressed in Hasidic garb—a long overcoat and velvet cap—bounded toward me and asked if I needed to cross the border. "No," I told him. "Why?"

"Because I've gotta get over myself," he answered in his thick Warsaw Yiddish, "and I'm looking to rustle up a convoy to rent a rig with me."

Hearing that, I decided to tell him the truth, and revealed that I wanted to get to Thorn.

"Nu," he said. "Why didn'tcha say so?"

Before I knew it, there we were, a motley crew sitting together in a carriage: the Hasid and I, a Gentile with three children, and another Jewish man—a baker—with his stout wife. When the two of them started to converse, I found that the baker was named Yekl, and his wife Keyle. We set off for a little village, a few versts[9] away from Aleksandrowo.

It was the middle of the night on a Thursday when we arrived at a low-roofed little guesthouse. It was thankfully very warm inside. My compagnons de voyage ordered tea, along with a bite to eat. I sat down on a bench beside the oven, and unpacked my bundle, where I still had a crust of bread and a bit of cheese in reserve, given to me at the start of my journey. I limited myself to ordering a cup of tea, for I knew that of my eight rubles, only four now remained, and who knows how much the *moylekher* would demand for payment.

All the others, though, ate a hearty supper, as I swallowed down my bit of bread with tea and waited to be shown to the spot where we would be sleeping. I was put up with the stout lady in one bed, while her husband bunked with the Hasid, and the Christian family took up quarters on the floor. Thus did we spend the night.

In the morning, the *moylekher* took a good look at us. Everyone had to tell him their destination. The Christian family was headed to Brazil; the Jews, of course, to America;[10] and I to Thorn, to the town's cantor. As soon as he received his pay from us, he went off to "sniff out" how things looked at the border—that's how he put it. "You've gotta' sniff out what clowns they've got on post today," he said, and disappeared.

Meanwhile, the innkeeper served breakfast. My heart was beating madly, hoping that she would not serve me any. But no amount of worrying would help—she dished me up eggs, a glass of coffee, and some onion *pletslekh*.[11] I gave in entirely, unable to resist the temptation of the hot food, and began eating with gusto. It all tasted so good to me—I ate it up and let out a great sigh.

"What are you sighing for, Miss?" the Hasid asked me. Oh, if only he knew that it was because all I had to my name were the four rubles floating around in my purse.

When I asked the innkeeper how much the breakfast came to, she responded, "Not now. Eventually you'll pay me for everything all together." Oy, I thought to myself. She must figure that we are going to be here for a long time.

And so we would be. When the *moylekher* returned, he bore some very bad tidings: the border guards were not taking any bribes, and something else made the present moment not at all a good time to try to smuggle across without their cooperation. A layer of frost had sealed up all of the snow so that when one walked on it, it made an awful crunching noise and left one's footprints clearly visible, making it easy for the guards to track the smugglers and shoot at them.

The news took all the wind out of our sails. The company asked the *moylekher* how long this new status quo might last, and he answered very coldly: "Sometimes a week, sometimes more! We'll have to wait for rain to break up the frost." Ha, just try waiting for rain in the dead of winter!

The news cut no one as deeply as it did our Hasid, though. He went into an absolute frenzy. Now, back in Płock,[12] where he had told us he was from, he had been his rebbe's chief follower.[13] You could also tell that he was quite a rich man, seeing as he wore a luxurious satin coat and velvet cap, with a yarmulke to match. He was tall, with a reddish throat and a pair of staring eyes. But as soon as this impressive, imposing Hasid heard the *moylekher's* news, he began wringing his hands and running around the room with such a wild look about him that he rather startled the rest of us.

Still, I was bold enough to ask him, "Tell me, my good man, what has made you so much more afraid than the rest of us?" But he said nothing, just continued darting about to and fro. Everyone thought he had lost his wits entirely. The *moylekher* took pity on him and consoled him, saying, "Keep calm, you'll be quite safe with me. And it could be that we'll be able to leave sooner rather than later."

The Hasid threw himself at the *moylekher* and covered him with kisses. Meanwhile, I thought to myself, "Who knows what our smuggler really got up to there at the border, that he should have been forced to flee and return to us so quickly."

I wanted to just go back whence I came but did not have enough money for the trip—a carriage to take me to Aleksandrowo and then a train ticket to Warsaw. So I remained where I was, waiting to see what would be.

At one point, the Hasid remarked on my apparent melancholy. He could see that I was nearly penniless, and said to me, "As long as we're here, Miss, eat and drink to your heart's content. We can settle up later." I did not care to ask him what exactly he meant for me to contribute eventually and decided to just consider his offer "good as gold," as they say. Now, at mealtimes, I ate without a care right along with everyone else. Of course, when a person's belly is full, their mood brightens. And so I began to sing again, too, just a little, to myself.

But the would-be emigrants, once they overheard it, would not leave me alone.

"Miss, oh Miss!" they would cry. "Sing something from the Yiddish theatre!"

And so I made them happy, and myself, too, by doing some of the lively songs written by Tsunzer, the beloved troubadour. I could also do a few of Goldfaden's theatrical numbers by then. It was like good medicine for me. And Mrs. Z--- started pampering me with the finest delicacies. Every morning she would pour me some milk as she delivered the refrain, "A glass of milk for our *zingerke*, our little singer!"

This went on for eight days while we stayed at the inn and prayed for rain. But as if out of spite, no rain fell, and the moon went on shining brightly every night. And as long as the weather remained like that, carrying out our clandestine journey across the border remained impossible.

# XV GOOD PEOPLE AND EVIL SPIRITS

One rather gloomy day, when the frost on the ground was beginning to melt, the *moylekher* said to us, "Gang, today we're going for a little walk."[1] We were all seized by sudden joy—I, too, of course, but I was also thinking: "My God, how shall I ever manage to leave this place if I have to pay for a whole week of my meals?" And indeed, the settling-up was soon upon us. I was the last to go.

"How much do I owe?" I asked.

But Mrs. Z--- just began to laugh, saying, "I wouldn't accept a single kopeck from our dear little singer, our *zingerke!*"

I was a touch ashamed to accept such kindness, but truth be told, it also made me very happy. We said our goodbyes, and I thanked our hostess for my room and board. She wished me well, adding that as she had gotten so used to having me around, and had no children of her own, what she really wanted was for me to stay back and live with her.

Soon all of us were seated on a long sleigh, and we set off for the nearby forest. We journeyed for three-quarters of an hour until we hit upon a narrow footpath. Then, leaving our luggage on the sleigh, we all climbed out of it and onto the path, forming a single file. I walked behind the Gentile family, the Hasid walked behind me, and Yekl and Keyle brought up the rear. We assumed Yekl and Keyle to be man and wife because they always ate together and paid as one.

Telling one of his associates to remain behind with the sleigh, the *moylekher* then gave his orders to the rest of us: "Gang, you'll have to move quickly now, really put down your feet."

I teased him a bit, "Surely you mean 'pick up' our feet?"

"It's no time for kidding around," he answered. "This is serious business. There'll be no jokes, in fact no talking at all. Voices echo in a forest."

His words cast a certain pall over the company. God alone could help us now, we all thought.

After walking on ahead for some paces, he gave a sign for us to follow him. And so off we tiptoed, one by one down the narrow trail. At every crunch of the snow under our feet, the *moylekher* shook his head and hissed: "Shh, shh, shh." Holding our collective breath, we finally reached a wider path.

"Children, now we have to really hoof it," said the *moylekher*. The Gentiles ahead of me did so, and I followed suit. I quickly overheated, dressed as I was in a long, fur-lined coat. Tossing it over my shoulder, I carried on. Eventually, we reached another narrow trail and hotfooted down that for a couple of minutes. Then, suddenly, the *moylekher* froze.

"Here, gang," he called, "you stay behind while I have a look-see to check whether the guards I paid off are still the ones on patrol."

He had already taken some of our money for the purpose, earlier that day back at the inn. No one ultimately knew how much he had demanded from each traveler. I myself had given him three rubles.

Now we all just stood there on the trail awaiting his return. Looking around, I realized I did not see stout Keyle, and asked Yekl, "Where is your wife?"

"Wife?" he responded. "What kinda wife? Anyway, she's probably just lagging behind."

Astounded, I asked him, "How do you mean? You left her alone back there? Why didn't you walk behind her in the first place?" These questions he did not answer, only saying that she must have gone straight when the rest of us had turned right.

It grew late, and still we stood there in the thick of the woods, hoping that stout Keyle might make her appearance. She was nowhere to be seen. But as we were afraid of crying out, all we could do was stand around and await the return of the *moylekher*. Once it became clear that Keyle was not coming, I turned to the others and said, "Surely you all realize that none of us are going to cross the border tonight, even if we could. I won't allow us to leave someone behind here, all alone in the forest."

Upon hearing my little speech, the Hasid began sobbing—truly sobbing, loudly, too—and said, "Miss, if we don't cross now . . . You see that shawl you're wearing on your neck? I'll take it and hang myself immediately from the nearest tree." I looked at him hard and could only reason that he had gone quite insane.

At this point, I was truly afraid of him, wondering, "Who knows what manner of thing this man must have done back home, that he is now so terrified of turning back!" But I stuck stubbornly to my position: I would not be crossing the border this night. After spending all this time together, how could we dare to leave one of our party to her own devices after she had lost her way in the wood?

Ignoring our instructions to remain quiet, I began calling out at the top of my lungs, "Keyle! Keyle!" My throat went raw from screaming, but aside from the forest's echo, there was no response.

At that moment, the *moylekher* came rushing up to us and gave us our new marching orders: "Run now, children. At once. The guards we have in our pocket are still on patrol."

My companions all fell upon me and started begging, "Miss, come on, let's go. You don't play around when it comes to crossing a border."

But I would not budge. Tears started streaming from their eyes as they pleaded.

"Let whoever wants to go, go," was all I said to them. "Who's stopping you?"

I do not know why no one would leave without my joining them—except for the Christians, that is, who did cross that night. But we Jews remained on the Russian side.

While being led back out of the wood by one of the *moylekher*'s associates, I wouldn't stop calling out for the lost woman. But she might as well have been swallowed up by the earth. We barely made it out of the dark forest alive, and once we did, where we expected to find the waiting sleigh with our luggage, the spot was empty. The shegetz who was supposed to be there could no longer bear waiting for us, and had returned to the village, to which we all now had to start making our way on foot. And quite the hike it was, so very late at night.

We finally arrived back in the village as dawn was breaking on a Friday morning. The innkeeperess was sliding her challahs into the oven. Stunned at seeing us at her door, she dropped one of the loaves, and asked us why we had not crossed, her voice choked with fear. I recounted the whole story to her: about Keyle, and the route we traveled, how we walked in a single file, she bringing up the rear, and how, when we turned onto a different path, she must have continued down the old one and gotten lost in the total darkness.

The woman clapped her hands together and exclaimed in the most plaintive tones, "Oy, *di nisht-gute* must have taken hold of her!"

"The who?" I asked her.

Tears streaming from her eyes, she answered, "The Unmentionable Ones! There are a great many in that forest!" She tried her hardest to convince me that dozens had been maimed by evil spirits in that forest before. Indeed, she told me so much about the Unmentionable Ones that I myself started to believe in all of it—how else could Keyle have vanished into thin air? Nevertheless, I started up again with my entreaties to the traveling party, asking that we all set off once more to look for her.

As soon as the day had fully dawned, the *moylekher* mounted a horse and rode off in search of Keyle. He went into the forest, going down the same path we had trod the day before. He shouted, called her name. He asked everyone he came across if they'd seen her.

None of it helped. He returned with no news. I was now moved to release the fullness of my anger upon Yekl the baker, cursing him out: "What's the matter with you? How could you let her walk behind you and not look back even once to check on her?"

"Well, why did you have to walk so quickly?" he responded. "Maybe she was incapable of following at such a pace."

Upon receiving such an answer, I went to sit down beside the window and remained there as if turned to stone. The Hasid noticed and approached me to ask why I seemed to be more affected by the woman's disappearance than her own husband was.

That started off a fight between the Hasid and the baker. The baker screamed, "What do you want from me? She's not even my wife! We just both happen to be trying to make it to America!"

I couldn't make heads or tails of any of it, and stayed in my seat beside the window. We were all cautioned against looking out, though. There was trouble if the Gentiles saw any unfamiliar people in town. I could only peek intermittently through a crack in the curtains.

Sitting there, I thought, I've been in this village now for eight days. No one at home knows where I am. My brother in Germany knows that I've left Warsaw, but am not at his yet either. Just imagine all the telegrams and letters flying back and forth, no one knowing where I've gotten to! And how could my sisters have done it, let an eighteen-year-old girl make such a long and perilous journey alone, crossing a border without a passport, and only eight rubles in her purse! Would my parents ever have dared to let me?

I broke out into tears over my bitter fate. The proprietress came over, sat down beside me, and began consoling me, telling me all was not lost. "If Keyle had not fallen into the hands of the evil spirits," said she, "they might have gotten you instead! Anyhow, do let's wait a day and see what happens before we get so upset."

And all over again, she begins telling me about the demons and ghouls that haunt the forest. She was absolutely convinced that these spirits had indeed hauled Keyle away to her doom.

As she was going on, when I turned to have a glance out the window, I chanced to see an open wagon rolling toward the house where the village mayor lived, just across from our inn. In the wagon were four gendarmes, and riding right between them—Keyle.

I screamed out, "There they are, your evil spirits!" It rather startled everyone present.

The *moylekher*, meanwhile, went right off to the mayoral residence, where he paid the fine of four rubles and fifty kopecks. Such was the penalty for someone caught attempting to cross the border illegally. In paying it, he freed Keyle, and brought her over at once to the inn.

How the woman looked, I am unable to describe. She could barely get out the words to explain what had happened.

But it amounted to this: she had fallen behind us for a good while, and then could not catch up with us. She was afraid to scream out. Eventually, the gendarmes caught her and brought her in. What they did with her next . . . Well, have a good guess.

Her story cut me to the core. I piped up to the *moylekher*, "Listen up, Reb Yeshaye (for Yeshaye was his first name), do you intend to bring us over or not? For if not, we'll all just set off for our homes, right this moment." I said it in a tone that would have announced to anyone: "Here is a woman whose pockets are absolutely bursting with rubles"—which couldn't have been further from the truth.

The *moylekher* thought a moment and said, "Fine. This Sunday, with the Almighty's help, I'll slip you all across."

And so, on Sunday, early in the morning, we were all led to the border. There, a long chain was lowered to the ground and our wagon went wheeling over it and across a little bridge.

"Gang," the *moylekher* said to us, "You are now in Germany."

I could not understand it: How could it be that on this side of that chain was Germany, and on the other Russia? But in any case, Germany was Germany! And if they all spoke German there, then I suppose it must be . . .

The *moylekher* then told us we all must set off individually, until each of us reached a certain German, Baumann. I dragged my bundle down from the wagon and set off to look for this person. Probably I would be walking right past a customs house, where I'd be able to ask after him. But once I reached it, and the officials inside asked me how they could help me, I just about went into a panic. A miracle had been at play, though: I'd spent the past few years laboring away in a shoe factory run by Courland Germans, and had picked up a bit of the language there. I took a deep breath and answered them, in my uncertain German, "*Ich möchte*, I would like to . . . to speak with Herr Baumann."

They exchanged glances with each other and whispered among themselves, "Ach, that Baumann hides too much of this Russian riffraff. They'll all have to be tossed back to where they came from eventually."

You can imagine how this hit me, like a blow to the heart. And yet—one of them did point out to me where Baumann could be found, and I went there. It was a German saloon with a couple of little overnight rooms for the weary traveler. The emigrants I had smuggled across with were already sitting there in the drinking den, their faces joyful, their hands clutching glasses of brandy. They handed me one, too. They'd already settled up the remainder of their fees with the *moylekher*. In the end, he demanded nothing more from me than the advance I'd given earlier.

Around noon, a great big wagon transporting beer to Thorn passed the saloon. I hopped on, took a seat on a barrel, and at long last arrived at my destination, with a single ruble still left in my purse. The driver delivered me to Schiller Street and pointed out number 40—the house where my brother lived.

As I approached the house, I heard my name being called from inside by a multitude of voices. They belonged to my brother's children. All at once, they came rushing out to me, took hold of my bundle, and led me into a beautiful, handsomely furnished apartment on the fourth floor.

# XVI IN THE HOME OF MY BROTHER, CANTOR OF THORN

My brother was delighted to see me.[1] He told me that from back home—that is, from Warsaw, for my real home was no more, now that my parents had passed away—he had been simply "bombarded" (to borrow his phrase) with letters from my sisters. They were sure I had gone missing. I briefly told him how things had in fact gone and what difficulties I had overcome in making my way to him. He was presently delighted even more in me, knowing how I had managed such a taxing journey while carrying only eight rubles, and not only that—arrived with one still remaining in my purse!

Eventually, he moved to introducing me to his wife and children. The wife was a modern woman, quite the little European, no wig, just long, long hair tightly braided and looped around her head. This was the mother of his five beloved children, all of them pretty as a picture. The eldest son was eighteen years old.

My brother was a very busy man: in addition to being a cantor and a kosher slaughterer, he also performed circumcisions and, from time to time, gave sermons—a real *Prediger*, as they called it in German, a preacher. But despite his many duties, he took the time to thoroughly ask me about how my life had been for me up until that point and what I intended to do with it now. I told him everything about my childhood in Porozove and afterward in Warsaw. I also told him of how I had nearly become a Yiddish actress. This last bit I was rather afraid of telling—he was a cantor and kosher slaughterer, after all! A religious functionary just like our father, though operating in a different world. I was nervous about the possibility of him flying into a rage and shouting at me, for he was a very strict and serious man.

But he just laughed heartily, and asked me, "What do you mean you wanted to be an actress? How did you even know you might be any good?"

So I told him of how I had been auditioned and found to possess a talent for singing.

Without overthinking the matter, he sat down at his spinet piano, struck a few chords, and told me to sing something. Now, I should note that my brother was one of the truly great cantors. Feeling quite sheepish, my cheeks flaming, I sang a song for him. When I finished, he came up to me, gave me a kiss on the head, and said in his own Yiddish-inflected German, "*Ja, liebe Schwesterchen*, my dear little sister. You have neglected a tremendous future. You might have been working full-time as an actress by now."

I couldn't understand him. Did he mean it or was he just having a laugh at my expense? I was so sure he would be angry with me and shout, "What do you mean, an actress?!" After all, I had heard the Yiddish artists who played at Warsaw's Eldorado Theatre being derided as mere "Broder comedians."[2] Decent people were fearful even of being on social terms with them. I remembered how when I was learning to read music from one of these artists, as I have told you, tongues soon got to wagging about me on Pawia Street. Folks would say, "Oy, it seems the little *litvatshke*[3] is straying from the proper path." Yes, I remembered all of that very well and was ready to hear the same from my eldest brother. But now, all of a sudden, I was hearing from this very intelligent man that I should very much regret not having tried to become an actress! I was positively shaken by his reaction.

I had come to my brother with quite a different intention, after all: I hoped that he might help me financially so that I could get married. But all of that could not have been further from my thoughts now. In my mind's eye, I could see rising before me the Theatre Bouffe at 25 Long Street in Warsaw, with its actors and actresses, its endless ovations. I thought to myself, "Now there is no one who can stop me from having that."

But in the meantime, I would be staying for a few weeks in the sleepy German town of Thorn. The children did their very best to provide me with opportunities for frivolity, taking me along with them to concerts and the like. Everywhere we went, they introduced me as their young aunt. They were very proud to be seen with me, for over the short period I had spent in their house, I had begun to speak German quite well, which brought them a great deal of pleasure. Their friends were always congratulating them on their "charmante junge Tante."[4]

We spent one evening surrounded by lots of young people and officers. Everyone was drinking and carousing, though many of us didn't even know each other, and started making raucous toasts: "To de helt of de lovely Russian gürl!" At which my brother's children said to me, "Auntie, they mean you!"

"Every city has its crazies," I thought to myself.

The fourth week of my stay in Thorn was Purim-time, during which my birthday happens to fall. Early on the morning before Purim, my brother approached my bed, wished me happy birthday, and handed me a whole hundred-ruble bill. My sister-in-law, meanwhile, gave me some beautiful material for a dress. Even the children presented me with gifts, each of them something different.

It was, it seems to me now, the one truly happy day of my life up until that point. I looked at the money and thought, "My God! To earn this I would have had to work a whole year in the shoe factory! And now, just like that, a hundred rubles!"

I could not fathom how I would ever be able to thank them profusely enough. My heart soared into seventh heaven. I kissed my brother and wept from pure bliss.

For the Purim feast, the most respected people in town came to my brother's house. After the company had enjoyed some tipples, my brother asked me to sing something for these very German, very assimilated Jews. I think I did the famous song from Goldfaden's *Almasado*,[5] the one that starts, "Elnt, kleyn, un nimes."[6] I had all of the guests on the brink of tears, these fancy German Jews and Jewesses, and they applauded me most heartily. I was in complete ecstasy myself, hearing their adulation, and went on to sing pieces from *Shulamis* and *Bar Kokhba*. As I filled my audience with wild enthusiasm, a certain feeling rose up in me, too. I felt like an *artistke*, a true artist.

Afterward, I heard one of the guests saying to my brother, "Herr Kantor, vhy don't you take de little Fräulein, your seester, and zend her to shtuddy in Berlin right avey?"

At which my brother called out to me in his beautiful baritone, "You hear what they're saying about you, Ester-Rokhl? That I should let you go and study! Well, what do you say?"

I was speechless.

Eventually, the guests left and I retired to my bedroom. But I slept very little that night. No, I dreamt while still awake. Why, the whole day had been like a sweet dream. The presents in the morning, with the one hundred-ruble bill among them! Then spending my night amid such a company! And all their cries of "Bravo, bravo!"

The next morning, all I could think about, most expectantly, was when my brother might return to the topic he had raised the night before over his glass of wine. But he never did.

Sad as it is to tell, I ultimately felt no great and lasting devotion from anyone in my family. They all loved me, to be sure, but whatever kind of love this was, I simply could not appreciate. I had a very good head for learning, and though my sisters were not rich, they surely would have sent me off to undertake a course of study had they truly cared about me, because how much could it really have cost in those days? Still today, I do not know whether they truly did not grasp my potential, or simply did not see the point of my progressing so.

And now, yet again, I would fail to advocate for myself as I needed to. Even at my rich, educated brother's, I lacked the audacity to say, "I want to stay here in Germany, I want to study." And so I carried on just as before.

Once I had been at his home for a month, I thanked my brother profusely for the hundred rubles he had given me, and his entire family led me to the train station. For this return journey, I had obtained a *pulpasek*, as they called it then—a passport for those who lived in border towns, allowing for free travel between territories, and bearing an assumed name. Yes, for a short time I became an entirely different person: Frau Fischel. I said my goodbyes to everyone, and my brother did not neglect to deliver this exhortation before we parted: that I should not go back to speaking Yiddish, seeing as I now spoke a fine German. I was such a naif that I promised to do just as he said.

He bought me a ticket for Aleksandrowo. After looking over my fake passport, an official called out, "Frau Fischel!" "That's me!" I said. The passport was stamped, authorizing it for travel as far as Nieszawa, just on the other side of the German-Russian border. On the train, however, I was able to buy a ticket for Warsaw. When the gendarme brought my passport back to me on the train, as was typical, he said, "Looks good, Frau Fischel," and asked for my ticket. I showed it to him. He asked me why it was not booked for Nieszawa, which was the destination marked on my passport. I was shaking with fear at this point and began to stammer. But I was very lucky. The gendarme detected my unease, took pity on me, and warned, "You'd better hide that ticket somewhere, it's no good." Whew, did I feel lucky. When I arrived in Warsaw and reached my sisters' building on Pawia Street, near Okopowa Street, named for the *Okopy*—the old Lubomirski Ramparts—I asked them how they were in German, saying, "Wie geht es?" They laughed at me. It made me rather embarrassed, not knowing whose example I ought to follow, whether that of my "German" brother, or my "Polish" sisters.

Soon I found myself in yet another pickle: I could not return to my old workaday existence after the smashing success that night in Germany at the Purim party. I could not bear starting all over again, scrubbing my sisters' children and sending them off to school every day, then managing the housekeeping all day long. I had come back only to find my life in Warsaw unbearable. I gave the hundred rubles to my brother-in-law to hide away and returned to my old profession: footwear. I was not given a position at the factory this time but rather was given materials to do piecework at home, producing little bows with which to decorate the shoes. And so I went on earning, more or less.

Soon I met a young woman who owned a fruit shop. She took a great liking to me. A couple of times she had me over to her family's house. There I met her brother, who sang in the operetta chorus of the Warsaw State Theatre[7] on Królewska Street. He was the company's only Jewish chorister, and even then, was only allowed in because he had a truly gigantic tenor voice.

It was not long before the young man fell in love with me. As we grew closer to each other, we started singing duets together. He fantasized about my becoming a performer, while I started concocting a plan whereby, seeing as he had such a beautiful voice, I could bring him to my brother in Thorn where he would train the young man as a cantor. We both figured such an arrangement could be a very gladsome thing indeed, and so we began asking permission for our getting engaged, I from my sisters, he from his parents.

My family did not say no, only that we should get to know each other better first. Meanwhile, the young man was already considering himself my fiancé. He would bring me to the theatre very often, including to the operettas in which he was singing. Poor thing, he had to buy tickets (in those days, complimentary tickets were not thrown around quite so liberally), though he always told me he was getting me in free. Ah well, if he wanted to puff himself up a little for my benefit, then let him!

Eventually, his company transferred to the theatre in the Saxon Garden. Who could possibly have been my equal then! Now, instead of having to peer in through the fence, as I once did, I was sitting in the very front row, leaning right up against the plush-covered bar that separated the audience from the orchestra pit—so close that I was very often able to pick out my fiancé's voice. *Seeing* him, however, was another matter. First of all, he was by no means a tall man, and second, though he was the finest singer in the chorus, these goyim would relegate him to the back line, making him stand behind the choristers with the rotten voices. That I didn't like one bit.

More than once, I waited for him after the performance ended and witnessed him emerging from his dressing room absolutely filthy due to the cruel torments his antisemitic colleagues in the theatre used to inflict on him. They would daub the inside of his top hat with soot, smear his clothes with schmaltz, steal his makeup, and play other lovely "pranks" like that.

My estimation of him plummeted on account of it. I would always upbraid him, saying, "How could a person let such things be done to him?" And I would nag him to lodge a complaint with the directors of the company. But he did not want to, and I never could understand the mysterious reason why.

# XVII AN APOSTATE FOUNDS A JEWISH THEATRE IN WARSAW

After a short while, my fiancé, the chorister in the Polish operetta company, helped me to revive my old connections to Warsaw's family of Yiddish theatre artists.[1] This happened to take place at a time when the actors were very much in need of my talents, and they were simply delighted to have me back in the fold. They all remembered me from my attendance at the rehearsals for Goldfaden's *Shulamis*, and without a word of discussion or debate, I became a member of the resident troupe of the Eldorado Theatre.

This new Yiddish theatre had arisen out of the following circumstances: the directress of the Russian troupe that had been performing at the Eldorado was a Gentile woman named Olginskaya. She was closely acquainted with a certain man who worked as a weighmaster.[2] He was a Jew who had converted to Christianity. Once, they got to talking about business, knocking their noggins together over what kind of enterprise they thought might stand to succeed at that moment in Warsaw. This was in 1892.

Suddenly the weighmaster pipes up to Olginskaya, "You know what? You have a lot of connections in St. Petersburg,[3] people with pull. If it's possible for you to get permission from the authorities there for a Jewish theatre,[4] you could become a rich woman."

And after a short time, Olginskaya did indeed receive permission for what was labeled a "Russian-German Theatre."

We heard she would be coming to our last rehearsal of *Yoysef in egiptn*[5]—Joseph in Egypt—the piece we were preparing. So we all, of course, dressed to the nines. When Madame Olginskaya arrived, Herr Vaysfeld began introducing the company in Russian, labeling all of us by the types of roles we would be taking in the productions. I was the last to be introduced, with these words: "*A eto nasha prima donna* (And here is our prima donna)—Mademoiselle Halperin!" Then he went on and on, enumerating all of my virtues: my fine voice, beautiful diction, command of German, and so on. I needn't tell you how red I turned at hearing all of this praise lavished upon me.

The *goye*[6] was positively kvelling, beaming with joy at the troupe she had inherited, as she witnessed a paradise of opportunity opening up before her. She spoke with me for a particularly long time and promised that a brilliant future lay ahead of me.

Eventually the rehearsal began. The conductor, Herr Lustig, sat himself down at the piano. The elder Shvartsbard arranged the members of the chorus and gave a blow on his tin whistle, which served as a pitch pipe. I should think that a good many veteran Yiddish performers still remember old Shvartsbard's tin whistle, with its three notes: la, sol, and fa. I can hear it still today, trilling away in my ears.

And so Shvartsbard gave out a pitch, and off the singers went, *mitn gantsn knak*, as they say—at full tilt. The first number was lifted from the opera *Les Huguenots*,[7] and ended with the words, "Von einem Vater zehn Kinder weiden ihre Schafe im Feld, jeder von ihnen nicht minder, mit Gottes Macht, ein starker Held!"[8] When the chorus finished singing it, Madame Olginskaya broke out in vigorous applause. After that came the dialogue between Joseph's ten brothers, spoken in quite correct German.

The roles were divided as follows: Yankev Libert played Reuben, Adolf Berman was Simeon, a certain folksinger named Sendik[9]—Issachar, Titelman—Joseph, Herman Berman—Potiphar, and playing Potiphar's wife Zulaika—none other than myself. Everyone's performance pleased Olginskaya very much, and she advised us to start preparing yet another piece very soon.

It was decided that we would do Goldfaden's opera *Shulamis*, and as Vaysfeld had already translated it into German, preparations could begin in earnest, and the roles were quickly decided upon: Shulamis, of course, went to me; Faynshteyn would play Avsholem, Shulamis's wayward beloved; Adolf Berman—Manoyekh, her father; Triling—Avigayil, her rival for Avsholem's love; Rotshayn—Tsingitang, Avsholem's comical sidekick. Our new leader, Madame Olginskaya, insisted that rehearsals begin immediately, on the stage of the Eldorado's summer theatre.

A week later, I had already memorized my part. But there was no director hired to stage the production anew, so at rehearsals, the company members would simply ask who remembered how things had been done under Goldfaden, and that person would then demonstrate to the rest of the group.[10] Of course, there were those who had remembered Goldfaden's production, among them our stage manager A. Maks; one of our choristers, a certain Rozenkvyat; and Gothard, the assistant prompter. But none had taken principal acting roles in Goldfaden's original. Those old stars of Goldfaden's troupe had nearly all immigrated to America,[11] among them: Jacob Adler,[12] David Kessler,[13] Tantsman, and Spivakovski.

You can already imagine what such a staging process was like. Everyone wanted to one-up everyone else with their own "inspired" ideas. When someone, for example, demonstrated a bit of blocking that they said they "remembered very well," like the back of their own hand, another would try to persuade us that he "remembered it better." God had blessed the chorister Herr Rozenkvyat with a talent for whistling but cursed him by neglecting to give him any kind of voice. The man couldn't sing a note. After the first choral number from *Shulamis*, "Ongelodn mit ales guts, mit di shtekns in di hent,"[14] he would lead the chorus back offstage, whistling all the while.

At that moment in the opera, Shulamis must lose her way in the wilderness. Rozenkvyat, still whistling, would return and walk about the stage, and I would follow his every step. As there were no mountains yet constructed on the set, he would conjure them with his whistling and his movement: here, we would be walking between lofty peaks; there, on our left, would be a boulder; and now on our right—a well.

I would stare at him with wide-open eyes and think innocently to myself: How could a boulder suddenly form here and a whole well be dug over there? But I kept all that to myself. I did not want to ask him. I made it a principle: above all, do not ask questions, just be ready to work.

Well, what should I tell you? We fussed about like this for quite a few days, and nothing came of it. Hardly anyone knew what anyone else was doing. And so, gradually, the performers began to drift apart. Everyone returned to his or her trade. Faynshteyn went back to making his umbrellas, and Abelman his corks.

# XVIII ACTORLY SHTIK

Upon seeing that things were going badly and the company was starting to break up, the directress of our troupe, Olginskaya, opened up a tab for the performers in the theatre's restaurant. This restaurant was run by a fellow named Kotunski, who was like a father to the penniless actors of Warsaw. As soon as the troupe learned of the account Olginskaya had started, they flocked to the restaurant, and before long, Olginskaya had become quite a significant debtor. I never ate there, though lunch at the place cost no more than thirty kopecks.

It was not that I was richer than my colleagues, nor was I ashamed of eating with them. No, it was just that I was a *yoldevke*, that is: a decent girl, a bashful young lady. They called me the *litvishe yoldevke*, the prim little Lithuanian girl, in their actors' slang, laughing at me for being such a pious thing and not wanting to eat at Kotunski's, because he served unkosher food. But aside from me, nearly all of the actors ate there. The only other exception, if I remember correctly, was Libert, who also would eat no *treyf*.

The *goye* Olginskaya, knowing that she had accumulated some major debts over the few weeks that the account had been open, began going after the artists to collect. And how were they going to repay her? How else than by going back to work!

The weather had turned cooler, so we would now be gathering to rehearse in a hall suited for wintertime. We started chipping away again at *Shulamis* and made some progress, but a lot was still lacking. The company told Olginskaya that certain special set pieces and rare costumes were needed. She was nervous about being able to fulfill the request, and so directed the elder Shvartsbard to hurry and prepare a different piece.

It was a Wednesday—I still remember it exactly—when Direktorin Olginskaya came to us with Dovid Shvartsbard flanking her and gave this speech in Russian:

"Ladies and gentlemen, you should know that this Friday, we must play the operetta *Di bobe yakhne* (or as it's known in Russian, *Koldunya*, and in German, *Di Zauberin*—both meaning 'The Sorceress').[1] Are you up to the task of learning it in time for Friday? If not, our whole enterprise here is done for."

As soon as she finished speaking, a clamor arose from many of the assembled artists:

"Yes, yes, we are up to the task," they shouted. "We can do it! It will go up!"

I did not contribute a word. I could not understand what they all meant by it, nor what they hoped to achieve. When they noticed me sitting silently off to the side with my fiancé, they came up to me and asked if I would continue to be a willing participant in our work, so that we could all continue to exist. If so, I must memorize, by Friday, the role of Mirele, the orphan girl in *The Sorceress*.

Before I could answer, my fiancé spoke for me: "No, no. She will not learn it by Friday."

He rejected the plan because, as he was still singing in the Polish operetta company, he well knew how much time it takes to learn a whole piece of that genre—all the solo and choral numbers, and the prose, too, that is, the dialogue scenes. He made me so terribly afraid of the prospect that I repeated after him, mechanically, "No, I will not be able to learn it in such a short time."

But truth be told, I had not an inkling of what was going on, nor of what was yet to come.

# XIX THE FATE OF YIDDISH THEATRE DEPENDS ON ME— SO SAYS A *GOYE*

Perceiving that trying win over my fiancé would be a lost cause, my fellow artists waited for him to leave for the Polish theatre and then set to work on me.[1] They tried to convince me that the preparations weren't anything to worry my pretty little head over—just six musical numbers to learn and a few bits of dialogue. They knew what a talent I had for memorization, they said, and that I was very musical, to boot. So, would it really be that overwhelming a prospect to learn such a *kleynikayt*, a trifle?

Kaminski and Herman Berman were the ones doing most of the talking, and they did it for their own benefit. Kaminski wanted to play the part of Mirele's worldly and heroic lover, Markus, the man who rescues her from bondage, and Berman wanted to do the clownish peddler, Hotsmakh. For *them*, it was a trifle! They remembered it well from their time with Goldfaden. They talked so much and were so stubbornly persuasive that I finally answered them:

"As you will all be able to memorize it, so must I."

As soon as I said it, they broke out in such rapturous celebration, you would have thought they'd won the lottery.

The prompter, Gutman, who had a crooked back, handed me my script and said to me in his ringing voice, "Have no fear, Miss Halperin. I'll be sitting in my box and won't let you fall."

I couldn't fathom what he meant by it. He'll be sitting in his box and won't let me fall? What it meant was this, though I didn't know it at the time:

He would take care to prompt me well, being ready with all the words of the text in his little compartment below the stage.

Olginskaya then approached me, and taking me aside, said to me in Russian that whether or not there would be a Jewish theatre in Warsaw now depended entirely on me. If I took the role, and we performed this Friday, a little money would come our way, and the company could survive. But if not—then all our trouble was for nothing, all the work we had done rendered worthless. And to strengthen her appeal to my conscience, she surreptitiously prodded into my hand a long roll of coins that I assumed must be a wad of kopecks.

But then I took a look at the label: it was ten rubles. She had taken care that no one should see her giving it to me. My hand began to tremble. But hearing how seriously the woman had talked of the fate of the Yiddish theatre, and feeling her gift rolling around between my fingers—it did give me a certain thrill. And so, thanking her for the money, I promised her that I would do all I possibly could.

After hastily saying my goodbyes, I ran home. On the way, I entered the garden of the Krasiński Palace,[2] sat down, and looked at the part. After reading it over a couple of times, I felt I more or less knew it by heart.

When I arrived home, one of my sisters confronted me with the sourest expression on her face.

"Where have you been?" she asked. "I'll bet you haven't eaten a thing yet! What kind of mishegas has gotten into you? Something to do with the 'Tulderada'? (For that's what she called the Eldorado.) Thinking you'll disappear there for days at a time?"

Bumbling the name of the theatre in that way, perhaps she thought she could make it seem an ugly thing to me. But I said nothing in response, just went straight to my room—that is, the kitchen, where my bed was. There I found the sister in whose home I was living. She took quite a different approach:

"So, what's going on, our little artist? When are we finally going to get to hear you really and truly playing a bit of a role?"

That gave me rather a warm feeling, and I answered her, "Soon, dear sister. This Friday, in fact, you'll see me play in *The Sorceress*. I'm to be the leading lady."

Then I showed her the ten rubles I had received from the theatre directress. I cannot overstate my joy: my sister's words had sent me straight up to the clouds. I do not know whether she herself was excited by those ten rubles or by the future that was rising before me, but for the first time I heard her speak in this way to me:

"Now that you're earning some good money, we need to make sure you're being taken good care of. Drink milk. Have a bit more butter. You must have the strength to sing."

Her words were like a balm upon my heart. I had never heard her say such things. I handed over the ten rubles to her and asked that she might indeed use it to take care of me in the way she prescribed.

That afternoon, I left to meet with the chorus master, Lustig. In one hour's time, he taught me my three major numbers, so that when I got to rehearsal, I already knew half of my role quite well—a very prepared little prima donna. There at rehearsal, I found the German director Herr Oskar, and the German actor Herr Berthold, who was to play my father, Avromtshe. All the other actors were there, too, and we began to set the staging.

The ladies and gentlemen of the chorus were arranged into a dance circle spanning the entire stage, and they launched into the first choral number, in German: "Zu dein Geburtstag, zu deinen Feste, / Kamen sich zusammen deine Gäste," and so forth.[3] At this point, I was to appear onstage and be led around the circle to greet each guest in turn, as I begin my solo, also, of course, in German, as was required: "Was nutzt mir die Freude, auch alles gut, / Wenn ich mich erinnere an diese Minut," and so on.[4] Then the peddler Hotsmakh comes in with his German dialogue, "Wahre, wahre, ich verkaufe freilich, alles sehr billig un wer es wird wollen teuer, der soll brennen, wie a Feuer."[5]

After this he launches into the blindman's bluff number.[6] I still remember that when I heard Berman doing the part for the first time and singing the line, "Hotsmakh ist ein Blinder un hat eine Frau mit sechzehn Kinder,"[7] I could not help laughing. The director, Herr Oskar, approached me and asked in German, "Fräulein, werden Sie Freitag auch lachen?"[8] I could not answer him; I felt so guilty.

Soon we started on the second act. The director said to me, "When the music begins, you shall come onstage with the pail of water."

"But where will I be with my pail before that?" I asked, responding to his German with the same. "Where do I come on from?"

"From the *Kulissen*," said he.

What could it possibly mean, this word *Kulissen*? I could feel everyone's eyes on me, seeing how red I was turning at not understanding. Never had I heard such a word before: not in Porozove at my father's house, nor in Thorn at my brother the cantor's, and I did not dare to ask now. And so I took the pail in hand and just stood where I was. But Oskar could not stop bellowing, "From the *Kulissen*!"

Staring at him in utter confusion, I asked him quietly, "Please, would you demonstrate for me what I'm meant to do?" He took me by the hand

and led me to two strips of green curtain that hung at both the extreme right and extreme left of the stage, and instructed, "You shall come on from one of these side entrances." I realized those simple curtains leading to backstage—the wings—must have been the ominous *Kulissen*.

From that point forward, I was taken step by step and physically shown the actions I was to take in the role, and thus was taught the rest of my numbers. Meanwhile, my young gentleman from the Polish theatre had come over, directly from his own rehearsal. My colleagues began asking him if he would help me study the role in the two days that remained before the performance on Friday evening.

"And by the way," they added, "we'd like to offer you a place in our troupe. You shouldn't have to go on performing among goyim."

# XX A GENERAL AT THE REHEARSAL

Thursday, that is, a day before the performance, we began rehearsal at ten in the morning. This was called the *Generalprobe*, the final dress rehearsal. But I could not begin to grasp why it would have been called a "general rehearsal." I didn't see a general anywhere, though I looked for one in every corner. At any moment, I expected some broad-shouldered officer to march into the hall, the general for whom our rehearsal today had been named.

We rehearsed the whole day, not even going home for lunch. No—just a piece of bread in everyone's pocket, allowing us to work until six the following dawn. In the middle of the night, we had a break. A table was set up on the stage, full of tea and bread slices spread with butter. Gobbling that up, we had the wherewithal to go on rehearsing.

When I arrived home, the morning was already well advanced. I was exhausted, and everything was weighing heavily on my heart. My brother-in-law opened the door, giving me a welcome that was not at all what you'd call "warm." It is easy to imagine, after all, why it might not have been to his taste that I should be coming home so late. Typically, at such an hour, I would have already sent off my sister's children to school, but today it had been necessary for her to do it herself. He greeted me with these words:

"Nu, did you really have to come home so late? And to think that you haven't slept the whole night through."

I would hear the line again more than once that day. Did they think such reproaches could really have lent me strength after such a difficult night? But I did not answer them and just went on with my daily chores. I was not to have a moment's rest, for I soon had to start preparing for the performance.

Using my ten rubles, I went out and bought a couple of glasses of milk, which was at that time a rarity for me. Back home in my shtetl, I had often drunk the milk produced by our own nanny goat, but here it was to be a special treat that I allowed myself for my first performance. I also purchased myself a little box of white face powder and a bit of pulverized carmine, just as I'd been instructed. What I was then meant to do with these I hadn't the vaguest notion, for I had never used powder before in my life. I didn't even know what it looked like before that day.

I had not sewn myself any clothes for the performance because I had been furnished with a new costume made of some sand-colored cotton stuff. It consisted of a "princess" dress with a jacket. They told me I should wear the "princess" in the first act, although the first act of *The Sorceress* takes place in a brightly lit garden, and the dress was made of a very heavy cloth. For the second act, I threw together a shabby little dress, an apron, and a headkerchief,[1] and packed it all up into a bundle. When the time came to head off to the theatre for the performance, I thought someone from my family might accompany me, but who in that house had any interest?

Finally, my fiancé came and we took the bundle and went out to look for a droshky. We walked to Smocza Street because, on our stretch of Pawia, no such carriage could ever be obtained. But going to my grand début on foot somehow did not suit. And so we rode to the theatre, like real working actors, paying a whole twenty kopecks for our dear little droshky.

# XXI MY FIRST STEPS ONSTAGE

It was nearly impossible to make our way through the theatre's courtyard, packed as it was with people all the way out to Long Street.[1] It was only by a great effort that we managed to finally shove our way into the building.

Descending into the dressing rooms, which were located beneath the stage, we found all the actors already there getting ready. When they saw me, they rejoiced, and came to congratulate me and wish me success. Soon I was led to the cosmetician—Antoni was his name. He sat me down and began to smear my face with some kind of fat. Up until then, my face had never had anything on it besides soap and water. Then he rubbed my cheeks with the carmine I had bought, sprinkled my face with the white powder, and, using a matchstick, traced a black line under my eyes. After reddening the edges of my nostrils, and once again dumping powder over my entire face, he said, "Pani gotowa," Polish for: "The lady is ready."

I rose, went to look in the mirror, and let out a scream, a scream so wild that it terrified everyone around me—and myself, too. I simply could not recognize the woman looking back at me. As was typical, the actors had a good chuckle at my expense and called me by their old name for me, *yoldevke*—Little Miss Goody-Two-Shoes. I pretended I did not hear them and just went on combing my hair and pulling on my costume. When I was finished, I sat down to wait until I was called.

In the meantime, the conductor came down to see me, accompanied by the first violinist, Michał Shults. They played through my first two numbers for me, wished me success, and assured me we would all make it through just fine. Then up they went back to the orchestra pit (Figure 11).

I cannot possibly transmit with my pen all that I went through in the succeeding minutes before the performance—one would have to go through it oneself. Only my colleagues in this line, who have experienced it, could

FIGURE 11 The playbill for this very performance of *The Sorceress*, listed in both its German and Polish titles. The performance, the first starring turn of Kaminska's career, was given by the "Russian-German" troupe under the direction of the Russian, non-Jewish *impresaria* Madame O. N. Olginskaya, at Warsaw's Eldorado Theatre on November 4, 1892. Playbills were posted in both Russian and Polish—the one shown here is chiefly in Polish. Kaminska is credited, of course, by her unmarried name, as Miss Halperin. *Teater un* Kunst (Theatre and Art) (Łódź), no. 3, November 23, 1922, 2.

possibly understand it. But just try to imagine the position of a provincial twenty-year-old girl, a girl from the shtetl, grabbed up and flung onto a Warsaw stage where great artists such as Jacob Adler, Spivakovski, Grodner, Kessler, Vaynshteyn, the Tantsmans, along with so many others—so many giants—once performed. And now I was to perform here, after just two days of rehearsal, and in such an operetta as the famed *Sorceress*. I would simply have to rely upon God's good graces.

The bell for the audience members signaling that it was time for them to take their seats pealed for the third time. It was also my signal to begin the climb up the stairs to the stage. I felt my knees giving way under me, but their protest was in vain—there was no turning back now. I had soon ascended, and found myself in the wings, God be thanked. I was led onto the beautiful garden terrace that made up the set of the first act. The stage was splendidly decorated and hung with countless colored lanterns. The teeming chorus looked ever so handsome and dignified. The gentlemen were all wearing dress coats, and the women frocks in every color of the rainbow.

The orchestra dove into the overture, and Kaminski, who was playing my love interest, Markus, grasped my arm. I could feel his heart beating even more madly than my own and his hand trembling. It made it quite clear to me what an important step we were all taking.

When the music ended, Madame Olginskaya rushed up to us and said in Russian, "Esteemed ladies and gentlemen, give this your all, for our very existence hangs upon the success of this evening. And please: do guard yourselves against ever breaking out with some Jewish joke, or a Yiddish word, because General Kleigels, the prefect of the Warsaw police, has sent his 'specialist' here."[2]

We all keenly felt the import of her words.

Soon the curtain rose, and before we began to play the operetta, we sang the Russian imperial anthem, "Bozhe, Tsarya khrani!" (God save the Tsar!), there in our places on the stage. Then just as soon as we'd finished the last bar of the anthem, the chorus took up the opening number of the operetta: "Zu dein Geburtstag, zu deinen Feste," Mirele's birthday song. After the opening choral fanfare, I was given the opening chord for my solo and began singing . . . a whole half-tone higher than what was written. After thus botching the first verse and the short ritornello that comes after it, I managed to carry off the second verse correctly. I received a long ovation for it, too, which helped lift my spirits some and give me the courage to carry on.

Ultimately we closed out the first act with great success, and in the second act, I sang my number "Elend, von alle Bäumer weit"[3] in truly sparkling fashion, very sentimentally. It is the song of an orphan girl, after all, and harmonized with my own situation at the time. The audience was moved to tears, and things went along just swimmingly until the fourth act.

That act takes place in Turkey.[4] They dressed me in a pair of velvet trousers with a men's jacket, also in velvet. I took a look at myself, and immediately my mood soured. "Oy vey!" I cried out. "I should present myself in front of others wearing *this*?" But they reminded me I was now a girl singer who performs to the accompaniment of a barrel organ in the coffeehouses of Constantinople, and this is how such people dressed. My fellow actresses also managed to calm me down by telling me I had exquisite feet, and so should naturally feel confident performing with them quite bare.

While the costumier dressed me, Mr. Shults, the first violinist, went over that act's number with me, my last solo song—"Bei mein Vater war ich ein einziges Kind"[5]—as it was the one I had the weakest grasp of. Meanwhile, the third bell was ringing, and so I climbed up to the stage, heart pounding to beat the band. The fact that I barely knew what I was to do onstage, however, did not scare me so much as the trousers. My word, how could they put a girl onstage in a pair of trousers?! But whether I liked it or not, I was thrust onto the set, as someone called out to me from the wings, "Onstage, all is permitted!"

If I wanted to become a true artist, it was imperative that I learn to stop feeling shame.

"Very well," I thought to myself. "If that's how it must be, so it must."

Before long, the curtain came down on our first performance. The crowd applauded. I was called out multiple times, or, to put it more accurately, I was shoved out in front of the curtain and saw before me innumerable heads, each appearing so small that they looked like the heads of tiny pins, and as numerous as grains of sand on the face of the earth. I could not distinguish one head from another, and the number of them seemed to double before my eyes. The stage director, Herr Oskar, was also called out, along with Madame Olginskaya, the foundress of our troupe, who had initiated the whole endeavor. They offered up their thanks to all of us, though I didn't know why I should be the object of gratitude.

When I returned to my dressing room, I asked aloud, "How am I supposed to wash my makeup off?" At which Antoni, the cosmetician, came over and removed all the color by wiping my face with pork fat. I stood there rooted to the spot, my cheeks absolutely shining with grease. The actress Triling noticed and advised me to powder up a bit. And so I threw some powder on, then looked all together like a miller.

I was well aware that the assembled actors were chuckling to themselves at my expense, but it was a drop of water in the ocean in comparison with the prevailing mood of festivity. It is simply impossible to capture what state my mind was in on that one lovely night over thirty years ago.

After the performance, my fiancé escorted me home, as did Kaminski, since he also lived on Pawia Street. This time we walked, and shared with each other all our impressions of the performance: who was good and who managed to get out the German well, for in those days, that was a chief concern.

After arriving home, I quickly went to bed. But try as I might, I could not fall asleep until it had grown quite late. When morning came, the household did not wake me, letting me sleep in a bit. They had gained some respect for their little "artist." And anyhow, this was Shabbos morning, and on Shabbos it's acceptable to stay in bed a little longer than usual.

Around noon, the family finally barged in and asked me, "So, how did it all go, *artistke*? How much did you earn?"

But answer made I none.

# XXII NEW STARS

That Saturday night, of course, we repeated *The Sorceress*, but this time it went rather more poorly. I don't know why, but everyone played worse than they had at the première. Then on Sunday, the Russian troupe played in the theatre, and on Monday, it was back to us.

At that performance, we had special guests in the theatre: the famed actor Shlifershteyn,[1] from Lemberg,[2] together with his wife Finkl, the daughter of that city's chief cantor. She was a very musical woman with a beautiful contralto. The two Bruh sisters came, too. One of them also had a very pretty voice and was the prima donna of the theatre in Lemberg. Completing their party was a fellow named Eskrays, a baritone who also worked as a cantor in Lemberg.

These others had been brought along without our knowledge. All we'd been told was that Shlifershteyn would be there, and indeed he came up onstage on the day of the performance and introduced himself. The veteran actors, like the Bermans, Rotshayn, and Titelman, he knew already, for he had played alongside them in the very same theatre we were now playing in, under the directorship of Goldfaden himself. But the young people he was meeting for the first time.

This third performance went very well for me, and I overheard Shlifershteyn saying to Eskrays afterwards, "She will be a true artist. I think she could eventually be entrusted with the role of Dora." This was the heroine of his own play, as he had told us.[3] Upon parting that night, he said to me, "Just carry on performing. Someday we'll do it together, and make a killing."

Meanwhile, the material success of our present enterprise, over the course of these three performances, had been too good for words. Our houses were so overfull that management had to pay a fine for exceeding the maximum capacity of the space.

But we artists saw precious little of our terrific receipts. The young actors, in particular, were hardly treated with an excess of fairness. When one of us came to management to ask for his pay, he was told that as new actors had recently been engaged, they had to be given the substantial advances they'd been promised before the rest of us youngsters could receive anything. At that point, we all began to mutiny, insisting that it wasn't right, and that business was not being conducted at all properly. And so the administrators called in the stage director, Herr Oskar, and gave him money to distribute to the company as he saw fit. Oskar determined that I, though I was the leading lady, should be given no more than forty kopecks; Kaminski, in the lover role—thirty kopecks; and for each of the rest of the company, the piddling sum of fifteen kopecks. Today's generation of young actors never had to put up with the things we had to as we were just coming up.

After such treatment from the administration, the young members of the troupe turned to Herman Berman, who was, after Shvartsbard and Oskar, the oldest in the company. He advised us to simply stop performing. On Tuesday, the Russian troupe played, and on Wednesday we gathered in the theatre again, where, after some brief negotiations with the administration, we managed to reach an agreement. Each of us was given a few more kopecks for a day's work. It was furthermore decided that we would not play again until Friday, when we would début our take on *Shulamis*.

At this point, I was brought to one side and made to understand that I was not yet mature enough for a role of such weighty responsibility as the title part in that opera, the tragically spurned heroine. It would be given instead to Anna Bruh, who had already prepared the role, and I would play the secondary role of Avigayil, the well-born Jerusalemite woman whom the hero Avsholem, the true love of Shulamis, marries in her stead. Later, they said, I would get to play the heroine myself after being able to observe Bruh, and we could alternate in the role. I was rather hurt, because I had already studied the part, but there was nothing to be done about it.

For this production, Shlifershteyn took over the stage direction and began instructing us in our parts. He would also be taking the role of Tsingitang, the comic sidekick to the male lead, and Herman Berman would play the father of Shulamis, the old Bethlehemite shepherd Manoyekh. Eskrays, meanwhile, would take the lover role, Avsholem. By this time, my fiancé from the Polish operetta company was won over to our side, and he joined our troupe, too.

His first role with us was one of the three suitors seeking the hand of Shulamis in marriage. The first suitor, the warrior Yoyev Gidoyni, was played by Rozenkvyat, the same fellow who had used his great talent for whistling to help teach us *Shulamis* back when we first started rehearsing it. My fiancé played the second suitor, the wealthy landowner Avinodov, and the third, Nosn the deputy priest, was played by Adolf Berman. Rehearsals were conducted very properly, and we could quickly tell that we were in good hands under Shlifershteyn's direction.

Friday came, and there we were in the theatre, getting ready for the first night.[4] The aesthetic of this production was something altogether different. Now we were wearing long tunics, with turbans on our heads.

After the grand choral number that opens the piece, with the pilgrims making their way to Jerusalem from Bethlehem, Bruh, as Shulamis stranded in the desert, warbled her first aria, "Ikh bet dikh, groyser shtarker got."[5] Once she finished, I could only stand there, stunned by her singing. Perhaps her voice was no lovelier than my own. But with her, it was clear that one was watching a truly experienced and skilled artist. And unlike me, she had no fear of the electric stage lights and the massed heads of the audience members. She leaned out toward them from the boards, and I could not begin to comprehend her confidence. And she was so beautifully made up, whereas the first time I had makeup put on, my face looked like one of the masks we used to wear on Purim. But I started watching closely to see how she applied it, copied her exactly, and looked much better for it. Indeed, I learned a great deal from Bruh.

When she sang her duet with Eskrays, "O, der Brunnen, o die Katze!",[6] one could plainly see that, compared to her, he was a big old *drong*, as we say in our actors' slang—by which we mean, he had all the dramatic ability of a *stick*.[7] On the other hand, Shlifershteyn as Tsingitang quickly won fame throughout Warsaw for his performance. I myself thought there could be no greater artist than he in all the world. Can you imagine—an actor makes himself up as a black fellow with big white eyes and jumps about like a goat? Not to mention his dancing! I watched him as if he were a god.[8]

The first two acts of the performance went off with great success, and the third act gave us the chance to see the other new artists who'd been hired. When the eldest of the company, Rozenkvyat, who was playing Yoyev Gidoyni—the first of the suitors to come and claim the hand of Shulamis after Avsholem breaks his vow to her—entered the stage after the entr'acte, he just stood there as if he'd been turned to stone, with his mouth agape, and the other actors could not help but crack up as they watched from the *Kulissen* (by now I had it down pat that this word referred to the offstage wings). Consequently, by the time my fiancé sang the solo of the second suitor, the high roller Avinodov, he received a hearty ovation. Adolf Berman, too, playing Nosn the priest, dispatched his part with great panache.

In the fourth act, after I, as Avigayil, finished singing my big dramatic *scena*, together with Avsholem and the women sharing in my grief,[9] Shlifershteyn told me I had played it like a "true tragedienne."

# XXIII DESPERATE MEASURES

*Shulamis* carried on for a few performances with full houses, and the profits were scooped up by the more well-known artists who had come over from Lemberg. Those of us who had been in the company earlier, meanwhile, were given short shrift, puffed up with hollow promises that we would soon become great artists and win great roles—but for now, we little ones just had to accept matters as they were and not make a fuss.

But soon, the elder players in our company started raising a ruckus over this mistreatment, and the situation got rather ugly.

As the Austro-Hungarian subjects from Lemberg had no residence permit for living in Warsaw (in tsarist Russia, Jews from abroad could not enter the empire), one of our starving local artists betrayed them to the authorities, and they were soon ordered to pack up their things and leave within twenty-four hours. But management wanted to get all they could out of the foreign artists and begged the powers that be to permit the actors to remain in Russia a couple of days more. And so it was decided to travel to Łódź[1] for two performances, one of *Shulamis* and one of *The Sorceress*.

When the troupe administrators asked me to come along, I was stunned. As if it were a casual matter, to get up and go to the great metropolis of Łódź! Once I had received my family's permission, I eagerly set about packing my things, bought a couple of necessities, and made my way to the train. My Warsaw colleagues and I traveled, naturally, in third class, but the foreign actors were put up in second. I did not understand what a slight this constituted, but my older friends in the company were hopping mad, considering it a tremendous insult. For this injustice, they decided they were quite finished playing nice with the foreign artists. While still on the train, they began to plan what kinds of pranks they would pull on the *kires*,[2] as they called them—the damned Austrians—once we arrived in Łódź.

# XXIV MY FIRST TOUR OF THE PROVINCES

After arriving in Łódź, we were put up in the Hotel Viktoria. It was my first time ever staying in a hotel. The foreign actors were allowed to play a couple performances but then were quickly sent away from the country. These were the two Bruh sisters and their father, together with Eskrays, and Shlifershteyn's "wife," Finkl. Shlifershteyn was himself a Russian subject, but it turned out that he and Finkl had never been formally married, and her name therefore did not appear beside his on his passport, so she was thrown out along with the rest of them. Funny how he would just let her go like that while he himself was happy to stay behind.

And what's more, as was typical of male actors in those days, he accompanied her to the train, then immediately returned to the hotel . . . and the room where three of us girls were staying. These were Manye Triling, myself, and another whose name I can't remember.

"Ladies, here I am for the taking," Shlifershteyn announced upon entering. "My wife is well on her way out of the city."

I must add that he also had an actual wife back in Warsaw, and children, too—a wife he had not even divorced. These are deeply "backstage" secrets—yes, from way behind the *Kulissen*—but I cannot help myself. All—dead and alive, and for the latter, I wish many more years of life—must forgive me if I, turning over one page after another in the chronicles of my life, happen to thumb past some bad people along with the good. Their names are recorded here through the machinations of unavoidable fate, the fate that joined my path to theirs.

Once, after a performance in Łódź, a few young local men asked us to dinner at the Viktoria's restaurant. My fellow actors called these men *yoldn*—townies, civilians, chumps—in a word, nonactors.[1] These *yoldn* didn't invite the whole troupe, only me ("Miss Halperin," they called me), Miss Triling, Shlifershteyn, and Berman. But we brought along a few others. The finest drinks were soon ordered up, along with the loveliest dishes. All the performers began to stuff themselves—all except me. I just sat there, not knowing what to do, acting every bit the *yoldevke* that my fellow actors liked to call me—the same old Miss Goody Two-Shoes.

I quietly asked Triling if it was a Jewish restaurant. She told me it was not, and I found myself stuck in a moment of awful crisis. Still, I had not gone so far as to eat any unkosher meat. Soon our irreligious hosts began trying to get us girls drunk. But my sound and sensible *Litvish* brain told me what was going on, and I only had a few sips.[2] Triling had a little more and started in to cackling quite raucously. The townies, meanwhile, proclaimed themselves great devotees of our art, and by buying us a bit of food, thought they had managed to buy us, too. Seeing that we could expect nothing good from these gentlemen, I gave a tug at Shlifershteyn's sleeve. He understood and quickly led us back to our room, ordering us to lock the door and go straight to bed.

But I still had a very strange night ahead of me. I could not fall asleep and instead lay awake just observing my two roommates, who continued giggling to themselves until it was quite late and they finally fell asleep. Pondering the situation further, the same question kept drilling itself into my mind: Is this where I was headed? Was such a thing as *this* really to be my vocation?

# XXV GUESTS FROM RUSSIA

After playing several performances in Łódź, we returned to Warsaw. There, we found fresh talent for our company, newly arrived from elsewhere in Russia: Spivakovski, the elder Fishzon, his wife Braginska, and Gelis together with his wife and daughter.[1]

I do not remember where exactly they arrived from, but I think it was Odessa. Spivakovski, a handsome, burly man, wore a greatcoat in the Nikolaev[2] style and a top hat. Fishzon, with his broad nose, wore the same kind of coat but instead of the top hat, a stiff fedora, and on his fingers, massive diamond rings. Even on his pinkie—just on one hand—two golden rings studded with diamonds, stretching up the entire length of the finger! Braginska was a tall, pretty woman and dressed very elegantly. The Gelis family, however, was not quite so richly attired.

Everyone in this company spoke in a different dialect. Those from Odessa dropped "*h*"s where they should have gone and put them in where they should not have, saying *hoygn* for *oygn*,[3] and *arts* for *harts*,[4] and switched vowels around, too, saying the word *shabes*[5] as *shobes*. Those from the Volhynia region[6] shifted vowels, too, but quite differently. With them, *zen*[7] came out as *zin*, and *kez*[8]—*kiz*. The troupe ended up being quite the little grab bag of various vernaculars.

After we played *The Sorceress* a couple of times with Shlifershteyn, and our houses started to get smaller, we joined forces with the newly arrived actors and started to prepare a production of *Uriel Acosta*.[9] In the process, I experienced something quite new, as here, slowly revealed before my eyes, was an altogether different sort of play from those I had performed in before. Up until that point, I had grown accustomed to seeing plays with song and dance and simply could not imagine one without them. How was it possible to sit for two hours and not hear at least one musical number or see anyone shake a hoof or two? It was so surprising that I found myself having to ponder over the idea at length.

The roles in *Uriel Acosta* were assigned thusly: Herr Oskar would play Acosta, sounding just as echt German as he does in Gutzkow's original. Braginska would play Judith Vanderstraaten[10] with a thick Berdychiv accent,[11] and Spivakovski was Ben Akiva[12] with an Odessa accent. Everyone else, meanwhile, spoke with a Warsovian twang.[13] Three separate prompters had to sit in the box below the stage. Meanwhile, I had fallen from my great prima donna heights and was now acting in the ensemble, together with the ladies and gentlemen of the chorus, or in this case—the supernumeraries. I took it as a grave insult and felt profoundly hurt. But I said nothing and came to rehearsal as usual.

It would be interesting to describe how the rehearsals went. We, the young Warsaw actors, lacking fancy capes or diamond rings, soon realized that the big actors from elsewhere possessed in fact rather small talents, and we lost any respect we had for them. So, according to our usual custom, we started carrying out *grandes*—playing little pranks. The top *grande-makhers*, the biggest pranksters, were the brothers Adolf and Herman Berman, Rotshayn, Titelman, and Kaminski. After every rehearsal, one of our guest artists was invariably missing something, each time something different. Once, it was somebody's silk scarf missing from their neck; another time, it was someone's galoshes. Fishzon got it the worst of all. Very often, when he would go to put his fur on, it would be absolutely sopping wet, with who knows what. But all these actors were put through the wringer, aside from Spivakovski, who was left quite alone.

At the last rehearsal, during the second act, when Oskar as Acosta was doing the monologue, "Vos, a krist bin ikh?",[14] with all the other actors, as instructed, standing onstage with eyes as big as saucers and mouths hanging open, not understanding a word of his *Hochdeutsch*, especially not our thickly accented guests, suddenly Herman Berman gets it into his head to grab one of the furs, turn it inside out, put it on, then caper across the entirety of the stage with it flouncing about him. We couldn't help but break out in positively paroxysmic laughter. Our highly Teutonic Acosta, however, became more and more agitated and roared out in German in the authoritative tones of a stage director, "Take care, this will all be written up"—that is to say, we would be punished. But we all turned a deaf ear to him and just kept howling with laughter until tears welled up in our eyes.

When the Rabbi de Santos character had a line, our resident prompter would give it to him. When it was Judith's turn to speak, Braginska's own husband, Fishzon, had to prompt her because she could not understand a word our prompter said. In one such scene, when Fishzon was in the booth prompting Braginska, and her character's father, Menashe Vanderstraaten, was being played by Gelis (if I remember correctly), it was now Herman's brother, Adolf, who found it necessary to go down behind the stage, enter the prompter's box, and execute a prank so deranged that Fishzon found it impossible to carry on prompting. Berman began shifting his weight from side to side, spitting, and screaming out in Russian, "Pray what is the meaning of this vulgar display!?"

The hall erupted with gales of laughter, once again boisterous enough to interrupt the rehearsal completely. But still, this, too, was accepted as a joke, albeit a very unprofessional one. To put it mildly, the new actors could not expect any favors from us. They played out their performances of *Acosta* with hardly any success to show for their travails. And they were not given the opportunity to perform further with us, it having also become apparent that they knew no German at all.

Eventually, Spivakovski hired a few actors and moved with them to an auditorium on the same street as our theatre, a building known as the Château des Fleurs. There was a small stage there, and Spivakovski took it upon himself to put on *Shulamis* and assume the role of Avsholem, swathed in a red blanket, under the folds of which you could see his black trousers and gaiters. He looked so hilarious that I knew in a trice this was not destined to be a serious production.

And that is how there came to be two Jewish theatres in Warsaw. We carried on making fools of ourselves at the Eldorado, as did Spivakovski with his troupe at the Château des Fleurs.

# XXVI SETTING OFF ON A LONG AND THORN-RIDDEN PATH

One bright fine day, my young gentleman said to me, "I want us to sign our engagement contract."[1] He had seen how my talents on the stage were attracting interest and did not want anyone to wrest me away from him. So one day after a performance, we left the theatre and headed directly to my sister's house at 84 Pawia Street, beside the old earthwork ramparts, to get engaged. The whole troupe came along, too, and we all had a rip-roaring time. My sister and brother-in-law made a beautiful dinner and bought lots of liquor. Everyone got a little bit drunk and more than a little bit merry. Kaminski sang pretty folksongs and declared himself very jealous of my fiancé, who was taking such a leading lady as me for his wife.

We reveled the whole night through, and Libert, Rotshayn, and the Berman brothers had everyone in stitches. Kaminski was the last to bid me farewell as everyone left, and said to me in his familiar Warsaw accent, but in a tone that I hadn't ever heard him use before, "Miss Halperin, it's he who's gotten engaged to yeh. But I . . . well, I wanna marry yeh."

He confessed the same to my sisters.

We were scheduled to perform the next day. But that morning, Shlifershteyn called us all together to his lodgings at the Hotel Dresden, directly across from the theatre, and said to us, "Gang, we are not going to play today, or ever, if they don't start paying us a bit of money." We all agreed, of course, and he taught us a little theme that he wanted us all to sing. It was decided that when management came to call us to the performance, we would say nothing, just begin to sing this tune *piano*, quietly, quietly. Then, when this started to make them hot under the collar, we would again say nothing, but just keep singing, now *forte*.

And that is precisely how it went. When we were summoned to perform, all we did was go on singing our song. Then at eight that night, when the troupe administrators came and started to reprimand us, threatening that they were going to call the police, we sang *fortissimo* and made the hand gesture that signifies: show us the money.

Seeing that they were not going to get anywhere without it, they offered us fifty-two rubles for our company of thirty, which included the choristers. And once we had that money in our pockets, we went out and performed.

The accord did not last long, though, and the troupe fell apart. Shlifershteyn plucked one of his sisters and made her an actress, gathered together a few others, and took them all on a tour of the provinces. Fishzon, meanwhile, seeing that a few actors were still left in Warsaw, set about organizing a troupe himself. He managed to win over me and my colleagues by promising us great successes, declaring that he would introduce us to the wider world, where he had once traveled with Goldfaden's and Grodner's[2] troupes—to Odessa, to Berdychiv, and to Bessarabia.[3]

"You can only imagine," he rhapsodized, "what treats they've got to eat there in Bessarabia, and such wines! The grapes positively dangle from the vine, just waiting to fall right into your mouth."

Naturally, when our starving artists heard about such a Garden of Eden, they all seized the opportunity with both hands. But Fishzon was not able to get me on board quite so easily—first, he had to survive a battle with my family. What, let an unmarried girl simply venture off into the world like that? Preposterous!

But assemble a troupe he did, one made up of the following actors: Yankev Libert, Leyzer Rapel, Avrom-Yitskhok Kaminski, Adolf Berman, Shaye Rotshayn, Zilberberg, and Tshizhik,[4] joined by the actors who had come to perform *Uriel Acosta* with us: Fishzon himself, of course; his wife Braginska; and Gelis, along with his wife and daughter. Now it just came down to me. Once I joined, the company would be ready to hit the road.

The troupe began a fierce campaign of persuasion with my family, and it got so far as Fishzon guaranteeing my sisters that before long, I would be wearing even more impressive diamonds than the man himself. He was valiantly assisted by Libert and Kaminski, and finally, their combined efforts proved successful. They won my family over to their position, and I was given permission to join the troupe on its tour for a brief period of time. The entire troupe was delighted.

And so we began preparing for our journey, but a strange feeling held sway within me. On the one hand, I was excited about the great adventure ahead. On the other, I was gripped by an incomprehensible terror. I knew the journey would not in fact last for a brief period at all, but rather that I was tying myself to a long chain that would bind me ever tighter and tighter, and that in its grip, I would have to endure unfathomable hardships.

Yes, here was the start of my long, harrowing, and thorn-ridden path, to which I sacrificed the best and bloomiest of my years: the path that delivered me so many triumphs and blissful hours, together with so many torments, and limitless sorrows.

*   *   *

My first stop on this path was to be Łódź again. And right around this time, a change came into my life. My fiancé had suddenly grown cold, and for the life of me, I could not figure out why. He had decided to travel with us, but while we were on the road, I lost his affections. Some time later, I discovered that Kaminski had woven various intrigues in order to drive a wedge between the young man and me. Meanwhile, Kaminski was becoming my minder on the tour, explaining that my sisters had asked him to watch out for me, and he had given them his solemn word that he would. . . .

# XXVII UNDER FISHZON'S LEADERSHIP

Finally, the troupe arrived in Łódź. This time, we would not be staying at the same fine hotel where we had lodged before, but rather in some shabby hostel with very shabby little rooms. Fishzon claimed a big one for himself and his wife and invited me to stay with them. The idea was not at all appealing, but a space was fitted out for me all the same—a sofa with a screen surrounding it to lend a modicum of privacy—and I settled in. Fishzon booked another room for seven artists to share—Kaminski, Libert, Rapel, Adolf Berman, Zilberberg, Rotshayn, and Tshizhik—and a very compact little room it was, to boot. The Gelis family stayed in a third room, a large one where we ended up holding our rehearsals.

For our first *spektakl* (Fishzon never used the rather more prosaic word *forshtelung* when referring to a performance), our director selected an act from *Shulamis*, an act from *The Sorceress*, and to conclude, a little unrelated divertissement. He meant to stun all Łódź with this lively and multifarious program.

Fishzon had played in *Shulamis* before, with Braginska in the title role and himself as Avsholem, and did so again here. He was not bad in rehearsal, but at the *spektakl*, God himself would taken pity on the man for the way he performed. When he sang "In beys-hamigdesh, in a vinkl-kheyder,"[1] the music was on one end of the earth, and he on the other. When he went to look for me in the well, I was so stupefied by his dreadful singing that I did my call to Avsholem, "Ver iz dort? Got zol aykh bentshn!",[2] three whole tones higher than written. The remainder of the act from Shulamis went off in much the same way. Half the audience left their seats and fled the scene quite early.

But that piece's failure allowed the successful act from *The Sorceress* to stand out in stark relief, and it truly enraptured the audience members who remained. Fishzon was very good in the title role of Bobe Yakhne,[3] as were the rest of the performers in their parts. We never got to the divertissement, however, as it had grown quite late.

Still, our fate had been sealed by the flop of *Shulamis*: our schedule in Łódź quickly dissolved, and after just one performance, we were sent packing.

Gelis took off to seek out a second stop for us somewhere, while we remained in Łódź awaiting his news.[4] None of us mere actors had any cash to throw around, but as I was staying with our director, I did get some meals—such meals as I would only wish upon my worst enemies. A whole day, just bread and herring. Meanwhile, Fishzon and Braginska purposefully avoided going down to get lunch, for if they did, they would have had to see the others and get them something, too.

Once the other actors cried out to me, "Miss Halperin, see to it that the director sends us down a stipend for meals."

I found the mission very hard to carry out, but I put on a brave face and went off to the man. Appearing before him with eyes downcast in supplication, I said, "Herr Fishzon, our troupe is asking for a bit of money for meals."

I will not forget what followed for as long as I live. Fishzon pulled out a twenty-kopeck piece and gave it to me with the instruction that I should bring it down to the room where the seven actors were staying. I stood fixed to the spot with the twenty kopecks in my hand, not knowing what to do, whether indeed to bring it down to them or not.

But then I mustered up my courage and asked him, "What are they going to do with twenty kopecks?"

He answered, "Let them buy bread and herring."

And so I went down, opened the door to the actors' room, stuck in my hand, sputtered out, "Herr Fishzon has sent you twenty kopecks," and ran away.

The actors called after me, but I did not look back, and still do not know what took place in their room next.

Not long after, Gelis returned and told us that we would be leaving the next day to perform. It was a Friday, and before night fell, we left Łódź. Whither we were going, none of us knew. Zilberberg did not come with us. He decided to leave for home, still having some money in his pocket for the trip back to Warsaw. But the rest of us set out on the train to continue our tour. Before even an hour had passed, we were told to get off. I gave a look around: we were in Koluszki.[5] See, Fishzon stuck to a strange tactic: he never told the actors where we were headed and kept everyone's tickets on his own person. Whenever our train pulled into the station, that was when we would find out the name of the locality where we'd be performing.

This time, after alighting from the train, he had us all just remain in the Koluszki depot, sitting close to our bundles and keeping an eye on them.

"God in Heaven," I thought to myself, "the man isn't an emperor, after all! Why can't we just ask him why it is we have to sit here?"

The Warsovian youths, though they were by no means bashful, showed respect for our director's fancy fur cape. So they shoved me ahead to do their bidding, as usual, prodding me to be the hero by asking why we were just sitting there at the station.

And so I asked. The answer I received was that we were to play the next night, a Saturday, in Tomaszów,[6] but as Tomaszów was a small shtetl, we could by no means disturb its sacred tranquility by taking the train into the place on Shabbos. So we would stay where we were until the next evening, and then, when the sun set and Shabbos ended, take the next train to the shtetl and make our way directly to the theatre. When our starving artists learned that we would have to sit there until the next day, they were beside themselves with rage.

"What, and we don't need to eat?" they growled.

Now they demanded a meal allowance from Fishzon directly. Once they received it and ate their fill, we all stretched out on our bundles and spent the night right there at the train station. The next day, while others found something else to eat at the station, some of us were forced to fast—Libert and I refused to eat *treyf*. And so we passed the feasting day of Shabbos in a state of dire hunger. As soon as it was dark out and Shabbos had ended, we made our way to a certain Jew in Koluszki and had a bite to eat in his home. But shortly after, the train arrived that would take us to Tomaszów.

# XXVIII AN OFFICIAL SPARKS SCANDAL IN TOMASZÓW

Arriving in Tomaszów, we hired a wagon for our things and a sleigh for the women and children, that is, Braginska, Mrs. Gelis with her daughter and young son, and me—four actresses in total. That was the entirety of our lady personnel. The men were left to make their way on foot, and it was no mean distance from the train station to the theatre. Still, there our directors were, Fishzon and Gelis, lumbering after the wagon and sleigh right alongside the rest of the men. Only Kaminski was no pushover: he clambered up onto the running board of our sleigh and hitched a ride.

Finally, we reached the so-called theatre, which was located on the outskirts of the shtetl. Said "theatre" was actually a barn, clapped together from wooden boards. After alighting from the sleigh with our bundles under our arms, we descended upon the buffet that had been set up inside. We slaked our thirst with hot tea, had a bite to eat—on Fishzon's tab, of course—and proceeded to the dressing rooms.

We played *The Sorceress*, in German translation (or our closest approximation thereof), as was our standard practice. If we'd tried it purely in Yiddish, the government official would have forbidden the performance. Fishzon and his wife, Braginska, had the roughest go of it. They were natives of Berdychiv, and you couldn't get a proper German word out of them if you tried.[1] So it was decided, in order that the performances not be shuttered as soon as we began, that this time Libert should take on the title role of the witch, Bobe Yakhne.

And so he did, pulling on a skirt and going onstage, as we say it in our actors' slang, to *makh*[2] Bobe Yakhne in German. It was upon me to *makh* the ingénue, Mirele, and Kaminski her sweetheart, Markus. The other roles were divvied up among the remaining actors who had a decent grasp of German. It would have gone off fine except that the venue was clearly intended as a summer theatre, and we were in the midst of a winter storm. My costume was very flimsy and lightweight, and by the time we got to the third act, when my character has to go barefoot in the marketplace, the playing surface was covered in snow and ice. I had barely finished my song, wherein I beg for the aid and compassion of the market vendors and customers, when I already sensed that I had caught a serious cold. But, God be thanked, we did manage to get through the whole of the *spektakl.*

The presiding censor, a young and callow little officer, stood beside a couple of his colleagues in the frigid theatre and froze right along with the rest of the audience. After the performance, I went with the Fishzons back to the hotel, where a fine, warm room had already been prepared for them. The Gelis family had another room in the same hotel.

Attached to the hotel, there happened to be a rather nice restaurant, and after our second performance, it occurred to Fishzon that he should invite the censor to a dinner catered by it. He thought if he could get chummy with him at such a convivial little collation, the man might let it slide if Fishzon decided to slip "a drop of Yiddish" into our performances. And so he extended the censor an invitation, along with his fellow young toy cops.

Seated at a beautifully set table in Fishzon's own room were the following diners: Mrs. Braginska, Mrs. Gelis, the young Miss Gelis, and myself. To wash down our supper, we had a little to drink. The military fellows had a lot—of course—and soon showed what they were really made of. They began to "pester" the women. Mrs. Braginska managed to make a quick getaway with her daughter in tow, scrambled off to their room, and locked the door. The fellows amused themselves the most with me because I was able to speak German with them.

Then, one of them asked me whether or not I might like to take a little sleigh ride with him. Fishzon supported the motion heartily.

"*Ja,* Fräulein Halperin," he cooed, "why shouldn't you go on a nice little drive?"

I managed to conquer my embarrassment enough to answer him tartly: "Why don't you let your wife go on 'a nice little drive' with them? As for me, I hate sleigh rides."

Then I excused myself and went into the hall. There, I found, sitting in a corner, all our Warsaw boys who had come along on the tour. The first of them to approach was Kaminski, who rushed over to tell me that he had rented a room for me at a tailor's house for only three rubles a week, including board, and that if I wanted, I could head there right this instant. I was left in a serious pickle. How could I just up and leave the place that had been reserved for me at the hotel? But Kaminski was a pal—he strode into the suite, quickly returned to the hall holding his coat and hat, and led me right out, together with his fellows, to my new lodgings at the tailor's.

The next morning, I found out that quite a theatrical little scene had taken place at the hotel. The inebriated officers had gotten in a huff over all the ladies leaving, and made a shambles of the table, smashing all the glassware into smithereens. The ending was the richest bit, though: the censor forbidding us from playing at all, even in German.

Well, so it goes. We'd still already put on a couple of nice, appealing performances, and, for what it's worth, the troupe had earned some money. I never saw a groschen of it from Fishzon, though.

And he began acting rather odd in general, for instance, by putting Libert to work as his errand boy. Once, when a few of us were strolling about the town, we spotted Fishzon in his voluminous fur cape and, trailing behind him, Libert, carrying a massive hamper of dirty clothes over to the local laundry. It offended us terribly to see it. Adolf Berman and Kaminski were worked up enough to run up to Libert and demand that he drop the hamper on the spot, right there in the snow. "You're not his packhorse!" they spat out, in a rage. They managed to frighten him awfully, and he dropped the hamper on the ground at once. Old man Fishzon, poor fellow, had to stoop down himself, making his excuses all the while, stowed away the hamper under his cape, and trudged off with the dirty laundry quite ashamed, as all of us had a good laugh at his expense.

Thus ended Fishzon's direction of the Varshever Yinglekh,[3] as he called the troupe. Adolf Berman and Leyzer Rapel left Tomaszów for Warsaw, seemingly on foot. I could not do the same—I had too many things with me. Gelis, meanwhile, also parted ways with Fishzon, leaving with his wife and daughter, and I joined them. Together we set out for the Polish town of Nowo-Radomsk.

# XXIX *SHULAMIS* IN A BREWERY BASEMENT

Our troupe now had a few holes in terms of personnel, but after all, the show must go on. For our first performance in our new surroundings, we put on, as usual, *The Sorceress*, and Herr Gelis cast himself in the title role. As we were missing a woman, Libert rigged himself up in feminine attire and played the role of Bashe,[1] the ingénue's wicked stepmother. When we put on Shomer's *Revizor*—The Government Inspector[2]—I played various roles, including Berke to Rotshayn's Shmerke, which had us both pasting on beards. And so we went on treading the boards, and it was not long before some profits found their way to our pockets.

From Nowo-Radomsk, we traveled to Bendin,[3] where we ended up being allowed to give just one performance. After we did *The Sorceress*, the censor judged that our language was not coming out German enough, and that was it. By then, the members of the Gelis family were fed up with spending their days in such an oppressive country, and as we were close to the border with Prussia, they expressed their wish to steal across. They were adamant that I, together with Kaminski and a couple of others, should join them. Everyone agreed to the plan—everyone besides me.

I would not, under any circumstances, leave Russia without my sisters knowing. And besides, I still remembered all too well what happened when I illegally crossed over to my brother in Thorn. The experience with the *moylekhers*, those border smugglers and their shady agents, convinced me but good that I should never try to repeat the process ever again, not nowhere not no how.

Meanwhile, time did what it will when it came to me and Kaminski. I began growing . . . accustomed to him. He had shown me such friendship and devotion on our journeys. When I caught a cold, he did not find it an inconvenience to run and fetch me tea in the middle of the night. And even when it meant walking in shoes with rips running right through them, he would share his last groschen with me. When he did well at cards, he would say it was I who'd brought him luck—and would then go and buy me something with his winnings. It's only natural, when you receive such kindness from a fella when you're on tour, that, try as you may to fight it, you can't help but start to love him.

And so all my troupemates began urging me to join them in crossing the border, willy-nilly, and, once we were on the other side, to join Kaminski under the chuppah and wed him. But I did not want to take such a step. My sisters would understand it as me running off with God-knows-whom and would be ashamed to ever show their faces again on Pawia Street. The neighbors already talked enough about how such a pretty young "maiden" had cast herself out into the wide world and thrown in with some kinds of *komedianshtshikes*, two-bit buffoons. Throughout our tour, I could just imagine them wagging their tongues about it all. Pawia Street was an absolute fount of gossip then, just as if it were situated not in Warsaw, but rather in the tiniest provincial shtetl. I could not stand to bring such potential disgrace to my family by eloping across the border.

Moreover, we did not even have the means to get out of Bendin. So we rented out a brewery basement, the room where the malt was left to soak, and put on *Shulamis*. We constructed the requisite well for the set from a few boards, slapped together a few mountains, and then we were more or less ready to perform. Our ticket sales there were no joke: eighty rubles. And the proprietor helped by making sure that the police wouldn't put the kibosh on our performances.

When it grew dark on the evening of the first show, and the audience began to gather in the hall, we laid planks of wood across boxes and barrels of beer, on which the spectators took their "seats." I was already in my Shulamis costume, and Rotshayn had daubed on his soot to play the swarthy Tsingitang. The orchestra—a single violinist—had been set up atop the ovens where the malt was drying. The fellow's score was placed on a mound of barley. And we began to play.

We had brought our own curtain along with us, a bit of green chintz with a floral pattern. We hung it up by its rings on a string stretched across the space, thereby erecting the partition between ourselves and our public. That so-called curtain served us in our every moment of need. We would even put it up when giving a performance in a private home. And now, in the brewery, when the moment arrived, it was drawn to one side, and the violinist played our opening note for us.

All of the actors, waiting in the "wings" (such as they were), belted out the choral number that begins the opera—we had no actual choristers in our troupe—and received an enthusiastic ovation for it. After that, I sang my solo, then went to hide behind the plank-board well. But once the tenor, Avsholem, got through his song and his scene with his sidekick Tsingitang, water had begun streaming out of the big barrels of malt and onto the "stage," and as I crouched there, I was immersed in the muck.

When Avsholem found me and made as if to haul me up by the rope Shulamis ties herself to when going down to fetch water, I was sopping wet, just as though he were rescuing me from an actual well.[4] It would have been quite a neat little coup de théâtre had I not been completely covered in mud. In any case, we were able to get through the act.

In the second act, Rotshayn got the urge to do a jig as Tsingitang. But as the patrons were seated very close to the performers, almost right on top of us, he splashed their faces and clothing with mud as he performed said jig. Nonetheless, the patrons remained calm, like perfect martyrs, sacrificing themselves for this so-called art. They remained in their places and endured the entirety of the performance with brave faces, only stopping every once in a while to patiently wipe them clean of scum.

Afterward, they invited us all out to dinner, and at the night's end, we skipped home quite merrily, each of us with a pair of shining rubles in our pockets. But Kaminski realized something was missing from his: his passport. In those times, journeying about for even one day more without a passport would have been risky business. He had to return home.

Without him, we were no longer able to play. First of all, he was the leading actor of the troupe. And besides that, he was a dab hand at the whole business of putting on a show. No one could hammer together a makeshift stage like he could, nor bodge together a bit of scenery. And so we were all forced to return to Warsaw with him. But when we went to pay up for our lodgings in the shtetl of Bendin, we realized we would not have sufficient funds for the journey back.

It so happened that Kaminski was acquainted with a well-known clockmaker in the shtetl of Dombrove,[5] the next town over from Bendin, and it was decided that we should all go and stay with him. We hired a wagon, with two of us riding in it and the others walking alongside, and in this wise, we arrived at our new destination.

# XXX I MARRY AVROM-YITSKHOK KAMINSKI

It was already dark when we approached the shtetl, and I was frightened something awful by the immense fires I saw blazing out of the high chimneys—glassworks factories, I was told. Still, they sent such a chill down my spine that I did not want to ride any further.

So I got down from the wagon and we all walked, each of us with a bundle in hand, searching for the clockmaker. It was not long before we found him. He occupied a small shop, which boasted a diminutive worktable, a little stool, and a bench that served as a seat by day and then was covered with straw and functioned as a bed by night. It was here that we finally plunked ourselves down—I, now considered our Warsovian prima donna, and the rest of the troupe. I took the sleeping bench, and the rest scattered themselves around the room and found a few awkward spots to spend the night—a few sharing the one stool, others lying atop their bundles.

Early the following morning, the clockmaker set off for a certain moneybags in Dombrove for the purpose of getting him to invite us to give a performance in his home, so that we would be able to earn enough to return to Warsaw. And indeed, that very night, the old moneybags called up some fellow upper-crusters along with their families and we put on a little "amusement" for them, toting along our by-now historic curtain, a couple of kapotes, and some false beards with *peyes*. We decided to *knak*—bang out, as we put it in our actors' slang—the second act of Shomer's play *Der treyfnyak* (The Heretic),[1] and closed with a nice divertissement of folksongs.

Our audience was frightfully pleased with the entertainment and threw us a lavish dinner following, along with forty rubles in cash. We split up the money equally among ourselves and finally were able to set off for Warsaw, thank heavens.

When I arrived home, my sisters were thrilled to see me, as a wild rumor had been spread in the city that I had died while on tour. They had even sat shiva for me! But they later found out that it had all been made up. It was Purim-time, 1893, when I returned. But before long, as the troupemates began to spend time together in the city and enjoy each other's company, we started to think about taking our show on the road once more.

Soon a Russian producer, a certain Gorov, showed up in town, and made it known that he wanted to spirit off a Yiddish troupe to Płock for Passover—and wanted me as its leading lady. The players came to me, as usual, and begged me to sign the contract and join them on the road. But my sisters, likewise as usual, stubbornly resisted. They would not allow me to travel alone anymore, not unless I married first. And they meant Kaminski, whom, as it turned out, they liked quite a lot. My enormous attraction toward the stage conquered all, once again—and I gave him my hand.

Our wedding date was set for the first of the month of Nisan, in 1893. Before long, the rumor mill on Pawia Street was churning at full tilt.

"What's at play here?" our neighbors whispered. "A girl returns from a long journey with a young fellow—and now a chuppah already? Smells like scandal to me. . . ."

But here's the real scandal: if some mystery man had appeared before me then, God knows who, I would have gladly married him, as long as it meant I would be allowed to go off and play upon the stage.

And so the preparations rolled on. Everything that was needed for the wedding was slapped together in a trice, all of the formalities duly carried out—and in the Warsaw of those days, that was no easy thing. First of all, one had to send a notice to the police newspaper that announced Miss Halperin and Mr. Kaminski's intention to marry. When I asked why it was necessary to publicize this, I was told that it was so that any married man or woman could see if their spouse was planning to wed another, giving them a chance to state their objections before it was too late.

In the end, our wedding went off with a good deal of pomp. My sisters managed to throw together a truly sumptuous meal, in spite of my brother-in-law being an incorrigible miser. It seemed to me that he was giving in, just this once, so that he could finally wash his hands of me, together with my expenses. For a whole week we made merry, and how! After all, who knows the art of merrymaking better than actors?

When the week of festivities finally ended, we began making ready for our journey to Płock.[2] The only actual actors were myself, my husband, Ribalski,[3] and R. Rotbard. The rest we threw together from all and sundry.

One was a hatmaker, another a glovemaker, and they were joined by a couple of chorus boys and chorus girls. A boat was soon leaving for Płock along the Vistula River, and we embarked.

Rehearsals were underway for *The Sorceress* and *Shulamis* with this new assemblage. On the third night of Passover, we played the latter in a charming little theatre. Nice audience members, too, and the whole troupe brought them pleasure. Underneath all the beards and historical tunics, they couldn't tell who were the actual artists, and who the amateurs.

We spent a few days there in Płock, but when our houses started to thin out, we made our way back to Warsaw.

# XXXI UNDER OUR OWN DIRECTION

This time, I did not lodge in the sister's apartment where I had as a girl, but instead with the sister who had a little place just upstairs from her. I still had a couple of rubles from the money we had made in Płock, and it was enough to keep myself fed for a time. When it ran out, my sister provided. But I was not happy—so we began thinking about a tour again.

I had a husband now, too, after all, and so I didn't need to worry about damaging my reputation by going on the road. And just staying at my sister's, planning for someone to hopefully come book me on another job— well, that was no kind of plan at all.

Kaminski had once worked as a folksinger and had two friends, Sendik and Tshizhik, who were also folksingers. We decided to turn these two singers back into actors again, as they had performed with us before, and take to the road with them to continue putting on theatre. Kaminski even suggested we could pick up some additional work by singing at weddings as an ensemble, but the idea was not to my taste. So we concentrated on making ready for our theatrical tour.

It was getting close to Shavuos now, and we wanted to play somewhere on the holiday.[1] After collecting together all our capital, we found that my husband and I had only seventy-five kopecks to our name, left over from our time in Płock. Sendik, meanwhile, had thirty kopecks, and Tshizhik sixty. Oh, the possibilities! What sort of wonderful journey we could make with such kingly sums as these. . . . Oh pooh. But we totted up the figures for hours, calculating that to get to Zakroczym,[2] as each of us would need to pay about thirty kopecks for the steamer down the Vistula, we would in fact have enough. And so we packed up our few old things, and a couple of days before Shavuos, boarded the boat bound for Zakroczym.

The waterway it sailed down was that same thorn-ridden path I was to travel for the rest of my life.

Arriving in Zakroczym, we stopped over at an inn. Thank goodness that my sister had packed us a parcel of food; otherwise, we would have started to go hungry that very night. We washed up, ate our dinner, and got to work. First things first, we needed the usual performance permit. My husband put on the best clothes he had and went off to the local authorities to secure it. He came back not long after, his face drawn.

The authority had refused to give permission. However, my husband understood that with the help of a few rubles, perhaps that refusal could be magicked into an approval. Where would we get the money, though?

As we discussed the matter, Kaminski, who'd been in this town once before with his folksinging, suddenly remembered that he'd gotten acquainted with a certain local shoemaker, Skharyele. So, turning on his heels, he went off to ask the man if he might borrow five rubles. The shoemaker answered him that he would indeed lend him the money, on the condition that he become a partner in the "business." Kaminski, of course, promised him he could, took the five rubles, and returned to the official.

Before long, Kaminski came back to us with the signed playbills in hand. (At that time, no actual permits were distributed—one just had the playbill signed by the local officials, and the display of the signed playbills meant that the performance was authorized.)

How can I describe our joy! We could perform! Now we just had to figure out where. Kaminski went back to pounding the pavement of the shtetl, and found a rather large stable that had been constructed in a yard, made for the horses to rest in during long market days. It seemed it would be the most suitable place in which to put up a show on the holiday. The owner of the stable also happened to own a tavern, which had a room for rent.

"And ya know what, children?" said the man. "We'd like yehs to come stay with us there."

Of course, we very much wanted to take him up on the offer, but if we left the inn where we'd been staying, we'd have to pay up, and we didn't have the cash. What I did have was a pair of golden earrings that I had received as a gift from one of my fiancés. I pawned them and we settled up for the old lodgings, then moved to the taverner's. He was a terrifically decent fellow and did not even ask us whether or not we had money to pay. No, the first thing for him was to make sure we were fed, and he told his wife to add us to her list for the big holiday meal. As for the stable, he and I settled on a fee of a single ruble, good for the whole month.

# XXXII THE SHOW GOES ON . . . IN A STABLE

We quickly got to work and began transforming the stable into a theatre. Thankfully, no more than two horses were laying claim to the place at the time. We duly conducted them out to the yard, tied them to a tree, and rolled their manure out on wheelbarrows. After sweeping up inside, we bought a big bag of sand for a few kopecks and sprinkled it all over the floor. By the end, the great hulking horse barn had taken on an entirely different appearance, becoming something quite pristine.

Then the men took to constructing the set. There happened to be two broken sleighs just lying there in the yard out front. The men dragged them in, turned them upside down, and set them up as the foundation of our stage. We had also borrowed some planks of wood to use both for the stage and for seating. At the day's close, everything was nearly done. But I wanted it to look even more respectable, so I borrowed a bit of money from the taverner, purchased red paper, tore it into streamers, and hung them around the audience's benches.

In front of the stage, we placed our old green chintz curtain. But there was nothing to cover the plain wood of our stage's back wall. The men, poor things, had to trek to the nearby forest and cut down a bunch of little trees, then arranged them around the space—three each at stage right and left, to serve as wings, and two in the background. And so, we had a finished playing space, with every little comfort one could ever wish for.

With a couple of stage lights set up, it would have looked right theatre-ish, if not for the tall ladders that stretched from one corner of the ceiling to another, hung with bales of hay for the horses. Suffice to say that it profaned the look of our theatre somewhat. Kaminski, meanwhile, had made up a bunch of posters and we pasted them up onto the exteriors of various buildings in town.

Now all we were missing was music. We found the one musician in the shtetl, a flautist who could sight-read a bit, or at least enough to play the opening pitches of our songs. For our first performance, we had decided to put on *Shulamis*. But the music was too difficult for our man to learn. So Kaminski coached him on each number's brief instrumental introduction, and it suited—more or less. We engaged him for thirty kopecks a night, assuring him, of course, that we did not play on Shabbos.

By chance, there happened to be a great many Jewish soldiers in the shtetl at that time. They marched into the theatre one day and asked that they be treated to a special performance. Kaminski immediately seized upon a plan: to play for them during the day, forty of them together, each buying a ticket for one fifteen-kopeck coin, which would net us six rubles. It was enough to not have to let in any other audience members. We put on *Shmendrik*[1] for these forty soldiers, with the greatest of success.

I played both female roles—the mother, Brayne, and the bride, Rifke. The other roles were divided up among the three men. The soldiers left very happy, as did we, eyeing the first six rubles we'd earned in this shtetl. We divided them up evenly, with one ruble and fifty kopecks for each actor. With the three rubles my husband and I now had, we paid up all our debts in town, and still had a couple of kopecks left over.

The night Shavuos ended, we played *Shulamis*. We set the ticket prices very low, hoping to attract a bigger audience. The most expensive seats cost only fifteen kopecks, and the cheapest, five. Still, we did not sell many of the fifteen-kopeck seats, and earned no more than seven rubles in the end. But our expenses were minimal: thirty kopecks for the musician, ten for the lights, and that was all. We split up the remaining money among ourselves.

In the days after the holiday, we also put on a pair of one-acts, along with a little vaudevillian entertainment my husband knew, by Goldfaden, called *Shepsele nar*,[2] and we finished with some folksongs. For each performance of that mélange, we would bring in three rubles and often more. By the middle of the week, it was back to *Shulamis*. For that, we got five rubles a performance and extremely enthusiastic audiences. They used to come out saying, "Just the chance to gander at the little golden slippers Shulamis wore was worth doling out the ten kopecks for a ticket."

Speaking of gold, Warsaw was now abuzz with rumors that we were doing absolutely golden business in Zakroczym, positively raking it in. Some people who had seen us there told the actors back in Warsaw that we were packing the stable to the gills every single night. Hearing of our "good fortune," fresh actors from Warsaw scuttled off to join us. The first to come were Shvartsbard and his daughter Royze,[3] a very pretty girl. And soon after, Rotshayn came. They did not even check whether we wanted or needed them. But as I had always striven toward a better, more professional theatrical practice, we took them on, and began sharing our earnings with them.

Actually, it was for a couple of reasons that we accepted them. First of all, the new hires made us into quite a respectable troupe. We could start putting on plays requiring bigger casts. And—we wanted to boost our ticket sales even higher. On Saturday night, we put on *Mekhires-yoysef*—The Sale of Joseph.[4] The house was huge, and we took in over eight rubles.

In Warsaw, meanwhile, they continued to twitter about our "golden" successes, and again the boat sailing from that city unloaded unto us reinforcements: this time, the actors Titelman and Stambulko.[5] As our little company was now becoming quite large, we began thinking of transferring to some nicer locality.

After playing a few more performances at our stable in Zakroczym, we took down our sets and green curtain and the red streamers from the benches, and started packing. We paid up everything we owed, too, and I was even able to redeem my earrings from the pawnshop. Our host adamantly refused to take the one ruble for renting his stable. Instead, he repaid *us*, honoring the company by throwing us a luncheon.

After hiring a wagon for three rubles, we set out for Płońsk.[6] Once we were all seated and ready to go, the shoemaker who had lent us some cash came running up to the wagon and asked what we were going to do about our success. As he had recouped his investment of five rubles, he now wanted to invest ten rubles and travel with us as our business partner. It was the least we could do for him, he said. But when our Warsovian companions heard this, they began mocking him so mercilessly that he was lucky to just make it down from the wagon alive.

Meanwhile, our hosts had come by to deliver us a parcel of food from their tavern, and saw us off as we pulled out of the shtetl. Truly fine people they were, and I shall always remember their goodness.

# XXXIII THE THEATRE LOVERS OF THE SHTETL

We had an extraordinary journey. The sun hung high above us and warmed us with its rays. Green fields laden with tall stalks of rye unfurled on both sides of the smooth sandy road. Our wagon rolled over it so effortlessly that we wanted the day to stretch out longer and longer.

As the sand got deeper, the men climbed out to lighten the wagon's burden and accompanied it on foot. As they walked and we rode, we rehearsed songs from the operetta that we were to play in Płońsk, to the rhythm of our feet and rolling wheels. It was such a balm to our hearts that we felt we were the richest people in all the world. As the dusk began deepening, we finally sighted the shtetl.

The eldest of the company, Shvartsbard, was designated our representative, and as such, was the one charged with asking the authorities for our license to play. The task of coaching the musicians, meanwhile, fell to me.

But before arriving in the shtetl, I had noticed that Shvartsbard's stiff felt fedora, which had apparently once been black, had turned entirely green from age.

"Herr Shvartsbard," I said to him, "you know your hat is as green as these fields? You can barely tell the two apart."

Before I had quite finished with my teasing, Rotshayn swiped the fedora from off Shvartsbard's head and spun it far out into the field, where it landed somewhere among the thickly planted rye, lost forever. Our esteemed representative, poor thing, had to make his first appearance in Płońsk altogether bareheaded.

So when we arrived, our first order of business was to buy this appointed manager of ours a new hat, while the rest of us found our way to a tavern. In those years, the small Jewish shtetlach were not yet blessed with hotels, just Jewish-owned taverns that kept a few rooms in which to put up travelers. As soon as we had unburdened ourselves of our luggage in these rooms, we went off into the streets to look for a spot where we could perform.

As we wandered, we became acquainted with a couple of locals, "theatre lovers," as they called themselves. They duly led us to a high-walled barn that the local firefighters used to store their barrels of water.

But I would like to dwell for a moment on these so-called theatre lovers.[1] In that period, as still today, every shtetl boasted a category of people who had "discovered themselves" to be theatre lovers. These were primarily idlers, or sons of rich fathers, who had, for one reason or another, but mostly just because it pleased them to do so, crowned themselves the theatre lovers of the town. They would seize upon the opportunity, as soon as some troupe arrived, to crawl out of the woodwork and cling to the actors for dear life. One must acknowledge that they had a strange intuition for recognizing actors when they saw them, and an uncanny ability to sense their imminent arrival in the shtetl. And putting aside for now any harm these hangers-on may have done to the art form with their sycophancy, they did indeed render us tremendous services in the form of finding us theatres and helping us rent them out, securing us permission to play, and so forth.

Back to our barn, though. Inside we found a ready-made stage, with a curtain and everything, as the local Polish amateur troupe had often played there. We made inquiries as to whom we would contract with to rent it and were pointed in the direction of the local apothecary, the town's wheeler and dealer—he would be able to guarantee the "firemen's stable" for us, as it was called.

Now it was up to me and Shvartsbard to pay this apothecary a visit. The first thing he wanted to know was what language we perform in. I of course told him German, at which point he immediately advised us that we would be better off playing in Polish or Russian. I promised him that after every performance, we would put on some little Polish or Russian divertissement, and he would be assured of understanding every word of it. Moreover, we would be playing operettas, with music anyone could appreciate, our first being *Shulamis*, or *Sulamita*, as it was known to him from its performances in Polish.

And so he "deigned to" rent us the barn for a fee of five rubles a night. The number scared me somewhat, but having no other options, we had to risk it. After he handed us a note certifying that he had rented the theatre barn out to us, we headed directly to the local tsarist official so that he could place his authorizing signature on our playbill. That was not so easily done, either. But once we had received the permit, we set about inscribing all the details of our intended offerings on those yellow-green sheets that always served us as playbills, posted them up, and began preparing our *Shulamis*.

This Płońsk we now found ourselves in was not at all like modest Zakroczym. Here we could find a good violinist, a certain Leybele Pultusker, and a number of other musicians who were not bad at all. My husband went through the material thoroughly with them, using the charts that our chorus master Lustig had copied out so neatly. By the time we finished practicing the first choral number from *Shulamis*, the whole shtetl was peering intently through the windows of the tavern we were using for rehearsal.

Leybele Pultusker was a short, portly little Jew, whose height about equaled the length of his violin. When he would hear me singing one of my numbers, he used to nearly jump out of his skin in ecstasy. Things were going so well, we didn't have to rehearse long and wasted no time in getting started on the barn, dragging out the firemen's water barrels and a couple of hoses. Clearing out the space was not half so great a chore as it had been at the horse stable in Zakroczym.

With that done, we set about making some flats representing a couple of mountains, along with a well, and the very next morning, we played *Shulamis* to resounding success. And just imagine, readers—a box office of ninety rubles! The joy we all felt is impossible to capture in mere words. The government official and the apothecary were right there along with everyone else in the barn, applauding with great spirit. And when the official is applauding, as a sign of his approval of the troupe, everyone else in the hall feels comfortable doing so, too.

We ended up staying in the shtetl for a whole month. Unable to hold rehearsals in our theatre, as during the day the water barrels would be rolled back in and kept there, we would practice out in the open fields that lay just behind the shtetl. We performed only three times a week. Once we had played for two weeks, each of us had earned a couple of rubles.

Around this time, I began to have a good think about some other important matters. During the month in the shtetl, I took a day to travel back to Warsaw, where I bought a tallis[2] for my husband, a pair of candlesticks, candles to bless for Shabbos, and with the money left over, some clothes for the two of us. After I unloaded my bounty back in Płońsk, and saw my husband davening in that tallis, I positively swelled with pride.

A deep camaraderie was being formed between all of us in the troupe. If one of us bought something, or made something, the others would kvell for him. On evenings when we didn't play, everyone would come to my room. Inevitably, the party would grow to include some of the "theatre lovers," or as we called them, quite simply, the shtetl's *yoldn*: suckers. We would then have the precious opportunity of listening to the expert opinions of these *yoldn* and their unsolicited bits of advice. One of them, a teacher, who used to mutter in these horrible nasal tones, once called out to me:

"Will you listen to what I'm going to recommend to you? Put on Goldfaden's *Both Kunemerlekh* (for that's what he called the play)[3] and you'll sell out the place."

Naturally, I thanked him for the nugget of wisdom, but the roars of laughter we had at his expense were more precious than any box office haul!

Eventually, we finished our month of performances in Płońsk, bade tender farewells to the shtetl, then once again packed our few pieces of luggage onto a wagon, along with ourselves, and set off for the shtetl of Przasnysz.[4]

## XXXIV A BAREFOOT GIRL IN PRZASNYSZ CAUSES OUR DOWNFALL

After arriving in Przasnysz, we made our way to a tavern on a street corner, but alas, there were no lodgings to be had there. The barroom itself was quite large, though, with long tables and long red benches. "You can set yourselves up here for now," the innkeeper said to us. We had no other choice.

As it was Thursday, we had to make quick work of it so that we would be able to perform as soon as Shabbos ended. But God came to our aid—the overseer of the firemen's barn in Przasnysz was a Jew. He did not hesitate in granting us permission to perform there. The local government official also assented to the plan and signed our playbills for *Shulamis*, which had become our golden goose. With that operetta, we would routinely sell out the house.

There in Przasnysz, we managed to obtain a newfangled item called a "Caligraph."[1] My husband would write out our playbill in Russian on a sheet of paper, then would type it out on the Caligraph and fire off dozens of playbills, on paper of all different colors, and we would go posting them around town.

All of the performers got to work. Here, as in the shtetl just prior, the first step in preparing our playhouse was dragging the barrels of water out of the barn. But the situation was a little different this time: we had to plug our noses.

It appeared that Przasnysz belonged to that rare class of lucky shtetlach in which there had not been any fires for a very long time, and so its firefighters had spared themselves some effort by never stooping to change the water in the barrels. By the time we arrived, the stench of the standing water had quite neatly poisoned the air of the entire barn.[2] Still, after shlepping all the barrels out to the yard, shlepping in some benches and some chairs for the first rows, the place was already starting to look like a theatre.

I took on the task of preparing tickets. I cut out long strips of paper and wrote out prices on them, from ten to fifty kopecks. When people would haggle with us, we would drop the prices even lower. In those days, out in the provinces, no one knew from municipal taxes, so that was something neither we nor our audiences needed to account for.

Having seen to our material needs in the theatre, we turned our attention to the music. When we began making inquiries into the local scene, we were told there were two wedding musicians: a fiddler and a drummer. I sent for them immediately. But when we set the score in front of them, they didn't even know which side of the page was the beginning. And so, as before, my husband sat down with them to patiently drill the material. It was an effort just getting the fiddler to play the first two notes of each number that would give us the opening pitches. This time, it appeared that we would have to sing *Shulamis* a cappella.

On the first day of rehearsal, when we could hear that the fiddler did just nearly "pack" an opening note, that is, get a hold of it and scrape it out, we'd start to sing, but then as soon as we began singing, there he'd go again, trying to sound the note once more. It seemed he was getting the pitch from the singers, rather than the singers from him. And as many times as we went over it, it was the same story.

Having worked ourselves to the bone that day, we went back to the tavern to have a bite to eat—and to worry about how we were going to manage to get a wink of sleep there in the barroom. There was no option other than to stretch ourselves out on the long tables. Whoever had not brought any pillows along wrangled some from the proprietor. For Kaminski and me, now the directors of our troupe, a bed was fashioned from a door that had been brought down and set up on chairs that were placed in a small pantry—our new bedroom. Thankfully, I had brought some bedding with me. It was the first time I ever had the privilege of sleeping on a door.

That night, we managed to get some rest while sustaining only a few battered bones. But what did that matter to people as young as we were then, and so full of vigor! We all rose quickly, bolted down our breakfast, and got back to work: someone to cut out the paper mountains for the set, another to create the well. The "cat" that Avsholem and Shulamis pledge their love over we always brought with us. All we had to do was nail it up to a post and stick on little nubbins of candles to serve as the eyes.

All day Friday, we sold tickets, and on Saturday night, we headed off to the theatre. We made ourselves up, got into costume, and sat down to wait for our audience. But the clock struck ten, and there was not a living soul in sight. We had to wait for the Jews to finish the evening prayers and the havdalah service marking the end of Shabbos. Once they carried that out, at last, our Przasnysz audience gathered, and we began to "carry out" our *Shulamis.* I say "carry out" because that's the word the folks in this shtetl used instead of "playing" a show—"carrying it out."[3]

After all of his study, the fiddler's playing led us about as far from the written notes as the biblical land of Goshen. It was so bad that I begged him for mercy, telling him it would be better if he remained silent. And so we sang the rest of the performance entirely without accompaniment.

It didn't matter a whit. The folks in the audience were enraptured, absolutely beside themselves with joy. Even the typically stony-faced types—the local apothecary, the tax collector, and the fire chief—shouted a full-throated "BRAVO!" By the time we took our last bows, it was nearly daytime. And we had fetched a box office of forty-five rubles.

On Sunday, the premises were occupied by the firemen once again. And we did not play on Mondays, as it is an unlucky day. On Tuesday, we put on Shomer's *The Heretic* and had a great success with that, too. We ended up playing three times a week. Our takings, averaging to around thirty or forty rubles, allowed us to live in high style. At this time, our troupe consisted of nine people: seven men and two women. In *Shulamis*, I could play both Shulamis and Avigayil. When I was on for the title role, I was billed under my married name of Kaminska, and when on for the secondary role of Avigayil, under my maiden name of Halperin.

We could have spent a whole month there, just doing those two pieces and earning enough to live off of comfortably for a while, but we were itching to put on Goldfaden's *Shmendrik.* The problem was we had only two ladies. I could play the title character's mother, Brayne, and Miss Shvartsbard could play his unwilling intended bride, but we needed one more girl to play Shmendrik's girl cousin—the one his bride gets switched out for at the last moment. To secure someone for the role, one of our actors managed to get his hooks into some barefoot girl who used to loiter outside the theatre, her feet black with mud. I handed her a pair of my shoes and a skirt, and she was led onto the stage.

In the scene where the unfortunate Shmendrik covers his intended bride's face with her veil and he is conducted to the chuppah, she is famously snatched away, and in her stead appears another disguised as her, now being played by the girl from Przasnysz. The damsel was brought off to the chuppah just offstage, then was danced back onstage. I led the dance, partnering with the traditional large challah.[4] And the crowd went wild, absolutely melting with pride and delight.

At the moment when I set the challah down, lifted the bride's veil, and leaned in to kiss my son's new wife, a clamor broke out. My first thought was that the theatre was collapsing. Then the cries grew even more raucous: "It's crazy Beylke! Crazy Beylke!" I understood what had happened and shoved this new "castmate" off the stage. We could barely finish the act. All because we had enlisted that barefoot girl, apparently a pariah of the shtetl, we had so disgraced ourselves that we very quickly had to pack our things and skip town.

Not having time for any dillydallying, we quickly settled up accounts, each troupemate paying what they owed in the shtetl, and before you knew it, we were sitting in a stagecoach headed for Ciechanów.[5]

En route, seated in the coach at the head of our group, I felt for the first time that sitting there were not just Avrom-Yitskhok and Ester-Rokhl Kaminski, but perhaps another little creature, too.

"I don't know what's going on," I whispered to my husband. "Somehow I'm not comfortable. I don't feel quite right."

My husband held me tightly so that I wouldn't be tossed about too much, all the while smiling contentedly to himself. The whole gang quickly figured out what was up, and I was just about set aflame with humiliation. But they comforted me as only actors can: "*Narele*, you sweet little fool, there's no reason to be embarrassed! After all, this new state you find yourself in— why, it's nothing if not *Jewish*!"

# XXXV IN CIECHANÓW, WE'RE TOO "REVOLUTIONARY," AND IN MŁAWA, TOO "BIBLICAL"

Ciechanów. A small shtetl with a four-cornered marketplace. We unpacked, and sought out as usual the firemen's warehouse, but this time we could not procure it. It was already being used by the local amateurs. So we thought we'd try to win over the head government official in those parts.

To that end, Kaminski piped up and addressed us: "Kids! You want people to know we're here? Well then group up!"

We were all staying on the second floor of an inn, our rooms looking out onto the marketplace. After we gathered together beside him, Kaminski threw open a window and issued the command: "Now gang! Let's have a go at the first chorus from *Kuni-Leml*, and give it a good *knak*!" And so we opened our mouths and out rang the chorus, "Mir, yudelekh, koshere khsidimlekh."[1] Within the blink of an eye, the whole shtetl had gathered in the marketplace.

My husband did not waste a second. He went down to the townspeople and asked, "Jews, tell me! Who among you is acquainted with the high muck-a-muck in this shtetl?"

One of the crowd asked him, "What? Are you one of the famous Broder singers?"[2]

My husband answered, "I am the leader of the players who have lately arrived here. We are not Broder singers. We are Warsovian Jewish actors."

And as luck would have it, one of the crowd was indeed acquainted with the town's tsarist official. With this townsperson's help, we received the official's permission to play in the local theatre but for one performance only. That performance was to be a test, to see whether we really would be playing in German and not the forbidden Yiddish.

We quickly got to work. One, two, three, and our little theatre was ready with everything we needed—the same little theatre that still stands there today on that four-cornered marketplace.

There was a very fine violinist in town. All he had to do was crack open the score to *Shulamis* and off he went, playing marvelously. To make sure we were ready, we scheduled an extra rehearsal to air out our German a bit, so that we would not, God forbid, get our tongues in a twist at the performances.

The next morning, our show went off with great success. A box office of fifty rubles, but most importantly—the crowd was enthusiastic.

Meanwhile, the official hadn't forgotten to send along his language expert. Up until the scene with the shepherds, our German pleased this man just fine, but as soon as he heard the eldest shepherd's solo number, "Der yunger volf, er shloft nisht,"[3] it was as if someone had lit a match under him. Honestly, was it really such a "revolutionary" thing we were doing?

On the spot, he pulled out his notebook and jotted something down. Standing in the wings, where I had been supporting the sound with some offstage singing, I noticed his pen going, and I understood that the official complaint had just about been made. Still offstage, I began to prompt the actors who were on, shouting at them:

"Quit your shlepping and sing in German!"

But the die had been cast. I still didn't understand the reason for the ban on Yiddish being spoken or sung onstage, but when we went the next day to have our playbills for *The Sorceress* signed, the high official answered our request with this:

"Clear out. You oughtta be grateful that I haven't brought you all in for questioning and had you arrested."

No begging would help us now, nor any pull we might have tried to obtain with him. We had to pack our things and go. I thought it a great pity to leave this shtetl, with its very nice audience and very fine fiddler. I thought I'd ask the gang if we might consider at least bringing the musician along with us. And they obliged me! We wrangled him onto the wagon with us and off we clattered to Młava.[4]

There we made our way to a respectable hotel, with charming and clean little rooms. But we were afraid to unpack until we knew we would be allowed to perform. I only took out my husband's black suit, which served the special function of being worn to go out seeking a *razreshenie*, the Russian governmental permit.

And so my husband washed up, dressed up fine as any lord, grabbed the playbills we'd had printed in Warsaw, and went off to the local official representing the provincial government. There he was told that playbills had to be signed by the official representing the district government instead. We grew a bit dejected because we had heard that this man happened to be a notorious Jew hater. But we had also heard that if we sent a woman to persuade him, it was more likely we'd prevail. Just my luck.

I quickly got dressed, as they say, "in vinegar and honey," that is, to the nines, and sallied forth. My husband remained in the anteroom of the man's office, while a local constable led me inside.

There sat a Haman with a black beard. It gave me a start even just to look at him.

"Chto udobno?" he asked me in Russian. "What would you like?"

I laid out our prepared playbills, the same blue-green ones we'd used at the Eldorado Theatre in Warsaw. He asked me what we intended to perform, and I indicated the title on one of the sheets: *Shulamis*.

"Eto—nyet!" he answered tersely. "Not that!"

With trembling hands, I then pushed our second potential playbill toward him, *The Sorceress*, which he signed immediately. All he asked was whether we would be playing in German. Naturally, I assured him that yes, we would be playing it in the same *yazyk* (language, in Russian) in which we'd done it in Warsaw. I also asked him whether I should reserve a seat for him in the theatre.

"Nyet, ya uezzhayu," he answered. "No, I'm leaving town."

So I asked him if he would sign just a couple more playbills for us before he did.

"Which?" he asked.

I fanned out *Shulamis*, *Kuni-Leml*, and *Shmendrik*.

In the end, he signed the latter two of these, but *Shulamis* he again rejected, saying, "Tol'ko ne bibleiskaya!"—"Just not the Biblical one!"

I did not dare ask him why he was so angry at the Bible.[5]

*　*　*

As it was already Thursday when we arrived in Mława, we waited until Saturday night, after Shabbos, to perform, and were very warmly received by the shtetl's audience—our performance of *The Sorceress* was a palpable hit.[6] We had a man playing the ingénue's wicked stepmother Bashe, as we still had no more than two women. This meant Bashe's daughter, the wicked stepsister, had to be played by a man, too, but it all worked on the audience like an absolute charm.

Having finished our Saturday night show, we waited until Tuesday to play again—this time, *Kuni-Leml*. It was also well received, but now the audience was demanding that we give them *Shulamis*. We decided to take advantage of the district official being out of town and the provincial official taking over his duties in the meantime, and I, together with my husband, went off to the man's residence.

We did not find the provincial official at home, but his door was open. A large dog, meanwhile, was keeping watch at the front window. As soon as we stepped through the doorway and peered inside, the dog leapt down from his perch and stationed himself at the door, blocking our exit. And when we tried to leave, he began to bark. All we could do was sit and wait for his master to return home.

When he did, he smiled at us and his pet, explaining how well trained the beast was: it would let anyone in, just would not let them out again. The official gave us no trouble at all, and within moments, we had him signing our playbills for *Shulamis*.

As soon as we put them up, the tickets went like hotcakes. We planned to play Saturday night and on Friday we had already taken in seventy rubles' worth of advance sales. But some evil spirit just had to go and bring the district official back to town before we could take the stage. He returned on Saturday morning and immediately sent the constable into the streets to tear down our playbills from every building.

The shtetl went mad. I came again before the district official, this time weeping, pleading with him to let us perform the piece.

"What is this?" I sobbed. "You can see here on the playbill that Kleigels himself, the prefect of police, allowed us to perform it in Warsaw!"

"Ya zdes' Kleigels!" he bellowed back in Russian. "Well here, *I'm* Kleigels!" So loudly did he bellow that he set the windowpanes atremble.

He barged out of the room and left me alone there. But I would not quit the spot until he came back. When he did, I resumed my vehement pleas. In the end, he allowed us to perform in Mława one last time, but not *Shulamis*, rather some other piece, provided that the very next morning, we would hightail it out of his town for good.

We decided to play *Shmendrik*. Many went to refund their tickets. They didn't want to see *Shmendrik*. But it was a fait accompli. If the authorities wouldn't allow it, there was nothing we could do. With broken hearts, we began rehearsing the old comedy.

This time, to play the swapped-in bride, we dressed up one of our actors in drag—the "Przasnysz bride" was etched too deeply in our memories to think of doing otherwise. We had heard that the girl was harassed mercilessly in the days following the incident onstage with people shouting after her in the streets, "Little actress!" "Barefoot actress!" "Beylke the comedienne!" She suffered such grief from the teasing that she soon took ill and died. It was a harsh lesson for us, and from that time on, if we lacked a third woman in the troupe, we would always just throw a dress on one of our gentlemen to play the second bride in *Shmendrik*—which had the added benefit of absolutely delighting the audience.

Once the curtain fell on this iteration, we said goodbye to Mława, and likewise to our very fine fiddler, who returned to Ciechanów. Back onto the wagon we climbed, and "Giddy-up!" We were off to Pułtusk.[7]

These long journeys were becoming more and more difficult for me. My friends laid their entire collection of pillows underneath me, but it was no good: I could feel my very insides being joggled something awful.

# XXXVI IN PUŁTUSK, IT'S LIKE PULLING TEETH

After arriving in Pułtusk, a nice clean shtetl, I was finally able to sleep—and how! More than twenty-four hours passed in deepest slumber. When I woke the next evening, I had no idea where in the world I was. I was so worn out and exhausted from the journey that my friends were truly afraid for me and decided we would not be making any more journeys by wagon. But when it came time to start preparing the show, my freshness and health were renewed. Thankfully, everything went more easily here, even the renting of a theatre space.

It was to be a real theatre this time, with a beautiful stage, where a number of different troupes used to come to perform. The music turned out nicely, too, as there was a proficient orchestra in town. But our box offices were much lower, which prevented us from remaining there for an extended period. Before long, we were on the road again back to Warsaw.

We could have gone by train for about half the journey, but doing without would be far cheaper, and as we had made very little in Pułtusk, we were forced to go by canvas-covered wagon yet again. And what's more, the drivers warned us that we would have to cross a large forest, where passengers were quite often ambushed by waiting bandits.

This aggrieved me terribly, but I put my trust in God. We entered a couple of wagons at dusk, and as soon as night fell, I buried my head in the hay, wept softly to myself, and prayed to the Lord to let us all live for the sake of the little soul that I had yet to deliver.

My prayers were answered. We arrived in Warsaw in peace. The carriage let us off in the Muranów district, where we all hailed droshkies, riding off like perfect aristocrats. Who could have guessed from looking at us then that we were the sort that usually traveled crammed together into wagons!

We were to remain quite a short time in Warsaw.

For one, most of our troupe, though they were all Warsovians, had lost the homes they once knew.

Titelman, for example, came from very good parents and a lovely family, but as soon as he became a "comedian," as his relatives dubbed him, they renounced him. More than once, he was forced to sleep, as he himself told us, in a sugar barrel. Such barrels were to be found near his home, in front of an iron gate that faced the street. When people went to remove the sugar from them, they would leave the straw-lined barrels lying there, and he was not the only desperate individual known to pick one out to use as a bed.

I was also looked down upon back in the city. My sisters were bearable, but my brothers-in-law saw us actors essentially as Gypsies.[1] Whenever my husband and I would help out one brother-in-law with a ten-ruble piece we'd earned through our hard work onstage, he would demonstrate his gratitude by offering this remark: "Children, when the Lord lends you aid such that you eventually save up a hundred rubles out there on the road, you should immediately return to Warsaw and open up a stand selling soda water with fruit syrups. Start small, aim big!"

All of us in the troupe were subjected to such nuggets of wisdom from our families.

Nu, with all of our grand ideas and aspirations, with our fiery temperaments and vast stores of energy for the work ahead of us, were we really going to just sit there and listen to a bunch of blather like that? It quickly became obvious that we couldn't remain in Warsaw for long.

And furthermore, our amassed capital, such as it was, would not suffice without our continuing to go out and get further work. We took the time we needed to stretch our weary bones after our countless wagon rides, but then turned our eyes once more to the road.

Around this time, several new actors joined us, and our troupe now consisted of twelve people. Among the new additions were Adolf Berman and Manye Kaline. One day, the whole troupe gathered together, and each divulged what amount of cash they could contribute. It turned out that we would not have enough for train tickets to Radom,[2] where we had wanted to go next. Count and recount as we might, calculate and recalculate, the figures refused to add up.

It was then decided that I alone would travel by train, with the rest taking a stagecoach. But I refused to travel separately, and so it was to be the coach for us all, a large one with a linen covering.

It was equipped with springs, and we were traveling down well-maintained roads, but still, we got properly shaken up for a good fifteen hours. Occasionally, we would stop in a little village to let the horses graze, and we would get out to graze a bit, too, on things we had brought along or bought in the village. These stopovers would also be opportunities to sneak in a slapdash rehearsal of a scene or two, in order to incorporate the new recruits.

Finally, after this long journey, our coach came jouncing into the shtetl of Radom.

# XXXVII THE MUSICIANS OF RADOM GET INTO A TIFF

After arriving in the beauteous provincial capital of Radom, our coach let us off at a courtyard beside the marketplace.[1] A sort of flophouse was situated there, with little rooms for respectable guests, and for the less respectable regulars, a large dormitory hall filled with a bunch of plank beds—those kinds of wide benches you can sleep on. We checked into a number of the little rooms and ordered some food, accounting for these expenses with the profits we expected to earn in Radom.

After eating, we thought we'd rest a little, but the owner of the place came by and asked for our passports. He was a short, wide little Jew with a red face, and when he spoke, he shouted: "Nu, gang, it seems you've come here to play 'threatre'?"

I responded, saying that, well, yes, we had come to play *theatre*.[2]

He inquired further, "You at least a good bunch of players?"

I told him he would just have to wait and see.

But he wouldn't give up: "And how did you like your lunch?"

"It was quite good."

"For supper you can have roast duck, even a little goose—whatever your hearts desire."

I exchanged glances with my husband. We asked the man his name.

He gave it and added, "Everyone in town knows me. Even the chief of police, and the governor, too."

Somehow I found myself getting swept up into this inanity. "Tell me, Mr. B---, is the chief of police a good person?"

"By my reckoning, everyone's a good person!" he answered.

* * *

Soon my husband made a start, unpacking the playbills, grabbing a couple of the actors, and going off to the theatre together with our host. Every minute that passed, I would dash to the window and look out for them and the good news they might bring back. When I finally spotted them again, their faces were beaming.

"Everything, thank God, is in order! The playbills are signed, the theatre's big, and it's not a firemen's warehouse!" they reported. No, it was an actual theatre, built of fine thin boards nailed together, with a stage, and even dressing rooms. I sincerely rejoiced. Somehow everything was falling into place so easily!

But we were fated to suffer heartache from some other corner—this time, it turned out, from the music. Radom boasted two bands of musicians, and the two groups were, of course, mortal enemies. One band approached us first and we booked it at a rate of eighteen rubles a night. But then the other ensemble came running up shortly after, and those musicians offered a reduced bid of fifteen rubles a night. At that point, the first musicians came back and dropped their price to twelve. We accepted their offer, and they joined us to start rehearsing *Shulamis*.

As it happens, they played very well. But then the second band returned and dropped its price to eight rubles, promising an orchestra twelve players strong. I saw that unless we intervened, there would be no end to this bidding war, and so we tried making peace between the two bands. We passed out a quart of schnapps and something to nibble on, and all sat down together. But I stood off to one side and raised a ruckus, holding a glass in one hand:

"Okay, *labushnikes*,[3] y'ole tunesters, you! Time to get chummy!"

And indeed, after downing a couple glasses just as surely as they'd downed their prices, these sworn enemies became the best of pals, sealing their new friendship with kisses.

The next day, we selected the best of the lot, and they used their strengthened position (thanks to their recent unification) to up the ante to twenty rubles a night.

And they deserved it—they went on to play such a *Shulamis* as I had never heard before in Warsaw nor anyplace else. The performance was a success—the police had not a word of reproach for our German, and the box office was nothing to sneeze at. And who started following us around not long after? The local theatre lovers, of course—or as we called them, the "yoldn."

We got through several showings of *Shulamis* without much incident. As our repertoire still consisted of very few pieces, we decided to play *Shmendrik* next, or as it was called in Russian, *Mamen'kin synok*—Mama's

Boy. Tickets sold better for *Shmendrik* than they had been doing recently for our other pieces. But just our luck for the governor to show up, not when we were doing *Shulamis* or *The Sorceress*, no, no, but instead for *Shmendrik*.[4]

In the middle of the performance, once we had let loose and reverted to our native Yiddish, and you could see the *nakhes* on the audience members' faces, how they were simply radiating pride and pleasure at hearing their own language, the prompter hissed at us, "Speak German! The governor's here!"

The news hit us like a thunderbolt. It left the troupe paralyzed hand and foot—and tongue, too. I alone did not lose myself entirely. I pitched my voice as loud as I could to lend courage to the ensemble as I made the switch to German, the first to do so, with, "Schmendrickchen, komm doch mal her zu dein Mama."[5]

At which, not missing a beat, Kaminski answered for the actor playing Shmendrik, who didn't know a word of German and stood there as motionless as a dead man, "Ich gehe, Mutter, ich gehe!"[6]

Within moments, we had all shifted our *yo* to the German *ja*[7] and our *host* to the German *hast*.[8] We more or less swallowed the dialogue, though, and just barely got through the songs. All I can say is, well, may the governor have a life as chaotic as the mess we made of the operetta *Shmendrik* that night!

After the second act, thankfully, he left, and from the third act onward, we played in Yiddish. But our fears were not allayed. We felt that our next performance was likely to be in danger.

And so it was. The following day, the chief of police received an order to no longer put his authorizing signature on our playbills. The elder Shvartsbard slumped back from the man's office. The chief had told him that we were not sticking to the dictates of the government circular in question and were speaking, as he said, "in Jewish." When we sat down to lunch, the food caught in our throats.

The keeper of the flophouse, Shimshen-Moyshe, who meanwhile had grown quite pally with the troupe, addressing us all informally, commented that we looked like a bunch of stuck geese. He went up to my husband, clapped him on the shoulder, and asked, "What? What is it? Why the long face? If I want you to, you'll play!"

"What do you mean, if you want us to?" I asked him.

"This evening," he said, "you'll see."

It had only just begun to grow dark when he called us into the cafeteria on the second floor and told us to hand over the playbill of the show we wanted to perform. Then he called in a little girl, only about six years old.

He handed her the playbill, along with an accordion as big as she was, but which apparently she knew how to play—and charm her listeners with.

"Don't leave the man until the paper's signed," he told her. "You hear?"

Before even half an hour was up, the little girl returned with the signature of the chief of police. Soon a constable came, though, and told us in Russian that this would be our last performance in Radom. But no one could take our signed *Kuni-Leml* playbill away from us.

We got our revenge by playing the piece entirely in *mame-loshn*, our dear plain mother tongue. The folks in the audience were overwhelmed with joy, and we waved an emotional goodbye to them, though we dared not divulge a word of all the trouble that had beset us behind the scenes.

# XXXVIII WE PERFORM IN A BARRACK

We did not yet leave Radom, though. Some fellow called Halperin, my maiden name, found me and latched onto me, claiming he was my relative, and soon cozied up to the whole troupe, promising he could arrange a couple more performances for us in town. As a contractor who had dealings with the government, he said, it was a sure thing. And he did try hard, scurrying off this way and that to try to make something happen, but accomplished nothing.

Meanwhile, after a couple of days had passed, the few rubles we'd earned in town were eaten up, and we now lacked the money needed to get to another city. The government contractor refused to be proven a liar, and worked with such assiduity that he was finally granted permission to arrange a concert in Radom. But right around that time, the entire Warsaw Ballet had shown up to town and took up residency in the theatre.

An alternative plan quickly formed in Halperin's mind: seeing as he was working on the building of army barracks outside of town, surely we would be able to give our concert there. Unfortunately, the roofs were not yet finished, nor the floors, and windows had not even been installed. But of course that would not stop our Halperin. This was a person who didn't know from obstacles. He gave an order to his laborers, telling them to clean out the barracks worksite and pile up some beams and boards for the audience to sit on.

This was an invite-only crowd, made up of the shtetl's so-called intelligentsia, people like the schoolmaster and the local unlicensed doctor, together with their families, along with a few manual laborers, both Jews and Gentiles. The latter, poor dears, didn't understand a word, but Halperin told them they had to be there.

Before the performance, Halperin himself came to our flophouse and said, "Nu, my family, come on, let's go. I invited my guests to show up at one o'clock." (As it was a Sunday, all businesses were closed.)

"But first tell me, dear Halperin," I responded, "what are we to do there?"

"What do you mean? You'll put on some 'pernormance.'[1] I've arranged for a band and everything."

Well, what could we do?

My husband turned to me and said, "Let's give 'em Shomer's *The Heretic*." He started rummaging through our trunk full of beards with yarmulkes sewn onto them and long Hasidic coats. Then we called the actors together, packed into droshkies, four in each, and forward, charge! Off to the barracks.

Halperin stayed back to gather up the audience he'd recruited, making us the very first people to show up that day at the barracks. When I saw the slapped-together walls made of unfinished bits of wood, moss still hanging from them, and the ground so full of divots that when you walked on it you had to hop about so as not to break your ankle, I thought I would faint. But there was only so much we could do. We needed the cash in order to get to our next destination.

As we settled onto the audience seats—fresh beams of wood that still smelled of melted pine resin—reminiscences of my childhood years came flooding back. I was transported to Porozove . . . to its forests . . . where I picked berries . . . where I sang songs right alongside the Gentile youngsters. . . . I was overtaken by some strange and unexpected yearning.

But I was woken from my reverie by the voice of one of my colleagues, who called out,

"Tell us, Kaminski, will it at least be worth the trouble of lowering ourselves like this?"

"How should I know?" Kaminski responded. "But I assume that as this maniac considers himself my wife's friend, he'll at least understand that we don't work for free and won't expect us to this time."

Now, as soon as the droshkies had delivered us, they had turned back into town. But as we sat there and chatted, we heard one of the droshkies clattering back toward us again. It was returning with Mr. Halperin in tow, the mastermind behind this barrack performance. His guests alighted after him, carrying an ample basket brimming with bottles and packages.

When I saw the couple of guests, I cried out, "Kids, let's go get into costume!" But first, I made sure to ask the barrack builder, "Tell us, Mr. Halperin: Are we really going to perform just for this couple of characters?"

"Just you wait!" he answered. "There'll be more coming! But before you go and get dressed, you simply must have a toast of something strong and a nosh with us."

And so we descended upon the basket. The audience got, in a word, blotto. I also drank more than I was able to handle. I wanted to forget myself a bit.

Meanwhile, a few more guests turned up, along with a couple musicians. We actors headed to a different barrack, a longer one that contained more rooms, each opening onto another. We stationed ourselves in them and got into costume and makeup. You can just imagine how we looked, smack in the middle of the bright day, no ceiling above us, just open skies!

The elder Shvartsbard went out first, to ask the audience members to take their seats. Then we played the entirety of *The Heretic* for them, and afterward, sang a few comic songs in rhyming couplets, along with some duets. Some intermittent snacking on the provisions that had been brought allowed the entertainment to carry on until dusk.

Then we all returned to town on foot. The audience took up a collection and paid us a hundred rubles. Our joy was indescribable. They even told us they wanted us to extend our stay and remain until the Warsaw Ballet left town—maybe we would be able to put on some more shows in the theatre after they did.

But my husband never liked to overstay our welcome in any one place, and Halperin had already shelled out a good deal for our sojourn in Radom. He even ended up paying for some of the actors' lodgings. In the end, we exchanged very fond farewells with the truly fine people we had met in the shtetl, then traveled back to Warsaw, where we spent a couple of days before leaving for Ostrołęka.[2]

# XXXIX A BASKET OF OUR THINGS SAVES ME FROM CERTAIN DEATH

How the journey to Ostrołęka went, I do not remember in much detail, but I do remember this: I'd lent a couple of people money, and arrived in town with a single copper kopeck to my name.[1] Making our way to a shabby inn, my husband and I rented a room and left our things behind with the wagon driver. He took them over to keep at his stable as collateral, since we lacked the money to pay our fare.

I, meanwhile, collapsed into bed, having been indisposed by the rough travel. I really felt very poorly. I wasn't able to keep anything down besides cherries and pickles, which had to sustain me through long and difficult days.

The shtetl of Ostrołęka taught me a good deal about hard living. We were not successful in receiving permission to play there, the town having never hosted any Yiddish troupe before. And without the opportunity to perform, we were also left with no money to travel on from the place. Nevertheless, I did not lose courage, though I had to get through the whole of that long summer's day, our first full day there, with my only nutrition being half a pickle. I had bought it with my sole copper kopeck. My husband came to me at one point to ask if I was hungry. With a smile, I told him I was not.

There followed another whole day of running around, seeking any means by which we could perform, even a homey little spectacle, that is, an entertainment given in someone's private domicile. With nothing coming up, my husband figured it would be best to take my pair of golden earrings

with their little white imitation gemstones, which, brushed as they were
with gold underneath, shone like real diamonds—and give them to the
wagon driver to pay for our journey out of town. If he could only bring us
to Łomża,[2] they would be used to compensate him for both journeys, both
in and out of Ostrołęka.

So that's what we did. I surrendered my earrings to the cause, and the
deal was done. That evening, before leaving, we all gathered at the wagoner's
house. He was really quite a decent person, and knew he was dealing with
decent people, too—just terrible paupers. So decent was he that he even fed
us bread and milk before finally telling us to load into the same coach where
all our luggage was lying, still not unpacked.

It was a long wagon with two tall ladders stretching horizontally down
either side. On these ladders were placed boards to sit on, three people to a
board. A bunch of poles stuck out of the rear and sides of the wagon, with
our baskets, bundles, and boxes looped onto them. It was getting to be dark.
We all sat and waited for the driver to finish davening the evening service and
eating his dinner. Once he did, he led out his pair of horses, hitched them to
the wagon, bade farewell to his wife, and off we went, rattling down the street.

We were tossed about so wildly that I felt I would be sick again. But I was
able to change seats to a more suitable spot, and my husband held me tight.
The driver was constantly trying to put me at ease, saying, "Soon, soon,
we'll get past these cobblestones and we'll be driving over sand, and then we
won't shake even a bit."

At the end of the road leading out of the shtetl, beside Ostrołęka's post
office, the sandy path began. As we drove onto it, the wagon suddenly
overturned, and everybody inside was poured out, in one great mass,
onto the sand. You can just imagine the subsequent outcry from the entire
troupe, especially the female personnel. "Ay! Kaminska! Our Kaminska!"
they screamed in one united voice.

To this day, I do not know how I ended up directly under the wheels,
but thanks first and foremost to God, and second to all our big baskets
that were secured to both sides of the coach, I was not crushed. If not for
those baskets and boxes acting as a buffer between myself and the ground, I
certainly would not be around right now to write these memoirs.

Among all the clamoring voices, I heard my husband's, vying to outmatch
the rest: "Don't scream! Don't scream! I've got her!"

And indeed, there I was in his arms. While many others had been pretty
badly banged up, I wasn't hurt, thank God, in the slightest, just as if an angel
from Heaven had set a pillow underneath me.

But our misadventures didn't end there. It wasn't enough to have endured
this catastrophe of falling out of the wagon. Shlimazls as we were, we also

had to wake up the postal workers with our hollering. They ran out, hurling abuse at us in Russian. "Zhid parkhati!" (You mangy Yid!) More than once, they cursed out the names of our dear innocent mothers. . . . And as if that were not enough, they also sicced their great big dogs on us, at which point we again let the welkin ring with our screams.

All of this went on until the driver, who knew these postal workers personally, explained what had happened and got them to stand down: the four-footed curs, along with the two-footed ones.

As they retreated, they warned us that we had better make sure to keep our voices down now, for if not, they would arrest each and every one of us.

And so, quite quietly, we all resumed our former places, crossed our arms, hunched down, and off we went. Our man drove very slowly now, knowing what a beating the poor troupe had taken.

# XL THE GOVERNOR OF ŁOMŻA INVITES ME TO AN *UZHIN*[1]

The next day, we made it to Łomża, which was at that time a provincial capital. Driving into a large courtyard, we arrived at a long, low inn, stretching over two blocks. The driver led the way inside, called for the proprietor, and introduced us, saying, "These are the little con artists, but very good people all the same."

Then, indicating me, he went on, "I've got a pair of this one's golden earbobs here, sparkle just like diamonds they do. I accepted 'em to give to my missus. That was their fare for the drive to Ostrołęka. Now I'm due their fare for the ride here."

Kaminski approached, and exchanging a few words with the innkeeper, the latter accepted my earrings from the driver, paid the man for both journeys, and told us to get our luggage down from the wagon. The driver exchanged friendly goodbyes with us before parting.

We then asked the innkeeper if we could leave our things in his private residence as collateral for our eventual payment, but he was a very fine man and told us all to take them into our rooms with us.

"Not to worry, I know you won't run off without paying," he told us with a smile. We thanked him graciously while at the same time asking if he might bring us something to eat. He fulfilled the request within moments. After eating our fill, more or less, we rested our weary bones a bit, and then started up again with our usual itinerary.

The elder Shvartsbard went off to secure the performance permit and Kaminski the theatre. It was not long before both returned, thank God, with happy results. The playbill for *The Sorceress* was signed on the condition that it be billed up top by its Russian name, *Koldunye*, and below that, by "witch" in Polish—*Czarownica*. We were to begin playing on Thursday.

We had a good rehearsal. First of all, we had a very fine violinist—our old chorus master Lustig's brother. And the venue was very nice, too. We were playing in the city theatre this time. I was so pleased with it that I gave an order to the troupe:

"Kiddies! We've got to put on a really good show here!"

And they really did get down to work. We women gave our skirts a thorough scrubbing. The men all bought themselves new paper collars. We decorated the stage with colored paper lanterns. And we put on a German-language *Sorceress* with fire in our bellies!

But the little being residing inside my own body bore the brunt of it, squashed as it was by the soul-squeezer they call by the name "corset." I was forced to wear it because the two dresses I had to my name no longer fit over my frame without it, and I did not have the money to buy a new, looser frock. Well, as long as I still looked lovely and sang nicely—and I did.

After the third act, the one that takes place in the marketplace, where the sorceress Bobe Yakhne kidnaps me, the curtain was lowered and raised again countless times so we could receive more and more ovations. Then in the fourth act, when I appeared again onstage, this time in the clutches of the organ-grinder in the Turkish coffeehouse scene, I was greeted with entrance applause.

Along with our usual Jewish audience, there happened to be many Christians in the crowd. *The Sorceress* had also been performed successfully on Polish-language stages, and so they came out in droves, not knowing it was a Jewish show. And as we spoke in German, they never even suspected it.

After the fourth act, a waiter from the large restaurant attached to the theatre stepped up onstage and handed me a carte de visite. It was from the vice-governor, inviting me, along with a few other ladies, to dine with him in a private room of the establishment.

I immediately showed the card to my husband, and he told the waiter that as soon as the performance was over, we would be there. It was clear we'd had a roaring success once the final curtain descended. Everything had been good: the theatre, the music, the Bengal fire we used for the effect of the burning inn at the end[2]—in a word, it all went off with a *bang*.

Only one thing was not right: that after such a show, I was obliged to go and eat with these goyim, and moreover, in a private room. I just wanted to go home and unharness this soul-crusher, my corset, so that I could finally breathe—but now I have an *uzhin* with a vice-governor!

But we had to go. Our continuing permission to perform depended on it. And so, three other girls and I quickly got out of makeup, and the waiter, who stood there waiting for us, led us into a private little chamber, with a long table covered in a tablecloth, as if for, pardon the comparison, a Jewish engagement party.

And there at the table were our "in-laws," or the poor excuses for them: the vice-governor, a tall-statured, aging goy with a graying beard, by military rank a colonel; joined by the town druggist, a short-statured, corpulent man with muttonchops; and a long, lanky man with a blond mustache. As soon as we entered, they got up from their chairs, lightning-quick, and cordially greeted us, planting kisses on our hands. Then each of them sat down by the side of one of us ladies.

The vice-governor vacated his seat at the head of the table so that I could take it, just as if I were the mother-in-law of this little party. Then they ordered the glasses to be filled, and stood up again to offer a toast. It appeared that they had already drained a glass or two before we came in, as on our first glass with them, they already wanted to toast to friendship.[3] My fellow actresses drained their cups right along with the men.

But I knew exactly what these nabobs were up to. And knowing that our men were standing right outside the door, nervous as anything and hungry, too, I had no compunctions about suggesting that it would be more than proper to invite in the troupe's "masculine personnel."

This was not necessarily to our hosts' taste.[4] But it wouldn't look good for them to refuse, and so they agreed to let the men join us. I introduced my husband first. "Gospodin Kaminski," I called him in Russian—Mr. Kaminski. Hearing the name, they asked me what his relation was to me. I told them, of course, that he was my husband. The vice-governor twisted his nose up something awful, but it couldn't be helped. Everyone was already seated at the table, after all, and had already set upon the feast quite unceremoniously.

Once the goyim had finished stuffing themselves, they demanded that we sing something for them in Russian. So the men sang a little Russian ditty, which delighted our hosts. By now I could no longer remain sitting there, trussed up as I was. I gave my husband the sign that he must take me home. I really felt very uncomfortable, and showed it, having grown quite pale at the table. I quickly said my goodbyes. These Russians conducted themselves quite correctly, even escorting me to the door.

But that changed soon enough. When the other girls noticed me leaving, they got up, too, despite being a bit tipsy, and started readying themselves to go. This really killed the goyim, who were desperate for them to stay.

Before making my exit, I whispered to the elder Shvartsbard, "If you happen to have one of the playbills, hand it over to me so I can slip it to the vice-governor. He's soused, so he's sure to sign it."

And that's just what happened. I slid the playbills for *Shulamis* and *The Heretic* over to the vice-governor, and he duly scribbled his signature without even pausing to ask what they were. I wended my way home quite happily until I started to feel extremely unwell again. If I'd had to take two more steps, I would surely have collapsed.

Not long after making it back to the inn, I heard my troupemates returning to their rooms, all of them a bit drunk, especially the ladies. I don't know what happened in the restaurant after my departure, whether the girls had said anything amiss to the goyim, or the other way around. I only knew that within their room, these girls were now laughing like all-possessed. Their windows opened out onto the street and were positioned so close to the ground outside that the girls' voices carried out there easily. Meanwhile, the three goyim were waiting on the sidewalk, biding their time till the laughter quieted down so they could get in a coaxing word with the girls, or the devil knows what else.

These girlfriends of mine, meanwhile, had gotten their blood so warmed by the vodka and the wine that they started cackling even more loudly, until a constable barged into their room with an explicit order from the vice-governor to put a sock in it.

The elder Shvartsbard was sharing a room with his daughter, and these two girls were in the room adjacent. Hearing the constable give the order, Shvartsbard grew frightened and ran into my room lamenting, "Madame Kaminska, what are we to do? The ladies won't keep quiet, and a constable just came in to reprimand them!"

So I had to get out of bed to go and pay them a visit. As I entered the girls' room, the same constable entered it again himself and scolded them with this gentlemanly little speech: "If you Jewesses don't get a hold of yourselves this minute, I'm going to arrest you."

"We ain't afraid o' you!" my girls retorted. "We just came from dinner with the vice-governor!"

The constable reminded them that it was the vice-governor who had sent him in to tell "those Jewesses" to control themselves.

Hearing this made me very afraid, too. I feared that this would turn out badly for all of us and began to shout at the girls, insisting that they calm down. But just try and tell a drunk person what to do. They simply could not understand what was happening to them, their minds were in such a whirl.

When they threw themselves down into one bed together and got back to their shrieking and guffawing, I snapped their mouths shut for them and brought each girl back to her own bed. At last, they gained some composure and fell asleep. But as for me, I couldn't catch a wink.

# XLI THE POLICE CHIEF OF ŁOMŻA AND THE VICE-GOVERNOR QUARREL

By the time day finally broke, I had worked myself into a state over the news it would bring us. A certain dread reigned over me. But when I walked out into the street that morning, all I heard, everywhere, was an exhilarating buzz about how we'd performed the night before.

Then I walked over to the theatre and learned that tickets for *Shulamis* that night were going like wildfire. By the evening, there were almost no more to be had. And we were able to put on *The Heretic* the night after, as the vice-governor had signed both playbills in the restaurant when he was well in his cups.

But when the elder Shvartsbard went to his office to get a playbill signed for yet another performance, the man threw him out on his ear, and our old comrade, poor dear, came to me quite crushed, saying in his distinct Warsovian accent, "You know, Madame Kaminska, you were right! Those nasty little wenches brought about this disaster with their hysterics. I fancy they'll have to go see him themselves. He happens to be serving on his own at the moment, as the governor's on leave. So now he's the macher around these parts—can't get nothin' done without his sayin' so."

As for myself, I was afraid to approach him. And anyhow, I was told that here in Łomża, we'd be better off making our case to the police chief, who was supposedly a fine individual. And so I went off to him, and though he was unfortunately not well, he received me. I told him the whole story of what had happened with the vice-governor, the fancy dinner in the private room, and the rest of it. Of course, as I told it, I broke into genuine tears. The police chief took pity on me, grabbed one of his cartes de visite, and scrawled a message on it to the vice-governor, asking him to sign the playbill.

Getting from the police chief to the vice-governor meant a walk from one end of Łomża to the other. And at this point, walking was not the easiest thing for me. But I took the carte de visite in hand and struck across town anyhow. I was barely alive when I came dragging into the vice-governor's office.

The police chief's card granted me admittance to the inner sanctum. I entered, walked right up to the vice-governor's desk, and reintroduced myself to him. I was sure he would offer me his hand in recognition and be at least a little bit cheered by my presence, as he had been in the restaurant. But what did I know! He didn't even invite me to sit down— and here I was, barely able to stand upright. Instead, he simply asked me what I wanted.

"What do you mean," I asked, "what do I want? I want you to let me put on a few performances with my troupe, so that we'll have the money to leave this place!"

He answered shortly and sharply that he would not suffer Yiddish to be spoken on a stage in his domain. We would have to perform in Russian or Polish. To add insult to injury, he was still frightfully irritable from the night before and wouldn't even let me make any answer. Then, to top it all off, he ordered me to leave the room. In other words, he gave me the boot.

I did not retreat to the inn but rather headed right back to the police chief and reported the whole of our conversation to him. I did not neglect to mention that after completely ignoring his carte de visite, the vice-governor had ejected me.

My words worked on the police chief like a wayward spark on a barrel of gunpowder.

It had now become a matter of pride for him. He put on his uniform and made ready to drive off to the vice-governor's office himself, telling me to come along. I followed him eagerly, of course. When he entered, I waited in the foyer and listened to the police chief tearing into the vice-governor thuswise in Russian:

"What do you mean by all this nonsense? What is it you have against these people? Have you no conscience? A pregnant woman has been running around all day sobbing, begging to be allowed to earn some money so she and her company can continue their travels."

In the end, they ended up doing quite a good bit of squabbling, after which the police chief finally ran out bearing the signed playbill, calling to me, "Go print up copies, at my expense!"

And so we did, and pasted them up all over town. We decided to bill the show as our farewell performance, given especially in my honor,[1] and of course, we quickly sold out. After all, the whole town knew by now of the story with the vice-governor, and how the police chief had stood up for the Jewish troupe. Everyone had waited with great impatience to find out how the saga would end. Upon seeing our playbills posted, the streets were absolutely filled with jubilation, as the people realized that the police chief had come out victorious. Everyone hated the vice-governor, as he was a virulent antisemite. And they all kvelled at his defeat, wearing a look of gleeful triumph as they sat there in the audience. It need hardly be said that our final performance came off marvelously, and brought us in more than enough for the journey to Suvalk.[2]

# XLII LEFT IN THE LURCH

For a change, we made our journey to Suvalk in closed carriages on springs, like respectable folk, instead of wagons. For half the time, we were traveling down a brand-new highway freshly covered with gravel. It turned out that something terrible had transpired on this road two days prior. A stagecoach of the speedy variety known as a "diligence" had tipped over on the strewn pebbles, and the driver, who was thrown to one side of the coach, fell victim to the accident. The coach was carrying heavy cargo, and when it went down, the entirety of it fell upon the driver and crushed him, and he died.

It seemed our own deliciously witty driver just had to recount all this to us and, what's more, joked that he hoped it wouldn't happen to us.

"Oh go on, you idiot Litvak, what are you blathering about now!" I called up to him.

But before I even managed to finish my little speech, our carriage started leaning to one side, and it seemed that at any moment we, too, would be lying upside down in an overturned carriage.

For now, though, the carriage was just lurching from one side to the other, and we could feel our insides lurching right along with it. You can imagine the screams that emanated from my fellow passengers at every tilt it gave. I was the only one who would never scream, because I was not the nervous type. I always had a very casual outlook on everything.[1] It was a miracle from Heaven that I had such a character, for if I had not, I would certainly not have been able to bear the bundle of troubles that was still to come my way in this life of mine. I calmly accepted every wallop, large or small, that fate was so generous as to offer me in abundance. It may be that the distinct equilibrium in my character will yet someday be upset, that one more terrible lurch shall manage someday to overturn me. But in the meantime, I shall make the effort to remain as cool and collected for as long as I have the strength to do so.[2]

In the end, somehow, we made our way to Suvalk in one piece. After checking into a hotel called the Gostinitsa[3] Franka, we settled into handsome little rooms, got the rest our bodies needed, and began praying to God that we would come by a performance permit easily this time. Before we could be sure that we would earn money to live off of, we did not have the courage to ask the hotel staff for anything to eat. The only question I could manage now was, "Do you have a decent fellow as police chief here?"

The answer came quickly: "Is he ever, Madame! We've struck gold with our police chief, we have. He's a German, name of von Berger. May no harm come to him, not even to his littlest fingernail! He's like a father to the Jews here."

Feeling a weight lifted from my heart after I heard that, I found it within me to order something to eat—for myself and the whole company, too.

Everything ended up going just as the staff had suggested it might. We received our permit with no difficulties at all. By the third day in town, we had already "knocked out" our first *Shulamis*, with terrific results. The police chief himself was in the theatre and applauded for us right along with the rest of the audience. And as he was a very fine man, he assured us our so-called German was just fine, too.

In a word, we felt *wonderful*.

The next day, the town of Suvalk was suffused with a festival air, a general feeling of, "That troupe must really be something! If the Chief von Berger himself was there clapping and cheering, they're bound to be good!"

And so we ended up staying in Suvalk rather longer than at some of our recent stops. We played a few times a week, and when it came time to get our playbills signed for *The Heretic* or *Kuni-Leml*, the police chief would say to us in German, "Das ist doch ganz gewiss jüdischer Text, werde ich lieber ins Theater nicht kommen un lässt euch nicht stören. Ich werde dabei nicht sein."[4]

He was sure we would be speaking Yiddish onstage, so, not wanting to disturb our work, decided simply not to show up. And indeed, we were not *gestört*, not disturbed a bit, as we rapped out those performances, blissfully at ease, in our treasured *mame-loshn*.

# XLIII SOMEONE SEEKS TO BUY ME AWAY FROM MY HUSBAND

Now in Suvalk, as in prior towns, there was the usual claque of self-styled theatre lovers, those folks who so "admired the art of acting."[1] (But more to the point: admired the *actresses*!) But here's the irony: in the period when I had gotten through long summer days on just half a dill pickle, there was no one who would lend me even five kopecks to buy a crust of bread. But now that we were, praise God, earning enough to make a living, there was a passel of very rich young people who would not even begrudge us a bottle of champagne. And their wining and wooing repeated itself day in, day out.

There was one young man in town who fell so head over heels in love with me that he sought to buy me away from my husband, and pay good money, too. I was to come as a set together with my yet unborn baby. I am not joking or telling tales. I am relating a cold, hard fact, a thing that truly happened to me in Suvalk in the year 1894. My friends who performed with me then, and are still living today, would surely recall this bizarre tidbit— and this most curious customer.

And the young man made the offer quite earnestly! For right around the same time in Suvalk, something similar had taken place: a certain landowner had bought another man's wife, also an actress, paying for her with his own real estate holdings. Now, this other fellow sought to become contestant number two in this unusual game, with me as the grand prize.

Of course, as soon as my fellow actors and actresses found out, knowing what a catch this man was, they made every attempt to reel him their way, and the whole time we were in Suvalk, they didn't lack even "bird's milk"— that is, they had absolutely everything they could have ever wished for.

He opened up tabs for them under his name at the restaurants, the confectioneries—even saw to their carriages! He hired a team of coachmen for an entire month and had them driving our artists to the theatre and back, as the venue was far from the center of town. We went on performing there, quite without incident, right until the High Holidays arrived.

But when they did, suddenly we all got very pious, including my husband and me, and felt we had to head home to Warsaw. Suvalk became the first town we left of our own free will. Up until then, the local police had forced us out of almost every place we'd been in due to our failure to refrain from performing in Yiddish.

I had saved seventy rubles in Suvalk, which I brought home and gave directly to my brother-in-law, instructing him to hold the funds in safekeeping for me in anticipation of a time when I could no longer earn money through performing. The first couple of rubles were to go toward childbirth expenses.

We stayed in Warsaw until after Yom Kippur. When Sukkos[2] came, we got the gang back together again, now with Hershel Berman and the actress Triling added to the mix, and returned to Suvalk. Some of the actors had to stay behind in Warsaw owing to various military obligations, and joined us later. In the meantime, we went on performing without them. The lack of men resulted in my having to frequently take on their roles onstage, especially as I could no longer play young ladies, owing to my evident condition at the time.

And so when we put on *The Sorceress*, I played Markus, the romantic tenor part, fitted out in a tailcoat. Truth be told, I looked splendid in that coat: the absolute picture of well-fed, robust young manhood. In *Shmendrik*, I played the equivalent young lover role, the groom Dovid. I essentially ended up playing all the leading men. In the operettas set in ancient times, however, I could still easily play the leading ladies because in those roles I could cover myself in a long, historically appropriate cloak. The voice, after all, was still very fetching.

I became very beloved in Suvalk, and we remained there in the summer theatre until it grew quite cold and the audience could no longer bear sitting through our shows in such a freezing spot.

There also happened to be a circus tent in town, and it was kept a bit warmer inside. The circus folk wanted to join forces with us, set up a stage, and perform one of our pieces together. But the authorities wouldn't agree to it. Still, we had to live, and none of us had any money. So the circus people invited us to put on a little act as part of their show, right there in the arena, sans stage. I was very reluctant. The only thing I'd agree to was some comical song-and-dance quartets we could slap together, something more suited to that peculiar setting.

In the end, we decided to throw on Hasidic garb and make a go for it. The foursome consisted of the two Berman brothers, Rotshayn, and me. We pulled little beards onto our faces, secured them with wires (which nearly cut right into my ears), tossed on the long black coats we had in stock, and got to rehearsing with the brass band, which was set up on a little perch overlooking the ring. We settled with the circus director on a performance fee of fifty kopecks per man, or better said, per person (for I was, after all, one of the four wearing the beards and kaftans!).

I will never forget the three nights we performed there, bounding into the ring just as if we were a pack of fearsome lions, to the oom-pah-pah of the big brass band. Our first number was a choreographed quartet called *Di brider yampelekh*,[3] and the second was *Der handlsmark*.[4] When the crowd applauded at the end, we ran back in to take a bow, then off again, then back again as they continued cheering. This repeated a couple of times. When it was clear they would not stop applauding, we decided to come back to stay and give them the encore they demanded. The three men did a few somersaults around the ring, but I stood there motionless, looking confused. I didn't know what to do: Should I imitate my fellow performers and also try a somersault, or just run off?

I chose the latter, and once I'd left the ring, I found tears welling up in my eyes. My God, why were we doing this? Why cheapen our art to this level, just to make a couple of groschen? Was there now to be no difference at all between putting on theatre and clowning? We could have at least left it at those two numbers we'd sung in the arena—sung them nicely, and honorably—and not returned to make a total mockery of ourselves.

My three partners sensed that the whole thing had distressed me, and consequently avoided me for the rest of the evening, unable to even look me in the eye. Of course, for our remaining shows in the tent, they would not engage in the high jinks they had at that performance. And so we continued playing there, receiving fifty kopecks every evening—until eventually I could feel that it was high time to bring a new life into the world.

# XLIV I AM A MOTHER!

The rest of the troupe set out for Grodno[1] and my husband escorted me back to Warsaw. He left shortly thereafter to join our colleagues, as they had already begun playing, while my sisters and I prepared to greet our little guest. She would not keep us waiting for long. In the year 1894, I brought her into the world: my first child, Leye-Shifre.

With her arrival, an entirely new purpose in my life revealed itself. A fresh fount of energy was tapped within me. I knew that from now on I must double all my efforts because now I had to care for two, think for two, live for two. But I could not sit and simply delight in my little girl for long. It was the will of fate, throughout my arduous life, that I could never depend solely on myself without needing to seek out work and audiences—and I would also never be able to devote myself entirely to my children. My walking stick never left my hand, and I was continually led back onto the road to tour. The result was that those receiving the smallest measure of my time were my children. Perhaps it was for that reason that God decided to punish me so gravely: I would end up losing one child after another.

In the meantime, terrible news reached me from the troupe in Grodno. Every day, business was getting worse, and if I did not return to them immediately, disaster was imminent. I had no choice but to set out at once. It was only the fifth day after emerging from my lying-in when I had to say goodbye to my baby and join the troupe in Grodno. I left Leye-Shifre with my sister. She had just lost a child of her own, and so she accepted my little girl to raise herself.

I am powerless to convey just how difficult it was to tear myself away from my firstborn. It was with a broken heart that I left for Grodno and resumed performing. When I did, business improved, but we could not remain in that city long, and set off on the road again. We wished to stop next in Białystok,[2] but the governor there was dead set against any rotten

Jewish performances being staged in his territory, and so we traveled on. Among other towns, we played in Bielsk,[3] where my sister joined us with my child. Throughout the time I'd spent away from my little girl, I had been seized by such an intense longing for her that I could not eat or sleep, and would surely have become a madwoman if she had not eventually been brought to me. From then on, the child stayed at my side and was dragged along over all of our long, dark, and winding roads.

Every city brought with it fresh troubles. At the moment, business was not terrible, but we were perpetually teetering on the brink of disaster. When we were allowed to perform in our own unique variety of "German," we were forced to tremble for other reasons. Sometimes we wouldn't be allowed to occupy the theatre, or even use the firemen's warehouse as a venue, and so we would have to put on unofficial, domestic performances, that is, in the private home of some affluent householder. We would set up shop there and put on a couple of acts from a play, sing a couple of comic songs, earn a few rubles, and then off we went, right back onto the highway.

But we never tired of traveling, and we never lost hope. Even if we were going to play an operetta and had no musicians, we found a solution: one of our actors would stand in the wings and incant the recurring accompaniment line, the ritornello, while I would sing the vocal line sans instruments. I even once sang the entirety of *Shulamis* to the bare accompaniment of a single French horn, played by a woman with a suckling child at her breast. That was, I believe, in Augustów.[4]

The worst of our troubles, however, was our fear of someone informing on us. In those days, there were actors who would jump at any opportunity to make a bit of quick cash, up to extorting other troupes for money. They would blackmail them, vowing that if the threatened party did not hand over the cash, these scoundrels would publicly denounce the company for claiming to speak in German onstage, but in fact performing in Yiddish. I believe that my troupemates will still remember a certain actor who truly *hounded* us. He would follow in the ruts of our wagon wheels and, like a leech, would suck out our hard-earned groschen. When we'd quit letting him suck, he would march off to the local authorities and snitch on us for playing in Yiddish. Of course, after that, we would no longer be allowed to perform in that area and had to hit the road yet again.

In summer, such constant traveling was bearable, but not so in wintertime, when we had to ride in wagons amid freezing temperatures, traveling 40 or 50 versts at a time.[5] During one such journey, my heart seized up and I became verklempt, looking at the little slip of a child lying across my knees, wrapped in a blanket. I held her so tightly to my chest, trying so hard to warm her with my nearness, to cheer her with the steady beating of my heart.

"My God!" I thought to myself. "Do I, a mother, have the right to deliver up my own child as a sacrifice to my art? Am I not committing a terrible crime by doing so?"

But then my train of thought was interrupted. It seemed to me that my child might have stopped breathing. I spent the rest of the journey in a state of mortal dread.

# XLV A GERMAN MAKES THINGS DIFFICULT

Arriving in a new city, we again were met by that "friend" I mentioned before, the actor-informer.[1] He would not stop his harassment, and as soon as we landed in another spot, there he'd be, waiting for us. There were even some actors in our troupe who talked about "neutralizing" this nefarious character. . . . But they were soon convinced it would be far smarter not to start anything with him, seeing as he had somehow managed to obtain such documents as would open any door for him, in some of the loftiest halls of power.

But an even higher power helped us. One fine day, the man vanished from the horizon, leaving nary a trace! It was only recently that I ever saw him again. It turned out he had really made a pretty penny off of us, which he had used to go abroad.

And so we rid ourselves of that plague of a man, but were soon confronted with a fresh new challenge. In a certain city—I cannot remember where now—our business manager had gone off to the local governor, as usual, to secure our performing permit. And as usual, our man presented him with the playbills that needed signing. But the governor threw them back in his face, thundering that he knew what kind of "German" these Jewish troupes performed in (namely, the kind that's half Yiddish), and that under no circumstances would he permit us to perform. Our business manager, however, had lived in Germany a long time and spoke the language well. Hoping to demonstrate to the governor that he was mistaken, he answered the man in his exceedingly proper High German, "Herr Exzellenz, ich möchte . . ."[2]

But as soon as he uttered the word *Exzellenz*, the governor leapt up, his face a murderous red, and began to bang on the table, shouting in Russian,

"Whaddya mean 'Excellency,' huh? I'm the Governor here, that's what I am. Now clear out!" And with that, he showed him the door.[3]

Our business manager was petrified, and remained standing there just outside the office, shaking like a leaf. He had thought that by speaking German, he would be able to win over the governor, who was himself of German stock, or at least that's what people said. But he had only managed to make a mess of things.

He returned to us dejected and recreated the whole scene with the governor. We all found it a very bitter pill to swallow. What were we to do now? The region was in the grip of such a severe frost at the time that it would be dangerous to set out on the road yet again. Our only possible course of action now was to send another from the troupe back to the governor, and obtain the permit by absolutely drowning him with tears— not an uncommon last resort for us. Sometimes we even went off to the authorities as an entire troupe, the women, too, with their children clutched to their bosoms. And if the official still would not give us the permit, such a cacophony would erupt from young and old alike that the man was routinely stupefied, and would quickly sign the permit, thanking God for liberating him from such an unholy caterwauling.

This time, the "pleasant task" of going off to the governor fell to Herr Gothard, our prompter, who enjoyed a reputation among us as rather a bold fellow. When he arrived, he launched into his opening statement, insisting that our troupe spoke a perfectly kosher German, telling the man he could come see us perform himself and would surely be convinced. He begged and bored the governor for so long that he wore him down, and the playbill was, at last, signed. As Gothard was leaving, however, the governor shouted back at him that we had better be quite careful, as a theatre expert would be dispatched to the venue for our performance, and if we let a single Yiddish word pass our lips, he would have us all clapped in irons.

That last bit of information hit us like a ton of bricks. We would have an expert there just to check on our German? It occurred to one of our actors that we should poke around town and find out who it was that might be coming as this "expert" to the theatre, and try to rendezvous with him before the performance, see if we could grease his palm a little. The people we asked pointed out a certain colonel of the gendarmerie, a Jewish convert to Christianity. He did not take monetary bribes, they said, but apparently wouldn't look askance at a drop of good brandy.

And so Gothard went off to see him at once, on the pretense of inviting him to watch us perform. The colonel broke out laughing and told Gothard that the invitation was unnecessary, as he had been ordered to come to the theatre anyhow as a military duty.

The next day, before the show, Gothard stationed himself outside the theatre, waiting for a chance to chat with the officer. We all agreed to not begin playing until our man gave us the go-ahead. Eventually, he managed to grab the colonel and suggest that he join him for a drink, as the performance would not be starting for a little while, anyway. The man hesitated at first, but in the end, his sense of duty was no match for the temptations of brandy, and the two of them went off to a restaurant, Gothard making sure to gesture to us first, cueing us to begin the performance. When he arrived back at the theatre, with the colonel in tow, the show, which of course we had done in "German," was already over.

The next day, the gendarmerie colonel made his official report, stating that the performance had been given entirely in a fine, error-free *Hochdeutsch*. This same routine was repeated every day we performed, and our run in that town played out quite without incident. If only we had been as lucky everywhere as we were there!

Our tour carried on for several months. We played in towns and cities from Brest-Litovsk to Kovno, from Mohilov to Chernigov.[4] In the Chernigov governorate,[5] we played all over but had consistently rotten luck in almost every town we visited, and consistently empty coffers for traveling expenses. Still, we managed to bounce from one town to the next with the promise that the drivers could collect on delivery—for in every town, there was always some "theatre lover." That individual would pay for the journey we'd just made, then arrange for us, together with our luggage, to be transported as cargo to another town. Once we arrived, another of the "theatre lover" variety would be waiting to pay for the journey that brought us to him. And so would we travel, until we had finally earned enough to stand on our own feet and pay our own way.

It is no joke, what I am writing here, but rather, the sad truth. That's exactly how it went, dear readers! That's how Yiddish actors once lived!

# XLVI MY FIRST CHILD DIES AND A SECOND IS BORN

The condition of Yiddish actors in those times would have been eased considerably had they only been treated as people. Unfortunately, actors were without rights. They were looked upon with disgust, and no respectable home would admit them, just as if they were some kind of bastard children. No press had yet been established that could educate the public and help to build bridges between it and the world of Yiddish theatre. With their walking sticks in hand, Yiddish actors had to beat a lonely path between governmental persecution on one side and societal indifference on another, with hunger and destitution looming everywhere.

More than once we had to wander the streets in the bitter cold until morning came, unable to find a place to spend the night. Hearing the word *artistn*—actors—people would slam the door in our faces, and flee from us as if from the cholera. "We will not admit *komedyantshikes!*"[1] we heard wherever we went. And if by chance we were admitted, the homeowners would lock up all of their valuables, so that the *komedyantshikes* couldn't get their paws on them, Heaven forfend.

True, in Russian Lithuania, people treated us a little more humanely, and we found many who sympathized with our plight, but it was a drop of kindness in an ocean of antipathy. I myself suffered terribly in the face of all this. I had imagined the actor's life quite differently, and would often seriously reflect on my choices and think, "What is all this misery for? Is it worth it?"

And as if all those torments were not enough, I was soon faced with one to devastate me. It was the first brutal blow I had been dealt since the death of my parents. At this point, having carried my second child for five months, my Leye-Shifre took ill in the town of Pyriatyn.[2] Dysentery. Within days, her little soul left her body.

When I looked at the pallid, unmoving face of my precious angel, it seemed to me that when she died, all of my happiness died along with her. Like the very sun had been extinguished. I thought, "If I had remained in Porozove, and never set foot in any big city nor any theatre, and I had a baby there in my shtetl . . . I would surely have been able to rescue that child from the claws of death. . . ."

Hot tears rolled down my cheeks. I pronounced myself guilty of my daughter's death. For a long time, I could not find peace. My husband, who was also in the deep throes of grief, nevertheless tried to console me. He did not take his eyes off me for a moment, and when he saw that it was no good, that I could not be soothed, he implored me to try—for the sake of our new child that I had yet to bring to the world.

And as I lay there drowning in my bitterest thoughts, an idea came to me: perhaps the child that still lived within me would bring with it some new happiness and renewed good fortune—that perhaps I would no longer know of such sorrow as I was then suffering. Imagining this possibility, I was finally able to find some distance from my anguish, and start coming to myself once again.

In the year 1895, in Bielsk, my second child, Regina, was born.[3] The joy she brought me did indeed help to dispel my grief, and, little by little, my still-fresh wound began to heal. It seemed to me that my troubles were now behind me. The heavens began to clear up. I decided, in spite of the pain and yearning it would bring me, not to shlep my new daughter along with me wherever the troupe went. Though she would not be sheltered in the bosom of her mother, she would be raised in an atmosphere of warmth and undisturbed quiet. She would not have to be forever jostled about as we traveled down our weary byways.

I did keep her at my side for a short time, but when she reached the age of three weeks, I sent her off to Warsaw, where, for the first few years of her life, she was raised by my sister. I would travel to see her very often, but I had made a solemn vow to myself that until she had gotten a little older, I would not take her with me on the road.

Once she turned three, she was brought to me, and I reclaimed her. We were playing at that time in Łódź. And from then on, she was always with me.

Soon after she was born, when we were playing in Bielsk, we returned to the cities we had visited on our first tour with the troupe.[4] We were already a familiar entity in those places, and now enjoyed great success in them. They received us quite differently than others did, as they knew us to be decent people. "These *komedyantshikes*," they said, "are nothing like the others. Why, looking at them is like looking at our own precious children!"

And so, little by little, we built up a reputation and a position for ourselves, and doing good business in these places was almost a sure thing. I say "almost" because, in the theatre, there is no such thing as a sure thing, and never has been. There were towns where, after the show, the audience would leave truly inspired, telling us that by the next day, we would certainly be enjoying sold-out houses. But God help us, when the next day came, the take at the box office had dropped considerably from the day before. Or it might happen that folks would advise us to travel to this or that town, promising that we would hit upon an absolute gold mine there. And so, we would leave for the place indicated, our purses puckered in expectation of all the precious metal. The result? We would not even make enough to leave the place.

All of this taught me that in the theatre, one simply cannot count on anything. One might always be met with disappointments such as these, disappointments one might hardly even have dreamt of.

# XLVII TRAGICOMIC EPISODES

Once, when we were preparing to play in a shtetl and could not secure the usual firemen's warehouse, my husband rented out a stable belonging to a local Jew. We shoveled out the manure, ramshackled a stage out of a few errant boards, set up benches, and there—we had a theatre. What we did not have was a roof—just some stray straw over our heads.

Our first offering was to be *Bar Kokhba*. As soon as we started to perform, we heard a rustling up in the thatch. Lifting our eyes, we noticed a strapping youth, lying quite comfortably up there, enjoying the show. We were dumbfounded. What was to be done about this whippersnapper? It was decided, in order not to interrupt the flow of the drama, that we wouldn't bother with the curious character until the act was completed. Instead, we'd just ask him, for the meantime, to lie there as quietly as he could, so as not to disrupt the performance. But he soon took up a different tactic.

Once the actor playing Bar Kokhba appeared onstage, the boy hailed him from on high and called out, quite loudly: "Long live the greatest of Jewish heroes, Bar Kokhba!" And when Papus[1] came on, the boy shouted again, mispronouncing the character's name, "Pakus! Little Pakus! May he live long, too, and get even redder in the face!"

All of us onstage were beside ourselves with anger, but nonetheless, could not help bursting out in laughter, howling so loudly and uncontrollably that the audience noticed and joined us in our mirthquake. And wouldn't you know? Our overhead guest, the turkey in the straw, quaked right along with them.

So quakingly did he quake that the thatch gave way, and the boy came crashing down onto the stage, where he lay prostrate before the throne of Bar Kokhba. Of course, the audience absolutely lapped this up and applauded raucously. The whole place was in stitches. Thankfully, I had not completely lost my senses and quickly ordered the curtain to be lowered. As soon as it came down, all of us actors descended upon our uninvited guest and let him have it so severely that one day he must surely have warned his children and his children's children, too, never to try any such tricks as he just had.

Soon we were in a new city—Berdychiv, if memory serves—and were met with the following situation. The municipal theatre was occupied at the time and we were left with no choice but to rent out a wedding hall and perform there. The lack of a stage was the main difficulty. But we found a solution: dragging together a pair of long banquet tables, we set them up on a kind of makeshift scaffolding, then rigged it all together, and voilà: a stage. And so that it would actually look like one, we hung some linen over the fronts and sides of the tables.

Then we realized we had entirely forgotten to arrange the prompter's box. But thank God, in that same building, there happened to be a little fruit and soda water shop. So we got our hands on a large box of lemons and set it up in front of the stage for the prompter, Herman Fisher, to station himself at. We covered that with linen, too, and so made it as one with the stage.

For a sign of when to raise the curtain, we decided the prompter would snuff out a little candle. But as fate would have it, the wind had its own way with the candle, and as soon as it went out, the stagehand in charge of the curtain, a local Ukrainian, yanked the rope, and up went the green chintz. The cries of the actors were useless. The stagehand could not have cared less about our success, and stopped up his ears. "The prompter," he said to us, "taught me just what to do, and told me not to listen to anyone, that I just gotta keep my eyes on the candle."

In case all that is not enough for you, it so happens that in the same city, in that same venue, the following took place. At that time, if I'm not mistaken, Abelman[2] was playing Bar Kokhba. Now, Abelman, as everyone knows, is no featherweight when it comes to the scale. At one performance, he was not being very careful and completely forgot that on our Berdychiv wedding stage, one must tread very lightly. And so, at a certain point in the operetta, standing on one end of a table, he stamped his foot a bit too hard. The entire stage swayed to one side under his force, as he tried to right it by planting the weighty bulk of his body on the other side. It was no good. Soon Bar Kokhba, in all of his majesty, was flat on his face.

The linen that had been hung up around the tables and the prompter's booth tore away, meanwhile, as the prompter sat in the now exposed box, convulsed with laughter. The audience, which always loves witnessing such catastrophes, erupted into such riotous cachinnation that it became difficult to finish the performance. It was only with great effort that we were able to quiet them down.

And of course, during this disaster, when it would have been the perfect moment for the Ukrainian to do his duty and lower the curtain, he—of course—could not manage.

Such tragicomic episodes as these followed us wherever we went.

# XLVIII THE CITY OF ŁÓDŹ

There was still no use talking of our performing someday in Warsaw. The city's chief of police now categorically refused to authorize the performance of any "German-Jewish" theatre. And so we set our eyes on Łódź.

We were always trying to seek out the permit to perform there. But we were not the only ones hungry for the juicy morsel that the city represented. Spivakovski, Fishzon, and others were also using every trick in the book to try to acquire the elusive Łódź permit for their own troupes. How we exulted, then, when we were informed that our efforts had not been in vain and we had finally been authorized to give a decent number of performances in the city.

And so we began to get together a troupe for Łódź. I must acknowledge that this was, for that period, a truly first-class troupe. And our repertoire, which was already nothing to sniff at, was made even more impressive with the addition of a few new plays, among them *Doctor Almasado*, in which I played the role of the daughter, Miryem.[1]

Our first venue in Łódź was the Arkadia, a summer theatre founded by the Polish impresario Sellin. Our sales there absolutely sparkled. At the Arkadia, we were brought back to life, and finally had the chance to rest our legs and stay a while after the constant shlepping about. We were even thinking we might settle in Łódź for good.

During this period, my husband took ill, which left him unable to carry out his management duties. And of course, there was no end of curious little circumstances to manage. Once, such a fierce wind blew that it carried away the Arkadia's wooden ticket booth along with the cashier as she sat inside it. That incident engraved itself deeply in my memory, owing to the nearly tragic fate of the girl. She was such a helpless, clumsy thing that she proved completely incapable of extricating herself.

We also performed for a spell in the Waldschlösschen[2] Garden, where today the Kalisher railway station stands.[3] There we played under the open sky, just as the ancient Greeks once had. It was not uncommon that we had to call off a performance due to rain.

And so a good bit of time passed. We played, and earned quite well, until we started to attract some crooked glances "from above."[4] There was nothing we could do about it, so we had to once again hit the trail. Unfortunately, on the journey between Lublin and Zamość,[5] I was robbed. Some thief managed to nab from my purse the entirety of the small sum we could call our own. Vicious wagging tongues would later spread the rumor that it was one of our own actresses who had done it. In any case, it left us in a desperate state.

In Zamość, my husband put on his new play, *Ibn Ezra*,[6] with which he enjoyed great success. Both cities, Lublin and Zamość, were able to get us back on our feet and, little by little, we were able to save up a groschen or two once more.

After a couple of months, I again gave birth to a daughter, and again my sister took the infant back to live with her in Warsaw. This little girl did not live long, and she died in Warsaw while in the care of her wet nurse. My rock of consolation remained Regina, who was growing up to be a clever and pretty girl.

# XLIX *CHERTA OSEDLOSTI* (THE PALE OF SETTLEMENT)

My long and perilous path, overhung by thorns, stretched out across cities and towns, amid fields and forests.[1] Winter and summer, autumn and spring, my walking stick remained in my hand. We had grown so accustomed to this life of ceaseless wandering that we had stopped even dreaming of a permanent home. The new theatre being built in Łódź, upon which we had pinned all of our hopes, was not yet finished.

A few months passed and—as was quickly becoming routine—I gave birth to another child. This time, however, it was a little boy: Yoysef-Hirsh. This was during the most bitterly cold days of 1897,[2] when the troupe and I were in Homel.[3] The child had barely reached two weeks when it was time for him to share our fate and join us in our life of exile. Our first journey with our newest recruit was from Homel to Chernigov, on a horse-drawn omnibus. The child was stationed in a corner of the vehicle with his wet nurse. Such a stabbing frost filled the air that all the passengers had wound themselves up tightly in their coats and never stopped tapping their feet on the ground in an effort to warm themselves.

Yes, such was the first journey of Yoysef-Hirsh—and his last. The poor soul was suffocated while nursing. It turned out that the wet nurse, having hunched over in a tightly coiled position, so as to protect herself from the cold, forgot about the child at her breast and had inadvertently smothered him. Others reckoned that the child had frozen to death, because on the same journey, the cheeks of Rotshayn's young son had been touched with frostbite.

Once my troupemates noticed what had happened to my little boy, he was already dead. But no one spoke a word of it to me until we arrived at Chernigov. Earlier, I had observed that my husband was deathly pale, and everyone else was trying not to meet my eye. My heart told me that some disaster had befallen us. When I asked what it was, everyone just told me about Rotshayn's boy and his frozen cheeks. But little by little, I began to guess at what had taken place.

Finally, one of my fellow actresses delivered the tragic news. Yoysef-Hirsh was buried in the Jewish cemetery of Chernigov. And on the day of his burial, I had to go and perform. We were putting on *Kenig akhashveyresh*—King Ahasuerus.[4] Even as my heart throbbed with grief, I went on and played Queen Esther.[5] It was no coincidence that the next day, people all over town were raving about how the queen had performed as though she were actually undergoing some excruciating ordeal.

It is worth noting that when I played Queen Esther, it was like celebrating my name day, my *imeniny*, as it is called in Russian.[6] I was named for Queen Esther, and deeply loved playing the role, which was also one of my best.

We played for two weeks in Chernigov then left for Niezhin.[7] There we battled numbingly cold temperatures in a venue designed as a summer theatre. No other theatre existed in the city at the time. My teeth chattered as I performed, and every minute I had to dislodge icicles from my nostrils. I recall a certain incident in Niezhin, when one of the place's most eminent citizens came running up to Kaminski during a performance, pointing to me and bellowing, "Murderer! What do you want from this poor creature? She'll literally freeze alive, right there where she stands!"

But just try and tell this conscientious "friend" that my husband himself was terribly ill, and for him to play under such conditions was far more dangerous than for me. After all, I was an extraordinarily healthy person, at least physically. There was a reason that people used to joke that Kaminska was simply *unable* to get sick. But there was no other option. The show had to go on, no matter the conditions. And if it didn't, even for a couple of weeks, starvation would follow.

But as with all things in this world, the cold soon passed, too. Winter yielded its place to spring, that season so lovely and so full of promise. And with the weather, my heart also became a less burdensome thing. A new ray of hope stole its way into me, and I thought to myself, "God! Perhaps the day has dawned at last when we, too, might enjoy a better life."

We came to Kiev. We were not permitted to play in the city itself, since it was, as they say in Russian, *vne cherti*, that is, beyond the Pale, being among those metropolises whose doors the empire had slammed shut to the Jews, who were forbidden from living or doing business within the city limits.[8] And so we rented a theatre in Slobodka, a suburb of Kiev, situated on the other side of the Dnieper River. Slobodka belonged to the Chernigov governorate, which was considered to be *within* the Pale of Settlement—or *cherta osedlosti* in Russian—the western outskirts of the empire where Jews were permitted to live. We stayed in Slobodka and performed there exclusively. We would spend whole days in Kiev, as we were able to walk about on its boulevards as freely as we liked, but as for sleeping, doing business, putting on theatre there—those things we could not do.

The theatre in Slobodka belonged to an engineer who happened to own some little boats. Quite often, we went out on the Dnieper in them, admiring the splendid city of Kiev. I still remember those evenings when the sun had just begun to go down, and its rays went bouncing off the cupolas of Kiev's countless churches, which were turned gold by the dimming light, as were half the heavens. Rare indeed that one gets to see such a dazzling panorama.

It is a well-known fact that it was precisely in those places near restricted zones where a troupe could do its very best sales. We had such a smashing success outside Kiev that we almost needed new purses to hold all the money we were making. And after giving a successful performance, it was always such a pleasure to watch all the boats launching onto the Dnieper, like swarms of locusts over the water, ferrying home those privileged audience members who were permitted to live in the city.[9]

In that city, a couple of new actors joined us, among them a young man by the name of Artshikhes, known today as Yulius Adler or "Yudke,"[10] as we all called him, and as we still call him today. He came to us in a frightful condition: clothed in rags, disheveled, and wasting away from hunger. Even just to glance upon him was startling. As we were acquainted with him from before and knew him to be a very musical young man, we hired him, initially just as a copyist of sheet music, a job in which he excelled. We also bought a bit of linen so that new underwear could be made for him. In no time at all, he felt at home among us. And being a very smart boy, he won our hearts, too. From that time on, he traveled with us everywhere, as a performer.

We played outside Kiev that whole summer, then when it got to be chilly and we could no longer play in the summer theatre, we traveled back to Homel. From there we carried onward to Vinnytsia.[11] It had no theatre, just a hall where Durov's circus happened to be playing.[12] It was doing brilliant business, and so Durov had no desire to give up its spot to us. When folks in the city interceded on our behalf, though, he relented, handed us the keys to the hall for a while, and went off with his circus to another town.

But of course, a new difficulty soon presented itself: Vinnytsia's mayor found out about us. After that, all of our arguments and entreaties proved worthless. We were denied permission to perform and had to travel on. But of course, a new difficulty soon presented itself: Vinnytsia's mayor found out about us.

# L THE WRITER DOVID FRISHMAN

We arrived safely in Łódź and began performing in the newly constructed Jewish theatre at No. 14 Constantine Street.[1] Never before had we played such a theatre, and it would be no hyperbole to say this venue could have gone right up against the best Gentile theatres in the land. It had a splendid stage with magnificent sets. The dressing rooms were big and bright. The auditorium had two tiers, furnished and ornamented in the most elegant style. I could go on and on!

And so we got to work, there in Łódź's grand new theatre. The makeup of the troupe was as follows: myself, my husband, and Herman Berman (the triumvirate directorship), Rapel and his first wife Ruzhe Horn,[2] Blifeld,[3] Yulius Adler, Herman Fisher, Gothard, Titelman, and others. Our repertoire at the time consisted exclusively of operettas, mostly Goldfaden's. As the local population's interest in theatre was tremendous, we did tip-top business there in Łódź. I was able to bring down little Regina from Warsaw, and from then on, she stayed with me.

One night, when I did my usual peek through the curtains before they were raised to see how the house was looking, I noticed a person who made me immensely curious. Then, all of a sudden, his eye met mine, this person I'd taken such an instant liking to. From the way he looked at me, I could sense that he would have a deep understanding of all that I was to speak and sing. We repeated this same routine for a number of nights, and he was always seated in the exact same spot.

Once I asked my husband, "Tell me, Kaminski, who is that gentleman who comes almost every night and sits in the same seat? He must be some kind of doctor?"

Why I guessed, quite out of the blue, that he was a doctor, I cannot understand to this day. Perhaps it was because he was wearing a pince-nez and had such refined, graceful features.

"No," my husband said to me, "that's a writer. Frishman, he's called. We're acquainted with each other."[4]

"Oy," I sighed. "He has such a nice, noble-looking face, like a doctor. I wouldn't mind getting acquainted with him, too."

A couple of days later, after I'd sung an act finale and the curtain was raised and lowered a number of times for the enthusiastic ovation, I noticed Frishman applauding for me with particular vigor. Shortly after, he ascended the stage to introduce himself to me, which left me positively blissful. I went on to finish the operetta with what I considered to be a double dose of success.

After the performance, my husband invited Frishman to follow us home. He did so—together with Hershke Epelberg,[5] who was later to become a theatre director in Warsaw—and we treated him to a fine reception.

From the outset, Frishman was absolutely overflowing with good-natured jokes. I can still hear them to this very day, wonderful and witty as they were. He told them in this unique, serious manner that made them even more delightful to hear. His entire style of speaking was calm, quiet, and unassuming. Among other things, he told us that he knew many actors and was close with Goldfaden himself. He had even helped the maestro finish his operetta *King Ahasuerus* and coached Mrs. Tantsman, the piece's first Queen Esther, on the text.

Thus unfolded the first evening of our acquaintanceship. When we said our goodbyes, I said to him, "Herr Frishman, I am ever so pleased that you came. How proud I feel that you have graced my home with your presence."

At these words, he pushed up his pince-nez, and answered me:

"If the tsar himself can take luncheon at Tantsman's place, then surely I can come eat at yours."

He said it so seriously that I truly believed that this luncheon had taken place. Then he repeated it:

"Yes, yes, Madame Kaminska, the actor himself told me that he had the tsar over for lunch."

When I noticed that everyone else had erupted into fits of laughter, however, I realized it was a joke.

After that, Frishman would regularly come up and see us in our dressing rooms, which were on the third floor of the theatre, off a long, dark hallway. There were always dozens of barrels of beer set up there, as the space served as storage for the theatre's concessions. And since the author was dangerously nearsighted, he would often stumble over a barrel and fall to the ground. But

it did not stop him from coming up to visit me along with the living quarters
of the actors, which were higher up in the same building, in little garret
rooms with windows jutting out onto the roof. Almost all of the actors in the
troupe lived there, including the Berman family, Rapel, Adler, and others.

Quite often, we used to all play cards together and chat about theatre. For
Frishman, there was no such thing as a bad actor nor a bad play. Everything
was good in his eyes, not, of course, because he lacked understanding, but
rather just the opposite. He understood the art so well, and therefore forgave
us so much. Our stage German amused him most of all. Not seldom, he
used to offer the actors corrections:

"Children," he would caution us, "don't say '*dos Platz*.' It is '*der Platz*,'"[6]
and other such things. And when we were eventually forbidden from
playing in Łódź, indeed because of our untidy Yiddish-German, it made
him so miserable, as if his own existence were tied up with ours.

But then fate parted us. We actors took our walking sticks in hand and
set off, as was our wont, into the wide, waiting world. When we returned
to Łódź many years later, I learned that Frishman had left town for St.
Petersburg and gotten married, receiving 10,000 rubles as a dowry.

"Nu," I thought to myself, "now Frishman certainly won't want to sit and
banter with the likes of us."

But years later, fate reunited us in Warsaw, where he was then living with
his very elegant wife. He had heard that we were playing in the Bagatela
Theatre and was the first to come calling on us.

But we will get to that eventually.[7]

How deeply aggravated he was by the press in Warsaw, when, since the
moment our troupe eventually settled there, it had ripped me to shreds. But
how happy he was years later, when I returned from St. Petersburg myself
after performing in the city, and he read the exultant odes I received from
the Petersburg press, which turned the tide in my favor among Warsaw's
journalists. His face beaming, he ran from one person to another and
exclaimed:

"Nu, what did I tell you about Kaminska? Is she a great artist or is she
not?"[8] (Figures 12 and 13)

But we will leave that for now to carry on recounting in the proper order.

And so, with heavy hearts, we left the city of Łódź, hoping to return there
as soon as we were able.

**FIGURES 12 AND 13** A studio portrait of Kaminska from her latter years, together with its original negative. It is labeled with the Polish name of the city in which it was taken, Baranowicze (now in Belarus, where it is called Baranavichy), as well as the name of the photographer, J. Ejgel. The subject is identified as "Art. E. R. Kaminska," the "Art." standing for the Polish *artystka*, equivalent to the Yiddish *artistke*—actress. Photograph and negative image (YIVO, RG 120, Folder 61, "Poland," Item 2).

# NOTES

## Introduction

1 The original title under which Kaminska's memoirs posthumously ran in the Warsaw daily *Der moment*, from 1926 to 1927, was *Derner un blumen: der veg fun mayn lebn—memuarn* (Thorns and Flowers: The Path of My Life—Memoirs).

2 One of Kaminska's biographers, Zalmen Zylbercweig, states that she was born on Purim, but her daughter Ida writes in her own memoir that her mother, who never used to give out the Gregorian date of her birth, would always say that she was born on *Tanes-ester*—the Fast of Esther—that is, the day before Purim. Other sources also state the latter, and Ida's specific memory of her mother's habit, and her obvious closeness with Ester-Rokhl, lends her account veracity. It seems likely to me from these differing accounts (Ester-Rokhl herself writes in the memoir of her birthday being celebrated on Purim) that she may have been born on the eve of Purim, at night, which would be coterminous with the close of the Fast of Esther, as Jewish holidays begin and end at sundown. It is also possible that she was born on the Fast of Esther during the day, but that any festivities on her behalf were postponed to Purim, the fast day naturally being a solemn observance, with any celebrations or feasting being impossible. It so happens that Zylbercweig dates her birth an entire month early, February 15, not heeding the fact that the year of Kaminska's birth was a leap year in the Hebrew calendar, and so both the Fast of Esther and Purim would have been observed in the added month of Adar II (in March 1870), rather than in Adar I (in February 1870). He also misreports the date of her death, which is accurately reported the day after it took place in *Der moment*, the newspaper that would publish her memoirs. Zalmen Zylbercweig, *Di velt fun ester rokhl kaminska* (The World of Ester-Rokhl Kaminska) (Mexico City: Imprenta Moderna Pintel, S. A., 1969), 7; Ida Kaminska, *My Life, My Theater*, ed. and trans. Curt Leviant (New York: Macmillan, 1973), 8; "Geshtorbn ester

rokhl kaminska" (Ester-Rokhl Kaminska Dead), *Der moment* (Warsaw), December 28, 1925, 1.

**3** *Tkies-kaf* (The Vow) directed by Zygmunt Turkow (Poland: Leo-Forbert, 1924), later rereleased with added sound as *A vilner legende (Dem rebns koyekh)* (A Vilna Legend (The Rabbi's Power)), directed by George Roland (Poland: Leo-Film, 1933; National Center for Jewish Film, 2002), DVD.

**4** Nahma Sandrow, *Vagabond Stars: A World History of Yiddish Theater* (New York: Harper and Row, 1977), 57.

**5** Alyssa Quint, *The Rise of the Modern Yiddish Theatre* (Bloomington: Indiana University Press, 2019), 119, 186, 192. Quint's study also provides extensive analyses of Goldfaden's operettas, which were the artistic anchor of the Yiddish theatre from its beginnings under his stewardship in and around Odessa from 1876 to 1883, and, during the following twenty years, the stock-in-trade of Kaminska's troupe.

**6** Translations are by Yashinsky in all cases, except where noted otherwise. Zylbercweig, *Di velt*, 82. In the first European production of the play in 1906, Kaminska played Mirele's unfailingly dedicated maid, Makhle, and she would first play the title role in 1908 (ibid., 74). She later played her in a now-lost silent picture, shot in 1912 and directed by Yiddish playwright Mark Arnshteyn, with her daughter Ida making her film début in the role of Mirele's grandson, Shloymele (ibid., 228).

**7** Ida Kaminska, typewritten Yiddish-language manuscript of memoirs (YIVO, RG 994: Ida Kaminska and Meir Melman, Box 8, Folder 10, 1). Later published in translation as *My Life, My Theater*.

**8** Zygmunt Turkow, "Der ondenk" (The Memorial) in Zylbercweig, *Di velt*, 216–17; Yoysef Sandel, "Fishl Rubinlikht" in *Umgekumene yidishe kinstler in poyln* (Murdered Jewish Artists in Poland) (Warsaw: Yidish-Bukh, 1957), 2: 113. Sandel writes that Rubinlikht belonged to a school of interwar sculptors in Poland whose chief goal was "to animate the material and bring forth the image in its rhythmic beauty." He was one of the artists encouraged by the great writer and convener of creative salons Y. L. Peretz, chiefly known for his short stories and poetry. Kaminska would eventually find herself in the same artistic circles that orbited around Peretz. In 1906, she performed, along with her then Warsaw-based troupe, in one of Peretz's typically literary and abstruse dramas *Di goldene keyt* (The Golden Chain), then known as *Der nisoyen* (The Test) (Zylbercweig, *Di velt*, 64). The sculptor Rubinlikht would eventually be among the first Jewish victims of the Second World War, when he was struck by a bomb during the German bombardment of Warsaw in September 1939, and, being left untreated at the city's Evangelical Hospital, died shortly thereafter.

9 There was a dispute between those among Kaminska's family and friends who were erecting her monument and an official at the cemetery tasked with ensuring that all gravestones were kosher. This official claimed that the lion's face was too like a person's, thus defying the solemn prohibition against creating graven images of human figures. Apparently, after some retouching of the marble, the monument finally passed inspection and was allowed to be unveiled on the planned date. Turkow, "Der ondenk," in Zylbercweig, *Di velt*, 216–17.

10 "The legendary figure of the movies." Rifke Zilberg (Kadia Molodowsky), "Greta Garbo" (YIVO, RG 703: Kadia Molodowsky, Box 4, Folder 68, 1).

11 Ibid., "Ester-Rokhl Kaminska," Folder 67, 2.

12 Ida Kaminska, *My Life*, 8.

13 Ibid., 1.

14 Zygmunt Turkow, *Fragmentn fun mayn lebn: zikhroynes* (Fragments of My Life: Memoirs), in *Dos poylishe yidntum* (Polish Jewry), ed. Mark Turkow, vol. 75 (Buenos Aires: Tsentral-farband fun poylishe yidn in argentine, 1951), 230. Zygmunt Turkow, also an actor, was at the time of his memoir's publication Kaminska's former son-in-law, having been married to her daughter Ida from 1918 until their divorce in 1931. Eleonora Duse (1858–1924) was a renowned Italian tragedienne, considered one of the greatest actresses of her day, and likened to Kaminska for the sensitive realism of their acting styles. Turkow adds yet another title to Kaminska's list: "the Jewish Komissarzhevskaya," Vera Komissarzhevskaya (1864–1910) being considered Russia's leading actress in the same period.

15 She was usually addressed as Rokhl by her friends and family, and especially in her youth, by the diminutive form Rokhele.

16 Ester-Rokhl Kaminska, "Kurtse avtobiografye fun ester-rokhl kaminska" (Short Autobiography of Ester-Rokhl Kaminska), *Literarishe bleter* (Literary Pages) (Warsaw), no. 87, January 1, 1926: 17, originally published in the journal *Teater* (Theatre) (Warsaw), no. 1, 1925.

17 J. Hoberman, *Bridge of Light: Yiddish Film Between Two Worlds* (Philadelphia: Temple University Press, 1995), 228. Hoberman cites other examples, writing that Kaminska, the actress-heroine of Sholem Aleichem's novel of the Yiddish theatre *Blondzhende shtern* (Wandering Stars, 1909–11), actors Boris Thomashefsky, Sigmund Mogulesko, and

Seymour Rechtzeit, and composer Sholem Secunda, who wrote the hit song "Ba mir bistu sheyn," were all the children of cantors or themselves served as *meshorerim* (choir boys) in their youth.

18  Sholem Aleichem, *Yosele solovey* (1889), in *Ale verk fun sholem-aleykhem* (Collected Works of Sholem Aleichem), vol. 3, *Stempenyu; Yosele solovey* (Moscow: Der emes, 1948), 201.

19  Zylbercweig, *Di velt*, 3–4.

20  Ibid., 3.

21  From 1882 to 1914, the population of Warsaw increased by 131 percent, with the increase of Jewish residents being markedly higher than that of Polish residents, 163.5 percent to 118.7 percent. Stephen D. Corrsin, *Warsaw Before the First World War: Poles and Jews in the Third City of the Russian Empire, 1889–1914* (Boulder: East European Monographs, 1989), 22, 24. For more on the acculturation of these new Warsovian Jews to the city's increasingly secular mode, see Corrsin, *Warsaw Before the First World War*, 31–8, and for further background, Piotr Wròbel, "Jewish Warsaw Before the First World War," in *Polin: Studies in Polish Jewry*, ed. Antony Polonsky, vol. 3, *The Jews of Warsaw* (Liverpool: Liverpool University Press, 2004), 156–87.

22  Scott Ury, *Barricades and Banners: The Revolution of 1905 and the Transformation of Warsaw Jewry* (Stanford: Stanford University Press, 2012), 56–8. For women's occupations, see Glenn Dynner, "Those Who Stayed: Women and Jewish Traditionalism in East Central Europe," in *New Directions in the History of the Jews in the Polish Lands*, eds. Antony Polonsky, Hanna Węgrzynek, and Andrzej Żbikowski (Boston: Academic Studies Press, 2018), 295–312.

23  Ury, *Barricades and Banners*, 61–4.

24  For a full translation of this seminal work's libretto, see Quint, *The Rise*, Appendix II.

25  Sandrow, *Vagabond Stars*, 57.

26  Kaminska, "Kurtse avtobiografye," 17. The name, often appearing as *yidish-daytsh-teater*, is also used to refer to this translingual historical form of Yiddish theatre more generally. Yitskhok Turkow-Grudberg, *Yidish teater in poyln* (Yiddish Theatre in Poland) (Warsaw: Yidish-bukh, 1951), 14.

27  When teaching the memoirs in a Yiddish course for the Workers Circle entitled "On the Road with Ester-Rokhl," I gave a lighthearted assignment: asking the students to pretend they were Ester-Rokhl's friend and help her craft a profile for a nineteenth-century dating app after kicking

several unworthy bachelors to the curb, as she does in the memoir. The results were as humorous as may be expected, with one having Kaminska promote herself thus (translated from the student's Yiddish): "Beautiful Jewish girl seeks a groom. I am fashionable and independent with a pious pedigree and the voice of an angel. Seeking men with manners who know something about theatre. Gold-diggers need not apply."

**28** Zylbercweig, *Di velt*, 201–2.

**29** Yitskhok Turkow-Grudberg, *Di mame ester rokhl* (The Mother Ester-Rokhl) (Warsaw: Yidish-bukh, 1953), 281.

**30** Ibid., 202–3. Turkow-Grudberg only got to a couple of chapters, with Jonas Turkow taking on the rest of the transcription and editing.

**31** Mirosława M. Bułat, "Turkow Family," translated from Polish by Michael C. Steinlauf, in *YIVO Encyclopedia*, www.yivoencyclopedia.org/article .aspx/Turkow_Family. Bułat was the first to publish a complete translation of Kaminska's memoir, which she did, into Polish, in 2020, under the title *Boso przez ciernie i kwiaty* (Barefoot Through Thorns and Flowers) (Warsaw: Wydawnictwo Naukowe PWN, 2020).

**32** I hold that the memoir years are themselves key to an understanding of Yiddish theatrical history, documenting as they do Kaminska's learning from the folk and the folk learning from her in the dissemination of early Yiddish theatre, even in the period when Kaminska was playing ingénues. I would furthermore not characterize the plays Kaminska put on in the period, operettas and melodramas and farces, already received as classics though having been written not long before, as "shund," trash, as neither Kaminska nor her audiences saw them this way. Another researcher, Shelly Zer-Zion, focuses on the mother roles that Kaminska took in the period of her later and greater fame, arguing that as audiences identified with and admired Kaminska's nobly suffering matriarchs, the Yiddish theatre gained a new level of respect. One colorful proof Zer-Zion brings is the great Yiddish writer Peretz—himself a sort of rebbe, or Hasidic master, to his followers, one who spiritually fostered new talent—attending a performance of Kaminska as Gordin's titular orphan girl Khasye in 1905 Warsaw, and, as witnessed by the writer Avrom Reyzen, being deeply moved by the performance: "I see tears in Peretz's large eyes. Big, shining tears. Peretz is crying. It was the greatest wonder, the greatest surprise: the rebbe was crying." Zer-Zion, "Ester Rokhl Kaminska and the Legitimization of Yiddish Theatre," *Journal of Modern Jewish Studies* 16, no. 3 (2017): 471, citing Zylbercweig, *Di velt*, 55–6 (translation here my own).

**33** Secretary of Abraham Cahan to Ester-Rokhl Kaminska, New York, February 5, 1924, YIVO, RG 8, Box 59, Folder 461 ("Correspondence, undated, 1918–1919, 1922–1925"), https://digipres.cjh.org:443/delivery/DeliveryManagerServlet?dps_pid=IE11102068. The phrase "oll rayt" (all right, A-OK!), by then having entered the Yinglish lexicon, appears in typed Yiddish characters like the rest of the letter.

**34** Ibid., May 20, 1924.

**35** Kaminska to Jonas Turkow, Warsaw, June 1924, in Ester-Rokhl Kaminska, *Briv fun ester-rokhl kaminski* (Letters of Ester-Rokhl Kaminska), ed. Mark Turkow (Vilna: B. Kletskin, 1927), 77.

**36** Y. L. Peretz, *Nokh kvure*, in *Di verk fun yitskhok leybush perets* (The Works of Yitskhok Leybush Peretz), ed. Dovid Pinski, vol. 9, *Dramatishe verk* (Dramatic Works) (New York: Farlag idish, 1920), 35.

**37** Fan letter on the occasion of a performance on October 1, 1914 (Odessa) (YIVO, RG 8: Esther-Rachel Kaminska Theater Museum Collection, Box 93, Folder 489), www.archives.cjh.org/repositories/7/archival_objects/1284786.

**38** Undated greeting card (YIVO, RG 8, Box 62, Folder 490), www.archives.cjh.org/repositories/7/archival_objects/1284787. If in the formal register, "dir" (to you) would appear instead as "aykh." One might expect that register would have been preferred here, used as it is for revered figures, people with whom one is not personally acquainted, and people of more advanced age, and Kaminska was all three to this crowd of admirers—but it would seem that a gesture toward familial intimacy is at play.

**39** Playbill for jubilee performance, "XXX-yeriker yuvl fun ester rokhl kaminski" (Thirty-Year Anniversary of [the stage career of] Ester-Rokhl Kaminska" (November 28, 1922, Warsaw) (YIVO, RG 8: Box 47, Folder 112).

**40** Ida Kaminska, *My Life*, 9.

**41** Ibid., 9–10.

**42** Michael C. Steinlauf, "Yiddish Theater," in "Theater," in *YIVO Encyclopedia*, www.yivoencyclopedia.org/article.aspx/Theater/Yiddish_Theater.

**43** Kaminska, "Kurtse avtobiografye," 17.

**44** For more on the particular reforms Gordin introduced into the Yiddish theatre, see Barbara Henry, *Rewriting Russia: Jacob Gordin's Yiddish Drama* (Seattle: University of Washington Press, 2011).

**45** Kaminska, "Kurtse avtobiografye," 17–18.

**46** Ibid., 18.

**47** Kaminska would later take the title role in a Soviet film adaptation of the play, playing opposite Yankev Libert. Zaynvl Diamant, "Z. Libin," in *Leksikon fun der nayer yidisher literatur* (Biographical Dictionary of New Yiddish Literature) (New York: Congress for Jewish Culture, 1963), 5: 44–9.

**48** "Yiddish Drama Tonight," *The Sunday Star* (Washington, DC), February 18, 1912, Part 2, 2.

**49** "Park Theatre," *The Bridgeport Evening Farmer* (Bridgeport, Connecticut), October 16, 1911, 5.

**50** Isidore Busatt, cartoon, "Libt er mikh, oder libt er mikh nit?" (Does he love me or does he not love me?), *Der groyser kundes* (New York), 3, no. 46 (November 17, 1911): 5.

**51** Cahan, "Ver iz a besere . . . ," *Forverts* (New York), December 9, 1911, 10.

**52** Ida Kaminska, *My Life*, 12.

**53** Kaminska, "Kurtse avtobiografye," 18.

**54** Turkow-Grudberg, *Di mame*, 255.

**55** Mikhoel Vaykhert, *Teater un drame* (Theatre and Drama) (Vilna: B. Kletskin, 1926), 1: 60, 62.

**56** Ida Kaminska, *My Life*, 13.

**57** Vaykhert, *Teater un drame*, 1: 60; Bułat, "Turkow Family."

**58** Ida Kaminska, *My Life*, 13.

**59** Ibid.

**60** Turkow-Grudberg, *Di mame*, 92, 281, 283; Zylbercweig, *Di velt*, 29–30.

**61** Ida clarifies that "Aunt Rivka's raising of the children was limited only to our physical development, not our spiritual one," and that though Ester-Rokhl and Avrom-Yitskhok had limited time for their children during the young ones' early years, "they were not stingy with love," particularly Ester-Rokhl. Ida Kaminska, *My Life*, 15.

**62** Zylbercweig, *Di velt*, 21.

**63** Ida Kaminska, *My Life*, 14, 17.

**64** Ibid., 14, 17–19; Kaminska, "Kurtse avtobiografye," 18. Kaminska was keen on her children being finely taught, Yoysef at conservatory to hone his musical abilities, Ida receiving careful tutoring up until the point of university, which, to her mother's regret, she did not attend, being primarily interested in acting. "Had you continued your education, you could have been a Prime Minister," Ester-Rokhl was fond of saying to her.

65  Kaminska to her children, Riga, September 8, 1908; New York, August 17, 1909, in Kaminska, *Briv*, 9, 17.

66  Ibid., Warsaw, March 23, 80–2.

67  The funeral and burial also took place in Łomża, the locals considering it an honor to have the theatre luminary laid to rest in their town. Ester-Rokhl, then in faraway Warsaw administering to their son Yoysef, who was afflicted with typhus, was not present at the ceremonies. Ida Kaminska, *My Life*, 39.

68  Kaminska, "Kurtse avtobiografye," 18.

69  "Jewish Actress Relates her Experiences in Russia and Ukrainia," *The American Jewish World* (St. Paul and Minneapolis), December 31, 1920, 13.

70  "Jewish Theatres in Soviet Russia," *The Jewish Monitor* (Fort Worth-Dallas), December 24, 1920, 1. Notably, both of these plays underline the bad behaviors and avarice exhibited by people involved in capitalist pursuits.

71  Undated playbill (Vilna) (YIVO, RG 8, Box 47, Folder 112), www.archives .cjh.org/repositories/7/archival_objects/1227436. The playbill, and many others like it, forms part of the Esther-Rachel Kaminska Theater Museum Archival Collection (RG 8) at New York's YIVO Institute for Jewish Research. This monumental collection includes materials digitized from the panoply of scripts, costumes, photographs, and theatrical ephemera that Kaminska's daughter Ida and Ida's husband Zygmunt Turkow established as a museum in Kaminska's name in 1926, just a few weeks after her death. The effort to organize the museum was part of the *shloshim* commemoration of the actress. Meaning "thirty," this is the month following a person's passing, during which the living may ensure for the deceased a bountiful share in the world to come by performing good deeds in their honor. The museum was housed in Kaminska's apartment at No. 1 Oboźna Street in Warsaw until its contents were donated to Vilna's YIVO Institute for Jewish Research in 1927. The collection was later transferred to New York and has since been largely digitized. Alyssa Quint, Elana Sara Weber, and Talia Goodman, "A Tale of Two Museums: Ester Rachel Kaminska Theater Museum Collection," www.ataleoftwomuseums.yivo.org/exhibits/show/a-day-at-the-museum

/polandyiddishtheater/polandyiddishtheatermuseum; "Esther-Rachel Kaminska Theater Museum Collection," RG 8, https://archives.cjh.org/repositories/7/resources/19907.

72 Mirosława M. Bułat, "'Cosmopolitan or 'Purely Jewish?': Zygmunt Turkow and the Warsaw Yiddish Art Theatre," in *Inventing the Modern Yiddish Stage: Essays in Drama, Performance, and Show Business*, eds. Joel Berkowitz and Barbara Henry (Detroit: Wayne State University Press, 2012), 117.

73 Kaminska, "Kurtse avtobiografye," 18.

74 Ida Kaminska, *My Life*, 64–5.

75 Ibid., 66.

76 Ibid., 70; "Geshtorbn ester rokhl kaminska," *Der moment*, 1.

77 *Literarishe bleter*, January 1, 1926, 1.

78 "Di grandyeze levaye fun ester rokhl kaminska" (The Grandiose Funeral of Ester-Rokhl Kaminska), *Haynt* (Today) (Warsaw), December 30, 1925, 2.

79 Ibid.

80 Ida Kaminska, *My Life*, 15.

81 Ibid., 228; Małgorzata Leyko, "Polish State Yiddish Theater," translated from Polish by Michael C. Steinlauf, in *YIVO Encyclopedia*, www.yivoencyclopedia.org/article.aspx/polish_state_yiddish_theater. Of the naming ceremony, Ida writes, "It was a great event for me, even though the memorial was nothing new. Various culture centers are named after her, and in Tel Aviv a street bears her name. My mother had always dreamed of a community-supported theater; she never dared dream of a state theater."

82 Turkow-Grudberg, *Di mame*, 283.


# Chapter I

1 Today known as Porazava, and situated in Belarus. In Belarusian, Volkovysk is known as Vawkavysk.

2 Ester-Rokhl Kaminska, "Derner un blumen: der veg fun mayn lebn—memuarn" (Thorns and Flowers: The Path of My Life—Memoirs), *Der moment* (The Moment) (Warsaw), June 11, 1926.

**3** Kaminska's usage here of the term "Gypsy" (in Yiddish, *tsigayner*) would not have been pejorative in this period and context, and her familiarity with Roma people would have been natural, as they have lived in Eastern Europe since the thirteenth century. Like the Jews, Roma were subject to exclusion, persecution, and even enslavement. Numbering perhaps a million people before the Second World War, at least a quarter of the Romani population was murdered by the Nazis.

**4** For more on the Eastern European Jewish charitable institution of the *hegdesh*, see Natan Meir, *Stepchildren of the Shtetl: The Destitute, Disabled, and Mad of Jewish Eastern Europe, 1800–1939* (Stanford: Stanford University Press, 2020).

**5** By a tradition explained in the Talmud, this is commemorated on the seventh of the Hebrew month of Adar, which falls in February or March.

# Chapter II

**1** A slaughterer of animals for kosher meat.

**2** A cantor in a synagogue. It was common in Eastern Europe for one man to occupy both of these positions.

**3** As Passover comes a month after the raucous carnival holiday of Purim, which Jews celebrate with feasts and satirical performances and masquerading (and the giving of charity to the poor).

**4** A dish of carrots stewed together with other fruits and vegetables, including potatoes and prunes, and sometimes meat, it is eaten especially on holidays—or, it seems, when one had a good enough store of dehydrated carrots, all winter long!

**5** A rabbi's wife, in the shtetl often tasked with administering advice to women and providing a traditional Jewish education to girls.

**6** This Torah portion consists of some early chapters in Leviticus and contains the story of the sons of Aaron the High Priest, Nadab and Abihu, who are consumed in a fire sent by God, punishing them for improper service in the Tabernacle. It is read out in synagogue in late March or the beginning of April, thus often signaling the start of spring.

**7** The fifth weekly Torah portion in the book of Numbers, it contains the death of Korah, who leads a rebellion against the leadership of Moses. It is read out in June or July.

**8** The evening prayer service, the last of the three requisite services of the day.

**9** Kaminska, "Derner un blumen," *Der moment*, June 18, 1926.

**10** Not kosher, not adhering to the Jewish dictates of slaughter and food preparation and thus unfit for consumption by adherents of Torah law.

# Chapter III

**1** Gentile girls and Gentile boys. The words—likewise "shegetz," the singular form of shkotzim—often have a pejorative edge, but not so in this chapter's admiring account of Ester-Rokhl's non-Jewish age-mates.

**2** Literally "watched" matzo, its ingredients and production are carefully inspected at every stage. *Shmure* matzo is considered to adhere even more strictly to the commandments of matzo-baking than any other kind of matzo and so is especially suitable for use in a rabbi's home or for display on the ceremonial seder plate.

**3** With only eighteen minutes allowed for the production of matzo from start to finish, any dough left behind and not baked immediately into matzos would render the next batch unkosher for the holiday.

**4** In the Yiddish dialect spoken by many Litvaks ("Lithuanians"), Jews of the former Polish-Lithuanian Commonwealth, within the historic borders of which Porozove is located, sibilant sounds like *s*, *sh*, and *ts* mingled, thus the discrepancy in the pronunciation of this woman's name. "Tsirlen" happens also to be a verb meaning "to twitter, to chatter," leading to Ester-Rokhl's wonderful wordplay in the following line, where she says that over the course of several weeks, the matter "hot . . . zikh . . . avekgetshirlt" (more or less: "was chattered away").

**5** A young Gentile man.

**6** Kaminska, "Derner un blumen," *Der moment*, June 25, 1926.

**7** Praising the Lord "who with His power and might fills the world," this blessing is uttered upon hearing thunder or witnessing hurricanes, earthquakes, and other extraordinary or potentially destructive natural phenomena.

**8** The ultimate credo of the Jewish faith, referred to by its first two words, meaning, "Hear, o Israel." In addition to being customarily said multiple times a day, it is also uttered at moments of distress or when one's life is in danger.

**9** A busy street in the shopping district of Warsaw's former Jewish quarter.

# Chapter IV

**1** A pogrom was carried out against the Jews of Warsaw on Christmas of 1881. It lasted three days and led to the death of at least one Jew, the ruin of many homes and businesses, and the flight of many Jews from the city.

**2** Meaning "peacock" in Polish (cognate to the Yiddish *pave*), this street was situated in the largely Jewish Muranów neighborhood of Warsaw, and later, during the Second World War, the Warsaw Ghetto.

**3** These pronouns characteristic of the *Varshever* (Warsovian) Yiddish dialect are distinct from those of Kaminska's native *Litvish* (Lithuanian) Yiddish (Kaminska's shtetl Porozove was situated in the historical domain of northeastern Europe known as *Lite*, Yiddish for "Lithuania"). The Warsaw Yiddish *yakh* is, in Standard Yiddish (which in large part resembles Kaminska's native *Litvish* Yiddish), *ikh* (I); *yo* (shortened from *iyo*) is a formal second-person singular pronoun in Warsaw Yiddish, appearing as *ir* in Standard Yiddish; *ets* also corresponds to Standard Yiddish *ir* (you, formal or plural); and *enk* to Standard Yiddish *aykh* (the objective form of you, formal or plural).

**4** This was the Great Synagogue of Warsaw, teasingly referred to as the "German Shul" for its more modern style of prayer, with a cantor leading a male choir (like Kaminska's brother's shul in Germany), and the elegant, formal manner of its congregants.

**5** Kaminska, "Derner un blumen," *Der moment*, July 2, 1926.

**6**  About halfway between Warsaw and Łódź.

**7**  The town served as administrative center for the district in which Ester-Rokhl's family lived.

**8**  A city now known as Jurbarkas, in modern-day Lithuania. It was common for yeshiva students from far-off places to have designated days for being fed at various family homes in the towns where they studied, a custom known as *esn teg* ("eating days").

**9**  This is a hallmark of *sabesdiker losn* ("Sabbath language") alluded to earlier in the divorce case of Tshirl aka Tsirl (see note 4, Chapter III). The dialect receives its name from the Yiddish word for Sabbath, *shabes*, and for language, *loshn*, being pronounced by its speakers as *sabes* and *losn*. This consonant switch characterizes the speech of many *Litvish* ("Lithuanian") Jews, that is, "Litvaks" (though not, apparently, that of Kaminska).

# Chapter V

**1**  A city then in the Grodno governorate, around 15 miles northwest of Porozove. Today, like Porozove, it is part of Belarus, near the border with Poland.

**2**  Kaminska, "Derner un blumen," *Der moment*, July 9, 1926.

**3**  Named for its sandy finish, from the Polish word for sand, "piasek."

**4**  Possibly a local word for the famous onion-topped flat roll known as a bialy, alternately referred to in Yiddish as a *bialistoker kukhn* (Białystok cake).

**5**  Kaminska, "Derner un blumen," *Der moment*, July 16, 1926.

**6**  The culture of the *Litvish* ("Lithuanian") Jews, or "Litvaks," was praised for its intellectual air, and mocked—by the Litvaks' coreligionists who came from parts south—for its coldness.

**7**  Litvaks were more likely to use Russian words in their Yiddish than Jews from certain other regions, who might more commonly have borrowed from any number of languages including Polish, Hungarian, and German, depending on where they resided.

# Chapter VI

1 Known in Polish as the "Krakowskie Przedmieście," which means the same thing as what Keyle calls it in Yiddish translation ("*krokover forshtot*").

# Chapter VII

1 A splendidly adorned public park in the center of the city. It was laid out in the late seventeenth century by Augustus II the Strong, king of Poland and elector of Saxony.

2 The French-language opera *Faust* by Charles Gounod (1859).

# Chapter VIII

1 Kaminska, "Derner un blumen," *Der moment*, July 23, 1926.

2 Avrom Goldfaden (1840–1908) is considered the "Father of Yiddish Theatre" for having first professionalized the form to a high artistic degree and popularized it throughout Eastern Europe and eventually the New World. By 1877, he was touring with his own troupe of actors performing pieces he had written himself, largely operettas and comedies. Seth L. Wolitz, "Avrom Goldfadn," in *YIVO Encyclopedia*, https://encyclopedia.yivo.org/article/1282.

3 Yoysef Goldshmidt, an early actor in the Goldfaden Troupe, originated the role of Elieyzer in Goldfaden's opera *Bar Kokhba* (1883), which concerns the ancient Jewish revolt against the Romans, led by the eponymous hero.

4 Also in a heavily Jewish area of Warsaw, just a few blocks away from Pawia Street where Kaminska lived with her sisters.

5 *Shulamis, oder bas-yerusholaim* (Shulamis, or: The Daughter of Jerusalem) (1881), set in biblical times, is perhaps the most famous and well beloved of Goldfaden's operas. The title character is a passionate woman who loves but is deserted by a man above her station. The title of this choral number translates to "Laden with all kinds of good things" and is sung by a group of pilgrims from Bethlehem traveling to Jerusalem for a religious festival. A complete translation of the operetta by Yiddish theatre historian Nahma

Sandrow, which was produced at Harvard in 2009 by Debra Caplan, another Yiddish theatre historian, can be found at Sandrow's website, www.nahmasandrow.com/yiddish-plays-translated-and-edited/shulamis-or-the-daughter-of-jerusalem/.

6   The Jewish neighborhood centered around Smocza Street was known for its poverty and high rate of crime. There, tens of thousands of Jews lived packed into the characteristic residences of such neighborhoods—groups of three apartment buildings surrounding a central courtyard, or *hoyf*. Benny Mer, "Reimagining the Lively Character of Pre-War Smocza Street," *The Forward*, May 2, 2017.

7   In Polish, *Ulica Długa*. Kaminska refers to it by its Yiddish name, *Lange gas*.

8   Avrom-Yitskhok Tantsman (1857–1906) was a Yiddish theatre star born in Warsaw. Chronicler of the Yiddish theatre Zalmen Zylbercweig, in an article that appeared in 1929, called him "der libling" (the darling) of the Polish Yiddish theatre audience of his day. "Avrom-Yitskhok Tantsman," in *Leksikon fun yidishn teater*, ed. Zalmen Zylbercweig (Warsaw: Hebrew Actors Union of America, 1934), 2: 852–3.

9   A holy day commemorating the destruction of the two ancient temples in Jerusalem, as well as other calamities throughout Jewish history. Tisha b'Av and Yom Kippur are the two days on the Jewish calendar on which full sundown-to-sundown fasts are observed.

10   Yiddish actress Berta Tantsman (1856–1926), wife of fellow Goldfaden actor Avrom-Yitskhok Tantsman, with whom she later established an eponymous ensemble of their own. "Berta Tantsman" in Zylbercweig, *Leksikon*, 2: 854; Anna Kuligowska-Korzeniewska, "The Polish *Shulamis*: Jewish Drama on the Polish Stage in the Late 19th–Early 20th Centuries," in *Jewish Theatre: A Global View*, ed. Edna Nahshon (Leiden: Brill, 2009), 84.

11   Yankev Spivakovski (1852–1919) was a Goldfaden actor who in 1887 toured Yiddish theatres in America with scenes from the composer's operettas, including *Bar Kokhba*. He was one of the best-known Jewish theatrical entrepreneurs in Russia, performing throughout the Pale during the years of the ban on Yiddish-language theatre. Spivakovski led one of the first Yiddish companies to return to St. Petersburg in March 1905, when the ban was widely (if erroneously) believed to have expired. "Yankev Spivakovski," in Zylbercweig, *Leksikon*, 2: 1528–35.

# Chapter IX

1. Kaminska, "Derner un blumen," *Der moment*, July 30, 1926.

2. Delfina Potocka (1807–77), Polish socialite and noblewoman, was a muse to such artists as the composer Frédéric Chopin.

3. A Yiddish songwriter and folk bard (1836, Vilna–1913, New York) popular among the Jewish masses of Eastern Europe, who called him Lyokemke Badchan. Paul Glasser, "Elyokem Tsunzer," in *YIVO Encyclopedia*, www.https://encyclopedia.yivo.org/article/1155. A badchan (or *batkhn*) was a clever rhymester hired to entertain the guests at a wedding, raise toasts to the bride and groom, and stir up all the celebrants to extremes of joy and sorrow through his improvised verses. The art of the badchan is considered one of the precursors of modern Yiddish theatre.

# Chapter X

1. Ultimately named after Jan Grzybowski, the seventeenth-century Warsaw *starost*, or district governor, Grzybów was home to a large population of Jews during Kaminska's lifetime.

2. The nom de plume of Nokhem Meyer Shaykevitsh (1849?–1905), a Yiddish and Hebrew novelist, playwright, and theatre director. In 1882, he worked with Goldfaden to found a Yiddish theatre in Odessa, and would later settle in Warsaw, where he oversaw productions of his own work. Shomer's literary creations were wildly popular but scorned by more highbrow Yiddish authors as *shund*—a term used for pulpy, lowbrow fiction or theatre, often sensationalistic or sentimental.

3. Dovid Shvartsbard was born in Warsaw, and after his time in the needle trades, attended rabbinical school and served as the conductor of synagogue choirs. In theatre, too, he worked largely as a choral director, and often served as the representative of Kaminska's troupe in seeking permits to perform when touring the Polish provinces. "Dovid Shvartsbard," in *Leksikon fun yidishn teater*, ed. Zalmen Zylbercweig (New York: Elisheva, 1959), 3: 2127.

4. Moyshe Vaysfeld, one of the first major Yiddish theatre directors in Warsaw.

**5** Italian-French opera singer (1843–1919), a major celebrity known for the purity and satiny smoothness of her voice.

**6** Max Gustav Shvartsbard (1867–1932) was a major Yiddish actor of his day; he played lover and hero roles, and would later act in the silent film *Tkies-kaf* (The Vow) (1924). Kaminska also starred in the picture, her only major appearance on film. In it, she played the mother of the character portrayed by her real-life daughter Ida Kaminska, the preeminent actress of the Yiddish stage following her mother's death. In 1934, owing largely to the film's importance as a rare record of Ester-Rokhl Kaminska's performing, spoken dialogue was added and the film was rereleased, newly titled *A vilner legende* (A Vilna Legend). Max Gustav was the son of Dovid Shvartsbard, another chief artist in Kaminska's troupe.

**7** Miryem Triling (*c.* 1875–1920), born in Warsaw, would go on to enjoy a long professional association with the Kaminski troupe. As a young woman, she worked at a milliner's. Like Kaminska, she would later distinguish herself in the title role of Gordin's *Mirele Efros*. Three of her children with the actor Hershl Berman also acted and danced professionally, in Soviet as well as American theatres. "Manye (Miryem) Triling," in Zylbercweig, *Leksikon*, 2: 896.

**8** Hershl (Herman) Berman (1859–1923) performed with Goldfaden's troupe in Warsaw, and introduced Miryem Triling, whom he later married, to the stage. He enjoyed a long career as an actor and singer. Hershl's younger brother Adolf Berman (1872–1942) performed frequently with the Kaminski troupe as an actor, and as an operetta singer in Łódź and other Polish cities. He was active in Poland's Yiddish Actors Union. A man of advancing age at the time of the Nazi invasion of Poland, he remained in Warsaw and died in its ghetto after suffering vicious beatings by Nazi officers. "Herman Berman," in *Leksikon fun yidishn teater*, ed. Zalmen Zylbercweig (New York: Elisheva, 1931), 1: 205; Jonas Turkow, "Adolf Berman," in *Farloshene shtern* (Extinguished Stars), in *Dos poylishe yidntum* (Polish Jewry), ed. Mark Turkow, vol. 95 (Buenos Aires: Tsentralfarband fun poylishe yidn in argentine, 1953), 1: 227.

**9** Yankev Libert (1874–1946) got his start in the Yiddish theatre with Goldfaden's troupe in Warsaw. He toured extensively with the Kaminski troupe and attracted critical notice in their jaunts to St. Petersburg. He toured to the Russian heartland just prior to the First World War and worked in Soviet Yiddish theatres in Ukraine and the Caucasus after the Bolshevik Revolution.

**10** Kaminska, "Derner un blumen," *Der moment*, August 6, 1926.

**11** Like his father, who manufactured spats for a living. Ida Kaminska, *My Life*, 12. Kaminski was a major actor-director who would go on to found touring companies and a theatre in Warsaw with his wife, the author of these memoirs. He also wrote a number of plays put on by his and Ester-Rokhl's troupes. The only published one, drawing on their shared experiences, traverses very similar territory as that which Ester-Rokhl does in her autobiographical writing. Earlier known as *Di yidishe aktern inem kleynem shtetl* (The Yiddish Players in the Small Shtetl), the three-act comedy was first published in the Warsaw journal *Roman-tsaytung* (Novel Newspaper) as *Yidishe aktern af der rayze* (Yiddish Players on the Move) in 1907, and later in book form by the Warsaw press Bikher far ale (Books for All) in 1908. Kaminski was born in 1867 in Wola (in Yiddish, Volya), today a district of Warsaw, and died following an asthma attack in Łomża, Poland, in 1918. Zalmen Zylbercweig, *Hantbukh fun yidishn teater* (Manual of Yiddish Theatre) (Mexico City: Zylbercweig Jubilee Committee Under Auspices of Los Angeles YIVO, 1970), 163; "Avrom-Yitskhok Kaminski," in *Leksikon fun yidishn teater*, ed. Zalmen Zylbercweig (Mexico City: Elisheva, 1969), 6: 5254-81.

**12** Beni Abelman (*c.* 1865–1929) was born the son of ox dealers in the Praga suburb of Warsaw. He was highly regarded, as a singer-actor, for his enchanting voice. "Beni (Borekh-Moyshe) Abelman" in ibid., 4855–69.

**13** Shayele Rotshayn (1870–1942) was born to Hasidic parents in Warsaw and sang in choirs as a child. Later, he performed in the choral ensembles of Goldfaden's works after the composer arrived in Warsaw. When Kaminska's troupe was formed, like other former choristers who were expected to advance and meet a growing demand for stars (after many Yiddish performers of great renown had fled for America), he transitioned to become an actor in principal roles. In 1906, he founded a Yiddish children's theatre in Warsaw. When officials of the Warsaw Ghetto arrived at his home to conduct him to a deportation, he suffered a heart attack and died. "Shayele Rotshayn," in *Leksikon fun yidishn teater*, ed. Zalmen Zylbercweig, vol. 5, *Kdoyshim-band* (Martyrs Volume) (Mexico City: Elisheva, 1967), 4260–4.

**14** The "Herbstlied," with words by Karl Klingemann, a German poet and friend of the world-famous composer Felix Mendelssohn, a German of Jewish descent. The song, which compares the passing from spring to fall with the fading of eager romance into sad longing, was published in 1845.

# Chapter XI

**1**  The father of Moyshe Polakevitsh (1890–194?), an actor in Yiddish traveling companies, was the owner of a manufacturing business.

**2**  In Polish, "Ulica Bonifraterska."

# Chapter XII

**1**  Kaminska, "Derner un blumen," *Der moment*, August 13, 1926.

**2**  Founded in 1871 by a group of Polish composers, the Warszawskie Towarzystwo Muzyczne (Warsaw Musical Society) devoted itself to establishing programs of musical education, promoting Polish music, and erecting monuments to celebrated artists like Chopin.

**3**  An imperial Russian unit of weight that equaled 40 Russian pounds, equivalent to about 36 pounds in the system used in the United States.

# Chapter XIII

**1**  The mourner's prayer, recited by bereaved children every day for a year following the death of a parent.

**2**  As Nisan is a time of great festivity—Passover, the celebration of the Jews' redemption from slavery in Egypt, is observed from Nisan 15 to 22 (somewhere between late March and mid-April)—there is a custom not to visit cemeteries throughout the entire month.

# Chapter XIV

**1**  Kaminska, "Derner un blumen," *Der moment*, August 20, 1926. Rosh Chodesh is the holiday celebrating the new moon and with it, the beginning of a new Hebrew month. Iyar is the month following Nisan and falls between April and May.

**2** Credo of the Jewish faith, recited upon waking and going to bed at night. Its words are also supposed to be the last that a Jew speaks when death is imminent.

**3** From the Hebrew word for "seven," this is the week of mourning following a death, when the family gathers in the home of the deceased for prayers and visits from the community.

**4** Situated on the Vistula River, it is today known as Torún, and is in northern-central Poland.

**5** From this station, one could take the Warsaw-Vienna Railway, a train stretching from Warsaw in Congress Poland—part of the Russian Empire—to the borders of the Austro-Hungarian and German Empires.

**6** There were a number of towns and villages named Aleksandrowo in Congress Poland. This likely refers to the Polish town known today as Aleksandrów Kujawski, some 18 miles to the south of Torún (Thorn) and on the opposite side of the Vistula River. It boasted an impressive train station.

**7** Then part of the Russian Empire and today part of Poland, some 10 miles east of Aleksandrów Kujawski and 22 miles south of Torún (Thorn). It is on the Vistula River, and like Aleksandrów Kujawski, on the opposite side thereof from Torún.

**8** From a Hebrew word meaning "to accompany, to march someone somewhere" or "to lead a beast of burden," this slang term is common in *ganovim-loshn* ("thieves' language"), the professional argot of the Yiddish-speaking underworld.

**9** A unit of distance in imperial Russia, equivalent to about 0.66 miles.

**10** During this period, the mid-1880s, a great many Jews were leaving Eastern Europe for the United States, seeking economic stability and freedom from pogroms and other forms of antisemitic persecution.

**11** Flat, circular bread rolls, in this case covered in diced onions.

**12** A city in central Poland, also situated on the Vistula like Thorn. It boasted a very large and quite ancient Jewish population, dating as far back as the thirteenth century, even before the Polish king Casimir the Great (1310–70) famously welcomed vast numbers of Jews into his territories.

**13** A rebbe is a rabbi who has the distinction of leading a Hasidic sect. The rebbe is typically surrounded by a court of trusted acolytes, though all the members of the community are considered to be his followers—his Hasidim.

# Chapter XV

**1**  Kaminska, "Derner un blumen," *Der moment*, August 27, 1926.

# Chapter XVI

**1**  Kaminska, "Derner un blumen," *Der moment*, September 3, 1926.

**2**  The Broder singers were a class of wandering Yiddish performers, of whom one of the most famous was Berl Broder (*c.* 1815/17–68, born Berl Margulis), a former employee of a pig bristle factory. He hailed from a shtetl near Brody, in Austrian Galicia, now in Ukraine. This city lent him both his stage name and the name of this category of troubadours who earned their keep doing ballads both comical and tragical at a succession of inns. Though they were an important predecessor to the full-fledged professional Yiddish theatre, they were not considered to be the most sophisticated of performers and were often seen as less than savory individuals on account of their itinerancy and choice of vocation. "Berl Broder," in *Leksikon fun der yidisher literatur, prese un filologye* (Biographical Dictionary of Yiddish Literature, Press, and Philology), ed. Zalmen Reyzen (Vilna: B. Kletskin, 1928), 1: 395–401; David G. Roskies, "Berl Broder," in *YIVO Encyclopedia*, www.yivoencyclopedia.org/article .aspx/broder_berl.

**3**  That is, a female Litvak—one who comes from the region known historically to Jews as *Lite*, or Lithuania. The Jews native to Warsaw, on the other hand, would have identified as *poylishe yidn*, Polish Jews.

**4**  In German, "charming young aunt."

**5**  *Doktor almasado, oder di yidn in palermo* (Doctor Almasado, or: The Jews in Palermo) is a historical operetta written in rhymed couplets and first performed in St. Petersburg in 1882. Unlike Goldfaden's earlier, more farcical entertainments, *Almasado*, along with *Shulamis* and *Bar Kokhba*, are grand-scale works with a grand ambition: to give artistic expression to the Jewish national character. In *Almasado*, the heroic Jewish physician of the title comes to the rescue of his persecuted community in Spanish-ruled Sicily.

**6**  "Lonely, small, and despised," the song is about the persistence, faith, and survival of the Jewish people in spite of the torments of its oppressors.

**7** The Polish National Theatre (Teatr Narodowy) was founded in Warsaw in 1765 and still exists under that name today. In the period from 1838 to 1915, it was known as the Warsaw State Theatre. B. I. Rostotskii, "Polish National Theatre," in *The Great Soviet Encyclopedia* (translation of *Bol'shaia sovetskaia entsiklopediia*), ed. Aleksandr Mikhailovich Prokhorov (New York: Macmillan, 1973), 20: 333.

# Chapter XVII

**1** Kaminska, "Derner un blumen," *Der moment*, September 8, 1926.

**2** An official charged with the keeping of the public scales or the administration of a weighhouse.

**3** The capital of the Russian Empire, of which Warsaw was then a part.

**4** That is, one composed of Jews and committed to repertoire originally written in Yiddish. This company, however, like many in which Kaminska would take part, performed, at least nominally (though not always with great linguistic fidelity), in German, owing to the tsarist ban on Yiddish theatre. This ban was imposed throughout the Russian Empire in 1883 as part of a wave of anti-Jewish policies called the "May Laws," which purported to suppress public disorder that had taken root after the pogroms following the assassination of Tsar Alexander II in March 1881. It was only during a period of newly extended freedoms in the wake of the Russian Revolution of 1905 that the statutes began to be relaxed and authorities granted permission for Yiddish theatre to be performed in the major metropolises of the empire. Before that point, Kaminska and her fellow performers had to stake out territory and win audiences for their art in corners of the provinces, in stopgap playhouses in the shtetlach, in the shadows of the censors. This early portion of her career—the only portion of her acting work that is described at length in this memoir—was carried out entirely in this highly charged, cat-and-mouse atmosphere of governmental suppression. Her latter, post-ban years, ones marked by greater artistic freedom and fame, are left unchronicled in the memoir's pages, as she did not finish writing before her death.

**5** A biblical operetta by Yoysef Lateiner (1853–1935). The story is drawn from the Book of Genesis account of Joseph's abduction by his brothers, being sold as a slave to passing Egyptians, and subsequent sojourn in the land of the Pharaohs. The narrative was a popular topic for the very earliest *purim-shpiln*, dating back centuries—plays performed on

Purim, retelling biblical stories in rhymed couplets and song. Programs documenting performances of Lateiner's modern variation may be found at YIVO, RG 8.1: Esther-Rachel Kaminska Theater Museum Collection, "Performances of Yiddish Theater and Music: Plays, Programs, Playbills, and Posters," Joseph Lateiner, Folder 4518, items 176202–39, https://digipres.cjh.org/delivery/DeliveryManagerServlet ?dps_pid=IE3177880.

**6**  Gentile woman.

**7**  "The Huguenots" (1836), libretto by French authors Eugène Scribe and Émile Deschamps, music by German-Jewish grand opera composer Giacomo Meyerbeer (born Jakob Liebmann Meyer Beer), who was hugely popular in his day. Depicting a doomed romance between a Protestant and a Catholic, the formerly much-beloved opera takes place during a period of heightened violence against Protestants in France, culminating in the St. Bartholomew's Day Massacre of 1572.

**8**  "The ten children of one father graze their sheep in the field, each one of them no less than a mighty hero, by God's power!" As the line does not seem to match any lyric in *Les Huguenots*, it is likely that only the melody was lifted from that opera, to which were added new lyrics related to Lateiner's story of Joseph and his brothers.

**9**  Iser Sendik (1871–?) had a brief career as an actor in the Kaminski troupe before returning to his career as a folksinger. "Iser Sendik," in Zylbercweig, *Leksikon*, 2: 1513–14.

**10**  Having a director was by no means a given in the professional theatre of this day, with it often falling to the stage manager to dictate the actors' movements onstage and ensure all elements of the production were in place, often drawing on notes from prior productions or the company's recollections from having performed the piece before.

**11**  As many stars of the Yiddish stage did, eager to work outside of the shadow of the tsarist ban on Yiddish theatre, and, like many of their coreligionists in the 1880s, to escape pogroms and poverty in Eastern Europe, seeking a safer and more prosperous life in the New World. The mention of leading actors having sought fairer fields in America is significant. Kaminska and her fellow performers in Eastern Europe were a diminished lot following such mass immigration, making their accomplishments in growing the incipient art form of professional Yiddish theatre all the more impressive.

**12**  Or in Yiddish, Yankev Adler (1855–1926). One of the most revered Yiddish actors of his day, he was most famous for his title role in the

Shakespeare adaptation *Der yidisher kenig lir* (The Jewish King Lear). His daughters Celia and Stella Adler were also famous performers on the Yiddish stage, and the latter would go on to become one of the most prominent American acting teachers.

**13** One of the great actor-managers of the New York Yiddish scene, David (in Yiddish, Dovid) Kessler (1860–1920) got his start acting in traveling troupes in Europe. His Kessler's Second Avenue Theatre would compete ably with the Lower East Side theatres of such fellow actor-impresarios as Jacob Adler and Boris Thomashefsky. During a Brooklyn performance of Gordin's *Di kreytser-sonate* (The Kreutzer Sonata, based on the Tolstoy novella), Kessler complained of intestinal pains, and, following an operation, died two days later. "David Kessler Dies; Noted Yiddish Actor," *New York Times*, May 15, 1920, 15.

**14** "Laden with all good things, and our staffs in our hands." Earlier, when describing her audition for Goldfaden, in which she sang this piece, Kaminska remembers the first half of the line, meaning the same thing but slightly differently worded, as "Ongelodn mit al dos guts." In the printed libretto, the line appears somewhat differently still, "Ongelodn mit al dem gut, mit di shtekns in der hant," which, besides the slightly different grammar at the start of the line, gives the singular *hant* (hand) instead of the plural *hent*. Such variations in the sung text are expected, each troupe often working off a different set of memories or copy of a handwritten prompt book, and often not in possession of an authorized printed score or libretto. Avrom Goldfaden, *Shulamis oder bas-yerusholaim—ayne muzikalishe melodrame in ferzn un in 4 aktn un 15 bilder* (Shulamis: or, The Daughter of Jerusalem—a musical melodrama in rhymed verse, in 4 acts and 15 scenes) (London: R. Mazin & Co., 1902), 3.

# Chapter XVIII

**1** Another Goldfaden operetta, also known in Yiddish as *Di kishef-makherin* (The Sorceress), and known in English alternately as *The Sorceress*, *The Witch*, or *The Witch of Botoșani* (1878). *Di bobe yakhne* roughly translates to "The Grandmother Yakhne," but here, by association with the Russian folk figure Baba Yaga, "The Witch" or "The Hag." A very popular piece in Goldfaden's day, it tells the story of a wicked, scheming procuress, Bobe Yakhne, who works her dubious "magic" to lure the motherless ingénue,

Mirele, into her clutches (after having her father wrongfully sent to jail), eventually selling her to a white slaver in Turkey, all to make an easy buck and, it would seem, for the pure pleasure of bringing down the privileged bourgeoisie of her Romanian city, Botoşani.

# Chapter XIX

1  Kaminska, "Derner un blumen," *Der moment*, September 22, 1926.

2  The garden served during this period as one of Warsaw's public parks, surrounding the baroque palace that had been built in the seventeenth century for the aristocratic Krasiński family.

3  "For your birthday, for your celebration, / Your guests have gathered." In the original that has become familiar as the Yiddishist community's birthday song, this appears as "Tsu dayn geburtstog, tsu dayn yontef haynt, / Hobn zikh farzamlt dayne gute fraynd" (For your birthday, for your celebration today, / Your good friends have gathered). This is sung by the chorus to the protagonist, Mirele, in the garden outside her opulent middle-class home in the city of Botoşani, Romania. She is celebrating her sixteenth birthday, a signal of her family's modernity, as birthdays are not generally occasions of great festivity in traditional Ashkenazic Jewish life.

4  "What good is this gaiety, and everything that's fine / When I am remembering at this time . . ." Between the verses of the joyous birthday song, the forlorn Mirele cuts in to recall the death of her mother and describe how she cannot be happy at her party while her beloved progenitress is absent therefrom. In an autobiographical sketch of her life published in 1925, Kaminska recalled playing Mirele a few years before, in 1922, at a celebratory jubilee performance of *The Sorceress* honoring her thirty years of acting, since her principal début in the role in 1892. Owing to her "German-Jewish Theatre," as her former troupe designated itself, having had to perform in German to adhere to the tsarist ban on Yiddish-language performances, in preparing for this anniversary performance, Kaminska was only able to remember the German words of this solo, from her salad days, instead of the original (and by 1922, far more well-known) Yiddish lyrics. Kaminska, "Kurtse avtobiografye," 17.

5  "Truly, truly, with a happy heart I do sell all my goods at cheap prices, and whoever wants something expensive, may he burn like a fire." The

German that Kaminska quotes retains features of Yiddish, for example: adjectival endings that are not quite correct in German, "un" for German "und" (and), and "a" for German "ein" (the indefinite article "a"). This may be due to Kaminska knowing German imperfectly and thus not exactly remembering how the German was rendered in the script. It is also possible that the script's translators themselves were speakers of German as a second language, or chose to inflect the German with certain features of Yiddish diction or grammar, to lend a Jewish quality to the operetta's characters, even as they are singing and speaking in German. At other times, the "German" scripts submitted by the Yiddish theatre artists to the censor in St. Petersburg were simply Yiddish texts hastily transliterated into something resembling German orthography. The line from Mirele's solo, cited earlier, also bears some discrepancies from what might be expected in standard German: "an diese Minut," instead of the more correct "in dieser Minute." The same is true of other instances of German text performed by the actors that Kaminska quotes throughout the memoir.

6   At the birthday celebration, Hotsmakh stops the selling of his haberdashery to entertain the guests with a comic song followed by a game of blindman's bluff, or as it is known in Yiddish, *blinde ku* (blind cow).

7   "Hotsmakh is a blind man and has a wife and sixteen children."

8   "Miss, will you also be laughing on Friday?"

# Chapter XX

1   Mirele's father is arrested in the middle of her birthday party, owing to a conspiratorial plot hatched by Mirele's stepmother and Bobe Yakhne, the fraudulent "sorceress" of the title. In the second act, the girl slaves away as a Cinderella-like figure in her own home, cruelly dominated by her stepmother. The act's opening finds her clothed in rags with her hair in disarray, bending over a pail as she washes the floors and laments her bitter fate in a pathos-filled aria. Avrom Goldfaden, *Di kishef-makherin (tsoyberin)—operete in 5 aktn un in 8 bilder* (The Sorceress—operetta in 5 acts and 8 scenes) (New York: Hebrew Publishing Company, 19–?), 15.

# Chapter XXI

1   Kaminska, "Derner un blumen," *Der moment*, September 29, 1926.

2   The Russian imperial ban on Yiddish theatre was communicated in a secret government circular that was never made public, which meant that its enforcement was capricious, and often left up to local officials, whose susceptibility to bribery (and tolerance of Jewish theatre) was not always predictable. The "specialist" to whom Kaminska refers would be working as a censor, cracking down on the performance if he discerned that Yiddish was being spoken onstage. Infractions could incur fines, arrests of the actors, and closure of the theatre. See John Klier, "'Exit, Pursued by a Bear': Russian Administrators and the Ban on Yiddish Theatre in Imperial Russia," in *Yiddish Theatre: New Approaches*, ed. Joel Berkowitz (Oxford and Portland, OR: Littman Library of Jewish Civilization, 2003), 159–74.

   The imperious Hermann V. Kleigels headed the Warsaw police from 1888 to 1895. Later, as prefect of the St. Petersburg police and then governor-general of the Kyiv guberniya, he violently suppressed student rebellions and was, at best, dangerously indifferent to anti-Jewish pogroms. Malte Rolf, "Glossary of Names," in *Imperial Russian Rule in the Kingdom of Poland, 1864–1915*, trans. Cynthia Klohr (Pittsburgh: University of Pittsburgh Press, 2021); ChaeRan Y. Freeze and Jay M. Harris, Introduction to *Everyday Jewish Life in Imperial Russia, 1772–1914: Selected Documents* (Waltham: Brandeis University Press, 2013), 36.

3   "Lonesome, far from all the [other] trees," Mirele's allegorical song about a solitary sapling on a hill, which appears at the top of the second act, after Mirele's father has been arrested in the birthday party scene for a crime he did not commit, and she is made to scrub the floors in the home now ruled by her stepmother. "Bäumer" is another instance of Kaminska reproducing the German translation in somewhat Yiddishized fashion, as "trees" is *Baüme* in German, but *beymer* in Yiddish.

4   The wily Bobe Yakhne, the "sorceress" of the title, has assisted Bashe in ridding the latter of her meddling stepdaughter Mirele. In the operation, she gains a bit of extra lucre for herself by taking the girl captive and then selling her to an Ottoman organ-grinder, who accompanies Mirele as she warbles and wiggles for spare change in a café hazy with hookah smoke.

5   "I was my father's only child," Mirele's busking song in the café, a slow and plaintive number like most of this character's music.

# Chapter XXII

1   Adolf Shlifershteyn got his start putting on productions of Goldfaden's works with other then-amateur actors, many of them factory workers. Quint, *The Rise*, 193.

2   Known today as Lviv, a major city in Ukraine. In the period of which Kaminska writes, it was in Austrian Galicia.

3   *Dora, oder zibetsn yor in ostrog* (Dora, or: Seventeen Years in Prison), a drama in four acts, with songs.

4   Kaminska, "Derner un blumen," *Der moment*, October 8, 1926.

5   "I beg you, great and mighty God."

6   "O, the well, o, the cat!" Shulamis, lost in the middle of the desert, has been found and rescued by Avsholem, and, having no human witnesses, they pledge their commitment to each other by the things nearby them in the desert: a well and a wildcat.

7   Like *yold* or its female equivalent *yoldevke* that appear elsewhere in the memoir, this word features in *teater-loshn* (theatre language), the argot of Yiddish stage actors. Meaning literally a "stick" or a "pole," the popular London Yiddish playwright Shmuel-Yankev Harendorf defines it as a "bad actor" in the glossary of such terms that appears at the back of his theatrical memoir. Sh. Y. Harendorf, *Teater-karavanen: mayselekh un epizodn fun mayne vanderungen mit yidish teater* (Theatre Caravans: Anecdotes and Episodes from My Wanderings with Yiddish Theatre) (London: Farlag "fraynt fun yidish loshn," 1955), 230.

8   Influencing Kaminska's depiction of the player as a god may be the fact that his character, Tsingitang (perhaps related to the Yiddish *tsig*, "goat," or *tsung*, "tongue," pronounced *tsing* in the standard Yiddish theatre dialect), Avsholem's stuttering, buffoonish companion who serves as the comic relief of Goldfaden's opera, is something of a goat-man, akin to the rambunctious Greek god of the wild, Pan, or the faun, a mythic character that proliferates in European mythology. The character's caprine nature would have also been partly why the actor playing him typically performed in blackface, though racial stereotypes likely contributed to the practice, as well.

9   In these, her final moments in the play, Avigayil has lost the second of her children with Avsholem (both destroyed in ways that recall the witnesses of Avsholem's vow to Shulamis: the first is killed by a wildcat, and the second falls into a well), and sends her husband away so that he may reunite with Shulamis and thus lift the curse that has plagued all of these characters' destinies.

# Chapter XXIII

**1**  A beacon of the industrial revolution in Poland, the city transformed into a true textile powerhouse in the last quarter of the nineteenth century, fueled largely by Jewish tycoons and workers. Like most Polish cities and towns mentioned in the memoir, it was, during the period of which Kaminska writes, part of Congress Poland, a client state of the Russian Empire formed by the Congress of Vienna (1814–15), but is today located in the third independent Republic of Poland. At the time the memoirs were written and originally published, Warsaw, Łódź, and many other such places that Kaminska travels to in the course of her narrative were also in an independent Polish republic, the second, that lasted from 1918 to 1939.

**2**  *Kire*, an acronym for the words *Keyser YoRem Hoyde* (Hebrew, "The Emperor, may his splendor be exalted"), is used in Yiddish to refer to the Austrian emperor as well as his empire. It was also, as here, used by Jewish subjects of the Russian Empire as a slur for their counterparts of the Austrian Empire. *Verterbukh fun loshn-koydesh-shtamike verter in yidish* (Dictionary of Words of Hebraic and Aramaic Origin in Yiddish), ed. Yitskhok Niborski, 3rd ed. (Paris: Bibliothèque Medem, 2012), s.v. "Kyr"h/ kyrh [kire]."

# Chapter XXIV

**1**  In Standard Yiddish, *yoldn* means something like "dolts" or "suckers" (with the adjective *yoldish* meaning "simple-minded"), but in *teater-loshn*—actors' slang—it often refers derisively to nontheatrical folk, or indeed actors who behave like them, being bourgeois and ignorant of life onstage. As we have seen, Ester-Rokhl's troupemates call her a "yoldevke," the female form, in the days when she first begins to tread the boards. Playwright Shmuel-Yankev Harendorf's entry in the *teater-loshn* glossary at the back of his memoir reads, "'yold,' 'yoldn,' 'yoldevkes'— naive, balebatishe mentshn" ("'yold,' 'yold' in plural form, 'yold' in plural feminine form—naive, bourgeois people") (Harendorf, *Teater-karavanen*, 230). The word was likewise used in *klezmer-loshn*, the professional argot of Eastern European Yiddish-speaking musicians, to mean nonmusicians, the ones engaging them for gigs; or to refer obliquely to someone's husband (*yold*) or wife (*yoldevke*). In *ganovim-loshn*, the argot of Yiddish-speaking thieves, it referred to a non-thief,

or an inexperienced thief. The word may originate in *yeled* (boy,
in Hebrew) or in a Russian slang term for "penis," *yelda*. Robert A.
Rothstein, "Klezmer-loshn: The Language of Jewish Folk Musicians," in
*American Klezmer: Its Roots and Offshoots*, ed. Mark Slobin (Berkeley:
University of California Press, 2002), 29–30.

**2** The Litvaks were known for their cold and rational demeanors, while Polish
Jews from more southerly places like Łódź were popularly considered to be
warmer and more emotional and, at times, more prone to drink.

# Chapter XXV

**1** Avrom Fishzon (1843?–1922) was born in Berdychiv. It was there in
1875 that he performed a "Jewish concert" of songs and short scenes
with Yisroel Grodner, which Fishzon argued was the true beginning
of Yiddish theatre. After 1883, he toured the Pale of Settlement with
a changing cast of actors in a troupe that, like Kaminska's Warsaw
company, pretended to perform exclusively in German. His wife, Khine
Braginska (Braginskaya) (1867?–1951), was born in Kyiv and made her
début in Goldfaden's company in 1882. She joined Fishzon's company
in 1883. After the Bolshevik revolution, the family made its way to
Harbin, China. Fishzon died there in 1922, while Braginska and her
adult children ultimately settled in New York. Leon Gelis was born in
the Russian Empire in 1857, in a town that Zylbercweig identifies as
"Bershan"—though as a town with such a name does not appear in other
sources, it is likely that this is a typographical error for the Ukrainian
town of Bershad (the letters ד and ן, representing the sounds "d" and
"n," being sometimes mistaken for each other in Yiddish texts), which
had a significant Jewish population. He made his professional début as
an actor in 1887. He performed in nearly all of the best-known Yiddish
companies in Poland and Russia, and later worked chiefly as a director in
London and France. He often worked together with his wife, Polye, and
their daughters. He died in Paris in 1925. "Avrom Fishzon," in *Leksikon
fun yidishn teater*, ed. Zalmen Zylbercweig, 7: 6312–42 (unpublished
page proofs at YIVO, RG 662), https://yiddishstage.org/encyclopedia;
Barbara Henry, "Avrom Fishzon, or the Berdichev Sheherazad," in
*Digital Yiddish Theatre Project*, https://web.uwm.edu/yiddish-stage/
avrom-fishzon-or-the-berdichev-sheherazad; "Khine Braginska," in
Zylbercweig, *Leksikon*, 1: 213–14; "Leon Gelis," in ibid., 497.

**2** Like nearby Odessa, Nikolaev is a port city on the Black Sea, in southern Ukraine. It is known in Ukrainian as Mykolaiv.

**3** Yiddish, "eyes."

**4** "Heart."

**5** "Sabbath." The Ukrainian Yiddish dialect wherein the sound "a" becomes "o" is known as *tote-mome-loshn* ("Fother-Mohther Language"), as in Standard Yiddish (and Litvish Yiddish), the words for "father" and "mother" are instead pronounced *tate* and *mame*.

**6** Today, corresponding to southeastern Poland, southwestern Belarus, and western Ukraine.

**7** "To see."

**8** "Cheese."

**9** A Spinoza-like figure known for his challenges to traditional Judaism, Uriel Acosta was born in Portugal to a Jewish family that had been forcibly converted to Catholicism. Seeking to live as a Jew, he immigrated to the more free-thinking, tolerant Amsterdam, but was later excommunicated by the Portuguese Jewish community there for his anti-rabbinical and reputedly heretical writings. His tragic life, which may have ended with suicide, was much dramatized, including in a German play written by Karl Gutzkow (1846). That play was later translated into Yiddish and became a favorite on the Yiddish stage, including in an operetta adaptation by Goldfaden, though what is performed here is the straight play, a version of Gutzkow's drama. In it, the young Spinoza appears as Acosta's pupil.

**10** The beautiful daughter of Menashe Vanderstraaten, a wealthy Jewish merchant in Amsterdam, she is one of Uriel Acosta's only supporters in the community. Eventually, she poisons herself after being forced to marry Uriel's rival, Ben Jochai, leading to the title character's own suicide.

**11** Often transliterated from Yiddish as Berdichev, it is now part of Ukraine and was at this time an overwhelmingly Jewish city in the Russian Empire. In the latter half of the nineteenth century, it was home to a thriving Jewish-owned industrial sector, including nine leather-processing plants.

**12** A hundred-year-old rabbi.

**13** An indication that, contrary to popular belief, there was not always a set dialect for Yiddish actors that all troupes relied upon, though in time a *bine-yidish* (stage Yiddish) formed upon the basis of southeastern Yiddish came to be considered the standard in certain sectors. At this time, the players in Kaminska's troupe all performed using their native pronunciation, leading to the linguistic mishmash she describes (even more of a mishmash considering the Yiddish-speaking troupe is purportedly acting in German).

**14** "What, am I a Christian?"

# Chapter XXVI

**1** Kaminska, "Derner un blumen," *Der moment*, October 15, 1926.

**2** Yisroel Grodner (1841?–87) gained early renown as a Broder singer and actor. He worked with both Fishzon and Goldfaden in the earliest days of the Yiddish theatre in Berdychiv and throughout Romania, before parting ways with them and organizing his own theatrical troupes. Until 1883, he traveled the Russian Empire with a shifting cast of performers. Later, Grodner and his wife Annetta toured Warsaw and London, where he died. "Yisroel Grodner," in Zylbercweig, *Leksikon*, 1: 508–15.

**3** Bessarabia, a region of Eastern Europe which lies today mostly in Moldova and partly in Ukraine, was part of the Russian Empire during the time of which Kaminska writes. It was well-known for the growing of grapes and the production of wines.

**4** Imonuel Tshizhik (1867–?) was a son of the renowned Bunem Badchan and toured around shtetlach with his father, both performing comic songs as "freylekhmakhers" (merrymakers) in shows and plying Bunem's namesake trade (i.e., as badchanim, linguistically dexterous wedding entertainers). Later he joined Fishzon and Gelis's company as an actor and toured with the Kaminski company. "Imonuel Tshizhik," in Zylbercweig, *Leksikon*, 2: 900–1.

# Chapter XXVII

**1** "In a corner room of Jerusalem's Holy Temple" is the first line of the enduringly famous lullaby "Rozhinkes mit mandlen" (Raisins and Almonds), which was introduced in *Shulamis*. The song went on to enjoy a glorious life beyond Goldfaden's opera as one of the most celebrated of all Yiddish songs, even being recorded by Judy Garland as "Sleep My Baby Sleep" in 1938. In the original, Avsholem describes the widowed "Daughter of Zion" crooning to her son Yidele while promising him a successful future trading in raisins and almonds. The boy's name is an affectionate form of the name Yehude—Judah—and the child thus figures as a stand-in for the Jewish people, for whom the mother predicts a future of blessings, despite its present state of exile and torment.

2   "Who goes there? May God bless you!" Shulamis, who has descended into a well and cannot get out, overhears Avsholem preparing to drink from it, and shouts out this line to him from the depths shortly after he finishes his aforementioned lullaby ("In beys-hamigdesh," aka "Rozhinkes mit mandlen"). In the printed libretto, "Got zol aykh bentshn" appears as "Ikh vel aykh bentshn"—*I* will bless you. Goldfaden, *Shulamis*, 8.

3   "Grandmother" Yakhne, like many other roles of old ladies, hags, and witches in European opera and ballet of this period (and still today in British pantomime), is traditionally played en travesti, that is, by a man in drag.

4   Kaminska, "Derner un blumen," *Der moment*, October 22, 1926.

5   A town some 12 miles east of Łódź. Its chief distinction was serving as a railway junction between larger cities like Warsaw and Wrocław.

6   There are at least a dozen towns and cities in Poland bearing some variation of the name Tomaszów. The one referred to here appears to be Tomaszów Mazowiecki, a town in the voivodeship of Łódź.

# Chapter XXVIII

1   Braginska was actually born in Kyiv and raised in the Ukrainian town of Fastiv, some 40 miles outside of it. Her first language was Russian, and by her own account, she had to learn Yiddish to become an actress, making German an additional challenge. Khine Braginskaya-Fishzon, "Di ershte trit fun idishn teater in rusland" (When Yiddish Theatre First Took to the Stage in Russia), *Der tog* (The Day) (New York), February 25, 1934.

2   Yiddish, "do."

3   Yiddish, "Warsaw Boys."

# Chapter XXIX

1   This role often appears in an alternate pronunciation, as "Basye."

2   Shomer's play (published in 1883 in Odessa) was a popular adaptation of Nikolai Gogol's Russian-language satire of the same name.

3   Today known as Będzin, a city in southern Poland.

4   Kaminska, "Derner un blumen," *Der moment*, October 29, 1926.

5   A southern Polish town known today as Dąbrowa Górnicza.


# Chapter XXX

1   A *treyfnyak* is literally someone who eats *treyf*, or unkosher food—or
    someone who is themselves *treyf*, a nonbeliever, a heretic, someone who
    does not observe the dictates of the Jewish faith. Indeed, an alternative
    title for Shomer's play was *Der apikoyres* (The Heretic). Score of *Der
    apikoyres, oder der treyfnyak* (Vilna: 1900–1906) (YIVO, RG 7, Folder 310),
    https://digipres.cjh.org:443/delivery/DeliveryManagerServlet?dps_pid
    =IE11070064.

2   Kaminska, "Derner un blumen," *Der moment*, November 5, 1926.

3   Mordkhe Ribalski (1870–1933) was a runaway cantorial student from
    Fastiv, today in Ukraine. This "Yiddish Chaliapin" (his voice was compared
    to that of the celebrated Russian basso profundo, Feodor Chaliapin) began
    his stage career with Olginskaya's company and performed for many years
    in Fishzon's troupe. In 1921, Ribalski celebrated fifty years on the Yiddish
    stage. By 1927, he was living in the town of Nevel in Soviet Belarus in
    extreme poverty, with only a meager state pension to sustain him. He
    took his own life in 1933. "Mordkhe Ribalski," in Zylbercweig, *Leksikon*, 6:
    4979–82.


# Chapter XXXI

1   Shavuos is a springtime festival that takes place seven *weeks* (the meaning
    of the holiday's name) after Passover. It commemorates the receiving of the
    Torah at Mount Sinai and is celebrated by studying holy texts all night long,
    decorating the home and synagogue with greenery and flowers, and eating
    dairy delicacies.

2   A town in central Poland, situated on the Vistula.

# Chapter XXXII

**1** Goldfaden's very popular play *Shmendrik, oder di komishe khasene* (Shmendrik, or: The Comical Wedding) (1877), set in a small Polish village among a family of Hasidic Jews. It concerns the nebbishy title character's being set up by his devoted mother to marry a girl whose heart belongs to another, and the girl's machinations to avoid being wed to said Shmendrik. The play was so popular that the name came to be a very common bit of slang in Yiddish (and Jewish-inflected English), referring to a hapless or foolish person. The play can be found in a bilingual edition with translation by Fernando Peñalosa (McKinleyville, CA: Tsiterboym Books, 2017).

**2** "Shepsele the Fool."

**3** Earlier, the memoir referred to the girl as "Ruzhe," when Ester-Rokhl was first introduced to Dovid Shvartsbard and his brood.

**4** Another name for the biblical operetta by Yoysef Lateiner that Kaminska had described the troupe performing earlier, *Yoysef in egiptn* (Joseph in Egypt). A program for a production of the Lateiner piece in Poland in facts lists both Yiddish titles, along with their translations into Polish: *Sprzedaż Józefa* and *Jòzef w Egipcie*. YIVO, Joseph Lateiner, Folder 4518, Item 176223, https://digipres.cjh.org:443/delivery/DeliveryManagerServlet?dps_pid=IE3177880.

**5** Harris Stambulko (1876–?) was a Warsaw-born actor and singer who as a youth sang in synagogue with other actors mentioned in these memoirs, among them Adolf Berman and Herman Faynshteyn. He got his start onstage in the children's choruses that sometimes took part in Yiddish theatre, as his father, a printer, produced posters for the productions. In 1892, he helped to found Olginskaya's company. After performing in a musical quartet at the 1900 Paris Exposition, Stambulko made his way to Buenos Aires. There, the local Jewish press managed to briefly shut down his company's production of Shomer's *Der yidisher porets* (The Jewish Nobleman), over objections to how the play represented the religion. He settled in the United States in 1913, where he took up a career as a businessman. "Heris Stambulko," in Zylbercweig, *Leksikon*, 2: 1462.

**6** A town in north-central Poland, famous today as the birthplace of Israel's first prime minister, David Ben-Gurion (1886–1973). He would have been a child of about six when Kaminska's troupe came to town in 1893.

# Chapter XXXIII

**1**  Kaminska, "Derner un blumen," *Der moment*, November 12, 1926.

**2**  A fringed shawl worn traditionally by married men during the morning prayer service.

**3**  The *yold* is garbling the name of Goldfaden's famous farce, *Di tsvey kuni-leml* (The Two Kuni-Lemls) (1880), which concerns Karoline setting her sights on the gentleman who is tutoring her in German, Max, preferring him over the match her wealthy Hasidic father has made for her with the stuttering Talmudic scholar Kuni-Leml, Max's cousin—and spitting image. Max takes advantage of their resemblance by disguising himself as Kuni-Leml and thereby, after a number of reversals and amusing complications, finding his way to the chuppah with Karoline.

**4**  A town now in north-central Poland lying some 60 miles north of Warsaw and some 35 miles northeast of Płońsk.

# Chapter XXXIV

**1**  An early American typewriter model. An advertisement from within a couple years of its 1880 release boasts that "it is a machine invented to take the place of the pen . . . operated by touching keys as in playing the piano." Advertisement for the Caligraph, American Writing Machine Company, *American Railroad Journal* (New York), January 7, 1882, 13.

**2**  Kaminska, "Derner un blumen," *Der moment*, November 19, 1926.

**3**  *Praven* (to celebrate, to carry out, usually used for holidays or other observances), for example, *praven a seyder* (to carry out a Passover seder), but here: *praven shulamis* (to carry out a performance of *Shulamis*, almost as if it were a holy rite).

**4**  This is the so-called *koyletsh-tants* (challah dance), in which a woman dances backward in front of the bride and groom while holding an enormous braided challah, leading the couple back to the festivities after the chief wedding ceremony has taken place. Sometimes salt is carried, too, to complete the blessing for the happiness and prosperity of the couple's new household.

5 A town only about 15 miles from Przasnysz, in north-central Poland. It boasts a fine red-brick castle dating from the beginning of the fifteenth century.

# Chapter XXXV

1 "We little Jews, kosher little Hasidim."

2 See note 2, Chapter XVI.

3 "The young wolf does not sleep." The line is given in Yiddish, the language, it would appear, that this actor has shifted to for his song.

4 Only about 19 miles from Ciechanów, this is another north-central Polish town. It happens to have been the birthplace of Yiddish novelist Joseph Opatoshu (1886–1954) and dramatist Tea Arciszewska (1890–1962), whose play *Miryeml*, about child survivors of a pogrom, has been translated by Sonia Gollance. Both noted Yiddish authors would have been children when Kaminska's troupe performed in the shtetl.

5 Tsarist Russian theatrical censorship restricted all representation of religious subjects, both Christian and Jewish, on the "profane" stage, regardless of the language of performance.

6 Kaminska, "Derner un blumen," *Der moment*, November 26, 1926.

7 A picturesque town then in Congress Poland, about 45 miles southeast of Mława. Located on the river Narew, it has occasionally been called the Venice of Poland, on account of its canal-skimming gondolas and old Italianate architecture, which have historically attracted holidaymaking Warsovians seeking a weekend's respite from the nearby capital.

# Chapter XXXVI

1 *Tsigayner*, a neutral term for the ethnic group in the Yiddish of Kaminska's day, though taking on pejorative tones in certain contexts (often connoting such qualities as itinerancy and irresponsibility). Its equivalent in German, *Zigeuner*, is today considered an ethnic slur, like its English counterpart. The word's appearance here, referring to the persecuted ethnic group, reflects the deep historical antipathy toward actors.

2 A city in east-central Poland. It is about 62 miles south of Warsaw.

# Chapter XXXVII

1 Kaminska, "Derner un blumen," *Der moment*, December 3, 1926.

2 The man had referred to their trade as *treyater* (also sometimes seen as *triater*), a corruption of the standard Yiddish word *teater*, and used mistakenly by those unfamiliar with the art form, or to mock those who take part in it.

3 A word borrowed from *klezmer-loshn*, the code language of klezmorim, or traditional Jewish musicians. *Labushnik*, denoting a musician, is from the Russian *labat'*, to play an instrument. Rothstein, "Klezmer-loshn," 29.

4 As *Shulamis* and *The Sorceress* both have long stretches of song (typically easier to deliver in a foreign language than speeches are, as the rhythms and inflection are built into the music), they might have been easier for the troupe to do in German than *Shmendrik*. The latter, though also considered by Kaminska to be an operetta, contains less music and is packed full of spoken text, relying on salty and richly idiomatic Yiddish dialogue for its humor. There also may have been a more firmly established German translation of the two other operettas than there was of *Shmendrik*, which perhaps had the added danger of coming off rather sillier and less dignified than Goldfaden's entertainments more renowned for their music and grand, exotic or historical settings.

5 Kaminska's not entirely perfect German for "Little Shmendrik, come over here to your mama."

6 German, "I'm leaving, Mother, I'm leaving!"

7 In Yiddish and German, respectively, "Yes."

8 "You have."

# Chapter XXXVIII

1 Halperin, something of a *yold*, seems to be mispronouncing *pyese* (play) as *pyesne* out of ignorance, but his utterance resembles a bit of *teater-loshn*, Yiddish actors' slang: the playwright Harendorf, in his lexicon of the argot, translates the almost-identical *pesne* (also likely stemming from a humorously corrupted form of *pyese*, or from the Russian *pesnya*, "song") as a "shlekhte pyese" (bad play). Harendorf, *Teater-karavanen*, 231.

2 A northeastern Polish town, located about 75 miles northeast of Warsaw. Like Pułtusk, where the troupe had performed not long before, it is situated on the banks of the river Narew.

# Chapter XXXIX

1 Kaminska, "Derner un blumen," *Der moment*, December 10, 1926.

2 Yet another town situated on the river Narew in northeastern Poland, only about 20 miles from Ostrołęka. Łomża boasted an ornate Great Synagogue, constructed in the 1870s and 1880s and eventually incinerated by the Nazis. It happens to be the town where Avrom-Yitskhok Kaminski would pass away, in 1918, then in his early fifties.

# Chapter XL

1 Russian, "dinner."

2 A powder used for pyrotechnic effects in nineteenth-century theatre, consisting of saltpeter, the bright yellow powder known as flowers of sulfur, and red arsenic. Owing to its noxious fumes, which could be dangerous for actors and audiences alike, theatres were advised to open their windows during the intermission following an act finale in which the fire had been used. E. Douglas Bomberger, "The Neues Schauspielhaus in Berlin and the Premiere of Carl Maria von Weber's *Der Freischütz*," in *Opera in Context: Essays on Historical Staging from the Late Renaissance to the Time of Puccini*, ed. Mark A. Radice (Portland, OR: Amadeus Press, 1998), 167. *The Sorceress* ends with the title character and her accomplices setting fire to an inn in which the recently liberated ingénue Mirele and her family are staying. The "good guys" manage to escape while the "bad guys" burn to death in the fire they started themselves.

3 The Russian tradition is to offer toasts according to a set order, beginning with a toast to the gathering itself and to meeting each other, followed later by a toast to friendship, then to love and women.

4 Kaminska, "Derner un blumen," *Der moment*, December 17, 1926.

# Chapter XLI

1  Yiddish troupes would often bill a certain performance as a *benefis*,
   a benefit evening, given in honor of some member of the ensemble,
   who would receive a share of the box office that night and often be
   bestowed with special gifts and monetary contributions from admirers
   in the crowd. The theatrical producer Nokhem Lipovski, who at
   various times acted with or served as a business manager in Kaminska's
   troupe, remembered that owing to the many such gifts she received at
   the *benefisn* in her name, she was in fact the group's richest member. On
   that account, writes Lipovski, it was often her bit of wealth, however small,
   that served to cover the troupe's travel expenses and venue rentals. This
   claim is borne out by the memoirs, which see her occasionally worrying
   over what capital she herself possesses, and whether it will be enough to
   sustain the activities of the collective. Zylbercweig, *Di velt*, 23.

2  Known as Suwałki in Polish, this is a large town in northeastern Poland
   some 90 miles from Łomża, 180 from Warsaw, and quite close to the
   current border with Lithuania. The picturesque Czarna Hańcza River runs
   through it.

# Chapter XLII

1  Had she indeed! Two chapters before (XL), Kaminska screams at her fellow
   actresses amid their drunken laughter, then is unable to sleep the whole
   night, and in this very scene, she curses out the driver of her carriage.
   And yet! She has indeed endured and shall endure a great deal, doing so
   with great hardiness of spirit; and even if we set that aside, her sometimes
   lavishly generous self-congratulation is very much a trademark of the
   show-business memoir and enhances the charm of her prose.

2  It is worth noting again here that Kaminska was battling cancer while
   writing these memoirs.

3  Russian, "hotel."

4  Though not entirely grammatical, and with the Yiddish *un* for the German
   *und* ("and"), this essentially translates to "It's quite certain that this is a
   Yiddish text. I would rather not come to the theatre, so as not to let you be
   disturbed [i.e. by his monitoring presence]. I will not be there."

# Chapter XLIII

1   Kaminska, "Derner un blumen," *Der moment*, December 24, 1926.

2   A Jewish harvest holiday, falling between late September and late October. To prepare for Sukkos, Jews construct huts outside of their homes, then eat and sometimes sleep in them during the holiday, to commemorate the makeshift dwellings in which the ancient Israelites lived during their wanderings in the desert after the Exodus from Egypt.

3   "The Brothers from Yampil." The latter is a town in Ukraine (then part of the Russian Empire) once famous for its Hasidic population, a group apparently satirized in this dance number.

4   "The Marketplace."

# Chapter XLIV

1   A city on the Neman River, now in western Belarus (and called Hrodna in Belarusian), then belonging to the Russian Empire. It served as the seat of the Grodno governorate, the guberniya in which Kaminska's home shtetl, Porozove, was located. Before the Holocaust, half of its population was Jewish. The notorious American gangster Meyer Lansky (1902–83) was born there, as was the Yiddish actor Herman Yablokoff (1903–81) and the aesthetic Yiddish poet Leyb Naydus (1890–1918), who would have been a tot when Kaminska's troupe came to town.

2   A major center of Jewish settlement in Congress Poland, in the northeast of the country, not far from the Lithuanian border. It was connected to Grodno, some 50 miles away, by a train line built in 1862. Białystok gave birth to the flat onion-and-poppyseed-topped roll known as a bialy and was an important hub of textile manufacturing, second only to Łódź in nineteenth-century Poland.

3   Today known as Bielsk Podlaski, it is about 30 miles southwest of Białystok, in Poland.

4   A town on the Netta River and the eponymous Augustów Canal, in northeastern Poland. The tsarist administration that governed it was located in Suvalk, where the troupe had performed earlier.

5   About 26 or 33 miles.

# Chapter XLV

**1**  Kaminska, "Derner un blumen," *Der moment*, December 31, 1926.

**2**  "Your Excellency, I would like . . ."

**3**  Russian officials had a prescribed list of terms of address, and using the wrong one would be taken as a grave insult.

**4**  These cities, identified by the names Kaminska uses for them, were spread out around the Russian-controlled Pale of Settlement, from the more westerly Brest-Litovsk (located today in western Belarus, on the border with Poland, it is also called Brisk in Yiddish and is known in Belarusian as Brest; the modernist Yiddish poet Anna Margolin, who lived from 1887 to 1952, was born there) and, some 200 miles north, Kovno (located in Lithuania and known in that country's official language as Kaunas), to the more easterly Mohilov (in eastern Belarus, which knows it as Mahilyow) and, some 180 miles south, Chernigov (today in northern Ukraine, and called Chernihiv). If lines are drawn connecting the four places on a map, they form a sort of parallelogram.

**5**  The guberniya east of the Dnieper River in Ukraine, with its administrative center in the city of Chernihiv (in Russian, Chernigov).


# Chapter XLVI

**1**  *Komedyant* (comedian) refers to a comedic actor or a sort of wandering minstrel who performs comic songs. By adding the Slavic diminutive *-tshik*, even further derision is intended, downgrading the status of these actors in Yiddish operetta to that of professional buffoons. The ill repute in which actors were held is symptomatic of a long-standing pan-European anti-theatrical prejudice but may have owed something, too, to the fear and wonder with which local populations in Slavic lands regarded itinerant performers generally. Historically, in Russia and Ukraine, minstrels called *skomorokhi* were associated with pagan customs and witchcraft. This did not mean that local people did not itch to see them perform, but rather that the delight they took in their spectacles (songs, puppetry, trained bears) was always tinged with fear. Russell Zguta, *Russian Minstrels: A History of the Skomorokhi* (Philadelphia: University of Pennsylvania Press, 1978).

2   Located on the Udaj River, it was then in the Russian Empire and is today
    in northwestern Ukraine.

3   Regina, after achieving some fame as an adolescent actress, died in the
    autumn of 1913. Most other sources record the year of her birth as 1894.
    "Regina Kaminska," in Zylbercweig, *Leksikon*, 6: 5282.

4   Kaminska, "Derner un blumen," *Der moment*, January 7, 1927.

# Chapter XLVII

1   A complex villain in the operetta, Papus is a disabled, embittered jewel
    merchant who plots with the Romans against his own people, the Jews,
    who are being led into armed rebellion by Bar Kokhba. His actions are
    partly motivated by his love for the Jewish maiden Dine—typically played
    by Kaminska in her troupes—who is in turn enamored of Bar Kokhba.

2   When we first met him, Beni Abelman was a cork maker living in Warsaw
    and working on the side as an actor.

# Chapter XLVIII

1   *Doctor Almasado* is set among the Jews of fourteenth-century Palermo,
    ruled at that time by the Crown of Aragon. The titular doctor is the
    only one in the city who can heal Elvira, the sickly daughter of the local
    governor, Don Pedro—despite the fact that the Jews have been banished
    from the city by royal writ. Miryem is Almasado's daughter, who is involved
    in a forbidden romance with his Gentile apprentice, Alonso.

2   German, "little forest palace."

3   Known in Polish as the Kaliska railway station, it was opened in the year
    1902, and served a line that connected the Polish cities of Warsaw and
    Kalisz, between which Łódź was a midway point.

4   That is, the authorities started breathing down their necks.

5   These two cities in southeastern Poland are, respectively, about 140 and
    180 miles southeast of Łódź, and about 50 miles from each other. Lublin,
    among the largest cities in Poland, was known for its famous Hasidic rebbe
    Yankev-Yitskhok Horovits (1745–1815), the mystically gifted "Seer of

Lublin," while Zamość, with its grand central plaza and baroque town hall, is remembered by many Jews as the birthplace of the classic Yiddish writer Y. L. Peretz (1852–1915).

6 Its full title being *Ibn ezra, oder der yidisher minister* (Ibn Ezra, or: The Jewish Minister), this unpublished play by Avrom-Yitskhok Kaminski concerned Yehuda ben Yosef ibn Ezra, who served as majordomo of the royal household of King Alfonso VII of León and Castile in the twelfth century, in which position he was able to combat the anti-Jewish persecutions of the encroaching Almohad Caliphate. The play was based on a novel of the same title by the Yiddish author Shomer.

# Chapter XLIX

1 Kaminska, "Derner un blumen," *Der moment*, January 14, 1927.

2 Director Nokhem Lipovski, who served as business manager in Kaminska's troupe at the time, remembered the year of this child's birth as 1900. Zylbercweig, *Di velt*, 22–3.

3 Today the second-most populous city of Belarus and known as Homyel in Belarusian, it was then a part of the Russian Empire. It is located along the Sozh River in the southeast of the country. Around the time that Kaminska's troupe was there, the city was about 56 percent Jewish, and boasted more than twenty synagogues.

4 Another Goldfaden piece, this was a Biblical operetta written by the composer after arriving in New York City for an ultimately disappointing stint in 1887, eager to find steady theatrical success in the United States.

5 Ester-Rokhl was a particularly popular member of the troupe, and as such, it seems that some would buy tickets specifically to see her. She was commonly expected to provide for her colleagues from her own coffer of monetary gifts from admirers. Therefore, if the troupe was not to go hungry, she would have to play, even under the direst circumstances. This defense of her actions is given by Nokhem Lipovski, who calls the "torments of the grieving mother on that evening . . . impossible to describe." Zylbercweig, *Di velt*, 23.

6 The *imeniny*—the feast day of the saint who shares a given person's name—was celebrated with more fervor than birthdays among Orthodox Christians and many European Catholics. As Kaminska appears to have

been born on the Fast of Esther, her parents decided to name her after the day's eponymous heroine, and here she connects that distinctly Jewish choice to the distinctly Christian concept of a name day.

7 Today known as Nizhyn and located in northern Ukraine on the banks of the Oster River, it was then part of the Russian Empire's Chernihiv governorate, which had its administrative center in Chernihiv. That city is situated a distance of about 40 miles from Nizhyn, a center of the Chabad Hasidic movement in the nineteenth century. Nizhyn's Jews, who made up around 25 percent of the city's population, were viciously beset with pogroms that erupted in 1881 and 1905.

8 Geographically, Kyiv was deep within the Pale of Settlement, but it had special status as a "closed" city to Jewish residence. The directive governing this stemmed from a desire to limit Jewish mobility—geographic, social, and economic. Exclusion of Jews and limitations on their trades and education were intended both to prevent commercial competition with ethnic Slavs and to control the public disorder unleashed by anti-Jewish pogroms. John Klier, "Pale of Settlement" and "Pogroms," in *YIVO Encyclopedia,* https://encyclopedia.yivo.org/article/246, https://encyclopedia.yivo.org/article/260.

9 Subject to a number of restrictions, some Jewish members of certain groups were indeed given residence permits to live outside the Pale of Settlement and even within such closed imperial cities as Kyiv, Moscow, and St. Petersburg. Such groups included university graduates, military personnel, doctors, and prostitutes. The latter detail was crucial to the plot of the English dramatist Michael Morton's play *The Yellow Ticket* (1914) and its various filmed adaptations (including a 1918 German silent film starring Pola Negri, *Der gelbe Schein*), in which a young Jewish woman pretends to be a sex worker in order to gain the titular certificate—the identification document granted to members of that profession in the Russian Empire—that will then allow her to settle in St. Petersburg. Susan A. Glenn, *Daughters of the Shtetl: Life and Labor in the Immigrant Generation* (Ithaca: Cornell University Press, 1990), 13, 18; Klier, "Pale of Settlement."

10 Not to be confused with a later, more well-known Yiddish actor, also named Julius Adler, who immigrated to America at a young age and played the priest in the renowned Yiddish film *Tevya* (1939). Born the son of a bakery owner in Białystok in 1880, this Adler of the Kaminski troupe started performing as a young boy, in 1891, with a group of the itinerant Yiddish performers known as Broder singers. With that group, still a treble

and billed as "Yudke der alt" (Yudke the Alto), he served as prima donna, playing female roles. Later, in addition to acting with such troupes as the Kaminskis', he also wrote plays of his own and translated others, including Henrik Ibsen's *Ghosts* (*Gayster*, in Yiddish) and August Strindberg's *The Father* (*Der foter*). His family's correct surname was indeed Adler, but it was apparently known at various times as "Artshikh" or "Artshikhes" due to reasons pertaining to the tsarist army. "Yulius Adler," in Zylbercweig, *Leksikon*, 1: 11–13.

**11** Located on the Southern Bug River in west-central Ukraine, it was then a part of the Russian Empire. It is the largest city of the historic region known as Podolia, spanning western Ukraine and northeastern Moldova, and was the birthplace of Cubist painter Nathan Altman (1889–1970) and printmaker Todros Geller (1889–1949), who eventually won great success as an illustrator in Chicago, his adopted hometown.

**12** Vladimir Durov (1863–1934) was a Russian circus impresario who used his studies in zoology to develop a system for training animals to perform without the use of punishment. His Durov Animal Theatre, located in Moscow, is still in operation.

# Chapter L

**1** Kaminska, "Derner un blumen," *Der moment*, January 21, 1927.

**2** Lyric soprano Ruzhe Horn (*c.* 1873–99), born in Warsaw, began in the Yiddish theatre as a chorine. After her marriage to Leyzer Rapel, she played leading roles in Goldfaden's works. She died in her native city, of tuberculosis. "Ruzha Horn," in Zylbercweig, *Leksikon*, 1: 589.

**3** Character actor Yitskhok Blifeld (1875–1936) was born in the Ukrainian shtetl Yarmelinets, known in Ukrainian as Yarmolyntsi. His father was the owner of an inn. The young Blifeld's early admiration of a traveling quartet known as Di Brider Shvarts (The Brothers Shvarts) gave him the initial inspiration to become an actor. After performing in a number of companies, including the Kaminskis' and Fishzon's, he immigrated to the United States, as he wanted his children raised there. In America, he performed under theatrical giant Boris Thomashefsky in Philadelphia, and later toured such cities as Detroit (1928–9) and Baltimore (1929–30). "Yitskhok Blifeld," ibid., 183.

**4** Dovid Frishman (*c.* 1860–1922) was a highly prominent poet, critic, and journalist in Hebrew and Yiddish, and a translator of many works of European literature into Hebrew. Born to a well-heeled merchant family in the city of Zgierz, just north of Łódź, he worked in his home country as well as Germany and Russia to advance the cause of a modern Jewish literature more focused on aesthetic forms and universal ideas than on national and political concerns. He also translated widely from world literature, rendering into Yiddish works by Oscar Wilde, Heinrich Heine, and Shakespeare (including *Coriolanus*). He died of cancer in Berlin. "Dovid Frishman," in *Leksikon fun der yidisher literatur, prese un filologye,* ed. Zalmen Reyzen (Vilna: B. Kletskin, 1929), 3: 204–28.

**5** Heshl Epelberg (1861–1927) was raised in a Hasidic family in Łomazy, Poland, but upon moving to Warsaw after his marriage, he became involved in secular literary and dramatic circles. He worked as an editor, writer, director, and playwright; among his plays is *Esterke* (1890), about the legendary Polish queen who was said to be a Jew. Epelberg immigrated to the United States in 1921 and died in New York. "Heshl Ep(f)elberg," in Zylbercweig, *Leksikon*, 2: 1582–6.

**6** German (and likewise Yiddish) for "place." According to Frishman, the actors were giving it the incorrect definite article, using instead of the masculine *der*, the neuter *dos* (the Yiddish equivalent of the German neuter article *das*, perhaps a sign that the performers are also slipping into their native tongue).

**7** We will not. Kaminska was unable to complete her memoirs before her death, and *Der moment* published all that it had. This is the final entry. How wonderful, though, that she alludes in it to future freedom and success, after the tsarist ban on Yiddish theatre had begun to ease in 1905, the year the Bagatela opened. After all the seasons of endless wanderings, verbal acrobatics to appease the authorities, and physical exertions to prepare makeshift stages, she gives us a snapshot of life at the Kaminskis' own theatre, in her adopted hometown of Warsaw, where the troupe would finally play in its unfettered mother tongue. And then, a sentence later, we find her returning from a tour to St. Petersburg, of all places—that crown city so formerly blocked off not only to Yiddish cultural activity but also to Jewish residency generally. These are some of the very rare occasions on which Kaminska skips forward in her narrative to describe events that would occur far in the future, and how fitting that she does so now in the final entry, leaving the reader to dream of all that would be.

**8** Though Kaminska intended to cover far more of her career than her failing health ultimately allowed her to do, this does make for a poignant ending. It sees her finishing a successful run in Łódź, now as a well-known artist—the same city that hosted her first out-of-town engagement as an untested ingénue. She had spent earlier chapters, when just discovering the theatrical life, dreaming that she could someday attain the status of an *artistke*—an actress, an artist—on the Yiddish stage. And now, a famed Yiddish-language intellectual hails her with precisely that word, posing the clearly rhetorical question, "Iz zi a groyse artistke?" Despite all the thorns along her path, and the many that lay in wait to prick her, she has finally plucked this evasive flower, and many more would come to join it, in the great bouquet of her life.

# INDEX